C000260007

Tunku Halim was born in 1964. He lives nomadically but is a frequent visitor to his country of birth, Malaysia.

His previous books include several short story collections, his latest being *7 Days to Midnight* (2013), two novels, *Dark Demon Rising* (1997) and *Vermillion Eye* (2000), and the novella *Juriah's Song* (2008). His non-fiction books include *A Children's History of Malaysia* (2003) and a biography of his late father *Tunku Abdullah — A Passion for Life* (1998).

His first book with Fixi Novo was the bestselling mid-career retrospective *Horror Stories* (2014), followed by the novels *Last Breath* (2014) and *A Malaysian Restaurant in London* (2015).

FIXI NOVO manifesto

1. We believe that omputih/gwailoh-speak is a Malaysian language.

2. We use American spelling. This is because we are more influenced by Hollywood than the House of Windsor.

3. We publish stories about the urban reality of Malaysia. If you want to share your grandmother's World War 2 stories, send 'em elsewhere and you might even win the Booker Prize.

4. We specialize in pulp fiction, because crime, horror, sci-fi and so on turn us on.

5. We will not use italics for non-American/ non-English terms. This is because those words are not foreign to a Malaysian audience. So we will not have "They had *nasi lemak* and went back to *kongkek*" but rather "They had nasi lemak and went back to kongkek". Nasi lemak and kongkek are some of the pleasures of Malaysian life that should be celebrated without apology; italics are a form of apology.

6. We publish novels and short-story anthologies. We don't publish poetry; we like making money.

7. The existing Malaysian books that come closest to what we wanna do: *Devil's Place* by Brian Gomez; and the Inspector Mislan crime novels by Rozlan Mohd Noor. Look for them!

8. We publish books with the same print run and the same price as those of our parent company, Buku Fixi. So a book of about 300 pages will sell at RM20. This is because we wanna reach out to the young, the sengkek and the kiam siap.

CALL FOR ENTRIES.

Interested? For novels,
send your synopsis and first 2 chapters.
For anthologies, send a short story of between 2,000-5,000 words on the theme "KL Noir."
Send to **info@fixi.com.my** anytime.

HORROR STORIES

Tunku Halim

Published by
Fixi Novo *which is an imprint of:*
Buku Fixi (002016254-V)
B-8-2A Opal Damansara, Jalan PJU 3/27
47810 Petaling Jaya, Malaysia
info@fixi.com.my
http://fixi.com.my

All rights reserved. Except for extracts for review purposes, you are not allowed to duplicate or republish this book, in whole or in part, without the written permission of the publisher. Although to be honest the idea of pirated books is kinda cool and we'd secretly take it as a compliment.

Horror Stories
(c) Tunku Halim 2014
www.tunkuhalim.com

First Printing: February 2014
Second Printing: February 2014
Third Printing: April 2014
Fourth Printing: June 2014
Fifth Printing: July 2014
Sixth Printing: December 2014
Seventh Printing: March 2015
Eighth Printing: June 2015

Cover and layout: Teck Hee
Consultant: Izaddin Syah Yusof

ISBN 978-967-0374-54-3
Catalogue-in-Publication Data available from the National Library of Malaysia.

Printed by:
Vinlin Press Sdn Bhd
2 Jalan Meranti Permai 1, Meranti Permai Industrial Park
Batu 15, Jalan Puchong, 47100 Puchong, Malaysia

Acknowledgements are due to the following for permission to reproduce stories which appeared in the following publications:

"Biggest Baddest Bomoh", "The Rape of Martha Teoh", "The Width of a Circle", "Watching the Doll", "Ladiah", "Four Numbers for Eric Kwok", "Night of the Pontianak", "A Labour Day Weekend", "Malay Magick", "44 Cemetery Road" and "Plane Load" from *44 Cemetery Road: The Best of Tunku Halim*, published by MPH Group Publishing in 2007.

"The Laughing Buddha", "Haunted Apartment", "Mr Insurance Man", "Mr Petronas", "A Sister's Tale", "Strangling the Soul", "This Page is Left Intentionally Blank", "The Woman Who Grew Horns" and "Gravedigger's Kiss" from *Gravedigger's Kiss: More of Tunku Halim*, published by MPH Group Publishing in 2007.

Contents

INTRO

"I was sick ... I felt that my senses were leaving me.
The sentence — the dread sentence of death ..."
— *The Pit and the Pendulum*
Edgar Allan Poe

It's been awhile, my friend, since you and I sat down to a quiet heart-to-heart.

In fact, its been more than six years since we chatted. The last time was when I released my twin compilations, *44 Cemetery Road* and *Gravedigger's Kiss*. So now that that we've selected twenty stories from those books and compiled them into this single, user-friendly volume, it's time we had a good talk.

As for me, I'm still writing and imagining terrible things and awful creatures. I recently released a new collection of short stories called *7 Days to Midnight*. I didn't include an introduction to that book because quite frankly, at that time, you and I weren't really on speaking terms.

We had become somewhat estranged.

But today, on this sunny day, as I sit at my desk staring out the balcony door at the waves, listening to them wash against the rocks beside my house, I'm thinking of you and only you. My first thought is that I hope you're still alive. That's because life has this rather annoying tendency to bring about death. Sometimes unexpectedly but always inevitably. I know this is shockingly bad news. It might even spoil your day.

You might need to update your Facebook status: *I just found out I'm going to die.* Don't be surprised if you receive a whole barrage of comments, asking if you're terminally ill. Nobody wants to know they're going to die. In fact, I dare surmise, nobody wants to die at all.

This is the reason, some say, that horror stories are popular. Because it's through such disturbing tales that we confront our fears and our greatest fear is not the death of our loved ones, which is heart wrenching in itself, but our own finite time on earth.

Our own death.

And that, my friend, is as scary as hell.

So often, we take refuge in heaven.

In religion, that is. Perhaps in the words of spiritual gurus or the consoling text in religious books. But many will unknowingly, unwittingly, turn to a horror tale thinking that it's pure entertainment, something to pass the time, a bit of fun perhaps, when the real reason is in fact much deeper, darker and dreadful.

Just as there are many shades of fear, there are similarly many different flavors of scary stories. You'll find a whole variety of them here, from the extreme horror of "Gravedigger's Kiss" and "Four Numbers for Eric Kwok" to the more playful "Mr Petronas" and "Biggest Baddest Bomoh" to the more Gothic-like

"Malay Magick" and "44 Cemetery Road". There's even a non-horror tale to thumb through: "This Page is Left Intentionally Blank". It's slotted in just for a bit of friendly contrast.

My favorite tales in this collection are "The Width of a Circle", "Ladiah" and "The Woman Who Grew Horns" amongst many others. Well, the truth is that they're *all* my favorites. Each story is like my own child, brought to life from the musty dark chambers in my mind, draped in cobwebs where grotesque creatures merrily creep.

So, my friend, do take the time now.

It's best late at night when we won't be disturbed. Find a quiet corner. Let a single light bulb burn. Let the rest of the room be shrouded in darkness and all is quiet outside but for a faint howling, almost mewling sound, in the distance.

Start turning these pages.

Then you and I, ah, we can be such good friends again.

Tunku Halim
Tarooma, Australia
December 2013

BIGGEST BADDEST BOMOH

Idris Ishak had this crazy thing for Zani Kasim. When she walked past nonchalantly as usual, his heartbeat would stop in its blood-filled tracks, and her smile would cause his breath to get caught in his throat like a struggling frog. She extruded a subtle, sensual perfume he found himself longing for while he lay blissfully in bed, thinking of her warm dreamy eyes, which was far, far too often.

And that was why he found himself on a Singapore-Kuala Lumpur shuttle flight this Friday evening with the other holidaymakers and balik kampung commuters. But Idris was on no holiday. He was on serious business. Business that made his hairs stand every time he thought of it and made him almost quiver in delight as he thought about the bounty that would be offered to him.

It all started with Zani, of course. That was a given thing. The day she joined as the Managing Director's secretary was the day Idris fell head over heels in love and in absolute wanton lust for her. She wore a yellow blouse and cosmetic pearls with matching earrings and she whiffed of that special perfume of flowers and musk. He was gone. It was oblivion at first sight. Her skirt fell just above her knees and Idris spent that entire afternoon admiring her slim, well-shaped legs, watching them swish against her skirt. The next morning found him gazing into those warm dreamy eyes, longing to caress her gleaming shoulder-length hair, yearning to press his lips against her fair, smooth cheeks, not to mention those full, cherry-red lips.

There was nothing Idris could do but beg for a date. Being only a clerk in Accounts Receivables, he did not feel particularly confident on whether she would assent. Idris though was quite simply in love and love did strange things to people, and lust produced even weirder behavior. Idris plucked up his courage while hovering over the humming, chemical-belching photocopier. He tucked his bundle of accounts under his arms as if it contained the secrets of a dark universe and ambled over to her.

She had just taken a message over the phone and was tearing out the ubiquitous WHILE YOU WERE OUT slip when Idris found himself in front of her gleaming white desk. His eyes fell longingly on those fair, smooth cheeks, and then strayed across to her warm, dreamy eyes.

"Hi, Zani! I'm Idris," Idris said in a bright, cheerful voice, which he hoped would radiate confidence and friendliness, and mask that blind desire bubbling just below the surface.

"Nice to meet you, Idris," replied Zani. She quickly looked up, and as quickly looked away.

"I'd like to welcome you to Solid Equipments." Idris wore a Cheshire-cat grin as he imagined himself lying next to that gleaming long hair, stroking it ... oh stroking it ...

"Thanks," Zani replied, eyes not leaving the newsletter in her dainty fingers.

"Will you have lunch?"

Zani glared up at him with a puzzled look, the cosmetic pearls and her eyes flashing angrily.

"Lunch, you know," Idris elaborated. "Have lunch together, you and I—eating together ... get to know each other. My treat!"

"No, thank you," Zani snapped, swiveled her chair to face the computer screen and began typing fastidiously — even arrogantly, if one could do that.

"Next time perhaps," Idris said, his smile dropping like a shattered rock.

"Maybe, maybe not," muttered Zani as her dainty fingers ran rings around the keyboard.

Idris was crestfallen. Zani was obviously not interested in him. He crept away towards Finance, hoping that the carpeted floor would swallow him whole.

"That girl not your type."

Idris turned around to see fat Cindy Lam from Marketing with a half-eaten biscuit and a cup of milky sweet tea.

"What do you mean, not my type?"

"Not your type, very action one. I heard she got three or four boys chasing after her, but she only like rich people."

"How do you know this?"

"I've been sitting in the cubicle opposite her," Cindy replied, "heard all her phone calls. Don't waste time."

"Okay, I won't waste my time with her," lied Idris.

He was not going to give up so easily. Just the sight of her warm, dreamy eyes and long gleaming hair would lift his spirits and bring a song to his lips. Every effort he made would be worth it. She was going to be his. He knew it. It was just a question of time and effort.

Not wanting to appear too keen, Idris made a tactical decision not to call her for the rest of the week. On Monday, he called her extension and in a deep and confident voice asked her for lunch. He was turned down, the slammed phone ringing like a bee in his ear. He refrained on Tuesday. Wednesday saw his roti canai luncheon request rejected. It was going to take more bloody effort than he thought!

By the time Friday arrived, Idris was in the darkest of moods. Zani had rejected all lunch dates and ignored him when he came up to her with a bunch of fifty-dollar orchids. She just dismissed him as if he was an office boy and the orchids ended up petals first in the bin. To make matters worse, his workmates giggled, even laughed at his every approach.

Cindy Lam kept repeating "I told you so" all through lunch until he felt sick in the stomach and offered her his nasi lemak, which she soon consumed without ceremony. "Not enough chilli," she said as she chewed the last mouthful.

"I'm going to get her," said Idris. "She's mine."

"How? She ignores you all the time."

"Somehow, she will be mine. I'll go to a bomoh."

"A bomoh, a shaman, a magic-man?" asked Cindy with eyebrows raised.

"Just joking lah," said Idris as he stood to get up.

"Wait, wait, you sit down." Cindy watched Idris reluctantly climb back onto the wooden bench with a fed-up expression. "If you are serious, I can help. My uncle's driver knows a very good bomoh. He call him the biggest baddest bomoh in the world!"

"Sounds like a Michael Jackson song," muttered Idris.

"Don't be stupid," said Cindy with blazing eyes. "If you really want this girl, this bomoh will get her for you. You know my uncle's cousin dying from cancer last year, you know. Went to the bomoh, five days later, cancer gone! Just like that, doctors call it a miracle. I call it magic. Powerful magic! Not called the biggest baddest bomoh for nothing!"

And so on a taxi with torn plastic seats leaving Subang airport and onto a rattling bus departing Puduraya, Idris's eyes were transfixed on a hazy image of Zani, her gleaming hair billowing in the wind, but just out of reach. He headed south in a speeding bus to a hotel in Seremban, a lodging house with eight rooms off a busy street with a rusty air conditioner and thin musty towels. Idris slept restlessly, tossing and turning as the air conditioner stalled, started, changed gears, hummed and clanged. How he wished he was tossing and turning with her, pressing his mouth against her fair, smooth cheek, her cherry-red lips. *Soon, soon*, Idris whispered, the flashing lights outside falling upon his face in a spectrum of garish colors so he looked like an extraterrestrial guest star from *The X-Files*.

A tired, bleary-eyed Idris found himself in a rusty, battered taxi with its Mercedes-Benz star missing on the bonnet and a relic of a Chinese driver in singlet at the wheel with one tooth missing. And then up along the windy tree-filled roads, towards Simpang Pertang. Then a turn off into a lane, a dirt track road, scaring a chicken which jumped over the taxi, squawking hysterically. Squeezing past a stubborn goat which no blaring of the horns would budge. Its big glassy eyes, as they crossed paths, transfixed on his, fluttering its eyelids, letting loose a couple of flies that circled the simmering air.

You here to see the Biggest Baddest Bomoh? He heard it say, swishing its beard from side to side. *Power corrupts, absolute power corrupts absolutely. You better know what you're doing! Absolute fool!* The goat nodded its head and pointed its bitty horns at Idris. Idris fell back on the plastic-coated seat, he could have sworn it spoke and the damn goat was now chuckling away!

Finally they found the house, which to Idris's disappointment was quite ordinary, one in a row of eight, with nothing different about it. Washing on the line, tricycle at the front, slippers and shoes entangled at the front door. This could surely not be the Biggest Baddest Bomoh's house, cancer-curer, witch-doctor extraordinaire. He called out a greeting anyway, removed his shoes and entered.

On a hard, old sofa, below a rotating fan, in front of a large old television, with children yelling next door, Idris was dismayed. This could not be the powerful shaman Cindy boasted of. He had been taken for a ride, all the way up the bloody peninsula. All this way for nothing! Pak Hitam was about thirty-five, lanky, and wore a thin-lipped smile on his spotty face. He served tea clumsily, spoke with a thick, high-pitched Negeri accent and said that only true love would win Zani over. True love! What bullshit!

Idris repeated his story with all the semblance of patience he could muster, telling Pak Hitam what he wanted, what he needed. Zani, of all things, Zani, shapely legs, dreamy eyes and all. Pak Hitam talked of love. Idris wanted potent potions. Idris argued that he had exhausted all love's avenues, all jalans, all lorongs. Pak Hitam had to help or he would kill himself, added Idris for dramatic effect. Yeah, jump into the Gombak river, people did it all the time! That worked like a little miracle. Pak Hitam agreed, taking Idris quite literally and seriously, the fool. Now for the true test. Did this rambling man have the magic?

At first Pak Hitam lit a black candle, muttered some words, made strange gestures with his hand, inhaled deeply and blew the dancing flame out, saying Zani would now be attracted to Idris. With the black smoke drifting by his lips, Idris stopped a curse in his throat. This was not the deal. Attraction was not enough. It was just allurement and others could just as well entice her. After all there were four other men to contend with. Rich guys too!

Another spell, that was what was needed. What kind of spell? An iron-clad guarantee of her, no matter what. No matter what? Yes, she would be his, without fail. Those are difficult spells, Pak Hitam countered. Nothing was too expensive to have Zani. Idris had come all this way, not for a possibility but *certainty*. And surely the Biggest Baddest Bomoh, cancer-curer, witch-doctor extraordinaire, could do this. So you want her, no matter what? *No matter what*, replied Idris, licking his tumescent lips.

Pak Hitam, with great care, led him behind the house, and up a verdant hill, towards a sacred site teeming with mosquitoes. They climbed a twisting, narrow track for forty minutes and reached a sudden clearing with six red, half-rotting posts surrounding. With each step of their uphill, and somewhat sweaty journey Pak Hitam seemed to grow taller, frame bulkier, voice deeper and on reaching the clearing, he was a different person, with authority and eyes sparkling with power. Absolute power!

Sitting on the damp ground beside a burner, smoldering charcoal, gray smoke blustering up the branches, acrid fumes filling his nostrils, a teary-eyed Idris heard the chanting. The voice rose and fell in dreamy waves and Pak Hitam's eyes, bloodshot and puffy, closed and opened, like the mouth of a hungry fish. The words were a jumble, some with meaning, others a cacophony of tangled words.

When he was done, Pak Hitam uncrossed his legs, stood up and approached Idris and coldly whispered: "She is now yours."

She was. For as soon as Idris was back in modern, flashy Singapore, away from jungle, chickens and talking goats, Zani called.

He had just returned that Sunday evening to his one-bedroom flat, when the telephone rang. Zani did not even ask if he was free, she was going to come over *right now*. Idris just said *yes*, of course, sure thing, anytime, no problem. He abandoned his half-eaten meal of fried rice in the kitchen and paced up and down, straightening posters, stacking magazines, lining up shoes and slippers, spraying air freshener indiscriminately.

Everything was just right. He put on some light background music, combed his hair, changed out of sarong and T-shirt into casual trousers and tennis shirt, with the Lacoste crocodile grinning. Bed made, cushions arranged, curtains closed, lights dimmed. It was going to be perfect. Absolutely perfect. *Pak Hitam came through!*

The door bell rang and Idris tactically waited a few seconds before opening it. *It was Zani in person!*

Idris could hardly believe it. Here she was — glamorous, gorgeous, voluptuous. Glistening eyes, soft skin, full cherry-red lips longing to be kissed, black gleaming hair. And that was just the top, below that was a most alluring and shapely body Idris had ever seen. The red blouse and black skirt would soon be off and he would ...

The phone rang. Idris cursed himself for not putting the answering machine on. He reached for it signaling Zani to come in.

It was Cindy Lam.

"Can't talk now, I'm busy."

"How did it go? Did you meet Pak Hitam?"

"Yes, yes," said Idris impatiently, "I've got to go now."

"Did he agree to help?"

"Yes, yes he did." He looked back at Zani and grinned. Just ravishing.

"How much he charge you?"

"Not much, not much," Idris replied as he motioned Zani to enter. Two hundred ringgit was peanuts for *this*.

"You waste your money."

"Why?" countered Idris.

Zani smiled adoringly as she came in. Idris's heart soared. It was going to be a heavenly night. He would soon be lying next to that gleaming long hair, stroking it ... oh stroking it ...

"Waste your money."

"Cindy, I'm willing to pay ten times that. She's here," Idris said triumphantly, "Zani is *here* in my flat!"

"Oh no, dear God!" hollered Cindy.

"What do you mean?" asked Idris irritably, angry at himself for letting her keep him on the line. Zani closed the front door with a thud that jolted Idris's heart like a gunshot.

"Zani died in a car crash on Friday after work."

The phone clanged onto the tiled floor, leaving Cindy's hysterical warnings flying aimlessly like a buzzing insect. Idris's mouth was dry and gaping like a hooked fish, his eyes wide with terror. Sweat dripped down his white face.

Zani smiled, the long gleaming hair creeping down, her incisors, long and sharp flashed in the fluorescent light. Her eyes blinked, reddened and turned crimson; from her face, like a rotten egg cracked all over, thick green liquid oozed out, spilling in huge globules down her blouse.

"Oh darling, I'm yours."

"No, no!" shrieked Idris, as he backed away.

She floated slowly across the room to him, gleaming hair billowing in an invisible wind, arms reaching for an embrace.

Even as Idris felt the hard concrete wall press against his back, he cursed the bomoh ... the bloody awful power ...

Zani floated down from the ceiling with a hungry smile, mouth open wide, incisors long and sharp, lunging longingly for his throat.

And all Cindy could hear was screaming.

NIGHT OF THE PONTIANAK

"Let's go pontianak-hunting!"

Fauziah slapped the plastic table and her eyes flickered like dark flames so we knew a refusal was out of the question.

Neither Julian nor I had seen her since she became a remisier three months ago at the stockbrokers where her father knew the MD, and I was surprised that the once-gentle girl had become loud and aggressive. Corporate life had changed her.

"Why?" I asked. "Sounds gila to me."

"It'll be exciting, Azman. Much more fun than sitting here eating supper."

"Eh, I'm enjoying my food," Julian said, as he tried with his sticky fingers to tuck his shirt beneath his burgeoning belly. "I love satay after a few glasses of Heineken. It's a Gomez tradition!"

"Well, hurry up then," she said, tossing her hair over one shoulder. She fished a compact from her new red handbag, blinked at the mirror and ran pink lipstick over her lips, smacking them together as she put the cosmetics away.

We were at a Kampung Pandan stall beside a row of shophouses. Some had tattered **To Let/For Sale** signs stuck to the metal roller blinds, but most were occupied — there was a 7-Eleven look-a-like, a Thai Kitchen, a shoe shop filled with bright fluorescent slippers and a Maybank. Cars were crammed into every corner and the sound of traffic buzzed like angry insects around us.

I stared at her enviously. All of us had graduated together with Accounting degrees but neither Julian nor

I had found jobs and we always got better marks than her.

"No such thing as pontianaks anyway." I said. "They belong in old Malay movies. Now we don't even bother with such things. We need to forget this VHS stuff."

"VHS?" Julian said as he waved his greasy satay stick in the air.

"Violence, Horror, Sex lah. You ignorant or what?"

"Azman, you're really talking nonsense," Fauziah said. "Why should we forget violence, horror and sex? These things are as real as the cigarettes you're chain-smoking. We, as a nation, can't be in constant denial."

"No lah. It's all bullshit. No such thing as violence, horror and sex in Malaysia. As for smoking, it just takes me to that blissful high country where the air is so clean and refreshing. Don't you know adverts never lie?"

I grinned stupidly at Fauziah which earned me a kick under the table. I said 'adoi' and pulled my legs away, although I did relish that physical contact with her, no matter how brief or painful. I'd once plucked the courage to ask Fauziah out to the cinema but she made excuses. A pretty well-to-do girl like her wouldn't want a son of a taxi driver for a boyfriend.

"You're both so childish," Julian said with his mouth full, satay sauce trickling down his chin.

"Hey, you don't talk," Fauziah said. "You're the one who's so addicted to Pokemon trading cards."

"That was a long time ago."

"Only two years ago, Julian."

"Okay, okay. Anyway, I agree with Azman. There're no such things as pontianaks." Julian took a long slurp of his sugarcane water and grinned, his fleshy cheeks wobbled delicately beneath the fluorescent lights.

Fauziah sighed. "You men think you know everything. You wait. I'll tell you what happened to a friend of mine."

"I don't want to listen to your long story lah," I said.

"It's not long! Anyway, my friend and his brother were driving home late at night. Then he saw a lady dressed in white sitting on a fire hydrant in front of an old colonial house. My friend likes anything in skirts, so he just stared lustily at her as they drove past."

"And then?" Julian said, a new satay stick poking from his mouth.

"My friend said to his brother: 'Hey look, a girl sitting there." But his brother refused to look. He kept driving, saying nothing. His eyes on the road. My friend turned to see if she was pretty. But all he saw was the back of her head. Her long straight hair falling to her waist. Even when the car took the corner, he could still only see the back of her head. It was as though she kept rotating her head so that he couldn't see her face. But this meant her head had to spin round her entire body!"

"Just like Linda Blair in *The Exorcist*!" I said.

"Yeah! But this was real. His brother had heard about a pontianak that haunted the area. So he didn't dare look. My friend was so scared that night that he wet his bed!"

"The hairs on my arm are standing, man," said Julian. Then he threw his head back and laughed. "There are hundreds of stories like this. Fools believe them. Educated people like us don't."

"I suppose neither you nor Julian heard about the lady who one night couldn't sleep. She sat on her balcony and saw a woman walking down the dark street next to a school field. This woman wore a white dress and her long hair was hiding her face. The lady was going to call out a greeting when she realized that the woman's feet weren't touching the ground!"

"She then rushed inside and wet her bed!" I laughed.

Fauziah again kicked me under the table.

"Adoi," I said and rubbed my shin. This one hurt a lot more that her first kick. "Why are you so violent?"

"That's because I believe in VHS."

"Very funny, Fauziah," I muttered.

"So, Fauziah, you believe in all this hantu stuff, huh?" said Julian, scratching his cheek and leaving bits of sauce there.

"Yes, of course I do. If we go pontianak-hunting I'm sure you'll see something. Then you'll believe me!"

"I don't want to go lah." I said. "A waste of time."

"Coward," she said.

So that's how we ended up pontianak-hunting at 2 in the morning.

I left my motorbike near the stalls and, as I headed for the passenger's seat of her Proton, Fauziah threw me the keys and asked me to drive. I was surprised. Was this a prelude to something more romantic? Then I chided myself for the stupid thought. She hadn't changed her mind about me; she just thought a woman shouldn't be seen driving men around.

As I made my way through the city which was brightly lit and getting ready for Chinese New Year, she fiddled with a big torchlight that took twelve batteries, a free gift with the VCD player she bought and now kept in her car in case of an emergency. Julian was at the back humming to himself and ogling at the shapely females on the street. His contribution to the hunt was a baseball bat which he kept in case there was a car accident and he got into a fight. I tapped at my pack of Salem's in my shirt pocket which I told them I needed in case I wanted to die from lung cancer instead of being slaughtered by a pontianak. They both laughed and said I was mad.

"Hey, slow down," Fauziah said. "There's a bump here."

The trees receded and we went over three road bumps. Then up popped a row of terrace houses opposite a dark school field. Wasn't there a school field in her story about the pontianak in white? Before I could contemplate the similarities, Fauziah told me to make a sharp left.

It was an inconspicuous turning which I could easily have missed. The road narrowed to a single lane and climbed steeply, winding away like a snake as it took us deep through a jungle.

Black branches brushed against the windows of the car. "You sure this is the right way?" Julian asked as he roughly scratched his head.

"Yeah," Fauziah said. "It's just up ahead."

The road got even narrower and as the bitumen gave way to dirt, the streetlights disappeared and except for the headlights, we were plunged into darkness. I saw nothing but a frenzy of branches, leaves, creepers and undergrowth and just as I was about to suggest to Fauziah that we turn back she said:

"Okay, you can stop over here. This is a dead end."

I stopped the car and turned off the engine.

Everything went quiet. "Ready?" Fauziah said.

I lit a cigarette and nodded.

"Sure thing," Julian whispered.

We got out of the car and the first thing that struck us was the high-pitched cacophony of insects. The second thing that hit us was the humidity which embraced us in its sweaty arms.

Fauziah, dressed in jeans and a blouse, led the way to the water tank. I was thankful for her powerful torch which, occasionally, she would flash at the surrounding foliage or allowed it to roam the top of the trees like a searchlight.

"Nothing," she said, as though disappointed some bloodsucking creature hadn't fallen on us and ripped out our throats.

Then I stepped on something soft and cursed.

Fauziah pointed the torch at my shoes. They oozed with mud.

"At least it's not shit," she said. "Anyway, don't walk so close to the drain. It's muddy there."

"I can see that," I grumbled. "You should have told me earlier. Now I have to wash them when I get home."

"Always complaining, aren't you?" she said. "Next time I'll remember not to bring you."

"Yeah, if there is a next time."

"Come on, quit it you two," Julian said, shaking his head. "Let's look around. So this is the lair of the pontianak, huh?"

"Yeah," Fauziah muttered. "I used to cycle up here as a girl. My friends always said a pontianak haunted the place."

"Schoolgirl talk," I said.

The other two said nothing. Perhaps they wished it was so. That pontianaks didn't exist. That they belonged in the black-and-white reels of Malay movies. That they were nothing but fables conjured into Malay folklore to scare unruly children.

Julian tapped his palm with his baseball bat as he walked, his stomach swaying about him. I hoped he wouldn't have the occasion to use the weapon.

We reached the fence.

I clutched the chain links and rattled them to show I wasn't nervous. They felt warm, perhaps from the heat of the day or maybe the rusty thing was coming to life? I quickly dropped my hands and then pretended to wipe them on my jeans.

Fauziah flashed the torch at the metal sign in three languages. A uniformed man pointed a rifle at someone running — *trespassers will be executed,* it seemed to say.

Julian tried to push the padlocked gate open. The chain around it rattled but the thing was locked.

Around us the shadows, the night sky, which we could only see past the tops of the trees, seemed to grow darker and an alluring perfume, which must have drifted from the exotic flowers in the jungle, permeated the air. The insect voices became a loud shrill.

"This way," Fauziah said.

I followed the beam of her torch as she led us on the narrow track that circled the water tank. Sometimes, she flashed the light at the concrete structure but all I could see was paint peeling off like giant swatches of dead skin.

I felt the hairs stand like bristles on the back of my neck but I wasn't sure why. What was there to be afraid of? I'd been an Eagle Scout in secondary school and we had to sleep in the jungle at night as part of the ragging. I was not scared then, so why now?

Suddenly, there was a loud beeping. We all jumped.

My cigarette fell into the dirt tossing up sparks like fireflies.

"Oh shit," said Julian. "My handphone!"

He rapidly spoke into it, making big gestures with his baseball bat while I leaned against the fence, trying to stop my hands from shaking.

"Just my mother," he said, when he had finished. "Worried about me. We're supposed to go to church tomorrow." He pulled a crucifix from beneath his shirt and gave it a kiss. "This will keep the pontianak away."

"No it won't," said Fauziah. "No Muslim prayers, no Christian crosses, no Buddhist charms, no Hindu rituals can repel the vampire. The pontianak is older than religion. Older than humanity! Older than time itself!" With that she shrank away from us.

I stared at Fauziah's receding shadow. I now knew why I felt nervous. Something was wrong with her. The Fauziah I'd known never acted in such an odd manner. Or spoke so strangely.

"Okay, that's it," Julian said, when we got back to the gate. "No pontianaks here. Let's go."

"Yeah," I chimed in. "Nothing here but mosquitoes."

"We can't go now, there's more to see." Fauziah flashed her torch at the trees around us as though it would reveal something more compelling.

Julian left the water tank, then turned to us. "Nice place, Fauziah. But maybe your pontianaks are on one of Azman's Salem holidays, visiting that high country where all the trees are chopped down and burning."

I proudly tapped my pack of cigarettes nestled in my shirt pocket but I couldn't help coughing.

"Let's get out of here," he said.

"How do you know there are no pontianaks here?" Fauziah said. "One could be right beside you."

"What are you people doing here?"

We jumped at the sound of the voice.

A man in a security-guard uniform stepped into the beam of light. His face was dark and hard and his stance aggressive.

I joined Julian and Fauziah. If there was going to be trouble, they would need my help.

"We're just taking a walk," Fauziah said.

"You people can't roam around here," the man said in Malay. He was portly with his shirt undone to his waist. "That's government property, you know."

"We know," she said. She turned to Julian. "Put your baseball bat down. Don't worry about this guy."

She flashed the torch at some bushes which revealed a young woman squatting with her face turned away. From her sarong and dour gray blouse I guessed she was a maid who worked in one of the large houses down the hill. The man was probably the security guard and this was their romantic hideout.

"You should go," said the man.

"No," said Fauziah. "You should!"

"Why?"

"Because I said so!"

The tough lines on the security guard's face crumpled. He cursed under his breath and disappeared into the darkness.

A few seconds later, there came a revving and a single headlight blazed. A scooter shot down the road bearing the security guard and the maid who sat behind and hid her face.

Again, Fauziah's dark silhouette made me shiver.

The security guard wasn't frightened of her. What I saw crawling like leeches on his face was not fear but *repulsion*. Once I had mistakenly gulped a glass of sugarcane water that had gone off only to be sick to my bones. This was how I now felt about Fauziah. Why did I feel this way? I couldn't understand it.

"Good riddance," she said, turning to us. "Just because he was in a uniform he thought he could order us around. See what a bit of power does to some stupid people."

"Wow!" Julian laughed. "He really buggered off with his tail between his legs! You were so damn fierce!"

"Yeah, you showed him who's boss," I said.

She flashed the torch in my face and I tried to smile. I couldn't get the idea out of my head that she had turned rotten. I could almost smell her flesh decaying. Was my imagination running wild? Or was there something else happening here ...

And a thought nagged my mind. She told us she had been up here as a girl so that meant she must have lived here. But did she *still* live around here? And the school field ...

"Fauziah," I said. "Your story about that lady seeing a pontianak."

"Yeah, what about it?" She turned the torch away and now I could see her face. She was grinning.

"That was *you* wasn't it? You saw the pontianak. That was your house at the bottom of the hill. You once told me you lived across from a school field."

"You've got a good memory, Azman."

Her eyes seemed unnaturally big.

"What are you guys talking about?" Julian said. "Listen, ... the ... insects, they've gone all quiet."

Julian was right. It was horribly quiet. And the air was hot. Sweat dripped down my forehead.

I lit a cigarette, but couldn't keep my hands from shaking. "Fauziah, did you really see a pontianak come walking past your house?"

"I did. And I didn't run back to my room. And I didn't wet my bed. I called out to it."

"Oh, come on," Julian said. "Don't bullshit."

"The pontianak, she turned and stared at me. Her eyes huge. Her mouth open. Her feet not touching the ground. I tried to scream but nothing came out. She floated across the road like smoke. I wanted to run but couldn't move. Her hair, it was so long, it danced in the wind. Her white dress twirled around her body. And her teeth ..."

"I don't believe you," Julian barked. "You're talking shit. You're here with us now — alive and well. Stop this joking, okay?"

"Julian." Fauziah slowly shook her head. "I'm not joking. When a pontianak attacks you, you don't always die. You can become one of them."

"Nonsense!"

"Really, Julian?" Fauziah laughed. It sounded more like a cat shrieking.

Her torch fell to the ground and buried itself in the mud beside the drain.

But the flame of my lighter still flickered in my hand and by its glow we could see how her eyes bulged. How her eyebrows like worms squirmed to her ears.

Her hair grew long and coarse, curling down to her hips. Surely this had to be some trick, some joke of hers.

She threw her head back and her jaws fell open like a python's.

Her fangs gleamed. But that was not what made me stagger back and moan. For then, her throat tore open as though a jagged blade had cut her flesh.

Blood!

Great clots of it slid down the curve of her neck, down her blouse, onto her jeans.

Her head spun to a cracking sound like joints and bones breaking and popping out of their sockets.

And at the end of this unbelievable revolution, she grinned and licked her lips.

This was no longer Fauziah. This was a demon whose eyes were so large they filled half her head and within those eyes squirmed a clutch of maggots.

"*NO! NO! NO!*" cried Julian.

He raised his baseball bat in the air and screamed as he struck her head with it.

There was a snapping sound as the weapon broke in two. She growled and slapped him with one hand.

Julian's body, heavy though it was, lifted high up before crashing on the road.

He cried out as he landed hard on his back.

She glided towards him. Her head, now no longer fixed to her spine but merely held to the shoulders by stretched tendons, bounced about her neck like a Jack-in-a-box.

Julian tried to crawl away.

His body shook. Vomit spilled down his chin onto his shirt.

Fauziah's head, laughing so horribly, echoing like screeching bats through the trees, sprang towards him, hair leaping, teeth gnashing.

I dropped the lighter and ran.

Behind me, Julian screamed.

I didn't look back. I knew the pontianak was upon him.

I jumped into the Proton and started the ignition. I did a three-point turn all the while keeping my eyes away from the jerking shadows and the awful, awful sobbing.

The back wheels got caught in the mud but somehow, in miraculous answer to my frenzied recitations of the Quran, it set itself free and I sent the car hurtling down the road.

In the rearview, I saw nothing but the top of the water tank submerged like a giant coffin beneath the sea of trees.

My heart pounded like bleeding fists in my head. The car skidded and swerved as I raced down the hill and I nearly got killed when it almost ploughed into the jungle.

I got to the bottom and turned right, past the terrace houses where Fauziah lived and opposite it was the dark school field. What cruel children roamed here, what dead things came alive, crawling out from the soil, pushing away the tufts of grass, in search of blood?

I half-expected to see the pontianak in white accompanied by troops of zombies floating down the road after me, but when I checked the rearview mirror I saw nothing but dark houses, the empty street and the numbing white glow of the streetlights.

Fauziah? A pontianak? Madness! I would surely wake up soon to find that it was all an awful nightmare. I would take a piss, drink some water and return to bed. I might even masturbate to get myself to sleep. In the morning, I'd phone Julian and Fauziah and we'd all laugh at my dream.

I took a corner and slowed down beside a row of well-lit shophouses. Brand new and covered in a montage of **To Let/For Sale** signs, it was fronted by desolate parking spaces and a cavernous monsoon drain. Come park here! The buildings whispered, black rectangular windows staring. *Come roam my dark empty shops. Everything very cheap-lah*. Especially your soul!

My hands trembled at the steering.

Just my imagination!

How ... how did I end up here in this dismal lonely place? I pressed my foot on the accelerator, keen to leave the squat structures behind.

I took a right and a left. The road plunged down and again I was going through jungle. I wanted civilization. Not this! It was too much like that track on the hill. But perhaps the main road was just up ahead. Down and down I went. Twisting and turning. Jungle all around. Soon I would meet other cars and traffic lights. I was sure of it. I prayed for it. I was far from the lair of the pontianak now. The water tank and the school field. I had left her far behind. I was safe now. Surely!

The road swung to the left past a white colonial house with a banana tree at the front. Houses! All I had to do now was ...

A bulky shadow.

It darted in front of the car.

I spun the steering wheel to avoid it. The car swerved up a grassy embankment. Rocking and bumping.

I hit the brakes but too late!

The Proton crashed into a wall, jerking my skull against the headrest.

I cried and fell forward on the steering wheel.

My neck hurt like hell but that was it. It was a close call but I was okay.

I turned the engine off and staggered out of the car to be greeted by the high-pitched whine of the insects. From further away I could hear the whooping of monkeys.

I ventured to the front of the car and found that it was crushed like a Coke can.

The moon drifted out of the clouds and I saw a sign above me. I glimpsed the words: *cadangan*, *arkitek*, *pangsapuri* — and I knew this was a construction site. From the rusty pilings, the unfinished brickwork, the twisted metal and weeds that had invaded the ghastly structure I guessed the condo had been abandoned.

Then the structure began to sway and the ground seemed to liquefy.

I held the car for support, gasping and heaving.

Sweat on my brow.

I waited until the grass, the gutted condo, the clouded sky stopped their horrible rocking.

The accident had shook me up.

After a while, I stood up and felt okay. The sick feeling was gone.

I reached for my Salems but I must have dropped the packet. Or perhaps they'd slunk back to that high country.

Then I noticed that the insects had gone quiet.

And I remembered the shadow.

It had jumped in front of the car!

I didn't want to see what it was, but I had to. Slowly, like a man condemned to the gallows, I turned to the road.

And gasped.

One pale arm lay crookedly on the bitumen.

I followed it to a wreckage of a body dressed in a white shirt drenched in what looked like chocolate milkshake, but I knew it was blood. The legs were bent over each other like broken branches.

Eyes, bulging like ping-pong balls, were buried in the bloody sockets as though someone had ripped them out and then rammed them back in. The tongue lolled from one side of his mouth like a huge slug and, for some inexplicable reason, I remembered Julian telling me how he had French-kissed a girl at a rave party, both of them mingling in the mellow mists induced from popping ecstasy pills.

Even at this distance, I could see his shiny crucifix draped on the road.

Where Julian's throat should have been was a mass of flesh, blood and cartilage.

Next to his mangled body was a grassy verge and a hydrant.

Gliding over the grass towards it from a banana tree was a hazy figure in a white dress.

Her long hair spiraled to her hips.

The head swayed from side to side at impossible angles as though the neck had been broken. A Jack-in-a-box.

This dreadful motion stopped as it reached the hydrant.

The head rotated to glance up at me.

Fauziah grinned.

She floated over the grass.

Body rising through the night air.

The hideous head spun around the body like a top in slow motion. Like a lazy Susan in a Chinese restaurant — but this one offered not halal food but dishes of blood and rotting meat.

"I'm all yours, Azman," came a voice.

A voice from between silky sheets.

I saw hair. I saw face.

Mine at last?

"That's right, all yours, my darling."

Hair. And face.

Flying across the road. Over Julian's mangled body.

Closer she came. White dress shimmering loosely in the moonlight.

Long hair. Rotting face.

Sweat poured down my cheeks.

Eyes bursting into mine.

Up the embankment she drifted. White dress twirling.

The dank smell of slaughtered pigs.

Hair. Face.

Maggots squirmed in the eyeballs. A clutch of them fell on the grass.

On the laces of my shoes.

The head stopped its gruesome spinning.

Her jaws flew wide open to reveal scalpel-like fangs.

I stepped back, quivering. I realized I was screaming. My throat was on fire. But wasn't I screaming all along?

If this was a nightmare surely, surely now I would wake? A liquid warmth spilled down my thighs and knees. Perhaps I was wetting my bed.

If only.

The head lunged for my throat. Perhaps for a long deep kiss.

My body crumpled to the grass.

My pack of Salems upon my cheek. So this is my high country.

Where the feasting begins.

HAUNTED APARTMENT

The Indian lorry driver stuck a hairy arm out the window, staring lecherously at me. Gleaming beady eyes, accompanying black bristles, greasy hair glistened sourly in the afternoon sun. His thick eyebrows arched as his pouting lips curled into a dirty smile, revealing shiny white teeth. The lorry growled out oil and black smoke as if warning me. I looked away. I hated it. Sometimes these workers called out as they drove past, hurling insults with the same mad look in their eyes. They had no respect for women here.

The heat and traffic pounded my head. Perspiration trickled down my brow. All I wanted right now was to have a cold shower and to slump on my bed in my cool air-conditioned room. My eyes blurred, my head was spinning. My boss, the nerd, was over-demanding. We were on a five-day week, but he liked us coming in on Saturdays. A sexist, good-for-nothing idiot. It was another stupid, meaningless day at the place we called the office. Any more days like these and I would be better off joining the civil service or becoming a nun. Did people still become nuns in this country? Did people still do crazy things like that? Who knows. Who cares. Thank goodness the weekend's finally here.

"Pamela, are you coming in tomorrow? We could discuss the Home Villas brochure then." My nerdy boss had a habit of calling out at me just as I was stepping out of the office.

"Sorry, I can't," I said as I brushed back my shoulder-length hair. He slowly walked up to me and had a habit of always standing too close, as if he was my lover.

Fat chance of that happening. My boss was a middle-aged Englishman who had stayed here too long, and didn't know how to go back to the land of rain and hail where the streets were meant to be paved with gold. Many from India and Jamaica went there and discovered the truth in the demoralizing dole queue. Perhaps my boss liked how some locals would kowtow to him and call him 'Tuan.' Maybe he thoroughly enjoyed his endless stengahs at the Royal Selangor Club. Or perhaps he just liked the girls here. More likely the latter.

"Why can't you? Have you a date with your boyfriend?" he asked sharply as he scratched his smooth pink chin.

"No, I'm seeing my doctor," I lied. I was annoyed. "And I haven't got a boyfriend!"

"No boyfriend? Pretty girl like you?"

"I don't need a boyfriend," I retorted. He faked a laugh and walked back into his office. He liked Indian girls. Mixed Indian girls like me were also to his taste. My mother was Chinese. He tried to ask me out once but I refused and I suppose he's always had that grudge against me.

I edged my red Kancil through the snarling traffic, trying to push my boss out of my mind. Hooting, racing, cutting in on the left and jumping traffic lights. I hated it. I had become one of them. I came to KL three years ago just after my father died. Was my coming here really the right thing to do? I'd asked myself this question many times. Maybe I was in too much of a hurry to leave the old memories behind and move on. Maybe I was just running from the emptiness in me.

I could still see the weariness in my father's face a few days before his death. Cancer is a horrible disease. It comes when you least expect it and then your whole world just collapses into dust. He suffered painfully and in the end the hospital couldn't do anything for him. When he finally died in my arms I cried for three whole days. On the third day, we cremated him. They had to stop me from jumping into the flaming pyre to join him in death.

For the next three months, I drifted in and out of life. I could not go to work, could not eat, could not concentrate on a single thing. Then slowly, grudgingly, I came out of my despair, my mourning. My family was around, coaxing me out of my grief. And finally, one morning, I woke up, ran to his picture and with tears streaming down my face, whispered goodbye. And to this day I'm sure I heard his voice say *farewell.* And I felt his smile.

My father always smiled so that it lit up his dark brown face. He loved carrying me when I was a little girl, always bouncing me up and down. I loved twirling my fingers in his jet-black hair, messing it up. He would laugh and hand me his comb. "Comb it back, you little mermaid," he would say. I would try to but we always ended up with a bigger mess. He loved telling me stories about a man named Mahatma Gandhi. And I would always be totally absorbed and asked many questions.

"Always be kind," he said gently. "And always look in the mirror to make sure that you're the person you believe in. And if you always stand up to your principles, nobody can take that away from you."

I didn't understand what he meant then but when I was older he made things clearer so that I understood. And he was always there for me, to protect me from the world. As I grew into an adult, his hair turned white and he started to go bald. But he always retained those large deep eyes. I felt that he could see right through me. Then the pain in his throat started.

I was almost home. The condominium stood tall against the hazy, cloud-filled sky. What would my father think of it? He would say something profound and meaningful like this was a testament to man's achievement or that man can create mountains but they had not yet learnt to move seas. We had put people on the moon decades ago, yet people still starved. Yes, he might have said something like that. My heart still ached for his words, his presence. Two years may seem a long time, yet I remember his passing like it was yesterday.

I drove past the gate as the security guard waved me in. I parked in my usual spot in the lower basement and took the lift up to the nineteenth floor. The numbers changed quickly. I was a daily mountain climber. Maybe also a corporate climber. Certainly not a social climber. Otherwise, I would be dating my boss. I shuddered at the thought.

Mrs Razak came out of her apartment as the lift door closed. She lived with her husband and two young sons in 19-01. As usual, she wore a loose-fitting dress not unlike a maternity dress that reached down to her ankles. Her hair was tied in a bun.

"Hello Pamela." She greeted me with a smile. "Hard day at work?"

"Yes, as usual," I replied. I liked her. She was the motherly sort.

"I'm baking a chocolate cake tomorrow. Would you like some?" She smiled warmly. It was good to have nice neighbors.

"Oh yes, Mrs Razak, I love your cakes. Your marble cake was delicious."

"Good, I'll bring some round on Sunday," she said. "The last girl that lived here liked them, too." She grimaced as if she had made a slip of the tongue. A momentary shadow passed across her face. "Oh, I'll see you on Sunday then," she hurriedly said and headed for the lifts.

Did she say something wrong? Was she hiding something? No, she couldn't be, she was far too nice.

I found my keys and opened the door to apartment 19-04. I dumped my bag on the carpet and entered the bedroom. My head hit my pillow and I exhaled, closing my eyes. I moved here a month ago. We had to move out of the house, so I had spent most evenings and weekends house hunting. I decided that I wanted a place of my own. No more cheap rentals for me. Sharing could be fun but it got tiresome at times. Our pile of unwashed dishes which everybody disowned made the place stink.

But house-hunting was not easy. The nice places were too expensive and the cheaper places were dumps. Luckily, I could afford this. The real estate agent said that it was below market value and Sue Lyn, my good friend who works in housing development, said that too. So I dug into all my savings and quickly put a down payment on it.

I liked this place straight away. It was in a good condominium with many expatriate neighbors. I liked that. I got another loan from the bank to do it up and spent a bomb. But the place was lovely. Except for one thing which I just could not place. A stupid yet unmistakable feeling. I didn't feel like I belonged here. Like I was intruding. Like this apartment belonged to someone else. It was another person's apartment. I was being silly again.

Then I started getting up at 4 o'clock in the morning. I could get up and hear the loud ticking of my alarm clock. And it would always be 4 o'clock sharp. The luminous clock face would stare at me as if asking "why are you awake at this hour?" I had no answer. Sometimes I could hear the sound of traffic below. Sometimes the sound of the wind would drown all other sounds. That was eerie. That was when I got scared. Silly to be afraid of the wind. But the howling of the wind sounded like an angry animal. Thankfully that only happened twice. I would fall asleep soon after.

All this started three weeks ago. The first week it happened once. Last week it happened three times. This week it has happened almost every night! It was becoming frightening. I could not understand why. Maybe I had been working too hard or had too much on my mind. I knew I somehow had to get rid of this habit of waking up at 4 o'clock.

I pushed away these thoughts and went into the lounge. I played a cassette and stepped out onto the balcony. A violin concerto blossomed out from behind me. This was probably the best thing about the apartment. The view was beautiful. There was still so much greenery in the city. I could see mountains in the distance. Not too far off I could see a housing estate being developed. To the right of it a tower block was coming up. It was probably an office building or another condominium. Another concrete mountain. Development at a rapid pace. What were the costs though? I looked down at the large swimming pool. It was peaceful and blue. My oasis in this increasingly maddening city. The pool was built so close to our building that I felt that I could actually dive straight into it. The waters were so inviting. I swam as often as I could.

The doorbell rang. I turned the music off and straightened my dress. It was Mrs Razak.

"May I come in?" she asked. She looked embarrassed.

"Yes, please do." She came into the lounge and sat uncomfortably down on the sofa. She studied my posters on the wall as if postponing what she had to say. "Would you like some tea or a cold drink?" I politely asked.

"No, thank you, Pamela." She examined her hands in thought. They were small and wrinkled. She turned her eyes to me and took in a deep breath. "Since you moved in I've been wanting to talk to you. But I never really got the chance."

"Talk to me about what?"

"About the previous occupant. The girl who lived here before you. It slipped out just now and I thought I'd better clear my conscience and tell you about her."

"What happened to her?" I asked curiously. This was all very strange.

"She was a nice girl like you. Went to work. Well brought-up. I could tell."

"Yes, but what happened to her?" My voice hid the cold feeling I felt in the pit of my stomach.

"She committed suicide. She jumped from that balcony over there." Mrs Razak pointed at my balcony, her hand trembling. "It was in the papers."

"Suicide — in this apartment?" I looked at her in disbelief. Yes, she had said it. The previous occupant had committed suicide in my apartment. I was shocked and speechless.

"Yes, I couldn't believe it," she whispered, "fell and hit her head on the concrete. Her body then rolled into the pool. It was quite horrible."

"But why are you telling me this?" I asked. I didn't really want to hear any more.

"Because you might be in danger. You see, I don't think she committed suicide. It has something to do with this apartment. I've never felt comfortable about it."

I didn't want to hear any more. It was hard enough having to deal with the fact that someone had committed suicide in my home. I wasn't prepared to listen to any ghost stories about it either. This was my apartment, it belonged to me, and I wasn't going to be scared away. Mrs Razak belonged to the older generation. She believed in old wives' tales and other superstitions. I did not believe in such things. I lived in a modern world of computers, laser discs and high technology. The dark tales of the ignorant past could remain dead.

I cut Mrs Razak's story short and politely showed her to the door. No, I had not experienced anything strange. Yes, I wouldn't hesitate to call her if there was anything wrong. She was a nice and caring lady. I didn't want to be rude. But I didn't want to be afraid for no reason either. People who live alone don't appreciate ghost stories. Especially about their own home.

I couldn't help thinking about the girl who jumped to her death. What a horrible way to die. Why did she commit suicide? The thought of my 4 o'clock problem came back to me. There could not be any link. Surely not. I was just overworked and hadn't been sleeping well. That was all there was to it. Or was there something more? I wished Mrs Razak had not told me. By trying to do good she only caused me to worry. It was stupid to be worried. There was nothing to be worried about. But I suddenly wished that I didn't live alone.

I called my friend Sue Lyn. I knew I could count on her. We met when I first came to the city. She was happy to have me come spend the night. I felt silly packing my bag. I knew I was running away from whatever was in my apartment. I had to admit that Mrs Razak had scared me. The 4 o'clock wakings were too much of a coincidence. And even if they were a mere coincidence, I wasn't about to take any chances.

Over dinner I told Sue Lyn all about it.

Her eyes were full of concern. She had short hair and a round face. Her Chinese upbringing allowed her to understand what was happening. Funny how we Asians are more prone to believing in ghosts. My boss would have laughed and called me a coward.

"Do you think there's something wrong with my apartment?" I finally asked.

"I don't know, Pamela," she said as she held my hand. "You know, I've heard that some buyers will bring along a baby when they visit a prospective home. If the baby cries it means that there's something wrong there and so they won't buy it. I'm afraid we didn't do that with your apartment, did we?"

"No, we didn't," I said as I took off my earrings and placed them on her table. "Look I'll just stay tonight, okay? I'm sure I'll be fine tomorrow."

"Stay as long as you like."

"No, I must go back tomorrow. I've got to face whatever's there, imaginary or not. I've got to face my fears. If I ran away now I'd never be able to look myself in the mirror ever again."

We talked a bit more until it was late. Her couch was comfortable and I slept well and I did not wake up at 4 o'clock. That alone should have served as a warning that something was wrong with my apartment. But it did not register then.

Sue Lyn had to go out early. I could not face returning home so I went to the office instead. My boss was surprised to see me. I told him my doctor's appointment had been canceled.

"Good, we can discuss that brochure then," he said with an irritating smile.

I tried to work on the Home Villas brochure but Mrs Razak's words kept creeping up on me.

"... you might be in danger. ... It has something to do with the apartment."

But I had to face my fears. I knew that. It was logic against superstition. Science against primitive fears. The illogical wasn't going to scare me, no matter how hard it damn tried. After lunch, I went home to *my* apartment.

My apartment looked just as I had left it. It felt normal, there was nothing strange and that was reassuring. Maybe there was nothing to worry about after all. I felt stupid, called myself a silly cow and laughed. It was a sunny day and I felt quite cheerful. Moreover, the breeze on the nineteenth floor was lovely. The afternoon was spent tidying up and reading my novel. In the evening, I made a simple TV dinner and watched a comedy. I knew I wasn't afraid any more as I laughed at all the funny bits. Before retiring for the evening, I had a nice warm shower. Everything would be all right. Or so I thought.

I woke up again that night. Automatically I turned to look at the alarm clock. *4 o'clock*. I was wide awake. I couldn't understand it. Why did I keep waking up? And why at 4? These questions wound tortuously through my mind. I must have asked *why* a hundred times. My luminous clock face continued to stare at me. With no answers.

And then it dawned on me. The Chinese superstition. *4 o'clock*. Four was the numerologist's nightmare. Four was death to the Chinese. My mother, being Chinese, always warned me of that number. She avoided that number whenever possible. Not on phone numbers, not on car numbers, not on bank accounts and certainly not on addresses. Four was death and death was four. That was when I knew that there was something really wrong with the apartment. The suicide was not a coincidence. Mrs Razak had tried to warn me. That was when I became frightened.

And something out there knew it.

I was listening to the ticking of the clock and the sounds of the traffic below, wondering what to do. I would move out in the morning. There was no question of that. It was foolish to come back. I should have listened to Sue Lyn and stayed with her. But what should I do now? That girl did not commit suicide — there was something wrong here. Something else lived here.

I decided that I would go to Mrs Razak's and spend the night there. She would not mind. She had said so. I knew I had to get out of here.

Just as I tried to get up, my breath caught in my throat. I heard my breathing, deep and loud. I was gasping for air. A weight fell heavily down on my chest. I tried to push myself up but could not. My arms were like lead. I was pinned down and no amount of struggling from me could relieve the pressure on my chest, arms and legs. It was as if a large, strong man was holding me down. Then the wind started.

A dark, threatening wind. It started softly as if coming from the road below. Humming, swirling and building up. It grew louder and louder, climbing higher and higher up the floors. It was wild and booming in my ears, building to a crescendo. Then it burst into the room filling it with raging fury.

The howling was deafening, not just like an angry animal but like an angry animal driven quite mad. And beyond it, something was laughing. A crazy, menacing laugh. That laughter rode on the waves of howling. The howling went up and down — the laughter was always there just beyond it. It was like some laughing demon riding this crazed animal. I started to sob uncontrollably.

And then I had a terrible feeling. A feeling I never thought I would ever have. A feeling that almost made me scream. *I felt its evil. It was definitely evil! And it was coming for me!*

That thought sent a cold convulsion through my body. Somehow in my fear I managed to get up. The paralysis suddenly disappeared. I threw the blanket off and ran from the bedroom. I flicked the switch but the lounge lights wouldn't come on. I tried to scream but it got caught like a bone in my throat.

I was about to rush for the front door when it turned completely quiet. No howling, no laughter. Nothing. It left as suddenly as it had come.

It was unnaturally silent. Everything remained dark but for the outside. The balcony door was wide open. I didn't remember leaving it so.

A misty green light swirled in the darkness beyond my balcony. The curtains billowed softly in the breeze.

The light was dancing. Dancing with the curtains. Dancing in circles.

Calling me. Calling me out.

I felt myself being drawn towards the balcony. My legs moved involuntarily, slowly, one at a time. I could not stop it. My mind was saying *No*. But it was calling.

And then I *wanted* to move. Wanted to go outside.

I stepped out onto the balcony. The lights were happy, the lights wanted me. It was beautiful. My hair and nightgown were caught in the wind. I held the rails for balance. The lights were dancing. Wanting to dance with me. It would be a beautiful dance. There was music playing — a delightful ancient melody. The lights continued dancing. Calling. Still calling.

Calling me down.

And the pool was lovely, inviting, welcoming. The pool lights were on and there were a hundred other twinkling lights swirling within the waters. The waters sparkled blue. The dancing lights were falling. Slowly falling. Calling to me.

Come Pamela. Come down. Join us.

I felt my body lean forward. I was on the tips of my toes. Yes, it would be lovely. To join the lights. To fall with it. In a glorious dance.

Yes, yes, come on Pamela. This is what you want, what you desire, what you dreamt of.

I felt my body slowly swaying off the rails. It would be incredibly beautiful.

Come on down. Let go of the rails.

I took my hands off.

I was about to jump into paradise when something said *No*.

I grabbed the rails just as I felt a tug to pull me down. I fell on the balcony floor. I pulled my face against the rails and looked down at the lighted pool. There was something dark and growing, spilling out from the edge of the pool. It was blood. Oozing through the blue waters. The water had been disturbed, as if somebody had jumped in. The pool lights were reflecting off the dancing waters, now filled with deep red blood. I fainted.

When I came to, it was nearly dawn. I saw the first glow of sunrise beyond the distant mountain peaks. It was red. And then I remembered the blood. I remembered last night. I looked down at the pool. There was no blood there. Not a trace of it.

What went on last night? What was I doing here? Had I imagined everything? Was it a bad dream? No, I knew it had all happened. This apartment was evil. It had been a living nightmare and I had almost jumped to my death. That poor girl had faced this same horror. It had killed her.

What had saved me? Someone had said 'No' just before I leaped. I could still hear the voice — it was vaguely familiar. I sat down wearily in the lounge with a cup of warm coffee. Whose voice was it? It was a familiar voice. Very familiar. I stared at our old family photograph which stood on the side table. Its silver frame was tinged in red, brightly reflecting the sunrise. And everyone was smiling there. I felt myself fall momentarily into its black-and-white world. *And then I knew.*

My coffee mug lay sprawled on the gray carpet. Black coffee spilled like a huge bloodstain. No, it couldn't be. It just couldn't be. But I knew it was. His voice was unmistakable.

It was my father! It was my father's voice! "No, little mermaid, no," that was what he said! I then felt the tears roll hotly down my cheeks.

I was sobbing loudly. Crying for my love for him. And I knew he loved me and was still with me, by my side, protecting me. And I cried with joyous relief. Despite my tears I felt the strangest sensation that everything was all right. It was the apartment, it felt different, like I belonged here. Without anyone watching me. The way it ought to be. I stood on the balcony and stared for a long while at the sunrise. It was beautiful and its warmth fell on my face. I was no longer afraid. He would always be here to protect me. This was no longer another's apartment. It belonged to me. It was mine.

Mrs Razak came over a few hours later. Her chocolate cake was delicious as I was sure it would be. I asked her to have morning tea with me.

"Sorry, Pamela, for scaring you the other day. You know we old people can be quite superstitious." She smiled apologetically.

"Don't worry," I said as I passed her the sugar, "I don't believe in ghosts."

"Oh, that's good," she said as she sipped her tea. "We Malays say if you don't believe in ghosts then they won't disturb you."

"That's interesting," I said as I helped myself to another piece of cake, "but it might not be entirely true you know." I was waiting for her to ask me what I meant. I would then have told her what had happened to me.

But instead Mrs Razak started telling me about how her son was putting on so much weight. She could not understand why. I did not mention her lovely cakes. I looked at my family photograph and saw my father smile. I somehow knew that I would not be waking up at 4 o'clock ever again.

A LABOR DAY WEEKEND

Arul and I are both in our early thirties. Both married for ten years or so with a couple of kids each. Neither of us would admit it to our wives but family life, sometimes — oh hell, a lot of the time — can be a bit boring and routine. If it's not my wife nagging about some minor transgression, like my failure to change a lightbulb or to send the car for service, or our two girls screaming over some new Barbie doll or her Pa arriving in his wheelchair with Lily and Albert for a surprise visit, then it's those tedious twelve-course family dinners her Pa is so fond of with fifteen around the table and everyone jabbering all at once and pretending to fight over the bill.

So one day, while we were having chicken rice, Arul said to me: "Eh, Hong — let's go on holiday this Labor Day weekend."

I spat a chicken wing bone on my red plastic plate, grimaced and shook my head. "No way. We'll all get on top of each other. Remember our trip to Cameron Highlands?"

"Yeah, only too well," Arul said, downing his iced Chinese tea. "But this time it's just you and me-lah. You know, just like our bachelor days."

"Sure," I said, staring at his wavy hair, at the sunglasses he had propped on it like a black tiara. "Why not? I'm sure Belinda won't mind. What about Moona?"

"Ah, I don't need to ask her. I just tell her what I'm going to do. She's lucky I even do that!"

"You're a real bugger, Arul. Anyway, where will we go?"

Arul excitedly told me that we were going on an unplanned holiday. "Just pack your bags for two nights. Then jump in my car and go wherever the road takes us, man."

I hoped Belinda wouldn't mind me taking off with my best friend for a couple of nights, as she was sometimes moody and unpredictable. So I chose the best time to ask her which was after our girls had gone to bed and she was enjoying her nightly cup of Chamomile tea listening to Pavarotti. I sat quietly, pretending to enjoy the pompous bellowing and as the opera singer's voice came to a climax and the strings of the violins died down, I casually mentioned Arul's plans for the coming weekend. Belinda, in the cascading folds of her white nightie and her thick plastic glasses edging down her nose, just glanced at me snottily and said:

"Sure you can, darling. Have a good time. You need a break from that slave-driving computer company you work for." And after a pause in which she ran her fingers through the coarse curls of her hair she said icily: "What's that you're holding over there?"

"Oh, just a list of government resthouses Arul asked me to get."

That's when she blew her top.

Now I have to explain. You see, Belinda, my dear wife, is one of the bravest and hard-headed persons I know but when it comes to ghosts or anything even remotely supernatural, she gets shit scared. She shivers when a funeral procession passes by and once we got lost driving around Jalan Dewan Bahasa and ended up next to some Chinese gravestones with photos of dead men and women staring, which was when she screamed and slapped me on the head. She refuses to watch *The Blair Witch Project* or *The Exorcist* when I bought the VCDs from the pasar malam, and she won't even allow me to watch *Millennium* on TV. I don't blame her. Some people are like that, they scare themselves silly.

So why did my darling wife blow her top? Well, you have to combine her irrational fears with Arul's uncanny interests. Ever since I've known Arul from secondary school, he's been keen not on History or Geography but on the subjects of Mysticism and the Occult. His bookshelf is stacked with works such as Richard Cavendish's *The Black Arts*, Colin Wilson's *The Occult* and Frazer's *The Golden Bough*. These books are just part of a much wider collection, and I'm only familiar with these titles because he tried to lend them to me. I said no thanks, for I knew Belinda would freak out and perhaps empty a glass of water over my head like she did when I once forgot to buy some nappies. That was, of course, a long time ago when Henrietta was two and Gillian was three months old. They're eight and six now and so I don't have that problem anymore.

Back to Arul. As I was saying, he has a keen interest in the Occult. In his living room, there is a small wooden chest in which he keeps a tattered pack of Tarot cards, a Ouija board, a pendulum, an assortment of crystals which he recharges every month beneath a full moon and a secret journal which he calls his Book of Shadows.

As for my Belinda, she is only too aware of Arul's interests because, on that ill-fated holiday at Cameron Highlands, he had brought out a crystal ball, lit some black candles and offered to contact Belinda's dead mother. Belinda screamed and ran out of the room and they weren't on speaking terms for the rest of the holiday. They haven't been too keen on each other since then. Ah, such is life.

Which brings me to the list of guesthouses I had in my hand. My dear wife believes, and I don't think she's too far wrong, that most of these government guesthouses are haunted. You should hear some of the stories that get around about these places, enough to make a grown man shiver in fright.

So, putting two and two together, Belinda blew her top.

Finally, after my dear wife had calmed down considerably and as I nursed my bruised arm which she had used as a punch bag, she said to me as we lay in bed:

"So, you two guys think you can go ghost-hunting without telling me."

"Darling," I pleaded. "I already told you, so many times, that we're not doing that."

"I don't want you meddling with this stuff and come back possessed by some spirit ... if you come back at all, that is."

"But darling, we ... we're not going ghost-hunting."

"Then why does Arul want that list of guesthouses? Arul wants to visit them to catch ghosts. So don't bluff me!"

"He ... he's never mentioned ghosts, Belinda. Not once. We're just going on holiday!"

"You promise?"

"I promise."

"I'll think about it. Turn off the light. Let's go to bed, it's late."

"Sure, darling."

The next morning, after I mentioned that we were going to get a three-month bonus this year, Belinda's mood changed and she told me that I could go. She even managed a smile. I kissed her and quickly left for office in case she changed her mind, jubilant at the thought of two nights away from home, away from Belinda!

On the day of our departure, black clouds covered the city and rain spilt from the skies, falling in torrents for hours.

Arul and I decided to wait until the rain cleared and by the time it'd stopped, which was about 4:30, floods covered much of KL. Arul wanted to head for the east coast but because of the terrible traffic, we decided to head south.

So we sped down the highway, agreeing that we'd spend the first night in Seremban but when we got to the Seremban turnoff, night hadn't yet fallen, and so we decided to continue our journey and took the route to PD.

On the way, I casually told Arul about Belinda's suspicions.

Arul hollered and thumped the steering wheel, his gold medallion dancing on his hairy chest.

"Eh, you shouldn't be so docile," he said. "Be the boss-lah, tell her what you want. Don't ask for permission. Don't even discuss it. Just tell her what you want. That's what I do. I don't lift a finger around the house, you know. I'm the king of my own domain!"

"I'm not like you, Arul. I'm not a dictator. Belinda and I have a partnership. We discuss things and come to a consensus."

"Yeah, like hell, Hong. I've seen how she bullies you. Don't take it, man. Show her who's boss."

"Anyway," I said, changing the subject. "You wanted that list of guesthouses just in case we needed a place to stay, right? Not for catching ghosts?"

"Come on, man. If I wanted to catch ghosts, I'd tell you. I just thought those places are so much cheaper than staying in a hotel. So, don't worry-*lah*, we're not going ghost-hunting, not this time anyway!"

With that he laughed and turned on the CD player. In his shiny red shirt, he looked like a devil up to no good.

"Well, that's a relief to know," I said without really believing him.

When we arrived at PD, Arul stopped the car at the first hotel we came to so that he could use the toilet. While he did his business, which I guessed was a big one because of the time he was taking, I sauntered over to the desk and asked the Malay receptionist whether they had any rooms for the night.

"Sorry, sir," he said in his ill-fitting green jacket. "All taken. Labor day weekend."

"Oh, I see," I said. "What about the other hotels?"

"None available. Whole of PD booked out." He grinned proudly and turned to a female guest with a servant and three children in tow.

"Thanks," I muttered and went in search of Arul.

Arul was in a cubicle doing his business and chatting on the handphone with his cousin. I interrupted him and told him the bad news.

"Let's get some beers first," he said and flushed the toilet.

So we wandered into the hotel bar and ordered our drinks from a sleepy middle-aged bartender. We took our seats in the rattan chairs and as we surveyed the empty lounge and tried to get a glimpse of the dark sea outside the windows, Arul and I chatted about many things. It felt just like the old days — two guys out for a drink with not a care in the world and even the prospect of no place to stay that night didn't bother us.

"So what shall we do?" I finally asked.

Arul put down his Carlsberg and wiped his mouth with a handkerchief. "We'll stay here all night drinking. Getting pissed drunk and in the morning we can take a dip in the sea — go skinny-dipping!"

"Come on get serious."

"Okay, let's head to Malacca. There'll be more hotels there. Bound to have at least one hotel room."

"Sounds good to me."

Watching the holiday crowd fill the bar and the musicians setting up on the stage, we had a couple more beers each and chewed hungrily on the nuts and crackers. We hadn't had dinner but we weren't too bothered. This felt like a real adventure and I was coming to appreciate Arul's unplanned holiday.

We listened to the band. The lead singer was a thin man with dark glasses singing almost angrily into the microphone. He had a great voice but, finally, we had to drag ourselves away as it was almost midnight and there was a long drive ahead.

As we left PD, heading further south, the streetlights disappeared and the road turned dark and we only had the car's headlights to help us see the way ahead. Without another vehicle in sight, the entangling jungle, the rigid shadows of the rubber and oil palm estates closed in as we made our slow progress to Malacca.

Not the moon nor a single star glimmered in the black sky. Occasionally, there was a flash of lighting which lit the trees and barren land. I glanced nervously at the host of shadows and I was sure we were being watched by evil things — spirits, ghosts, demons — that hid in the enveloping darkness. Would a pair of burning red eyes peer in through the window? Would a pontianak, with its intestines spilling out like a clutch of snakes, appear on the back seat and stroke my hair with its long sharp fingernails?

I shuddered. Perhaps Belinda was the sensible one. We were asking for trouble driving on this scary road after midnight.

Arul was unusually quiet. He may have been concentrating hard on the dark twisting road or perhaps he, too, felt nervous. We came across small villages with not a soul in sight and I knew if the car broke down we'd be in real trouble. The only sign of life were the scrawny cows and goats that wandered the night like lost souls. Arul flashed the headlights at a bull that blocked the road; it innocently stared back with its big round eyes and then, without a care in the world, it got up and sauntered away.

We drove through a town, where the streetlights blazed upon old shophouses and deserted streets, and although it was startlingly bright it looked like a ghost town washed in theatrical lights and was just as scary as the dark roads, which we soon found ourselves on again.

"You planned all this, didn't you?" I said.

"What? Taking this scary drive to Malacca? You gotta be kidding, man."

"I suppose you didn't, Arul. We headed to Seremban because of the floods, didn't we?"

"Sure did. And just because I'm interested in the occult doesn't mean I like to be scared."

"Maybe we were meant to come here. Maybe the floods, no rooms in PD, all of it was meant to happen, to bring us here."

"Maybe," Arul said. "But I doubt it."

"I suppose so. Belinda would really freak out if she was here."

"Yeah, she would!" Arul chuckled.

Neither of us said a thing as we passed a cemetery of pale headstones, wild grasses and trees that cowered beneath the sky. At a T-junction, we turned right which took us past a row of half-constructed terrace houses which, from the wild bushes surrounding it, had clearly been abandoned.

"Imagine," Arul continued, "if you went home and told her that we *had* been ghost-hunting."

"She'd be frightened to bits!" I smiled as I imagined her face, her hair like curly wires bouncing around her head.

"Man, Hong, I bet she would! Hey, imagine if you brought back a bottle and said that we caught a ghost in it. Tell her we went to one of those resthouses which she's so sure is haunted."

"She'd really go nuts!"

"I bet she would!" Arul burst out laughing and suddenly the road didn't seem so bad.

Soon we were driving along the coast, with stalls along the beach, and a plethora of cars and motorcycles joined us, honking, engine snarling, headlights blazing. Arul and I looked at each other and grinned.

We arrived in Malacca just after 1 that morning only to find that the Renaissance Hotel was booked out. We skirted several other hotels, motels and resthouses, including those on that list that so irked Belinda, only to end up without a room. We had to conclude that, like PD, Malacca's rooms were also full.

So like all good bachelors, not matter how fleeting or patently untrue, we slunked into a couple of bars, ordered beers by the jug and tried to feel up the GROs. Neither of us were worried about our accommodation for the night, as we talked, joked, looked back on our lives and wondered about the future.

When the bars closed their doors on us, there was nowhere left to go but the riverside next to the red-bricked Stadhuys, where we left the car engine and air conditioner on, tilted the seats back and tried to get some sleep. We weren't the only ones for there were three other vehicles parked close to us, one with three young children and a baby crying within. I only slept for an hour and ended up strolling by the river, listening to the slow gentle rhythm of the tied-up boats and later roamed around the Dutch building and, as dawn approached, I labored up the steep steps to the Portuguese fort amongst the early morning joggers and walkers.

Later that morning, we managed to get a hotel room and so after our showers and a buffet breakfast at the hotel, we went sightseeing. We strolled past old shophouses with their dark wooden windows and doors and later we visited a graffiti-covered St. John's Fort with its cannons pointing tiredly to nowhere. Dinner was at a nyonya restaurant followed by an early night in.

The next morning, after breakfast at a Malay stall selling cakes and nasi lemak, we took the North-South highway back to KL.

"Why are you grinning?" asked Arul as we sped by the Seremban turn off. For a second, he took his eye off the road to scrutinize me.

"You know I went to the toilet after breakfast, right?"

"Yeah, you did."

"Well, there was no water there. So I used the toilet at the Shell station. I found something on the window sill."

"What was it?"

I reached for the back seat, where my overnight bag was propped, pulled out the item and showed it to Arul.

"A jar!" he exclaimed. "You found a jam jar!"

"Sure did man," I said and stared through the clean empty glass. "I didn't think anyone would want it so I just took it."

Arul chuckled. "Man, Belinda will go crazy when you show up with that thing."

"I know she will!" I burst out laughing and tears rolled down my cheeks. "I ... I can just imagine her face when I tell her the story. She'll be so shit-scared she ... she'll do anything I say."

"Yeah, Hong, you're the man. You'll be the big boss of the house. She won't mess with you again!" Arul roared with laughter and he had trouble keeping the car steady. "You're going to have fun with that!"

We talked of many other things on the way back, but as the traffic built up upon the highway our voices became intermittent and, as we passed the Nilai turnoff, we fell silent.

I held the jar between my thighs and, with one finger, tapped the rusty aluminum lid while an image of her wire-like hair, her thick plastic glasses and her stare full of spite and ridicule came dancing down the highway. I imagined myself rotating the jar before her eyes and seeing her lips droop and alarm bouncing like a ping-pong ball around her face. She thought I was a weakling but this would teach her that I too could be cruel and dominating, that I was the man of the house and she'd better get used to it. Yes! Things were going to change. I would finally stand up to her!

Arul dropped me off at my house, one of many terrace houses on our street. So many streets in our suburb, so many suburbs in the city, so many cities in the world. But this house, this small plot of land with brick walls, tiled roof and crush of belongings, was mine — my castle, where I alone should be king.

Arul gave me a wave and took off. His parting words, before he wound up the window, were: "I'd give anything to see her face, man!"

I laughed as I stood in the middle of the road, bag slung over my shoulder, beneath the blazing sun but, when I turned to face the house, I shuddered. Perhaps

I should put the jar away? Then nothing would happen, everything would be the same, life would carry on unchanged: wife nagging, children bickering, relatives visiting followed by those loathsome twelve-course dinners.

But, like Arul, I too would give anything to see her face when I showed Belinda the jar. I would threaten to open it and release the fictitious spirit if ever she got out of hand. That was it! I'd use the thing as a weapon!

This was the *coup d'etat*, the bloodless revolution, the election where I alone controlled the press and TV — I'd install the Fuhrer, the dictator, the tyrant who would reign forever and a day!

Me!

I shook my head and these mad thoughts scattered away. All I wanted was to wear the pants in my own home. That was all. Was it too much to ask?

I pressed the bell and the maid, Ani, came out and unlocked the gate. My car looked as though it needed a wash. I would get Ani to do it this afternoon. I would start giving the orders around here.

I took off my shoes and entered the living room, Ani trailing behind.

Henrietta and Gillian would be at their cousin's place for their violin lesson so I had Belinda to myself.

"It's you," said Belinda when she saw me. She held a newspaper and with her eyes back at its rustling pages, she flippantly asked: "How was the holiday?"

"Great!" I said and put my bag down.

"Been doing anything I should know about? Like spend all our savings?" She took her eyes off the paper and pushed up her glasses to scrutinize me.

"Nothing dear except ..."

"Except what!" She folded the paper and got up. "Tell me what you've been doing!"

"Oh, eh ... Arul and I, we went ..."

"Went where?" Her fists were clenched so that I knew she was going to start hitting me on the arms.

"Ghost-hunting! We went ghost-hunting!"

Her jaw dropped.

"Ghost-hunting?"

"I know I promised not to ..."

"How could you! Why don't you listen, you dumb idiot!"

"But darling, I brought you a present. Look!"

I held up the jar.

"What's that?"

"We stayed in one of those resthouses, you know, one of those on the list. Arul did an exorcism. We trapped the spirit in this jar!"

I tried giving it to her but she backed off.

"Get it away from me!"

"It's a present, darling."

"Get it out of this house!" Tears welled in her eyes as she grasped at her hair.

And that's what I should have done. Walked out of the house and put it in the refuse chamber by the gate, come back in and ask for her forgiveness. But then what would have changed? What would I have achieved except for another bruised arm?

So I pushed the jar in front of her eyes. I was enjoying this. If I could reduce her to tears, what else could I do? So I unscrewed the lid. "Now I'm letting the spirit out!" I cried. I flipped the lid and it clanked on the floor. "Can't you see it flying out to get you!"

Belinda screamed.

I followed her terror-filled eyes to the jar.

I didn't believe what I saw.

At first I thought it was an insect, a black beetle perhaps.

But it wasn't.

It was a dark speck.

Growing bigger.

A shadow, swirling into a black cloud.

It was impossible!

Yet the thing grew blacker and heavier until the jar was filled with what I thought were a mass of black ants.

Then the blackness lifted out of the jar and floated, a miasma between my wife and I. From within the cloud, two huge golden eyes leaped at us.

I screamed.

The jar fell from my hands and smashed into pieces.

The eyes, the mass of cloud swirling behind it, lifted to the ceiling.

I smelled ash, charred burnt flesh and something else — the sharp odor of fresh blood!

Then the thing — the spirit — swirled around Belinda, a black tornado in a terrace house. Belinda shook her head in fear and revulsion. Round and round the spirit spun at an impossible speed. The sound it made was horrendous, like a plane crashing, like demons screaming in the bowels of hell. And through this, the two malignant eyes hovered three or four feet above her head, watching me almost gleefully.

I turned away for I felt its rancid being, its inherent evil, its corrupt and despicable soul.

When I looked up at Belinda, I couldn't see much of her except for her splayed-out arms for her body was wrapped by this foul blackness rushing at a thousand miles per hour.

Her body lifted three feet off the ground. She could have been an angel or a mere mortal who had mastered how to fly. For a second, I saw her face—her mouth was open in a soundless scream.

Then, the spirit vanished.

Belinda fell with a thud.

All was silent.

She lay motionless, curled up on the rug.

I then realized I was on my knees.

As I crawled towards her, a choking sound escaped from deep in her lungs. I touched her cheeks. It was cold.

"Belinda," I whispered.

Beneath her spectacles her eyes bulged like a frog's and then the glass misted over. She turned away from me and lay on her back.

Her hands suddenly flew at the air. Her legs kicked out as her body convulsed.

As I held her, cradling her in my arms, trying to stop her mad contortion I cried: "You're okay! You're okay! None of it's real! It was just a stupid, stupid joke!"

She suddenly froze. Belinda lay motionless, hands in the air, breathing hard. Then out came a shuddering breath, like a final gasp from a kettle before it automatically switches off, and her hands fell, followed by a hollow silence.

Behind me, I heard sobbing.

It was Ani weeping on the ground. When she realized I was looking at her, she turned to me and cried:

"Hantu! Hantu! Hantu!"

To this day, in our age of great science and medicine, the doctors still don't know what killed Belinda. Shock was one possibility. Perhaps it was fright. But I knew it was the spirit. The spirit in the jar I had so carelessly brought back with all my scorn and anger.

How did the evil thing get there? Could my ill feelings alone given it life? Or did someone capture the spirit and leave it in the toilet for me to find? Was it Arul?

I had no answers.

I saw Arul at the crematorium. All I could manage was "thanks for coming". The next day, he came to the house to pay his respects and I wanted to tell him about the spirit but nothing came out.

Months have passed and I've turned down all his invitations to meet up. I know it's wrong to blame him but I can't help it, I feel he egged me on. I know I'm being unfair. Finally, I agreed to meet him for a beer but we had little to say to one another. We may as well have been sitting across the table at a twelve-course dinner full of jabbering, munching mouths, all pretending to fight over the bill at the end. That humor, that touch of recklessness that sealed our friendship is long buried.

My two girls are motherless and I am without a wife. What was I trying to do with that stupid jar? I know Belinda had her faults, but so did I. There's nothing, nothing I can do to bring her back. And where has she gone? Has the spirit taken her to its foul and tortured lair or has she been mercifully sent to heaven?

Every once in a while, when a sudden midnight breeze blows through the window, as I sit on the sofa listening to Pavarotti and thinking of my dead wife and my two girls sobbing upstairs, I see a misty figure hunched up in the shadows by the curtains in a white gown. Her wire-like hair is a mess, her hands are balled into fists and her mouth opens and closes but I don't know what she's saying. Yet her eyes, burning through her glasses, chill my very blood.

She's just a figment of my imagination, I know she is. And I have no doubt I imagined everything — the spirit in the jar, my friendship with Arul, that one Labor Day weekend and her horrible death. All of it has just been one bad dream. I've told myself that a thousand times and I'll tell myself a thousand more times, just to keep myself from screaming.

Yet why, when I wake up in the morning to the humming air con and the neighbor's dogs howling, do I rub Tiger Balm on my arms, arms which are covered in purple bruises? And why, on most weekends, do I still find myself roaming like a lost goat on the narrow, verdant roads between PD and Malacca searching for answers? Answers — like love, friendship and laughter — which are gone forever.

THE RAPE OF MARTHA TEOH

He raped her but once. In darkened chambers, watched by a dark wooden clock. Martha's almond eyes hopelessly transfixed upon a black wooden screen of dancing maids with gentle smiles, sweetly waving silk before clumps of bamboo; and tears breaking the mother-of-pearl image apart. And the rhythmic pendulum — ticking — just beyond his grunting, panting; salty sweat trickling down her face, inhaling stale whisky breath; her mind reeling, screaming from his wicked intrusion. After an hour, crammed into mere minutes, Heng Wan slumped and fell away, singlet soaking, his white underwear from Robinson's twisted round a long, hairless leg; snoring.

Martha whimpered in the Sunday afternoon heat haze which filtered through the louvered smoked windows, her breath still, her body daring not to tremble, instead tensing against itself, locked solid in a rigid paralysis. The red scroll that read *Happiness*, doubled, circled, grew to gigantic proportions, sank to minute size and blossomed with the word *Hate*. It was a lie. If she could say she hated him with all her being, then she would be free.

Since that one singular rape she was trapped to him. What should have been a time for hate, anger and fear only reaffirmed her undying, blighted love for him. Heng Wan woke up, stretched himself and laughed as if nothing happened. He sang as he bathed himself, and Martha could only look at the ceiling, knowingly resigned to her fate; her small, round face, like putty, twisted in agony.

That was thirty-five years ago. Heng Wan was long gone, dead of cancer ten years now. He came home one day, coughed out blood and fell on the speckled terrazzo floor. “He was only sixty-two,” everyone had said. Martha nodded, grief-stricken, mourning for herself and a scarred life with him. She closed her eyes and his face emerged. His wry smile, sitting awkward on his hollow face, bright-lit eyes. The one the ladies found so attractive.

And there were plenty of those. It was not the calls, quickly put down, with the dialing tone buzzing in the eardrum, that annoyed her. Of course, it was maddening, with at least two or three a day. It was the lift in his voice, the gait in his steps, snippets of *Mack the Knife* whistled enthusiastically (how that tune would cut her) every time he was to travel outstation or would be out past midnight. He would not be traveling alone, he would not be at business dinners and drink without an escort. There would always be a soft, slender hand on his bony knee and cool whispers in his ear, in the dark corner of a bar as a waitress approached, balancing a round of twelve-year-old whiskies, ice cubes tinkling. Laughter, business cards exchanged for the umpteenth time, another round of drinks. He was happiest away from her and didn’t mind letting it show.

Martha would find lipstick on his collar, whiff remnants of perfume she never wore, and know. That was no problem for Heng Wan. He didn’t care whether she knew or not.

Sometimes, he would go out wearing a white shirt and return wearing a blue one. Sometimes, he returned home wearing clothes she never bought him and obviously not to her taste; modern, floral ties — colors clashing. Martha knew he had a wardrobe somewhere else; another home, another bed.

She had heard whispers, a mistress, a second wife, divorce. Martha knew better. Heng Wan would never divorce her. She was after all the perfect wife who somehow loved him, although she sometimes shuddered at his touch, and never mouthed the agony of his infidelity. If they had children, she would have been the perfect mother, but even without them Martha knew he was not going to leave her. And she was right.

The one who liked the floral ties was thrown out, after only two years of bliss. A new one, a Eurasian girl with hair to her hips, came along, and then another and yet another. Martha stopped counting. He was not going to leave her. She was an anchor in his sea of mistresses and one-night stands. She kept his home, ironed his clothes, made him delicious dinners on those occasions when he was tired or ill, and kept up the tradition of a family amongst the collection of antique rosewood furniture, marble tables and mother-of-pearl screens.

And then he died, leaving her alone with these memories. Not happy ones, for she loved him in a way that hurt her very being. Not a love that poured out of her heart but rather wrenched out of her wretched soul. An unhappy, tortured love that knew no way out of the hopelessness and despair. It was a prison of barbed emotion, that hurt every time she tried to pull away, to free herself from this person that was everywhere and in everything.

There was that one time when she could have left, after the singular rape, when she could have torn down the thick webs that suffocated and blocked her path and vision. But it only pulled her back, binding her to do his bidding. She knew then that her life was woven into the fabric of his ill-being and nothing could make her tear herself away, whether in distaste, horror or hate. The coils of this seething love bound her to him, to the darkest corners of the house in which he was the master.

For ten years now, Martha had stayed on. Her sister Audrey had asked her to move in with her but Martha refused. This was where she belonged. His memory shifted here, within its very walls, echoing within the hazel-wood wardrobes, creeping by the iron accordion gates leading to the front door. Her thoughts of him swam in the humid air circling the now-antique ceiling fan, his shadow elongating like bars stretching across the dining room floor.

His thin, knobby fingers had touched it all. His presence permeated everything, submerged her in his being — bubbling in the corpuscles of her blood, spinning, entangling webs in the fabric of her soul. Everything but her heart. It spoke of truth — he was a liar, a cheat, an adulterer; but she did nothing about it then and did nothing about it now.

Martha, now gray-haired and frail, chubby cheeks long deflated, lines crisscrossing her sunken face, sat by the window as always, looking out across the garden, past the large angsana tree, to the rusty front gate with the initials THW. She'd been sitting here for hours listening to the clock tick, watching, with empty eyes, the minutes pass as evening strolled in and mosquitoes rose above the shrill of insects, beyond the mournful call to prayers.

The white clouds above the neighboring houses took on a hue of dirty gray and small fruit bats swooped triumphantly through the air. Teoh Heng Wan was dusk, engulfing the day, seeping into every corner of dying light. Even with him ten years gone, she was trapped in his dark shadow. And shadows grew darker.

And then night came. The shadows in one particular corner by the red leather armchair, where he used to lounge before the television or read aloud from the paper, took on a heavy, watery blackness. The walls seemed to pull away in distaste, as the blackness grew, layer by sable layer. Every memory, every shred of his existence, every utterance or curse he hollered, drew together in a rancid, seething bonding. The air charged with a brooding malevolence and the inky darkness formed into a shape, tall and thin, quivering in the fading light. The blurred edges shrank away and there stood the unmistakable shadow of a lanky, slightly hunched man.

Teoh Heng Wan — still here — after all these years. It was perhaps the most natural, or unnatural of things. When his hunched figure first appeared three months after the funeral, Martha screamed and ran into the bathroom, locking herself in. She huddled in a corner, shaking and trembling, holding her head, certain insanity and its horde of diseases had found her. She didn't move from the cold, hard floor until the crack of dawn cast its first glimmer on the bathroom mirror. She had been planning to leave the house to live with Audrey, but after the appearance of his apparition those plans were laid to waste.

Every evening for ten years, just after nightfall, Martha sat like a bird with broken wings by the window in horrid fascination and dread, watching the despicable Heng Wan emerge from the inky blackness. Sometimes he did not manifest himself, those were the better days, but mostly he came. Sitting in the red vinyl armchair to gaze at her across the lounge through twin wells of penetrating blackness; goading in his mastery. No words passed but his voice in her said, *you are mine, you cannot leave here, ever.*

She would shudder, hands clutching tightly to the armrests, knowing she was trapped to him, to his memory, to this apparition. The dark figure would remain seated for about an hour or so, an hour in which Martha could touch every ghastly second that passed, and then without ceremony, the sable creature would dissipate into darkness. Martha, hands trembling, body shaking, would turn on every single light and feverishly pray he would not return. But he always did. And as the months passed, she became used to his nightly presence and soon it was like he never left.

Indeed he had not. He had always been there, just like tonight. Martha's eyes twitched, her eyebrows raised, her wrinkled, leathery fingers groped hopelessly for each other. Something was different, something was wrong.

Heng Wan should have in a singular long motion brought himself into his favorite chair. The red vinyl would creak as the apparition sat, as if adjusting itself into a comfortable position, to enjoy his dominion.

It did not. The figure hesitated. The murky head cocked itself into a position of thought, as if feeling out the house. *Something's here, Martha dear*, his voice whispered coldly in her head.

"What do you mean, Heng Wan?" she answered in a trembling whisper, her knees shaking.

The apparition took two steps forward, closer than it had ever been in those ten years. The figure was a watery darkness beyond the shadows, eyes like holes into a malignant black. It leered menacingly.

Martha's breath caught in the folds of her throat.

Someone's here.

And it laughed, an evil chortling of triumph and glee. *Young, nubile and innocent. Just how I like my women!*

It turned and strode away, that gait in his steps, towards the kitchen, towards the utility room. Except it wasn't a utility room anymore. She cursed herself then, in a way she had never cursed before. How could she have forgotten! It was the maid's room!

Emma, the Filipino maid that Audrey had insisted she take over. *You're seventy-two, Martha, far too old to look after this big house alone.* And being the docile one, Martha didn't refuse, didn't even think about Heng Wan in the brightness or sanity of day.

How ... how could she have been so stupid! With a face as white as ash, eyes wide in terror, she struggled out of her chair. Legs shaking, her head spinning uncontrollably, she was going to faint — but she pressed on ... she had to help the poor girl!

Mack the Knife whistled enthusiastically came rushing down the corridor like a whiff of rotten fish. Heng Wan going out to a 'meeting' ... going to meet his mistress. Heng Wan bringing out his fleshy knife.

Martha dragged herself down the corridor. As she passed her bedroom, the maids dancing upon the black wooden screen eyed her sympathetically, waving silk before clumps of bamboo offering to wipe her flood of tears that would inevitably follow. And the ticking, the infernal ticking of the wooden clock, the pendulum swinging madly, pounding nails into her head. She screamed and rushed to Emma's door, jerked and twisted at the handle but found it locked. She knocked with her fists frantically, calling for Emma to open it, to let her in, to run. But to no avail. All she heard was low gleeful laughter and Emma's young voice screaming out. Fear and pain in her hollering.

Martha fell to her knees, her fists warm and bleeding. Emma sobbing, begging for mercy that would never come.

And then silence. A dreadful hush fell over the house. The bed started to creak.

MR PETRONAS

Bobby lived among a blur of trees on the outskirts of Kuala Lumpur. His real name was Hazbollah bin Abdul Latiff Omar, new IC number 741336-13-5419, but we all called him Bobby.

"Please come now," he hollered.

"Why, Bobby?"

"It's important, please come."

"But ..."

Before I could continue, he'd hung up and I found myself surrounded by tables of ties and handbags, their proprietors slurping and talking and smiling and frowning, and always eating and eating and eating. Chopsticks, fork and spoon, messy fingers.

I tucked my handphone away and fought the escalator crowd into the spiraling heat. Instinctively, I craned my neck to see the Twin Towers soaring into the ebullient sky. Fountains splashed behind me and a playful breeze like a lover's fingers caressed my back. The crowds sat mesmerized. A security guard eyed a Malay couple walking hand in hand. An old amah, in danger of a heart attack, chased a child wielding an ice cream around the lake.

Bobby was my best friend. I knew that because he did the opposite of everything I told him. I said he was too young to marry but he went and got hitched to the receptionist where we worked. Although that was four years ago, I still called her Cik Normah. They wanted a baby but Bobby was still shooting blanks.

I joined the lines of cars, following the main roads, then took the winding bitumen until I came to Bobby's.

The house was small and cheaply built on mosquito-infested land left to him by his father.

My shoes obligingly joined a row of slippers.

"Eh, Ismail, how are you today?" a shrill voice called out.

"Fine, fine, Cik Normah."

"What's this Cik business, just call me Normah. Bobby's in the garden, at the back."

I followed her into a house permeated with the giddy fragrance of pounded chillies. Cik Normah wore a lot less make-up since she'd married Bobby, but she was still known as a great beauty. Her hair of henna and Sunsilk was no match for her mynah-bird eyes which made any male of the species want to covet and protect her in one embrace.

Bobby was in the back garden, thrusting his arms up and down, turning around, then jumping high. Trails of sweat ran down his thin back, his nose swiveled beneath the glimmering trees.

When he saw me, he karate-kicked the air and pointed his fists. I slapped my thighs, clapped and raised my tiger claws.

Bobby attacked, coming at me like a kampung chicken with its head chopped off. I danced away, hit the air and crouched low on the ground Silat Katak style. He kicked at my feet, and I jumped at him, both of us fell to the grass, laughing.

"Hish, macam budak," said Cik Normah before going back into the house.

Bobby got up and brushed grass off his Adidas shorts. "Thanks for coming so fast."

"No problem," I said, practicing a low punch. "So what's so urgent, you trying to fix me up with some girl again?"

Bobby laughed. "Well, I wish it was that."

"So what is it?"

"It's so unbelievable, I don't even know how to tell you."

"Just tell me."

"You won't believe me."

"Just tell me what happened!"

Bobby sighed. "Two nights ago, right in the middle of dinner, the phone rang. Normah picked it up. When she came back, her face was pale and her voice was trembling."

"What did she say?"

"Don't interrupt."

"She said 'Don't interrupt'?"

"No, you fool. She said ..."

Bobby sat down, his back on the wall of the house. He wiped the sweat off with a towel.

"Well, what did she say?"

"She said that someone on the phone said he was going to get her."

"What?"

"The person said he was going to get her. He said his name was Mr Petronas."

"Mr Petronas?"

"Yes, that's what he said."

"Maybe she misheard him. Maybe it was someone from the oil company, Petronas, calling her." The image of their headquarters, the Twin Towers sparkling in the sun filled my head. "Maybe he wanted to write her a cheque."

"Ismail, this isn't a bloody joke. He said he's going to get her."

"That's what he said." We both looked up. Cik Normah stood by the doorway, lips trembling, sarong tight around her slim waist. "He said his name was Mr Petronas and he's going to get me."

"But why does he want to do that, Cik Normah?" I asked. "And what the hell does 'going to get you' mean?"

She shook her head and sat down by the doorstep. "I don't know." Then she looked at her husband. "Tell him, tell him what happened last night."

Bobby wrung his towel. "We were asleep. Then I woke up to a sound, a noise at the window. I got up, drew the curtains and saw it."

"What did you see?"

"I'm ... I'm not sure. The first thing I saw were the eyes. Then, I saw the outline of a head and a face that was all black. Suddenly, the thing ran and jumped over the back fence."

"But Bobby, why do you call it a thing?"

Bobby bit his lip. "It was black and hairless. And the eyes, they were red, blood red, burning like hot needles into the back of my brain. That was no man."

I agreed to spend the night with them, just in case the thing returned. I sat in their kitchen drinking coffee and reading the *Malay Mail* while Bobby and Cik Normah waited in the bedroom.

Just after 1, I heard a rustling in the bushes outside. As I unlocked the door, Bobby appeared at my side. He gestured excitedly with his hands, I nodded, putting a finger to my lips.

I opened the door and we both stepped into the garden. We were met by a hungry darkness.

"Bloody mosquitoes," I said, slapping my face. "They're biting me all over."

"Look, Ismail." Bobby pointed to the fence. "It's there!"

"Where?"

"There, can't you see it?"

At first, I saw nothing, then a muscular outline of a tall man standing by a tree emerged. I decided that it, he, she, or whatever, must have been an *it* for when the figure looked up, eyes like bleeding crimson flames met mine.

I felt my bladder almost let go — until Bobby yelled.

"Get it!"

I stumbled after a sprinting Bobby.

At that very instant, the thing hurtled across the grass towards us.

Just as I thought my friend was going to crash into the figure, it leaped into the air.

We turned but it had disappeared. All we saw was the outline of Bobby's house beneath the night sky.

"Where's the damn thing gone?" Bobby shouted.

"Shit, I don't know!"

Then the clouds moved and a black figure squatting triumphantly on the edge of the roof revealed itself, a sinewy silhouette against the backdrop of a half-moon.

It peered down, red eyes blazing. Slowly, it reached forward as if to pick something and, all of a sudden, an object came soaring through the air.

"Shit," cried Bobby. "It's throwing down my roof tiles!"

We retreated to the fence as more tiles rained down on us. One hit the fence post and shattered. Another struck Bobby on the head, and he fell moaning on the grass.

Then came a crash as the thing leaped through the roof cavity, breaking through the ceiling.

"Normah!" gasped Bobby. "We have to help her, the thing's jumped into our bedroom!"

I rushed back inside the house, through the kitchen, down a corridor. Bobby followed, holding his injured head. I reached the bedroom and tried the door.

"Locked," I cried. "The stupid thing's locked!"

"Move aside!" Bobby stepped back and his leg flew at the wood.

Bobby dragged himself up from the floor.

Door one. Bobby zero. I madly thought.

Then out of the bedroom came a high-pitched laughter which turned my blood cold. I thought the bowels of hell had opened and the Syaitan himself had come to share a joke with us.

"Bobby, got a parang?"

Bobby stared wide-eyed at me, then as if he'd come out of a dream, he ran off and came back with a big spade.

"That'll have to do," I said.

Between the two of us and the digging implement, we managed to crack the door open.

But minutes had passed. Minutes in which anything could have happened to Cik Normah.

I gave the door one last shove and we both fell into the room.

In the ceiling was a gaping hole. A dark cloud partly hid the moon.

Bobby switched the light on.

Upon the bed, a figure hid beneath white sheets. Dark stains like leeches covered the material.

"No ...," Bobby whispered. He stepped forward so tentatively that I thought the floor was burning the soles of his feet.

I crept forward, my heart bashing away like a kompang. To my relief, there was no sign of the black thing.

Bobby reached the bed and pulled the sheet away.

Cik Normah screamed.

Dark patches covered a face riveted in terror. Beside her was a torn nightie with fingermarks on it. Then I realized she was naked and averted my eyes but not before seeing the same dark stains all over her body.

"I'll call an ambulance," I gasped. "You'll need to find some bandages to stop the bleeding."

"Please don't die, Normah," whimpered Bobby. "Please don't leave me."

"I ... I'm ... not hurt," she said. "I'm ... I'm okay."

"But the blood!"

"It's not blood, Bobby." I looked up and saw that Cik Normah had pulled the sheets over her body, she raised one hand and a slick of black slime flowed down her fingers. "It's, it's ... I don't know what it is!"

Bobby caught some of the liquid with his hand.

"What is it, Ismail?"

He passed me a couple of drops. I rubbed the greasy substance with my fingers, then put it to my nose. "Oil! It's black oil!"

"What happened here?" Bobby said to his wife.

Normah shook her head.

"What happened?"

"I was looking out the window at you both when it jumped through the ceiling. I tried to run but it grabbed me. It was strong and all greasy, and ...." She burst into tears.

"And?"

She shook her head.

"What happened Normah?"

She continued sobbing.

Bobby looked up at me. "Maybe you should leave us alone for a while."

I nodded and left the room.

Bobby didn't make a police report. He didn't think they'd believe him. How could they help anyhow? How were they going to arrest a mythical creature that covered itself with black oil so no one could grab hold of it? Or perhaps oil oozed naturally from its skin like it did from the earth?

After all, if man was fashioned from mud, then oil seeping from man could be conceivable. Yet could this not be some kind of awful joke?

Mr Petronas, indeed.

But no one was kidding. Cik Normah had been attacked and, although Bobby had not said it, I knew much more had happened.

This creature had raped her.

The unkindest of wounds came a few weeks later when we found out Cik Normah was pregnant.

As the months passed, her stomach grew bigger and, although Bobby tried to dismiss it as his imagination, he did say that she'd begun to smell somewhat oily.

Bobby was becoming even thinner. His hair was falling out. He said staying at home with Cik Normah was like living in an oil refinery. He'd stopped smoking too. He didn't want to burn the house down, he jokingly said but neither of us could manage a smile.

And his trembling hands weren't due to nicotine withdrawal. He was shit-scared.

We discussed abortion but Cik Normah refused to hear it.

"Maybe it's your child, Bobby," she said, eyes flashing. "How do you know it's not? You'd be killing our own flesh and blood."

She was right. We didn't know for sure.

It was during the sixth month of her pregnancy, when I was sending them home from work when Cik Normah screamed: "It's coming, it's coming!"

"What, right now?" Bobby yelled.

We were in a huge traffic jam in Jalan Ampang and I knew we wouldn't make it to the GH on time, not from the way Cik Normah was wailing.

"Bobby, she's going to need help now!"

I turned towards the nearest building. Drove down the side, stopped the car and we both helped her out.

The irony of it still fills me with anger and, dare I say it, a twisted kind of sick hilarity. Cik Normah lay there in Bobby's arms, next to the lake, her maternity dress from Metrojaya soaked in blood.

The fountains danced in the air while she kept on screaming.

I wanted to run for help but I knew our time was up. So I went on my knees to help bring the baby out.

A warm spray hit my face. Viscous liquid trailed down my cheeks. I rubbed it off and realized what it was. For no rhyme or reason, a ferociously stupid thought came to me ...

We've struck oil.

Then this tiny hand slipped out of Cik Normah and waved. That's right: it moved to and fro, so gracefully as if saying hello at a wedding at The Ritz-Carlton. Then the rest of the greasy thing spilt out, its body all black as it slid on the pavement on its protruding stomach.

A crowd had gathered by then, but they stepped back when the baby crawled across the pavement, a couple of times slipping on itself and falling face first. Then it got the hang of it and, like a monkey, sprinted past the bewildered faces, before leaping up a pillar.

It glanced at us with mischievous human eyes. That's right, human eyes no different from yours and mine. Pitying, intelligent eyes, it had.

And I only realized it had a mouth, when I saw its thick black lips stretch up its cheeks into a grotesque smile, a red tongue flickering inside.

Then, as if satisfied with what it'd seen, it reached out with one pudgy hand and started to climb. The umbilical cord trailing behind it.

I craned my neck as the 'bayi minyak' ascended higher and higher, leaving oil stains on the polished metal wall, now red with the setting sun.

As it went past the skybridge, it became nothing but a black dot. It climbed on and on, while the crowd below silently stared, mouths open. The baby scaled all 88 stories, occasionally stopping as if to rest, and then continuing until it got right to the very top.

For a few seconds it balanced itself like a tightrope-walker on the sharp tip of the spire. From there it could see beyond the city, beyond the scattered trees and hills, perhaps even the oil tankers plying the Straits of Malacca. Perhaps it could even see into our hearts.

Because then it jumped. High in the air, high above the tallest building in the world.

Before falling.

Before impaling itself on the metal rod.

I thought I heard it crying, a soft whimpering like a breeze through tired trees.

On the spire it melted. Whatever lubricant its little body held dripped down the metal cladding. The authorities sent a helicopter up but they only found stubborn oil stains.

Cik Normah died from internal bleeding. Bobby floated her in the lake and disappeared into the shimmering night. It took several days to get the redness and oily residue out of the water. No one ever heard from Bobby again.

As for me, I still can't visit a petrol pump alone.

FOUR NUMBERS FOR ERIC KWOK

Eric Kwok had two things on his mind. One, how he was going to wed the voluptuous Soo Lian and the other was how he was going to get the money to do so.

Sure, Eric had been trying hard for the past two months. He'd been working for the printers for over a year, and was paid a basic salary and commissions on top. Since he met Soo Lian in March he'd been working doubly hard, pushing his clients to print more, more stationery, more corporate brochures, more newsletters — shit, even more business cards. Luckily, he could get away with it. His clients liked him, liked his smart appearance, his easygoing manner, the small tokens of gratitude he often gave.

But it wasn't enough. His bank balance was rapidly falling, what with Soo Lian's enthusiasm for Max Mara dresses, Ferragamo shoes and Celine handbags. She would look at the items so longingly with her flashing eyelashes that Eric could do nothing but give her a lap-dog smile and present his Amex card, which, by pulling a few strings, he had recently upgraded to Gold.

A problem, but any problem was worth it to be with Soo Lian. Of course, her stage name was Veronica. Veronica the model, strutting up and down the catwalk at hotels and shopping centers. Eric admired her many talents which included acting and singing. She had appeared for a milk commercial once on TV and was auditioning for a Chinese movie set in Penang. On occasion she would do a few private strip shows for the towkays and bosses of public companies — the money was good and this started her off in her passion for the finery she wore.

But Eric had asked her to stop. *I'll buy those for you darling*, he had said, *you need never strip for anyone but me.* That was all well and good, but Eric didn't realize the prices for these lavish items. The first time she bought that black silk dress from the Renaissance Hotel boutique, Eric almost choked on his chewing gum. The expensive dinners were another thing. French, Italian, Mediterranean, Japanese, Thai — all at five-star hotels, all with a bottle of wine.

Eric was dreading his next Amex bill. He couldn't borrow from his family. They didn't have the money. And he couldn't borrow from anyone else, not from his friends, not from anyone. He even asked his bank manager for a larger overdraft, but was turned down. Then there were those other loans, the ones that could get you killed. He refused to go down that route. As his white-haired mother had said, he was silly, but not stupid.

Eric thought and thought. What was he going to do? Leaving Soo Lian was no option. She was his world, she was his everything. He only had to watch her waltz towards him through any chandeliered hotel lobby with that seductive smile, a silk dress flowing against her small breasts, and he was in heaven. But he was in danger of losing this heaven, and there was no way in he was going to let that happen.

Eric had been playing nombor empat ekor for as long as he could remember. It was no big deal, a few dollars here and there, once or twice a month when he felt like it, or when he was just passing the shop.

He won sometimes. Nothing big, nothing to shout about. Certainly never thought about it as a source of income. Until that one day when he won big. How he won probably had a greater bearing on things.

It was a hot, mind-numbing humid day, just like any other. The air conditioning was playing up again. The traffic was crawling past the nombor empat ekor shop, when he saw an empty car spot. He pulled into it, thinking of numbers he would bet on. He hadn't been having much luck with Soo Lian's birthday so far and he was considering using a different permutation when he saw it happen.

A blue Mercedes-Benz hit the back of a Proton as they were both trying to turn into Jalan Ampang. The two drivers jumped out with frowns and curses muttered under their breaths, then, like men used to the routine, they exchanged details and were gone. Eric was surprised there was no arguing or shouting, which often happened. They had an accident and they were gone, the Proton, of course, suffering much more in the collision. Eric had reacted instinctively; he pulled a sample letterhead from his file and quickly wrote down the numbers of both cars. The number for the Proton came out and Eric pocketed a cool thousand eight.

Since that day, when he wasn't out with Soo Lian or seeing clients, Eric would crawl along the choked-up city streets looking for accidents. He sometimes found them but there were always nosy cars blocking the accident scene with drivers jotting down the numbers and other cars madly honking away. He managed to get numbers at two accidents but they didn't come out. He used them again the following week but still nothing came of it.

Eric was desperate. His bank balance was falling like a rock, and Soo Lian's appetite for things expensive was growing — the other night she brought along two other models for dinner. The sake was heady, the bill horrific. Never have sushi at a hotel. He sold his shares, all at a loss. And the numbers just weren't coming out. Eric started to use every number he could find, various permutations of the many numbers he had: credit card, bank account, birthdays of friends and relatives, IC, driving license, birth certificate, gym club membership, even his bloody tax number. Eric wasn't a gambler, he wasn't addicted. He was simply desperate.

So desperate he mentioned getting numbers to an uncle.

"Why, you should have asked me earlier," said Uncle Bok. "I've never gone to get the numbers myself but my former colleague, Ang, is always getting numbers and he wins all the time. That's why he's driving a BMW."

"Really?" asked the wide-eyed Eric. "Why didn't you tell me this before?"

"You never asked before."

"I'm your nephew, you should tell me these things. How do you expect me to do well in life?"

"Winning on numbers isn't doing well in life."

"Okay, okay, you're right — tell me how does he get the numbers?"

"Through a medium."

"A medium?"

"Yes, a medium, the spirits talk to him in the cemetery, they give him winning numbers."

"And can anyone go to him, uncle?"

"Yes, yes, anyone can go."

"You mean that? He has no special clientele?"

"He's open to the public, anyone can go. But most don't."

"What do you mean, most don't? Uncle, if he's as good as you say, surely there'll be a long queue."

"Well, there used to be a long queue, that was many years ago. Then people stopped going for some reason, I don't know why."

"Maybe his numbers weren't winning."

"Oh no, his numbers always win, Ang will vouch for that."

"Then why don't people go, uncle?"

"I don't know. But I tell you what, I'll ask Ang to take you. I hope he will though, I haven't seen him for a while and I understand this medium is not a guy you mess with."

Two days after Eric's conversation with his uncle, the phone rang at his office, startling Eric out of his warm thoughts of Soo Lian. It was Uncle Bok.

"Good news, nephew. I've got hold of Ang. He refused at first, then he called back saying he'll pick you up tomorrow night!"

"Thank you, uncle! Thank you!"

"Don't thank me yet, wait 'til your numbers come out."

"Oh, yes, sure. But Ang always wins right?"

"Yes, he does."

"Wonderful news."

"Oh, Ang said he wanted to meet you first, today at 6 o'clock, at that Bukit Kiara horse-riding club. Can you make it?"

"No problem."

Eric was anxious and arrived at the club five minutes early. Ang was already waiting in the coffee lounge, which Eric thought was rather odd considering the Malaysian penchant for being late.

Ang's bulky frame was slouched in a rattan chair. He appeared to be in his sixties. He had distinguished gray hair, a round face on which sat a pair of silver-framed spectacles, and a thick gray mustache. He wore a short-sleeve shirt with a couple of buttons undone, black trousers and blue sandals. On his wrist was a shiny gold Rolex, which didn't look fake.

"Want a beer?" asked Ang, with a grin.

"Sure thing."

Ang ordered a jug of Carlsberg and the two drank like old friends. Ang told him about himself. He was in manufacturing for as long as he could remember until he got into trouble in the recession of 1985. He was made a bankrupt and then, quite miraculously, a cousin introduced him to the medium. Since then he pulled himself out of bankruptcy and money was no longer a problem. In turn, Ang had many questions about Eric's background, his work, his life, his love life, his current financial situation.

Eric saw no point in lying and described how he had been spending way beyond his means and how he had resorted to nombor empat ekor and how that had further aggravated his financial position. He even told Ang about how he had won that time when he witnessed the Mercedes-Benz knocking the back of a Proton.

"So now you know, winning is not just about being lucky," said Ang.

"I think it's about getting to the source of those numbers."

"Sounds like you'll do anything to get those numbers." Ang poured himself the last drops of beer from the jug.

"Yeah, I agree. Without money you can't do anything."

"And with money you can do everything you want to! Cheers!"

They brought their glasses together and finished their drinks. Ang glanced at his Rolex. "Time to go."

They shook hands at the entrance of the club. Eric watched Ang hop into his BMW. Not bad for an old man, thought Eric. He liked Ang, and he found the rich man down-to-earth.

Eric walked through the car park, not exactly sure where he left his car. Other than insect voices, it was quiet here. Night had descended hours ago and the lamps perched on poles offered little illumination. He admired the many expensive cars — once he paid his bills, he could think about getting something flashy, something Soo Lian would be proud to see him in. They had talked of many things, their friends, favorite hotels, TV shows, but they'd never talked of anything really important, like love or the existence of God.

He reached a dim section of the car park where it was too dark to identify the make of the cars. They seemed to press against him, their angular shapes poised like metallic monsters. He wondered if they were truly empty. Perhaps eyes stared from one of them, ears listening to the echo of his footsteps on the hard bitumen, waiting for him to come close before jumping at him, a knife flashing in one hand, the blade slicing through soft flesh beneath the dim fluorescent light.

Eric shivered.

His car wasn't there. He cursed his stupidity. He turned down another row and that was when he heard it — a dry creaking behind him. He spun around but saw no one, just the trees above the vehicles, their limp branches seeming to stroke the air.

He increased his pace, heading down another row of cars. It was his imagination, it had to be. Going to see the medium must have set it off at full steam.

Another creaking sound, like bones twisting in their joints.

Eric spun around.

Nothing at first.

Then he saw it from the corner of his eyes, a thin shadow slouching between two doors about ten cars down. He almost missed it, the thing seemed to be almost part of the darkness. Thing?

He didn't know why he thought this was a thing. But he was sure it was not human. Eric believed in good and evil, and this thing before him was so touched by evil, he could feel it coldly clambering on his skin.

He breathed in deeply, taking a step back, his eyes never leaving the figure.

This was not his imagination. It was right there. He took another step back, the figure remained stationary as if frozen by darkness. Eric knew he was a fool to have gotten himself into this financial trouble and perhaps even more of a fool to seek help from a medium, but what he felt here was true evil and he could never ...

"Can I help you?"

Eric spun around.

It was a security guard, talking to him in Malay, his lips twisted in a grin, his eyes blurred and watery as if he was suffering from conjunctivitis.

"There's something following me," Eric said. He turned and pointed at the figure, except there was nothing there but cars and shadows. If there was a figure standing there, it was now gone.

The man roughly scratched his bristles and looked in the direction Eric pointed with disinterest. "I don't see anything, are you sure you saw something?"

"I'm sure there was a figure standing there."

"Maybe it was a thief." The man's breath smelled of stale cigarettes.

Eric coughed and stepped back. "Maybe, you're right," he muttered, but he didn't think so. "I've lost my car, it's around here somewhere."

"Try the next row, there are more cars there."

"Thanks." Eric headed in that direction, glad to leave the guard's presence. He found his car in the next row, and he drove off thinking of Soo Lian, he would call her when he got home. The thing that had followed him slipped like a retreating coffin to the back of his mind.

Close to 11 the next night, Ang picked Eric up in his BMW and drove them out of the still-busy city. Ang wore a colorful short-sleeved shirt and what appeared to be the trousers and sandals from the night before.

Eric shifted uncomfortably in the leather passenger seat. He was not used to this luxury, nor did the thought of going to the cemetery at midnight ease his mind. Ang was jovial, treating Eric like an old friend; and his mouth would not stop moving, his gray mustache bobbing up and down as he talked about the economy, the stock market, politics, the PM, the latest movies out of Hong Kong.

A question burned in Eric's mind, which he didn't seem to be able to ask the previous night. Now he asked it. "My uncle Bok said that people don't go to him anymore."

"That's right, that's right. Nothing for you to worry about though. You're with me, I'll show you how to get the numbers."

"What do you mean, how to get the numbers?"

At this Ang just winked behind his glasses, gave Eric a sly grin and turned the music on. A famous Taiwanese singer took over, crooning a pop song. A drop of rain fell on the windscreen with a splat. Eric jumped back, his head hitting the leather headrest.

Ang laughed. "I think it might be a wet night." As if the clouds were waiting for his word, the downpour came. The road turned a shiny black like the glistening body of a cobra with a million diamond beads bursting upon it.

"Maybe we shouldn't go," Eric said over the singing. "Maybe I should just work harder at the office instead."

"Don't be silly Eric, we must go — the medium only comes once a month. If we miss him now we'll have to wait weeks. Think of how much money we would lose if we didn't go."

Eric looked at the wipers sweeping the rain hypnotically over the windscreen and saw an image of Soo Lian smiling.

He had to go, anything to keep a hold of her, anything to feel her silky dress against his body, her small breast soft against his chest. The Taiwanese singer was telling him that love was worth any hardship.

"Yes, we must go," he said finally. "Rain or shine."

They arrived at the cemetery just as the digital clock on the dashboard said 10 past midnight. They had been on the road for over an hour. The car went through a dilapidated gate and took a track which wound its way past dark mounds which Eric took to be hillocks and areas of rock and undergrowth.

The glow of the headlights cut a swath through the blackness, lighting up the drizzle and the muddy track ahead. Ang seemed to know where he was going. He turned onto a narrow pathway which could hardly accommodate the car. On either side poked large crumbling headstones engrossed with Chinese characters and faces. The photo of an old man stared at Eric, his thin lips seeming to want to scream at him to leave this place of rest, to get out of the car and run away as fast as his legs could carry him. They passed the tomb of a young woman with long raven hair, her teeth appeared unnaturally sharp against the marble headstone, her eyes seemed so alive.

The car pressed its way through the undergrowth. Ang continued talking about property investments and the rental he was getting from his three condos in Bangsar. Eric looked back, and swore her eyes were following him. Shadows shifted behind the car, merging and breaking as if the dead had risen and were mingling in its shadows.

Ang took another turning then stopped just beside a limp and twisted tree and turned off the engine. The lights disappeared and they were swamped by blackness. Ang opened the car door. The interior light came on; behind his glasses Ang's face appeared unnaturally old, his ever present smile had disappeared, his lips trembled below his gray mustache. Eric wasn't sure if he imagined it. Was Ang afraid or was his lips trembling with excitement? Ang got out and Eric followed, squeezing himself between the car door and the prickly bushes. Eric looked back anxiously from where they came.

"Don't worry," said Ang. "It's very safe here. Robbers don't come, they're afraid of ghosts."

"So am I."

"Don't be a scaredy cat, young man. The ghosts are going to give us numbers, real good numbers to win with. I tell you, you won't regret it."

"I don't understand why you're sharing these numbers with me?"

"Ah. So many questions. These things you cannot keep to yourself. You have to bring friends and relatives."

"I see," said Eric, feeling stupefied.

"Good, good. Come, this way."

Eric noticed that Ang had brought his briefcase out with him. "What do you need that for?"

"You'll see, young man. I'm carrying something very valuable."

"It's for the medium?"

"Yes, for the medium ... and his friends."

Eric didn't have time to speculate on these valuable items for Ang was ushering him onto a narrow path. The path could only be negotiated single-file and Eric followed his uncle's former colleague closely. The consequences of losing the man in this graveyard was more terrifying than anything that came to mind. Ang seemed to have regained his composure, whistling and chatting as if they were strolling through a shopping complex. This brought no comfort to Eric. He wondered if Ang was hiding something. The thought of what lay ahead brought a coldness to his veins. The gravestones stood on both sides, pressing against the path as if intending to suffocate him. Eric was careful not to touch any of them.

He heard a sound and glanced back. He swore he heard it. A kind of rustling, as if someone or something was moving through the undergrowth, following them.

Ang was well ahead and Eric had to rush down the path to catch up with him. He stole a look back and swore he saw a shape lurking in the bushes, another moving behind a headstone. Perhaps it was his imagination. Perhaps not.

Eric had the terrible feeling that whatever was hiding in the shadows was there to stop him from running back to the car. The only way to go now was to press onward. Eric wondered what the medium had in store for him.

Eric and Ang had to negotiate a slippery slope before coming upon a clearing of wild grass. A figure sat in its middle, cross-legged before a kerosene lamp where a yellow flame burned. The old man was hunched-up and muttering to himself, he was dressed in tattered gray robes, his spiky hair was a murky white, a pointed beard curled downward. On either side of him burnt what must have been a hundred sticks of incense. The musty smell reminded Eric of the temple on the hill he used to go to as a boy with his mother. She had taught him so many things he now couldn't recall — but he remembered her lesson about good, about right and wrong, about gods and goddesses.

The monk was chanting. Monk? He didn't know why he thought that. This was no monk, this was an old man who could grant numbers, someone who knew about the powers beyond the grave. A medium. And the smell, how could it have reminded him of the temple? It was pungent, wet — it smelt of something rotting. No gods or goddesses could possibly dwell here.

Eric suddenly wished he was anywhere else.

Ang called out a respectful greeting. The medium turned towards them, his eyeballs swiveling hugely in their sockets.

"It is you, Ang," the medium said in a deep guttural voice which reminded Eric of fiery crematoriums and hot dusty ash. "You have brought a young friend. Good. Sit down. Sit down."

Ang put his briefcase down and sat on the sodden earth next to the burning incense. He indicated that

Eric should do the same. Eric approached, feeling sweat on his palms. Slowly, he sat beside Ang, his eyes never leaving the medium. The smoke from the incense eagerly engulfed Eric. It was thick with a watery quality that bubbled corrosively in his lungs.

"And you have come for numbers?" said the medium in his reverberating voice.

"Yes," said Ang.

"Good," the medium said. "And for your young friend too?"

For the first time Eric saw the large eyes close up, they were gray, the pupils — were they red? They couldn't be, but they seemed so. Perhaps it was a reflection of the incense burning. "Yes, for me too, sir," he said, his fingers squirmed like leeches in his palms.

The medium smiled. "Good. That's very good."

"The last numbers you gave were excellent," said Ang. "Thank you."

"Aren't they always?" The medium grinned slyly. "Shall we begin?"

Ang keenly nodded.

"And you, young man?"

"Yes, sir," said Eric, feeling a tight coiling in his stomach.

"But there are two conditions. Do you want to know what they are, young man?"

"What is it, sir?" asked Eric, beads of sweat rising on his forehead. He noticed Ang nervously stroking his mustache.

"The first is to not call me, sir." The medium laughed, like a dog howling, the cavern of his mouth opening wide, revealing rotting teeth. The old man leaned forward. The light from the kerosene lamp threw dancing shadows on his face, and his spiky white hair seemed to tremble in anticipation. "The second, my young friend, I will only tell you after I've given you the numbers." He grinned, his tongue licked his bottom lip, curling over its contours; it seemed too long and unnaturally pointed. "Let us begin."

"But ..." The darkness seemed to be closing around Eric. "Shouldn't you ..." The smoke hurt his eyes, blurred his thoughts.

"Is there something wrong, young man?"

Eric said nothing. Within the gray smoke Soo Lian's eyes danced.

"Well, is there?" The medium's voice was sharp, razor-like, it seemed to crush any resistance Eric's brain put up. "Well, if there isn't, let us begin!"

The medium took out a yellow scroll of paper from within his robe, and placed it on the incense. Immediately the scroll burst into flames as if it was doused in kerosene. He let the ash fall to the grass before him. Some clung to the long blades of grass. The medium bent down studying the remains of the scroll. He stroked his beard and grunted, poking one finger into the ash as if looking for something. He picked some of it up and let it fall through the air, drifting back to the blades of grass. Then he grinned, tore a piece of a newspaper he had beside him, scribbled something on it and passed it to Ang.

Ang leaned forward, almost groveling, as he took the scrap of paper.

The medium removed another scroll, set it aflame on the incense, and again studied the ash, poking a finger at it, letting it drift through the air. His eyes phosphorus in the shifting light. He scribbled on another scrap of newspaper and passed it to Eric.

Eric hesitated. *There's something wrong here,* he thought. *I shouldn't take it, but Soo Lian ...*

"Take it!" commanded the medium.

Eric put his hand out. The medium pushed the paper between Eric's fingers and withdrew. Eric was left holding the scrap. Not wanting to look at it but, unable to resist, he opened it and saw the numbers written in a scrawny handwriting: 5328.

"Five, three, two, eight," Eric said.

"Those are your numbers, Eric," said Ang. "With them you will win."

"And now, young man, I have to tell you the condition." The medium smacked his lips.

"The condition?"

"Yes, the condition. Add together each number I have given you, what does it come to?"

"Five plus three plus two, comes to ten. Ten plus eight, comes to eighteen."

"Good. You can add, that is very important as you shall see. In one month's time, when you next see me, your body will become older — by eighteen years ... unless ..."

The medium smirked. His lips twisted gleefully.

Eric felt darkness leap at him, smothering his breath. His white-haired mother shouting at him, telling him what a fool he was to come here. He couldn't believe what the old man had just said. But he had heard it as plain as day, he would age by eighteen years ... unless ... A part of him didn't want to know, but the horrible truth was that it was too late not to know, he had already taken the numbers.

His words scraped horribly against his throat. "Unless what?"

"Unless the next time you see me, a month from now, you rip out the heart of a person who is connected to those same numbers. Then I want you to bring that heart to me."

Eric felt a claw tearing his brain. He bit his lips and tasted blood.

"You only have to make one kill every time you get the four numbers." It was Ang looking right at him, his spectacles reflected the incandescent yellow of the kerosene flame so Eric couldn't see his eyes. "It's not hard finding a connection, could be his car number plate, IC number, birthday, bank account number ... anything."

"And if I don't agree?"

"Then Ang will take you home." The medium grinned.

Eric jumped to his feet. "Bullshit! Ang will kill me right here!"

"Calm down, Eric." Ang was on his feet. "I have already killed my numbered person, he was a civil servant, it was part of his credit card number. I have no need to kill you. Killing you would be pointless."

"You're lying, Ang. You'll kill me because I now know your murderous secret!"

The medium laughed. "No, no, Ang will not kill you for that ... I will!"

Eric spun to face the medium. The old man was standing, his robes falling raggedly around him, his eyes burning a bright red.

"Listen, Eric you were the one who wanted to come." It was Ang, his voice pleading. "You have nothing to lose, I guarantee it. You have a whole month to find this person. There's no problem at all, I'll help you. Sure I've been unlucky a few of times and, sure, I've aged, but everyone grows old sooner or later ..."

"How old are you, Ang?"

"I'm thirty-two ..."

"What? You're younger than me? But you look like you're in your sixties! This is crazy!"

"Eric, I don't *look* in my sixties. I *am* in my sixties, my body is now that old, sixty-three to be precise. But listen Eric, I've been doing this for many years now. You were lucky to be picked. You can be rich like me! It's stupid to refuse!"

"I can't do it, Ang! I can't kill another human being!"

"I'll help you do it, the first time's the most difficult, then it becomes so easy, even enjoyable!"

"I cannot let another human being die, can't you understand that? It's wrong!"

"Then you will die, young man." The medium took a step forward and Eric saw the ivory hilt of a dagger poking from beneath the robe. This had to be a dream, a crazy nightmare — he wanted to wake up now.

"I can't do this!" he yelled at Ang. "Not for Soo Lian, not for anybody! This is madness!"

Ang shouted a warning.

Eric felt something hot plunge into his stomach. He looked down to see the dagger sticking out of him. Two parts of him surfaced. One that felt only pain and another that couldn't believe this was happening. His knees buckled and he fell on the ground, blood spilling on the blades of grass.

The medium stepped towards him.

Eric twisted on the ground, trying to get away. The earth was surprisingly soft, like his bed at home, the one where he laid many an afternoon in Soo Lian's arms. But that was in another time, another place. Here his clothes were soaked in his own blood.

"Now show me what you're brought, Ang." The medium said as he bent and pulled the blade from Eric's stomach.

Eric cried out in pain.

With trembling hands, Ang opened his briefcase. "See what I've brought you, master," he said.

The medium glanced at the glistening red lump about the size and texture of a rotten papaya. Several openings like sucker-like mouths sat on top of it, and its vein-like surface dripped with a dark fluid.

The medium shook his head and laughed. "You trying to trick me, Ang? This is a goat's heart! What numbers did I give you last month? Seven, four, nine, four—comes to twenty-four. Trying to save yourself twenty-four years, eh? I tell you what, I'll triple it! You will age by seventy-two years!"

"No, master!" howled Ang. "I brought you a follower, I brought you Eric! Please forgive me!"

"And what a useless follower Eric's turned out to be," said the medium, almost to himself. "We misjudged him, didn't we?" He turned to Ang. "Become older, by seventy-two years!"

The medium clapped his hands once, it was like a thunder-strike. His face was twisted with perverted pleasure. "Age my friend, until life is squeezed out of you. Come join us, come join the undead!"

Ang stumbled towards Eric weeping. "I'm sorry. I'm so sorry!" Ang's rounded face turned pale. It started to shrivel, holes blistering onto its surface. His gray hair and mustache turned white, and lumps of it fell on his clothes. Eric watched as Ang put on ten, twenty, thirty, forty years. His face was thin as if he'd just been released from a concentration camp.

"No!" cried Eric.

"What the hell is ..." Ang couldn't complete his sentence as bits of teeth flew from his mouth. His face was aged, like a man who'd just celebrated his hundredth birthday. Still Ang grew older, so old he should have died years ago, pieces of flesh peeled off his face, arms and hands. Still he didn't die, he stared hopelessly at Eric. But Eric knew Ang was no longer alive, but nor was he quite dead. His uncle's former colleague continued to rapidly decay until he fell to the ground, his legs no longer able to support him.

Ang was beyond skeletal, he sobbed as he edged forward, reaching out to Eric with a stick-like arm, his hand made of nothing but bones and a layer of pocked skin.

This was the man that had tricked him, who had brought him here to die. Even so, Eric reached out a consoling hand, but then a blinding pain sliced through his throat. He tried to say something to Ang but only manage to gurgle a mist of blood. Darkness engulfed him. Eric died before his hand fell limply back to earth, before the fountain of crimson fluid flowed over his cut throat.

The medium rose, wiped his blade and tucked it into his robe.

And Ang that was nothing more than bones and clinging tissue, slowly crawled from his clothes.

The medium strode over to him, his robe flapping in a sudden gust of wind. "You will now live here with the rest of us, Ang. Come out all of you! Come see what Ang brought us!"

Skeletal shapes emerged from the blackness, eagerly tearing themselves from it as if they were waiting for this moment. There were six of them, their faces horribly decayed, four crawled, two shuffled.

The medium put out a hand. One of the crawling creatures went up to it and with a tongue that looked as dry as sand paper, licked his palm. The other creatures hung back watching warily. The medium patted its head.

"I know you are all hungry," he said, eyes blazing down on them. "Tonight's meat will not be as tasty, but it's food all the same. You've all had your share of lucky numbers through the years. Now, we share this nourishment. But do not worry, in a few days you will have a fresh human heart! But for now, go eat what we have!"

The creatures made for the briefcase, though not as quickly as before. With bony hands they clawed at the glistening heart, elbowing and scratching each other as they greedily ripped off chunks of meat, all the while grunting and howling, their red eyes darting occasionally back to the medium as though fearful he would change his mind. When there was nothing left of the organ, they stole away like mongrel dogs to the edge of the clearing, their mouths and hands thick with blood. On their haunches, they licked the blood from their hands, then they ripped the globules of flesh with their bony fingers until these became tiny slivers which they then swallowed with saliva by arching their toothless heads back, making a gurgling noise which sounded like laughter.

Ang crawled to the medium's feet and stared forlornly up at him.

The medium patted him on the head. "Next time you must be faster. Don't worry, you won't starve, more food will follow in a few days. You will now live here with us."

The medium bent down to pick up the two scraps of paper, he looked at the numbers, tore them up and scattered them on the grass, his ferocious laughter caught by the wind, ascending up beyond the graves and into the night.

PLANE LOAD

Nadim reluctantly climbed into the seat of the Airbus, feeling the uncomfortable firmness that would hold his frame for the next nineteen hours.

He was thirty-four, of average build, average height, neatly cut hair, and had a once-handsome face that was now on the chubby side.

The phone had sung out loudly at 6 the evening before while he was busy watching a movie and yelling to the Indonesian maid to bring him a glass of Coke. It was the rasping voice of Harvey McNeil — Finance Director, and from its edgy tone he could tell something was up. And up it was.

The US auditors were querying a huge chunk of the Singapore accounts and so Nadim had to fly to San Francisco for an emergency meeting. Well, that was fine, tomorrow was a Monday and he'd rather be on the plane than going through spreadsheets and revenue contracts back at the KL office. He'd done this last-minute travel thing anyway, did it when the computer lost all the South Korean accounts and when the finance director in Beijing suddenly resigned. All part of a VP Finance's job.

What irked him though was that he couldn't get a seat on Business Class on any of the airlines. He was willing to connect from Singapore, South Korea, and Tokyo even, just to get a comfy seat but no, they were all taken. So cattle-class it had to be. He hadn't experienced the joys of its crammed-up comforts since his student days. He didn't mind not being able to use the lounge at the airport, nor even the queue at the check-in, but the narrowness of the confines, the push and shove and elbows, the crowd of passengers, what a shock it was.

So here Nadim stiffly sat watching the herd of travellers wander down the aisles glancing up apprehensively at the seat numbers looking for their rows, scrutinizing those they would be finding themselves next to for hours to come. The flight was almost full.

In his window seat, Nadim waited for his traveling companion. Would it be some fat American lady telling him about her wonderful holiday at Cherating, or some creative type with dark glasses and a snazzy laptop? Of course, a sexy babe with nice breasts would be too much to ask.

So Nadim waited and watched, taking the in-flight magazine in and out of the rear-seat pocket, glancing at the yellow flight routes like spider's legs across the map of the world, duty-free pens and perfumes and travel articles about some rundown village by a lake in India he had no interest in ever visiting.

What was his wife doing now? Probably ordering the maid around while their two kids pretended to research their homework on the Internet. Nadim had just got the two boys into private school. Not cheap, but nothing was these days. They lived in an end lot of a row of terrace houses. He would upgrade to a bungalow once the bank approved the loan. So work he had to. Emergency meeting in San Francisco? No problem.

One by one the seats filled up — a young Caucasian couple in leather jackets, T-shirts and torn jeans unable to keep their hands off each other, two hassled parents dragging along three children, none older than ten, chocolate ice cream smeared on their faces, an old lady with a large silver clip in her white hair carrying an oversized hand luggage. All heading past him — thank his lucky stars!

A tickling, a strange tingling, ran up Nadim's nose; before he could pull his large white handkerchief out of his pocket, he'd let out a huge sneeze that shook his body the way an erupting volcano would shake the kneeling ground.

Unfolding his handkerchief, he wiped the phlegm from his palm. He suddenly felt not entirely well. It couldn't be a cold, he thought, he hadn't been in the gym's swimming pool that long yesterday. Sure, it got chilly in that sparkling water on the 12th floor, especially when the wind gusted like a howling witch through the tower blocks, but nothing you could catch a cold from. It was perhaps the dust, dust from the blue seats which probably hadn't been vacuumed recently. Cost cutting — Nadim could understand that. But hygiene — well, that was another matter.

Nadim turned his attention to his fellow passengers. Most seats were taken. The two beside him were still empty. Maybe it wasn't going to be so bad. Maybe there wouldn't be anyone in those seats and he'd be able to stretch out his legs and get some shut eye. Hell, you couldn't even do that in Business Class. A male and female flight attendant were busying themselves with closing the entry doors when, frowning, they suddenly pulled it back open, admitting a man in.

The first thing Nadim noticed was the dark hat, black beard and black suit. Nadim thought him a rabbi or religious Jew in orthodox clothes at first. But the dirty black of his long coat, the thick necklace around his neck and the single gold earring told him otherwise. The man strode down the aisle and slotted himself into the aisle seat, next but one to Nadim.

Within minutes, the plane was airborne and they were soaring through clouds. The screen showed a graphic map of the plane's progress, then it flipped over to flight information: flight time remaining, height, speed, local time at destination — then back to the map. The seat-belt sign went off with a chime.

Nadim's traveling companion turned to him.

"Going to be a long flight," said the man.

Nadim nodded.

"My name's Ishmael. I'm going home."

"You're from San Francisco?"

"Yes ... that's right," Ishmael grinned. "It'll be good to get back."

Nadim felt the uncontrollable tickling in his nose which led to another almighty sneeze.

"Sorry," muttered Nadim as he wiped his nose and palm with a handkerchief. He wished he had brought some tissues.

"That's all right, quite all right," said Ishmael, "colds are a blessing — it helps remove toxins in our bodies."

"Really?"

"Yes, it's quite necessary, so our bodies can be healthy again. But sometimes it can be too much. Too much for the body to handle and this can lead to fever, it can even kill the man. So you see, the removal of toxins is important, but the body can be overzealous — so keen to get rid of the toxins that it destroys itself in doing so. This is when medicine helps. To keep the body in check ... so it exercises control. We need to remove the poison from the body at a proper pace — not too slow, so that the body is poisoned, and not too fast, so that the body kills itself in so doing."

"I see," said Nadim, putting away his moist handkerchief, not comprehending fully the discourse at hand.

Nadim felt a throbbing in his temple. Ishamel's bearded face for a moment swan and fell out of focus. He didn't feel good — not good at all — how the hell was he to survive the next nineteen hours on this claustrophobic plane? It would be hell, whichever way he looked at it.

"Maybe we can do something for you, my friend," said Ishmael with a grin Nadim didn't care much for. Ishmael reached into the pocket of his black coat.

As if he was performing a magic trick, he pulled out a small brown plastic bottle with a flourish of his arm. He pressed the white lid, unscrewed it, and then tipped a red capsule onto his large palm. Nadim couldn't help notice Ishmael's hairy wrists.

Ishmael flicked his eyes up at Nadim, his gaze penetrating. "This is the best for your flu," he whispered. "Believe me. Once you've had this you won't bother with anything else."

Nadim stared suspiciously at the shiny red capsule. "Are you sure about that?"

"Of course, I'm sure," said Ishmael. "This will cure your cold. I'm a doctor. I should know."

"You're a doctor?"

"Well, a doctor of sorts," whispered Ishmael with a sly grin. "Actually, I work for a pharmaceutical company. We do a lot of work there. More than those useless doctors."

"Oh, come on," said Nadim. "You can't mean it."

"Granted, those doctors do their best. But they are working with hands tied behind their backs. It's a useless battle for them. They don't have all the knowledge. They don't have the solutions. They're fighting without knowing who the real enemy is."

"So who's the real enemy then?"

Ishmael laughed. "That, my friend, is top secret. Company confidential. Proprietary information. If I were to tell you, I'd have to kill you."

"Yeah sure," said Nadim who couldn't help grinning. "So what's the top secret? I promise I won't tell anyone."

Ishmael, eyes burning bright, unbuckled his seatbelt and pushed his way into the seat next to Nadim.

"Do you really want to know, my friend? It's pretty shocking. Perhaps I shouldn't tell you."

"Oh, please do," said Nadim. "Now you're made me very curious."

"Okay, you must trust me then, my friend."

"Sure, I trust you. I have no reason not to."

"Then here's the medicine," said Ishmael. He held Nadim's wrist and dropped the pill into his hand. "Take it. I promise it'll fix your cold."

"Tell me first," said Nadim, staring suspiciously at the capsule which seemed to burn his palm. "If I believe you, then I'll swallow the thing. Otherwise, you can take it back."

"Okay, if you insist," whispered Ishmael. "This flu you have, we recently released the viruses in several locations in KL, Vietnam and Bangkok. You see the flu immunizations the doctors have been jabbing their patients with have been very effective. Too effective. This is not profitable for us. It doesn't help sell more pharmaceuticals."

He stared at Nadim, his eyes glowing bright.

"So our company releases a new flu virus every couple of years. The idea is to infect the population of a few countries. Naturally, the cold spreads across the borders, eventually making it a worldwide flu. It's a very different type of virus from the existing ones. With this new strain, the current flu immunizations won't work. So naturally the sales of our standard flu medications shoot up. And then to much acclaim, citing millions spent on research, we release the flu immunization for this particular strain. It'll cost a lot, of course."

"What?" whispered Nadim. "You deliberately create a new flu virus to make the population ill? You deliberately spread a new strain of the flu?"

"Sure, why not?" said Ishmael. "It's very profitable."

"You bastards. How could you do such a thing?"

"I know it's not the most ethical thing to do," said Ishmael. "But it puts a rocket under our stock price. And if we exercise our stock options, well, you see, there're millions and millions to be made."

"I don't believe you."

"I'm not asking you to," said Ishmael. "It's a simple fact. Companies will do anything to turn a profit. Sure, a lot of people get sick, but they don't die. Well, most don't. But business is business. Right, my friend?"

Nadim didn't know what to say. He felt the dark throbbing grow stronger in his head.

"And that capsule in your hand. Well, my friend, that medicine is for me. In case I catch the flu after I released the virus. You see, I broke the vial in the airport an hour ago. I did it in the café. The virus takes to the air, carried by invisible water droplets. It goes straight into the air-conditioning system. So I'm pretty sure you caught the bug. Your eyes are very watery. Your face is pale. I bet you're running a fever. It's up to you if you want to take it. But if you don't take it, you're going to be in pretty bad shape when they cart you off the plane in San Francisco."

Nadim stared at the capsule in his hand. It looked like a normal capsule. Nothing suspicious about it. He stared at his traveling companion. His heart was beating fast. His head felt hot.

"You are telling the truth, aren't you?"

"Yes, of course," said Ishmael. "But as I said, it's up to you."

Nadim stared at the capsule again. Was it safe?

He didn't know for sure. Would it jab this new flu bug? As long as Ishmael was telling the truth, it would. Why would Ishmael lie? There was no reason for deception. No motive.

Sometimes you had to take a risk. Nadim, VP Finance, knew that. *No pain, no gain*, said his gym instructor. *No risk, no return*, went the money-making mantra. But now his health was at stake.

Without further deliberation, Nadim popped the capsule in his mouth. He swallowed hard and the medicine slipped down his esophagus.

"Good," whispered Ishmael. "Very good, my friend."

He placed his hand on Nadim's leg and squeezed his thigh.

"What—what are you doing?"

"Oh, nothing," said Ishmael, slowly taking his hand away. "Just saying hello."

"Oh ... I see," muttered Nadim. But he didn't see. He took a deep breath. Then another one. A coldness tightly squeezed his belly.

"But how are you feeling now, my friend? The medicine kicks in pretty fast."

"I'm ... not sure." Said Nadim. "Starting to ... to spin a bit."

"Quite normal," said Ishmael, eyes glimmering, lips grinning. "Very normal. Very cool."

"If you ... say so," whispered Nadim.

Ishmael's face swam eagerly before his eyes, the earring, the necklace, gold burning brightly. The pattern on the seats crawled like an orgy of worms. The flight attendant drifted up and down the aisle like automations in slow motion, smiling masks on their made-up faces.

"Come with me, my dear friend," said Ishmael. "A walk will do you good. That's what you need."

Nadim didn't feel like a walk. He thought the floor would suck him in like quicksand if he got up. But he couldn't say no. No matter how hard he tried.

"I ... I don't need to walk. I just want to sit."

That was the best he could do. That was his strongest resistance.

"You must, my friend," Ishmael said. "You will walk. Come with me."

That's right. Ishmael was in charge.

Ishmael grabbed Nadim's arm and dragged him up.

Holding Nadim's shoulders, he led Nadim down the aisle.

Nadim stared desperately at the rows of faceless passengers as he stumbled past them. With headphones on, they were too busy watching movies. Too busy sipping drinks. Reading magazines. Snoozing under blankets.

"This way," ordered Ishmael.

When they got to the toilets, Ishmael pushed a door open.

"Might as well use the facilities," he said.

He ushered Nadim in. Eyeing the corridor and the galley, Ishmael followed behind, pressing himself against his prey. Nadim felt the man's hardness rub against his buttocks.

Ishmael pulled the bi-fold door shut. With a loud click, he locked it.

The light flicked on, like the opening of a sordid theatrical show. In the mirror, Nadim saw two grown men squeezed into the tightness of the toilet. Ishmael was salivating.

The dark gray of the toilet bowl pressed painfully into Nadim's shins. He wanted to vomit but couldn't. He wanted to scream but couldn't. Not without permission.

Ishmael would tell him what to do. Ishmael was in charge.

"It's a long flight," whispered Ishmael gleefully. Arms slipping round the front of his victim, he undid Nadim's belt. "We might as well enjoy ourselves."

"No," moaned Nadim. "No, no."

"Oh yes, we will. You're totally mine, babe. We can make as many trips to the toilet as we like. That is, every time I want you. No one's going to disturb us."

Nadim felt his trousers, his underwear shoved down his legs.

He wanted to cry.

Then he sneezed hard.

The drug, of course, didn't work for Nadim. It would be his longest flight ever.

For Ishmael, the drug worked wonders.

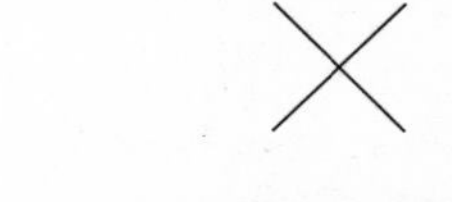

44 CEMETERY ROAD

Janice died a week ago. With this thought, I dragged myself from bed. I smiled grimly into the mirror and dropped my toothbrush back into its ceramic cup, fluorescent paste still hanging off its bristles. I grabbed my walking stick and the front door of our small cottage swung shut, thudding like a coffin lid behind me.

It was just past 6. Well before light. Before windows are lit and children are hustled off to school. Before sunlight glares between rooftops and cars speed noisily through roads. At 6 o'clock, darkness still reigns.

Before Janice died, I stayed in bed for as long as I could, enjoying lying against her soft sagging breasts, a wisp of her white hair upon my brow. Eyes half-closed, I would watch the crimson hue outside, like a flame, raze across our low iron fence.

Oh, that morning, how she breathed softly upon my cheek, whispering her secret. Her fingers held the pillow as though she were a child clinging to the remnants of a fairy-tale dream. With eyes closed she looked younger than her seventy-three years. That faint smile gave no hint of death.

Since the funeral, I have not dared stay in bed a minute longer. The sheets are cold and there is too much space on Janice's side. There she had read. There she had knitted. There she had been.

"Winter has come," I whispered to a streetlamp and its mosquitoes danced and flickered in an incandescent orange glow. "Will I die today. Or live again?"

At the roundabout, I turned left. Trying to keep my back straight, as if this would solidify me against what waited ahead. I shuffled past the dark playing field. Beside the swings and slides, a skateboard bowl had been dug out. After school and during holidays, the place was bursting with teenagers balancing like demons on mini-chariots. Even in the dark, the bowl trembled with energy. Ah, the relentless joys of youth.

What did Janice whisper on the day she died?

"I have a secret, my love."

"What secret?" I propped myself on the pillow and stared into her gray eyes.

"Meet me. In seven days." Her lips quivered and I could tell whatever this was disturbed her badly.

"Why? What are you talking about, Janice? I see you every day."

"In a week," she whispered. "At the ruins in the forest."

"How come? What's this all about?" My wife was behaving so strangely. So incredibly odd.

"Just promise," she said, taking my hand, hers coldly trembling. "Just promise."

"All right, all right. If it's such a big deal. But why ..."

"A week from now, my love. At the ruins. At dawn. No later."

"Oh, do tell, Janice. What the hell is this all about?"

And then she whispered a craziness that made my old heart shudder.

As I passed the scattered buildings of the nursing home, I saw most of the lights were already on. We old fogeys get up early. Perhaps we know we have squandered our youth, even our middle age, and now in our twilight years we know time is precious. That our remaining life needs meaning, so when Death comes pounding on our door we can look him squarely in the eye and know we're ready. And to you feminists, Death, I'm afraid, is a man.

I have one regret. Janice and I did not have children. We thought of adopting, perhaps a child from Africa or Asia. We even contacted a few agencies. But we had second thoughts. Would we be able to give the child enough of our love? In the end, Janice left it to me and I had my doubts. Janice was more disappointed than I thought she would be. Sometimes when we went shopping, I would find her in the baby shop, staring whimsically at shiny new cots draped in pretty fabric.

By now I had reached the end of the road. A dead end except I knew, hidden behind a clump of bushes and a tired-looking sign, was a dirt track that cut through the forest. I stood before it, breathing hard, not to catch my breath, although at my age this would only be normal, but because I was sure I felt a cold hand stroking my spine.

"You can't believe this nonsense, Janice," I had snarled that morning. "This is madness."

But she didn't answer. She just turned away.

Half-bewildered, half-angry, I stormed out of bed into the study. Her secret, it was the most ridiculous thing I had ever heard. I couldn't concentrate on the biography, for her words darted like irritating wasps in my head.

I put the book aside and when I crept back to the bedroom, I found her lying sprawled out on the twisted sheets, window wide open, lace curtains billowing like tortured sails in the wind. Her eyes stared icily at the ceiling, lips curled into a dreadful grin. I cried out and held my dead wife, trembling in the shafts of sunlight while her body grew colder and colder in my arms.

The ambulance men said there was nothing they could do. The coroner could not find the cause of death. A mystery disease perhaps. Did the bruises on her throat have anything to do with it? What bruises? I hadn't seen them before. They showed me, hidden beneath her hair, black marks on her neck. The doctor wasn't sure what made them. Nobody could be sure of anything. So many mystery illnesses nowadays.

Wiping wetness from my cheeks, I started up the track. The silhouettes of houses fell back and shadows of trees encircled me like vengeful ogres. Wild grasses swept by my boots. Frogs whooped and a lonesome bird called an incessant warning. I took my time with the steep climb, shoving my walking stick into the dark earth to heave my stooping body forward. My legs ached. My hips were sore. Had I taken my arthritis pills this morning? I couldn't remember.

A rustling in the bushes. I almost cried out. It could have been a dog or some wild animal. Too dark to see. Or was it something more sinister? My heart was beating fast. No use dying of a heart attack. Not now. When I was so close. I breathed in deeply to calm myself but instead the smell of dead things and feces filled my nostrils. I bent over, clutched my hat and heaved up whatever was left of last night's dinner. It was mostly liquid. Pathetic really.

I picked myself up and steadied my old body, bile burning in my throat. I glanced at my watch, my trembling hand making it hard to tell the time. An anniversary gift from Janice so many years ago. Not quite sure which one though. But we were on holiday somewhere by a sunlit beach. Was it in this country or not? I couldn't be sure.

"Oh, Janice," I said. "Our life has become a huge blur."

One thing I still know though: this dirt track had a name. It was called Cemetery Road because it led to a small cemetery on the hill deep in the forest. Only one of four roads in this once-thriving village. A village that existed two hundred years ago. But after the forest fires which destroyed half the homes, things turned bad. Folks moved to the big town, abandoning their broken-down timber houses. Making any kind of living here was hard.

In the last few decades though, as the big city relentlessly sprawled northwards, people returned with their cars and mortgages. In this new suburb they built their roads, houses and shops. As for Cemetery Road, it lay buried in the forest reserve, a mere track for hikers leading past the ruins of a mansion.

I plodded uphill, breathing hard, my old bones stiff and aching. Although chilly, my bald head beneath my hat was hot and my hands had grown sweaty. Dawn crept its way up through the leaves and branches.

Just before I reached the graveyard, the entrance leered over me, its lopsided post threatening to crush my skull. I stepped back, startled. I had arrived all too quickly. No, I didn't need to remove the strangling foliage to know the numbers carved into the mossy stone.

"I've arrived, Janice," I whispered.

44 Cemetery Road.

As a child, we had gone into the ruins on a dare but barely made it up the gravel path. The place scared us, even more than the cemetery next door. Zack, the pluckiest of our group, claimed he had seen strange lights, like candles flickering in the windows and shadows, gliding to and fro as though restlessly waiting. I didn't believe this nonsense. But there were stories about this sad place. Stories whispered only after a couple of whiskies.

Who knows if they were true. But history there was. Eamon Fitzgerald had come from Perthshire, Scotland. He worked as a kitchen hand before striking it rich in the gold fields. He bought the only land available then, twenty acres next to the cemetery, and there built the biggest and only stone house in the village.

After Eamon died, his son George made several extensions to the home. When George found out his wife Vera was having an affair with the gardener, he cleaved her head with an axe and threw her body down the well. He died in prison before he was hanged and with no offspring, the mansion was left empty. Then came the forest fires and the village was soon abandoned.

I pushed open the rusty gate which creaked out a guttural warning. Whether for me or someone or something else I wasn't sure. My shoes crunched upon the gravel buried by wild grass. Otherwise, it was silent here. Too awfully silent. No birdsong. No frogs whooping. And colder, too. Icy and damp it was. A trembling grew in my bones.

If I was to turn back, now was the time. To retreat through the gate and scurry down the track. Past the nursing home and playing field. My warm cottage behind the low iron fence would be waiting. I would make some tea, pick up a book or flick on the telly. The morning programs could sometimes be interesting. But the years ... they would ravage me. And I had promised Janice. Yes, I had promised her. That was my excuse. I knew better though. And so I heard my footsteps drag my old bones up the old driveway.

Dawn filtered through the foliage. I could take no solace from that. For now I could see a thick mist hung like a dismal cloak through the thick trees ahead, where the garden had been reclaimed by forest. The skeletal remains of rose bushes stripped by winter clawed their way to the stone ruins. I shuffled past the fallen remains of a pergola overgrown by creepers.

I groped at the timber post and part of it crumbled into dust. Age, it does such things.

Birth and death is the normal cycle of life. But Janice had other thoughts ...

"I met someone yesterday," she whispered. "At the ruins."

I knew Janice often went by the old mansion on her hikes and meeting other hikers was not unusual.

"Oh, who was it?"

"No one we know," said Janice. "It was a lady dressed in white. She gave me something."

"Oh, what was it?"

"Everlasting life."

"Ever ... what?"

"Everlasting life. When I see you in seven days, I'll pass this precious gift to you."

"What the hell are you talking about, Janice! This is crazy!"

"Is it crazy to want to live forever? It'll be you and me, young again, and living 'til the end of time!"

Young again? Until the end of time?

That was why I stood here trembling, at this dreadful desolate place, at this appointed hour.

Here to confront her madness!

Or was it mine?

I pushed my way past the groping branches into what once was the main part of the garden. I felt a tingling on my neck, as though someone was watching me. My eyes darted about but I saw no one, just overgrown bushes and white drifts of mists like malevolent ghosts. I drew my coat tighter against my body and my breath hung in the air. I cautiously crept down one of the broken footpaths.

A bulky shadow loomed ahead of me. Was it a vicious creature waiting? No. Just a fountain with a fallen pedestal. Murky water, brown and oily, stagnated there, giving off a foul odor that grabbed at my guts. I clutched my mouth to stop myself from vomiting again. It wasn't the smell that made me want to retch. It was fear.

Suddenly I was surrounded. Trapped! I spun around and gasped. Figures encircled me, their faces lunging forward. I was about to flee when I realized that the threatening figures were but sculptures.

Through the heavy mist the stone shadows stood like sentinels. Sad gray faces peered through foliage. An ear, an eye, an elbow, a foot, protruded from the bushes. A lion with one claw. A rat in its mouth.

"Janice," I whispered, holding back my tears. "What insanity awaits here? Why have I come?"

As if in reply there was a queer sound. Like someone laughing.

I looked up to see a figure in a white dress dart before me.

"What the—" I gasped.

I stumbled backwards from the fountain and knocked into something hard. I screamed.

A face peered right into mine. A stone face.

In its hands it held a jug of wine. A Greek-like sculpture with flowing robes. Discolored and chipped by time and the beating of the sun and the drumming of rain.

I glanced around me but she was gone.

"Where is she?" I whispered. "What am I doing here?"

"For me, my love," a familiar voice said. "For me."

I turned and gasped.

It was Janice. But not the Janice who had laid in my bed, a wisp of white hair on my cheek, soft sagging breasts on my chest. Not the Janice who knitted and did the crossword puzzles and made endless cups of tea.

This was the Janice I married fifty years ago.

Radiant and alight with energy. A red dress flowed about her slim body. Her hair blonde and shining even in the dim light. Her skin glowing like moonlight.

Oh, how young, how so alive, she looked!

"Surprised?" Janice said. "I told you I'd be here waiting."

"Yes, but ..."

"Everything I told you is true. Everlasting youth, my love. That's what I promised you."

Before I could ask her one of a thousand questions, Janice took my hand.

Her hand was freezing. I tried to yank mine away.

She gripped my fingers harder.

"Come, my love. Come with me."

Walking briskly ahead, she pulled me through the entangling trees, past its watching sculptures, to the fallen masonry walls. I dropped my walking stick but she didn't heed my protests and kept pulling me. My legs had trouble keeping up with her lithe dancing movements and I stumbled twice.

Up the once-grand entrance steps she drew me. The building had lost most of its roof and, beyond the crumbling brick structures, gloomy clouds like giant ghosts swept by.

We entered what must have once been the kitchen. The rusty remains of a stove slumped like a dead thing in one corner. The floor was roughly tiled and covered in bits of broken wood. In another corner were some broken ceramics, a fork and a metal cup.

"Let's wait here, my love."

"Janice," I said. "How ... What ..."

"Shhhhhh ..." she said and put a finger to my lips. The appendage felt icy. And since when did Janice paint her fingernails? Almost never. But hers were now painted red and they were long like claws.

Then I noticed her eyes. Now I could see them properly. How unlike the rest of her they were. Not young and vibrant like the rest of her body. Her eyes seemed unnatural. Older than those of my departed wife. Older than old.

They were dead.

"Don't ask questions, my love," she said. "You'll soon meet my new friend."

By now the sun had risen but because it was kept hidden by layers of swirling clouds we were in a world of neither light nor dark. As for the mist, it encircled our limbs, gripping us in a damp coldness.

Janice didn't seem to mind for she grinned at me expectantly, her lips bright red.

"Thank you, Janice."

I turned to see who spoke and there standing behind me was the woman dressed in white. My throat went dry.

"Hello," I stammered.

Despite my fear, I couldn't help noticing how stunning the woman was. Raven hair cascaded down in flowing curls. Around her neck she wore a gold locket of a strange design. But what I noticed most were her eyes, dark and penetrating as though she could see into the depths of my soul. But, like Janice's eyes, they appeared to be dead.

"Nice to make your acquaintance," she said in a low voice. "I've heard a lot about you. My name is Vera. Do you know why we've brought you here?"

"For everlasting life," I said. "So that I don't ever grow old. So that time can go to hell and Janice and I can live together forever."

"That's right!" laughed the woman. "Time can go to hell. I like that. You know what you want, old man, don't you? But do you know how I'll achieve it?"

"Yes," I said, drawing in a quick breath. "I saw the bruises on Janice's neck. You're a ... a vampire. You're immortal. Anyone you kill will also turn into a vampire. I know the legend. I've read about it. Am I right?"

"A legend is only a legend," said Vera. "Like all things in this world, parts of it are true. These vampire myths remain hidden in the human subconscious. All cultures have vampire legends. That should provide a hint that we are real. But humankind has forgotten us. Consigning us to mere stories and teenage movies. So much the better. We are safer than ever before."

"So you *are* a vampire!" I drew in a deep breath. My conclusions, insane though they were, were correct. My hands began to shake. "Will ... will you give me everlasting life? Will you make me young again? I want to be with Janice 'til the end of time."

The woman laughed. "You are indeed persistent for an old man."

"He's always been like this," said Janice, smiling at me. "Ever since we met. I love him dearly."

"Thank you for bringing your husband to see me," said Vera, stepping towards Janice. "I'll be forever grateful."

Vera embraced my wife. Janice stiffened and her arms flew up flailing at the air. She tried to fight against Vera but couldn't. Vera stepped back and Janice collapsed to the ground.

I stood frozen in horror. In the half-light I could see Janice's neck had been ripped out.

Vera turned.

Then I saw her for what she was. There was a wound in the side of her head covered in black blood. Then it vanished and she was beautiful again.

"What the hell have you done!" I yelled. "You killed my wife!"

"I've done what I'd always planned to do," said Vera, wiping the blood from her mouth with a white handkerchief.

She stepped slowly towards me, eyes shining bright.

Her mouth opened impossibly wide to reveal fangs. Long and sharp.

"Why?" I cried, stumbling back, pulling myself along one wall. "Why did you kill her?"

"Kill her? She was already dead. She was the undead. Just like I am. How cursed I am to wander aimlessly through time. Cursed to feed off animals in the wild or to take the occasional child, the homeless tramp or wandering backpacker. Never letting on that a vampire dwells among you pathetic humans. I used your dear wife to bring you to me."

"Me? Why me? What do you want with me?"

Vera continued stalking me. I had retreated into the remains of another room. From its sprawling dimensions I guessed it was a grand living or dining room. At my feet the broken masonry of a fireplace were scattered over white marble. Through the French windows the dark shadows of the forest beckoned.

"You are the last descendant of George Fitzgerald. When my husband split my skull with an axe and threw me down the well, I yearned for revenge. I killed him in his cell and promised to slay all his descendants. Then came the fires and the mob to hunt me down. So I fled and stayed away for so many years. But I always remembered to return to finish the work. You are the last descendant of George Fitzgerald!"

"You're wrong! I'm not a Fitzgerald. George Fitzgerald had no children."

"No legitimate ones. Your grandfather was George's son. His mother was the maid. She was dismissed when he found out she was carrying his child. So you see, you have come home at last. This is the house of your ancestors!"

"No!" I cried. "This can't be real."

Vera glided towards me, arms reaching out, and tongue licking her bright red lips. She grinned, "Revenge, after so many years, how sweet it feels."

I tripped and fell painfully on my back.

"No!" I groaned. "Please ..."

She stood over me, chest heaving, running a finger down her long curly hair. "I wonder how much blood is in that thin old body of yours."

Just as her fangs flew to my throat I heard a terrible ripping, a shrieking that filled the dawn.

The ground trembled.

The vampire fell back, hands clutching at the walls for balance, hair thrown across her vile face.

"What's this!" she moaned. "What's happening?"

With my last vestiges of energy, I got up and threw myself out of the house and back into the forest. I ran, hobbled, fell and ran again. I heard the vampire cursing behind me, giving chase.

Still I forced my legs to move. I must have come out the wrong way for the trees suddenly opened up, and instead of the track I was confronted with white gravestones. But something terrible was happening here.

The ground was shaking. Clumps of earth were thrown high in the air as if the place was being hit by artillery fire. If only that were true for the reality was far more terrible ...

Bodies in half-rotten clothes pushed themselves out of their graves. Worming their way out, clawing at the soil. Eyes wide and eager.

I turned to flee but Vera stood behind me, blocking my path. She was not grinning though. Her body shook, her face wild.

"No!" she cried. "This is impossible!"

"We have come for you, creature of evil," a dreadful voice echoed. "Harlot of the devil, we will destroy you!"

I spun and beheld a hideous figure, rotting flesh draped off its chest. A gray organ pulsed horribly within. It raised its thin arm. A crooked finger pointed accusingly at the vampire.

Eyes, large and bloody, stared angrily from a skull-like head. A few strands of hair hung off it. Upon its arms and legs were patches of shining white, bones showing through. Swatches of cloth, once fine clothes, still clung to the figure.

"You do remember us, don't you, darling Vera?" it growled. "Now it's our turn."

It clenched its hands into bleeding fists.

Behind it, several other figures, all rotting beings, groped their way forward, moaning and groaning their curses as they surrounded Vera.

"Return to your graves!" cried the vampire. "You are all dead! I killed you centuries ago!"

"Yes!" cried the figure. "We are indeed dead. But we are alive again to rip you off this living breathing earth."

Before the vampire could reply, the figures fell upon her.

I ran for the forest.

I heard a terrible shrieking and thumping.

And finally the ripping of flesh.

I knew as I fell moaning upon the track that the figure that spoke was George Fitzgerald. My ancestor. Did he come to protect me or did he wait through the centuries for his own revenge?

By the time I stumbled down Cemetery Road, the forest was awash in sunlight. Birds chirped in the trees. A yellow butterfly drifted innocently by. I could feel a warmth creeping back into my bones.

What had happened up there at the ruins? I didn't want to think about it. There would never be any answers.

I stepped out of the forest into the bright morning of suburbia. Up the road I trudged, already missing my walking stick, which I would never retrieve. My body ached painfully. Vehicles sped about. Children being hustled to school. I shuffled past the old folks' home. A man in a bright yellow T-shirt was watering the rose garden.

Beside the playing field a car stopped, its lady driver asked if I needed help.

"I'm fine," I said. "Couldn't be better."

"Are you sure?" She looked like a doctor or a vet. Maybe a psychiatrist.

"Perfectly fine."

A little girl in a pink dress waved from a child seat. I grinned at her. She could have been my granddaughter.

"Thank you for caring," I said to her mother. "This can be a lonely road."

I carried on. I could see my house now. A small cottage with an iron fence. There Janice and I had lived. There I will make my cups of tea.

There I will past the time. There I will eventually die.

THE WIDTH OF A CIRCLE

1. THE ZOO

The cold pillow miserably stroked Adam's cheek. He struggled for warmth within the three heavy blankets, his large brown eyes blinking at the huge casement window that kept out the winter's night. He wondered as only a child could do, honestly without a tinge of self-pity. This is England, home is far away; I'm thirteen years old and alone.

Adrift like a young leaf, fallen from the protective branches of a mighty tree, blown by the cold currents of an unforgiving wind, knowing something had ended and something was just beginning. But Adam, beyond the recognition of his present circumstance, knew there was something else, quite disturbing, like a door opening into blackness, and from the other side foul eyes were peering.

The dormitory, called "The Zoo" for more than thirty years, contained six junior boys. Lights out at 9:15 and voices in heavy darkness passed from bed to bed. All apprehensive about school the next day, but it didn't keep out a few jokes or discussions on Masters at College. Some boys had been here the term before and filled the others in. These innocent voices drifted in the dark until eventually the consensus was to be quiet and sleep.

One or two softly snored. They all looked the same, blond- or brown-haired, with milky-pink white faces. Adam had brown tropical skin, with jet-black hair neatly cropped for school.

He shivered thinking of the icy wind sweeping across the rooftops, of coconut trees that would not survive a minute here. His eyelids grew heavy, his body curled, hugging his cold pillow for comfort. Just as sleep crept his way, Adam remembered him. The strange old man. His eyes jumped wide awake. The door to blackness opened and a figure peered out. Somewhere beyond the Zoo echoes of creaking emerged as the house settled itself into the long winter's night.

2. ON THE PLANE

The loud humming filled Adam's head. The dim light strangely hurt his eyes. The aircraft was like a bustling wet market found in any major suburb. Instead of shopping baskets brimming with vegetables and dead chickens, this crowd carted duty-free plastic bags with bottles of whisky, XO, cartons of cigarettes and perfumes sold by alluring, heavily made-up ladies in white uniforms.

Passengers muttered as they passed the slim, smiling air hostess with dark eyes that said *I will take you there, and everywhere*. An old Chinese lady stubbornly tried to stuff a huge bag into the overhead locker while fellow passengers attempted to squeeze past her. Adam could just see them wrestling her to the ground, punching and kicking her. *Get out of the way old bitch, get out of the bloody way!* But they just waited, bags heavy in hands.

Adam and his father passed rows of seats, some empty, some filled with excited or tired people. Theirs were by the window. Seatbelts clicked into place. Adam's father scratched his sideburns and flipped through the in-flight magazine. A proud man, escorting his son to a public school in England — it took money to do that.

As Adam opened his Alfred Hitchcock book, a rasping cough filled the cabin and a thin figure approached. The pretty stewardess offered no help, she stood smiling blankly — *I will take you there, and everywhere*. The old Malay man hobbled down the aisle, leaning occasionally on his shiny wooden cane. He may have looked distinguished if not for his white crumpled trousers and a gray jacket, a size too large. The gray beard was old, unkempt but his eyes brightly lit, like an old lion looking for young, injured prey.

His slow footsteps, like an irregular heartbeat, shuddered down the plane. It was rude to stare, and Adam was about to look away when *the old man stopped*, his gleaming eyes met Adam's. They widened and a strange, frightening expression crossed the old man's face. Adam quickly glanced away, his thoughts in turmoil, his body tingling nervously.

Why is he looking at me? Why is he staring? Icy fingers crept up Adam's spine and he shivered. *He's only an old man*, Adam desperately rationalized. *Maybe he isn't staring at me. Maybe he's looking at something else behind me. Maybe. Maybe not.*

To be sure Adam glanced up, and there he was, the old man peering at him. No mistake. The strange, frightening look fixed like scars on the old face. Gray eyebrows hung like hoods over his eyes, and those eyes, like a cavern filled with bats, bore down on Adam as if reaching for his soul to twist it out from Adam's body.

The boy, for he was a boy of only thirteen, could do nothing but stare at the old man, trembling, not daring to turn away. The old man's mouth opened as if to say something, dry lips opening, revealing a tongue on which sat patches of white, with strands of saliva dripping from the roof of his mouth. Then the mouth closed and the old man mercifully looked away, his thin body lackadaisically creaking itself into an empty seat ... only three rows in front of Adam's.

The boy wished the old man had sat far away behind in the bowels of the plane. But no, the old man sat right in front of the boy with a hideous form like a septic wound. Gray hair gleamed with Brylcreem and when he turned, Adam could see the deep wrinkles like jagged ravines etched around large probing eyes. Hungry, soul-wrenching eyes.

Adam felt a jolt and the plane roared like a winged and fiery monster down the runway. The wheels took to the air and the passengers climbed into the night. The Klang Valley appeared below like a sprawling carpet of fairy lights. Adam decided that each single light was a single house with a family watching, hearing and living TV, absorbed in its electronic fantasy. And each single light was surrounded by tributaries of unending streetlights. The aircraft banked to the right and the Valley lights were left behind. Adam despaired to see them disappear into the black horizon, as if the last glimmers of hope were being finally swallowed up.

The boy kept vigil on the old man for a reason he could not fathom, a reason other than unadulterated fear. Fear though was certainly at work, like a tapeworm squirming away in his guts. The old man's eyes were fortunately closed as if in deep meditation; occasionally, the dry lips moved as if repeating some verse from the Quran. But Adam doubted it, more likely it was some demonic spell. This was interrupted by fits of coughing, probably from the dust of his musty moth-eaten jacket. This attire was not that of a wealthy man.

At thirteen, Adam already knew money talks. Three years later, he would counter that with: *Money doesn't talk, it swears;* the lyrics, this one by Dylan, would teach him philosophy, life, politics. But this was before he heard those songs, no, *lived* those songs. Adam had just an instinct now, an underlying feeling about wealth.

At school, most boys took the bus. They formed disorderly queues of blue shorts and bright white shirts in the piercing afternoon sun. These were the fortunate ones who could afford the private school buses. Those that could not had to pack themselves into long, smelly, grimy, public buses with cigarette smoke and swearing bus conductors. The luckiest were fetched by parents outside the school gates. Door-to-door service. And some, like Adam, were fetched by drivers in big, air-conditioned cars.

His friends would exclaim when they saw the shining green Mercedes-Benz. "Wah, your car so big lah!"

Adam would be embarrassed and say, "No lah, company car," as if that would negate the prestige, as if it was a valid excuse for being rich and pampered. All the boy wanted was to be no different and to belong. But there were other rich kids too, their *drivers* (for *chauffeurs* was too tongue-twisting to say with any confidence) carried their school bags all the way to the classroom door. Adam was glad not to be put through that ordeal.

The boy slept uncomfortably on the economy seat. His father didn't intend to spoil his son on business class and, in any case, it wouldn't be reimbursed by the company; the auditor would never allow that deduction. Anyway, there were many other expenses to take care of and boarding school was not for the financially faint-hearted.

Once or twice Adam woke up when certain eyes were on him. Once he looked up and saw the head of gray hair slowly turning away as if satisfied with what it had seen. The cane held between heavy palms, its hook revolving methodically, his gnarled fingers twitching with a sordid eagerness. Adam could feel that cold, wooden hook around his neck, pulling him to the old leering face, right up to those big devouring eyes. He squirmed in his seat at the thought of the putrid warm breath on his face, the smell of his moldy checked jacket filling his nostrils.

After what seemed an endless flight, and to Adam's relief, the indicator to fasten seatbelts finally came on. The boy's father slept most of the way and only woke for meals. He now folded his blanket and examined the contents of his travel wallet. Passports, visas, landing cards — they were all safely still there. "We're landing soon," he said to his son, "better put on your seatbelt."

The aircraft started its descent into the morning fog. It reminded Adam of a Jack the Ripper movie. He killed those girls in the same dense fog, their warm blood trickling from the knife wounds onto the cold, cobbled pavement. And he was never caught.

Adam's wide eyes found the old man smiling to himself and decided not to think of Jack the Ripper anymore.

3. FOLLOWED

Airports are strange places. Full of people wanting to be somewhere else. One half rushing to get out, to get home or to the waiting comforts of a hotel room. The other half impatient to board a plane to jet them to some faraway country, where another airport awaited. And once there, to be met by a large group of other people eagerly waiting to be flown away. And so it goes on. Adam would ponder this a year and a half later, while waiting to fly back for the summer holidays. But for now, it was just a place full of people, where airplanes landed.

This airport was particularly strange to Adam due to its sheer size. The airport bus with automatic doors dropped them near the 'Arrivals' sign and an escalator swept them up with the crowd. The cold groped with its icy greedy fingers and Adam was glad for the warmth of the new blue sweater. Adam thought that everything seemed new when going to public school. *Except myself*, he surmised, *I am still the same*.

His father led the way and they followed the queue of people in front. They got off the escalator and into a corridor, more than twice as wide as the aircraft, but really the same to Adam. Here the market had a big sale on. Passengers lugged baggage in a frantic race. Their expressionless faces on big, tall bodies. Not like the airport in Kuala Lumpur made of smaller men. No, they were big here, and all in a hurry, passing quickly by like fleeting shadows. The wheels of baggage trolleys clicked monotonously on and on over the tarmac.

"Ayah, I've got to go to the toilet," Adam said pointing desperately to a sign.

"Okay, I'll wait here," his father said putting the bags down. "Don't be too long."

The boy went inside and relieved himself, glad to be on the ground. *No funny-looking airplane toilets here*, he mused. He rinsed the soap off his hands and glanced at the mirror. He almost screamed. *It was him!*

Brylcreem hair, gray beard, eyes like a cavern of hungry bats. If it was not for the fact that Adam had just used the toilet, he knew he would have wet himself.

The boy closed his eyes, waiting for the dagger in his back. *Or would it be the throat?* He hoped to die quickly, painlessly, saw his parents in tears, the gathering, prayers in the house, the bundle of white cloth covering him in the grave.

He waited for the blow ... waited and waited ... but nothing came. He opened his eyes, the face was miraculously gone. Adam, his entire body shaking, spun round expecting the old man to be hiding in one of the cubicles, but they were all empty. His thoughts jabbed at his brain.

He can't have left the toilets. I'd have heard the door creak open.

Then the door *did* creak open and a man with a suit and briefcase entered. He glanced at Adam strangely and the boy quickly left the toilet.

The floor spun as Adam stepped into the corridor, his father a mere shadow approaching. The cold came in repeated waves, beyond that echoed the roar of aircrafts and the constant clicking of luggage trolleys. Everything swam, the light started to fade. He was heading for blackness when hands were on his shoulders.

"Are you all right, Adam?" It was his father. "You look very pale."

"Oh ... I'm ... I'm okay. Just a ... headache," Adam weakly replied. Everything came back slowly, grudgingly, into focus.

"You don't look well, you must have been tired out from the long journey." He felt his son's temperature with his hand.

After sitting his son down to rest, they queued at immigration for an hour. Adam looked anxiously for the old man but he had disappeared. *Maybe he went into some other queue,* thought Adam. But he doubted it. As the Indian immigration officer stamped their passports, the boy suddenly realized he had left his Hitchcock book on the plane. He was about to tell his father when he stopped. That exciting book had suddenly become nothing of any significance. It was as if Adam had deliberately turned off the TV during the last few exciting moments of *MacGyver*. What was exciting was now boring. Adam did not know it, but he had grown up a little. Just a little, but enough to get him past the first few days at the new school.

The boy, although now not a hundred percent boy — but not a man either — pressed himself against the cab window, taking in his new surroundings. The sky wore a hideous gray, he counted four planes taking off behind them. Not much to be seen on the roads, only cars and the rooftops of houses packed together; no tall buildings or beautiful palaces like he expected.

"Is this London?" Adam quietly asked his father.

"No, Adam," his father replied and laughed. "It's about thirty minutes from here. I'll tell you when we get there."

All Adam could say was "Oh!" and continued staring out the window, looking for London.

Adam's father forgot to tell him they were in London when the black cab merged into its traffic and narrow streets, but the boy knew they were there. He didn't see any palaces, just shops and dirty-looking streets with people in sweaters, scarfs and gloves, carrying plastic bags from supermarkets, their warm breath like cigarette smoke. All kinds of people of different colors walked the streets, black, white, brown, yellow. It was a surprise, for Adam thought London was full of whites.

The next day, they drove out of London. It was cold and it took some time for the heater to warm up. Adam thought of his things tucked away in two huge suitcases in the trunk of the red Avis car. That was all he had and he did not know where he was going. To school, yes, but what would it be like and what awaited him there? Snow covered the ground as they sped on the motorway.

Adam, despite this great adventure, wanted to be back home in Bangsar, that suburb for the well-off in Kuala Lumpur. He had a large room where the windows were always open and the fan was constantly on. It was always terribly hot and the call to prayers would fill the air. And the neighbor's dog barked persistently late at night. Suddenly Adam wondered whether he could still call it 'home'. And he almost cried.

They had been driving for about an hour when they came upon a small town. The roads were narrow, with more people strolling than cars. Adam's father was telling him to study hard and to write home as often as he could. The boy nodded obediently, staring out the window. An old lady with a poodle walked so slowly that Adam thought she was sleepwalking. A man was selling fruits, apples and oranges and all kinds of vegetables were displayed in his tiny store. As they passed a newsagent Adam almost yelled out. His mouth opened to scream but nothing came.

A figure stood hunched by a doorway, eyes upon Adam, following the boy as the Avis car went past. Adam knew he was not mistaken. It was the same old man on the plane, gray beard, ravenous eyes. Even from this distance, those eyes burnt with a horrid intensity, the lips curled up into an evil smile. The figure's hands tucked deep into a heavy gray coat and the face was cold like a corpse's. Adam wanted to tell his father about the old man but decided not to.

Ayah would say I'm stupid with my overactive imagination. But what was the old man doing here?

Adam remembered those eyes and realized he was trembling uncontrollably.

"Are you cold, Adam?" his father asked as he signaled left and turned the corner.

"Yes ... I ... uh ... think so. Did you see the ... the old man there?"

"What old man?" his father questioned as he took his eyes off the road and looked at his son inquisitively.

"That old man ... by the newspaper shop," Adam said, already regretting telling him about it.

"No, I didn't. Why?"

"Nothing, he just looked ... uh ... strange."

"There are lots of strange people here, Adam," his father said, "you'll get used to it." He glanced at his son with a frown and turned the heater up.

4. ST. CHRISTOPHER'S

In the Zoo that night, this frightening, leering old man with the hooked walking-stick filled Adam's thoughts and chased sleep away. He shivered under the blanket and tucked himself in deeper, trying not to think. The Zoo lay quiet now but for the odd restless creaks of the floorboards. Tonight was an event in Adam's life. He would later as an adult recognize it as *a pivotal point in life* and although the coming days would be of greater significance, it would seem like a blur to him only to be realized in the strangest of ways.

Now all he felt was confusion, a strange feeling of loss, but oddly enough, not such a bad feeling. He felt swept up by the strange events since he boarded the plane, and the knowledge that they still lay uncoiling before him did not placate the boy. Finally Adam yawned. Tomorrow would be his first day at St. Christopher's College and with that thought he fell into a deep sleep.

St. Christopher's College sat old and gloomy on the crest of a hill. Gray clouds blanketed the sky, hanging there as if waiting to descend, to swallow up the school, its boys and Masters. Adam's face shivered against the icy wind. He tucked his gloved hands into his jacket and strode quickly up from Hazelwell House, where he stayed, to the Dining Hall, commonly known as 'DH'. He was with David Scott and Peter Osborne, both new boys in the Zoo who had joined that spring term. They wolfed down the eggs, toast, cereal and coffee and stepped out of the DH feeling warmer.

The boys returned to Hazelwell for housework. Adam's task for the week was to sweep the Fifth Formers' corridors. This was easy. David had to wash the House Prefects' pots and pans, grimy with dried tinned spaghetti and baked beans. St. Christopher's after all provided an all-round education. If Adam had arrived five year's earlier he would have found himself warming the toilet seats for Prefects. Fortunately, this form of housework was banned. The public school system had changed considerably since Tom Brown's days, but certain remnants persisted.

The school bell jangled, the boys rushed for their books and a stream of green jackets trudged up College Road to the College buildings. Besides the DH, a former chapel complete with stained-glass windows, the only other building of architectural significance was the new chapel made of sandstone with huge windows divided into quarters and crowned with circular fenestration. Below its great vaults and arches rose columns upon columns of brass plaques with messages such as *Richard William Davies born 1898-1917, Hazelwell.* Remembrance for the dead from the Great War and the Second World War, college boys in regiments, many mowed down in the trenches in the Somme or on the beaches of Dunkirk and Normandy.

Adam did not know it as he passed the chapel with books tucked under his arm listening to Peter's tales of fast cars, but he would be polishing the same brass plaques three years later on a community service Wednesday and be struck by the solemn history of the college.

Beyond the chapel, more boys from different houses streamed along the playing fields towards College. The three rugby fields lay frosty and bare before the uninspiring gymnasium building. It was in College Two in the Fifth Form when Adam would break a scrum half's collarbone with a high tackle. He regretted not having a chance to apologize, for the injured player from Malvern was quickly taken off and sent to hospital while Adam walked aimlessly in a daze over what he had done.

Time shot by that first morning. Many new things had to be learnt. For a start he had a new name, for 'Adam' was pronounced '*air-dem*' instead of '*are-dam*'. He tried correcting them but the boys and teachers looked at him strangely. So he gave up.

Having to learn everything in English was a traumatic experience for young Adam. When the teacher at Adam's first lesson started teaching Geography in English, it sounded like a foreign language. Fortunately, he got used to it and the morning lessons went well. But Adam was to find out that he still had much to learn.

The queue for lunch was long as usual. Boys waited hungrily and impatiently. To Adam the useless heaters in the DH seemed like air conditioning gone wrong.

The DH being a former chapel had a high ceiling and Mother Mary and the Saints stared from stained glass windows above. Adam stuffed his hands into his pockets to keep warm, feeling homesick for chicken curry with coconut milk. The boys, Adam and David Scott, were in the same Chemistry class. It was a double period and finished just before lunch. David's stomach rumbled. He was brawny and sporting, and played rugby for his last school.

"That's Lawrence, he's a Prefect. I heard that he's a big bully," David whispered, nudging his friend.

"He can't be that bad," Adam replied with a mock wise-look on his face.

"Yeah, you say hello to him then."

David's dare was too hard to resist. Lawrence was tall, thin and blond, with blue-green eyes staring from a pale white face. Adam nervously edged up to him.

"Hi, Lawrence," Adam said with a big grin. Lawrence abruptly turned, staring hard at the junior in disbelief.

"Don't talk to me, arsehole," he said in a deadly whisper. Adam was speechless and stepped back in horror. "Get out of my face, slanty-eyed," Lawrence continued. "You don't belong here!"

"That *chink* from your house," growled Fowler, a fat boy with brown hair next to Lawrence. He turned menacingly at Adam and barked: *"Why don't you go back to the jungle you came from!"*

He gave Adam a shove and the junior boy fell, his bottom sliding on the polished wooden floor. There Adam sat on his arse in complete bewilderment like an idiotic clown, his legs sprawled out stupidly before him. The queue of boys stared like a pack of dogs, some smirked, some chuckled.

Adam got up and ran with Lawrence's high-pitched laughter chasing at his heels. He stood outside the DH in the bitter cold, panting, his icy breath heaving out in the yellow lamplight. Warm tears rolled down his cheeks. It was not the pain but the humiliation, the thought of not belonging, being different. Being a *chink*.

"Adam, are you all right?" It was David.

"Go away ... I'm okay!" Adam said angrily.

"They were real bastards, bloody bastards!" David exclaimed. "Forget about them, they're just idiots. I shouldn't have dared you."

David sat down uneasily on the iron bench beside the Chapel. In the darkness, Adam could see that the delicate white petals of the snowdrops had become tiny blobs of gray. The branches of the oak tree threw eerie shadows over them. In the daytime this place was beautiful, night made it dreadful.

"Well, I'm not going back in there," Adam replied as he brushed away his tears with a sleeve. "Not with them laughing at me. I won't go in."

"Let's not go back then," David answered. "We can always go to the fish and chips shop down the road. I've got two pounds ... that should cover us."

Adam looked at him with a concerned expression.

"Don't worry, all the Masters and Prefects are at the DH so we won't get caught," David said reassuringly as he got up and started to walk down the steep cobbled steps that led away from the College. Adam followed. He was after all not going back to the DH, ever.

It was a short walk to the fish and chips shop and Adam soon forgot the incident at the Dining Hall. They hungrily ate the hot chips with oily fingers, each one taking turns at the chunk of battered haddock.

"Ah, that was good," said David as they walked back to Hazelwell. "Much better than bloody DH food."

David threw his friend an invisible rugby ball as he ran forward. Adam chased after him kicking the ball in the air as he sprinted forward. David waited with his arms outstretched for the tackle. Before Adam could avoid him David's arms were round his waist and Adam was pulled to the pavement.

"Well tried, my Malaysian friend. Got to do better next time," David said as he laughed. He turned round and accidentally tripped on the pavement and Adam laughed loudly.

As the boys were about to turn into the drive leading to the House, a figure stepped out from the shadows. They were about to turn and run when the figure called out. "Hey, stop! It's me, Nigel."

Nigel had a cigarette in his mouth. He blew a curl of smoke in their direction. Nigel sometimes skipped lessons and almost got expelled twice. Whenever any of the juniors wanted a cigarette Nigel would always be there to sell it to them.

"I wouldn't go through the front if I were you," Nigel said as he flung his cigarette onto the road. The sparks bounced like fireworks in the dark.

"Why not?" asked David.

"Well, George Sims is waiting there for those who are late for prep. Go in the front and you're guaranteed a detention."

"So what do we do?" Adam asked.

"Round the back, Einstein. Just follow me, no one'll see us." Nigel led them round to the back of the House. They helped each other over the concrete wall into an overgrown and thorny garden.

Nigel was the last over. He jumped and landed on his backside. Adam laughed and David joined in. Nigel got up and brushed the mud off, looking embarrassed.

"You both owe me a pack of Marlboros for saving your skins," Nigel rebuked sharply as they entered the back door. His pride regained, Nigel quickly led the way down the corridor to the prep rooms where homework was done. David went next, indicating Adam to follow. Adam motioned to him to carry on as Adam, being the last, had to close and lock the back door.

All was quiet with everyone doing their homework. Through the open back door, shadows shifted in the overgrown garden. The twisted limbs of trees stood menacingly. A breeze blew in, the leaves started rustling in the darkness and everything came alive. Adam's eyes were pulled to a dark corner. A shadow had moved. He was sure of it. He quickly pulled the door closed, locking it behind him. Adam was about to follow the others when he hesitated. A chill fell on his neck, and he felt an irresistible urge, as if something was pulling him, to look back through the window.

The overgrown bushes cowered in the darkness. The trees twisted out of the earth, their branches locked angrily in the frosty air. Initially, he only saw a bare outline of a shadow beside a tree. The boy peered harder with the cold of the windowpane on his face. Then he saw it, *the figure*.

It was bent over with a hooked cane. The head slowly raised itself revealing a face white as a ghost's, its ravenous eyes meeting Adam's, piercing him right through his own eyes, into his brain. A blinding light exploded with a soul-wrenching scream, echoing in the complete blackness of his mind. Adam reeled back, almost falling; his breath caught in his throat, his body shaking in terror.

Adam, his mind in shambles, could do nothing but run. Rushing up the stairs to the Zoo, leaping up as many steps as he could, his running echoing down the stairwell. With each step he leaped, with each thud he made, a semblance of thought returned. When he reached the top floor, Adam's heart was thumping so wildly, he thought it would crawl up his throat and leap out of his mouth. He jumped into bed, his body shaking crazily as if it would never stop.

He knew that gray-bearded face, those black eyes like a cavern of bats. *It belongs to the old man! He's followed me here, and he's coming to get me.*

Adam pulled the pillow over his head and whimpered. He could see the stooping figure approaching from the garden.

He was entering the house.

This old man ...

He was coming.

This old man came rolling home ...

Up the steps.

This old man, he played two ...

He could hear the footsteps echoing.

Louder and louder ... it echoed up.
Give a dog a bone ...
His knife, sharp and glinting in the dark.
This old man came rolling home ...
Help me!! Help me!!!

5. WAITING COFFINS

Adam was deliriously ill. Maggie, the house matron — a kind and gentle old lady with white hair and large spectacles — brought soup and hot meals. Outside the wind howled and the window rattled uneasily in its wooden frame.

The other beds were empty, like waiting coffins. Adam could almost hear the bed legs trembling on the floor in anticipation. The blankets being warmed up, awaiting lively occupants — certain that they would come, just a question of time. The boys with their young, tender flesh, to wrap them up snugly, to smother them, and rot them into decay. In time their small skeletons would crumble under the weight of the blankets, and decomposing bones would fall silently onto the now-soiled underblankets. And on the cold pillows would lie the skulls alone with orbs gazing in defiance.

Adam felt his stomach retch. He heaved his body out of the blankets and vomited the morning's breakfast of bread and fried eggs into the bowl Maggie had thoughtfully placed beside the bed. When he was done, Adam fell on his pillow, perspiration on his forehead, an ugly rancid taste in his mouth.

After the mess was cleared, Adam was able to sit up and read. In fact, he felt a little better. He was able to have soup for lunch. David and Peter came to see how he was.

"You're a lucky bloke to miss double Chemistry," David said enviously.

Adam nodded, smiling weakly. He hadn't told them about the old man. They would surely laugh at him.

"There's lots of flu going around," Peter added. "If I were you, I'd go home until I was better."

"Malaysia's a bit far," Adam quipped.

"Oh yeah," said Peter, with a foolish grin. "I suppose it is, isn't it?"

"He'll be fine here, boys. We'll have him back at lessons in no time." It was Maggie, with a cup of tea and some biscuits.

David and Peter said their farewells, gathered their books, and trudged off to the afternoon lessons.

"Now, you get better dear," Maggie said. Her kind eyes twinkled behind the thick plastic glasses. "You'd better have this hot water bottle. It's a little nippy today, isn't it, dear?"

Adam was glad for the hot water bottle for it chased away the cold dampness. His temperature was still high and the doctor came carrying a bottle of vile-tasting medicine.

The boy swallowed it without complaint for his thoughts were but on one thing.

What was that evil old man doing at St. Christopher's? *What does he want?*

He felt weak, scared, not knowing what to do. A shiver broke through his body and in fear, tears streamed down the boy's cheeks.

Over the next two days, as he recovered, Adam felt the need to tell someone about the old man but every time he opened his mouth words would not form. David and Peter and even the Housemaster came to visit him but Adam did not say it was not the flu that made him ill, it was the evil old man from the plane who had followed him to St. Christopher's. The old man who was going to kill him.

Adam heard snatches of rock rising from one of the studies below, the screech of the guitar, the pounding drums, clash of cymbals. *Well, I cried for all the others till the day was nearly through and then I realized that God's a young man too!* the singer whined and screamed. A guitar riff took over. Adam had never felt so alone or forsaken and wanted to go home.

Adam thought of telephoning Malaysia, where it was sunny and warm and no old men followed him around. Mother would be cooking curry like she normally did every Friday and Father would get home around half past 6 in the chauffeur-driven green Mercedes-Benz. Father would shower, then watch the news. During the commercial breaks, he would check on Adam, to see if he was doing his homework. Once he was caught reading comics and was given a real scolding.

"You better do well in school," he said, pointing his shaking finger at Adam. "I want top marks from you. Only top marks will do!"

Adam sat in the corner with the *Beano* slipping from his fingers. He said nothing but stared shamefully at the study table piled with discarded homework.

His father towered over Adam like an angry giant, his voice though hardly rose. "You're going to go to a top university to learn business. Then you can help me in my company. Get back to your homework now."

His father walked away, closing the door behind him. Adam turned to his homework and in that moment decided that he hated it. All Father could think of was his business. He never saw Father except when homework was being checked. That was all he was to Father. Homework.

Adam decided not to call home. He played the conversation in his head. He imagined telling Father all that had happened. *Be brave, son,* his father would say, *and don't let this distract you from your studies, you must be strong and brave.* Strength and Bravery were good for business. Father was an avid reader of Sun Tzu's *Art of War*. If business and war were the same thing, then Adam did not want any of it. *Be strong and brave? How could I when that terrible old man was waiting outside?* But Adam had to. He could not hide in bed forever.

Adam knew, in a wave of determination, that he had to face him. If he came across the old man he would gather every ounce of bravery and, although he would be quaking inside, he would fiercely ask at the top of his voice why he was being followed. He would say the headmaster knew and the police were out to arrest him. Yes, Adam was certain the old man would be afraid of the police.

The boy closed his eyes and wondered if he could be so brave.

Will I be able to do it when the time comes? Will I run or will I confront this evil old man?

He did not know at this point in time. But the thought of such a confrontation made his blood run cold.

6. CONFRONTATION

Feeling stronger and better, Adam was at lessons again. Tuesday morning saw an appointment with the doctor, a check-up to see how he was getting on, so he skipped the first lesson at College.

"Well, young man, you do seem to be much better," the doctor said brightly. "Don't know what you caught. Must have been the new climate. Well, you'd better get on to your lessons. Can't have you missing all of them on my account." The doctor smiled and packed up his bag. Adam followed him out; the doctor was telling him how he had been to Singapore twenty years ago, but not Kuala Lumpur, but they were planning a trip out to Thailand in a couple of years. He got into a brown Volvo and Adam waved as he drove off.

Adam gathered his books and walked up an overcast and gloomy College Road. The College was mercifully quiet, for the boys had been herded into their respective classes. It was strangely peaceful. The end of the rugby fields with flags at each corner could hardly be seen for the morning mist softly blanketed the grounds. The icy wind swept across Adam's face and he hurried his pace.

Adam froze on the first cobbled step leading up to the Chapel. In the distance by the sandstone wall, a thin figure of a man sat on the iron bench beside the surrounding snowdrops, a white scattering on the grass. The mist shrouded the figure so that Adam only saw a small, dark shadow beside the oak tree. He could not discern the face for the distance and the mist. But he knew it. Knew who it was. Recognized the figure immediately. The old man. Bent over and leaning forward against his hooked cane.

Fear rose up in the boy like an uncoiling snake and the boy's books fell. They scattered on the pavement, the wind wildly ruffling through the open pages, as if rapidly reading its contents and discarding them as useless. He almost turned and ran. To run for the station, a train to London, a flight to Malaysia — to be safe again, where there were no horrible old men following with soul-wrenching, ravenous eyes. But Adam did not run.

Somehow he knew that if he ran now he would be a coward forever. He was sure that if he bolted, the old man would always be right behind him, hovering just behind his left shoulder, waiting to tap him with gnarled fingers when Adam least expected it; and he would turn to face its awful deadly grin and scream. He had to bring himself to face the old man *now*, criminal or mad man.

The boy also knew that if he ran away, he would be running for the rest of his life, from all the awful, tearful things; from people like Lawrence and Fowler, from injustices, unfairness and all the hurt this cruel world could muster. This, of course, he did not articulate there and then, for it was just a feeling, but a feeling so strong it gave rise to a determination to face the old man.

Adam took a deep breath and with legs that felt like lead, took his first step forward. Moving one leg before the other, he slowly started to climb up the steps. His heartbeat pounded like marching drums in his ears. His breathing, fast and heavy. Each pace, like a giant step, requiring a huge effort. With each pace forward, he felt the overwhelming urge to turn around and run as fast as he could. But he fought the feeling and carried on climbing. Somehow he *had* to face him.

He was close to halfway up the cobbled steps. From this distance he could now see the large, deep eyes, unkempt beard and gleaming hair he had first seen on the plane. Adam's breathing became more regular, the pounding in his ears was but a dull ache. He climbed faster now. Determination rising. The old man continued to sit staring out at the playing fields. A raucous cough shook the old body.

Adam built the strength and will to confront the old man with every step he took on the cobblestone. He would shout, demand to know who he was and why he was being followed. He had climbed more than half the steps and the old man seemed less frightening, more frail and old. He sat there without noticing the boy approaching.

It occurred to Adam, as he hurried his climb — keen now to confront the figure — that the old man may not be mad or evil at all. *Just an ordinary old man*. Maybe a senile old man following a boy he saw on a plane. Adam felt his face flush as anger rose. Anger at himself for being afraid and outrage at the old man for following him, for scaring the hell out of him. Adam started to run, his footsteps pounding on the cobblestones.

As Adam reached the top he saw the face clearly, not more than twenty feet in front of him. Wrinkles etched deeply in his face, eyes with a faraway, tired look; not burning and intense as Adam remembered. The old man did not see him. The sun had come out from the gray, blanketing clouds and the snowdrops were dancing brightly in the wind like a hundred white fairies upon the grass. The branches of the oak tree threw long, thin shadows across the lawn.

The old man pushed against his shiny, hooked cane and eased himself from the bench, his gray coat flapping in the wind. *This was not an old lion but a lame deer*, thought Adam, now not more than a few feet away.

As the old man rose, his body jerked, he stumbled two steps forward, his cane fell silently on the grass. Agony raked his entire face, the muscles twitching in a tremor of pain. His body swayed, the hands grabbing desperately at the air, the gnarled fingers curling, uncurling as if trying to grab for support.

Adam's anger vanished then and, without hesitation, he rushed over to help the old man, trampling on the delicate snowdrops and as he reached him, the old man fell towards him. Adam stretched out his hands, arms open wide to catch the body, hoping to support the weight.

As the old man fell into Adam's arms and as Adam caught him, the body paled, shimmered and, incredibly, started to evaporate. Adam's arms were outstretched, his body ready to catch the weight, but he felt nothing, absolutely nothing — but air, and caught in his arms was nothing but a pale outline of a body. The outline softened, rippled and disappeared.

Adam stood there alone, dazed, unbelieving. Doors slammed and loud voices filled the air. The first morning lesson had just ended and crowds of boys were streaming out into the sunshine.

7. ST. CHRISTOPHER'S REVISITED

I am here again at St. Christopher's. Not once been back here since I left school. That was a strange day in itself. We had drinks; they even allowed us champagne on the lawn outside Hazelwell. Of the six boys from the Zoo, only four remained. Now what was the reason for that? If my fading memory serves me correctly, one went to another school and another left for some other reason, financial trouble in the family was the rumor. It was a sunny summer's day, I remember, and we took photos. I still have them at my daughter's house.

On that day, I walked around the House, the College, DH, Chapel, the classrooms — knowing this would be the last time I would see these places again. Trying to imprint them on my memory, to visualize these places again, places that were so much a part of me. Was here for five years, almost an eternity to a boy my age.

The place where a boy became a man. I'm quite sure of it, for when I left at eighteen, I was a man. Maybe a naive, shy, young man with so much more to learn. But nevertheless, still a man.

And oh, I was in the College Rugby team with my friend, what was his name now, can't quite remember, ah yes, David. My friend David. We had a good team, didn't we? Even won a few games. Played much rugby in the fields over there. The pushing, the shoving and ah, the running. The wind in my face, the force in my legs, the ball in my hands. Those were good times.

Then there was that prefect Lawrence, yes, that was him. A racist. Got expelled for cheating in a History of Art exam. Made no difference to me. Later, I too became a prefect. I wasn't a racist. But an idealist. That may have been my life's undoing. My father, who died a long time ago now, wanted me to do Law and an MBA. I chose Philosophy.

After university I worked in London for a magazine. Life was exciting then. Restaurants, pubs, plays, bookshops, art galleries. So much to look forward to. That came to an end when I returned to Kuala Lumpur. My father got so mad when I refused to join his business. We didn't speak for a year. Old men can be so stubborn, can't they? I should know. Anyway, my work gave me a regular column in a local paper. "Adam's Apple" they called it. Never liked it myself. That went on for a few years until I got bored. Or did they get bored with me? Who knows, probably the latter. I became a full-time writer. That was way back.

So many years have gone by. How can I tell you all the other important things in my life? I could list the factual details but that would miss out the greatest things. Like the night, when researching a travel article, I walked beside Tasik Chini and watched the sunrise shimmering over the red and white lotus flowers. Insect voices everywhere and the breeze refreshingly cool. The first glimmer of light reflected off the waters and I watched the colors change. The jungle turned gray then green and the sky a crimson red. I stood there for a long time almost in tears, for life, if you gave it a chance, could be so beautiful. That too was a long time ago.

I've had a few books published on various subjects, not quite sure how many. Even a novel. Nothing you would have heard of though. They didn't do all that well. I've had to live a simpler life. The creation of wealth was never my strongest point. But I've had a good life, a happy one, most of the time. It's funny how in your old age everything can become so clear. Sometimes I feel that my life has passed with the blinking of an eye. What I thought would last forever in my days at St. Christopher's just went by like sand through these fingers. Some of my memories blur while others are so clear like yesterday.

Looking back I see those times — those important events that steered my life and gave it direction. Like when I got married and then divorced four years later. Ah, it was a turbulent relationship, it was inevitable. Pretty important, pretty eventful times, I'd say. Blissful and dreadful yet both a marker on life's undulating journey.

I am now pretty close to my journey's end, I'm sure of that, and I've had but one wish and that is to return to St. Christopher's. The place where a boy became a man.

I've been here but a few days. My daughter begged me not to visit England in the winter time.

"It'll be too cold for you, Ayah," she said.

"I have to go, it's the last chance I'll get to see the old place," I replied. I was pretty determined to go.

"You're not a young man anymore, you're eighty-two — it's a long journey and who will take care of you?" My daughter has three children, my teenaged grandchildren, and she tries to mother me too. She's grown up to be a wonderful person, wife and mother.

"I'll be just fine, I'll only be gone for just two weeks." I pulled her to me and kissed her on the forehead. She had tears in her eyes. She can be a little silly, sometimes.

And my son? There was my son and I lost him at seventeen. Died in a car accident on the Federal Highway. A three-car pile-up. He'd been out with friends. What could one do but be there at the hospital, identifying the body, sobbing in the bathroom with a broken mirror and bleeding hands and all I could say was: *why him! why not me!* The pain, the sorrow, the anger — they all dulled with time, with the passing years. My son, there was nothing I could do but carry on without you, and not a day has passed without me whispering your name, thinking of the times we never shared. Life can be so damn cruel. Must not cry now, my tears will freeze in this cold.

So here I am at St. Christopher's to see the old places. Managed to visit Hazelwell. Completely different, could not recognize any of it except the garden that's still overgrown. The College though is mostly the same. There are a few new buildings but nothing more. The Chapel and even the DH looks as it did sixty over years ago. History has been preserved here. Maybe I am not so old.

Even the tiny, fragile snowdrops are here like snow on the ground. And I can't quite believe it. This surely must be the iron bench from my past. It has to be. It looks exactly the same. Must have had a few coats of paint. Sad though about the oak tree. It has gone. It used to be on that very spot right there. Perhaps it was rotting and threatening to fall on the Chapel. Some days I feel like I'm rotting too. But not this morning.

It's been a misty one. From this bench I can hardly see the other side of the playing fields. I'm glad I brought my walking-stick. I've done too much walking and my back hurts. It's getting chilly now. Time to get back to the hotel. Oh my, the sun has come out all of a sudden. The snowdrops look lovely, dancing brightly in the breeze. Reminds me of that time at Tasik Chini with the lotus flowers. Life can be beautiful too, if you only give it a chance.

I push against my walking-stick to slowly raise myself. Being bent and old makes it so difficult. As I stand up, a crushing sharp pain bolts in my chest. It is as if my heart is being torn out of my body. I gasp for air. Colors are bursting in my mind. I stumble forward and my walking-stick drops from my grasp. I feel myself falling, I'm clawing the air madly. Everything turns black as I hit the grass. My heart has stopped beating.

8. DARKNESS UNVEILED

It is as if a veil of darkness is being drawn from my face. The light hurts my eyes. And I am hobbling down the aisle, slowly, but easily; never easier. My trusty hooked walking-stick is with me. It is a narrow passageway. The loud humming permeates everything. People, children, young and old are sitting on my left and right; seatbelts are fastened. They don't seem to see me. They can't hear my rasping cough. It is so familiar.

I see a boy. He is staring at me. *He sees me!* His eyes are large. Something about him. *No, it can't be. It just can't be. Could it be? Could it possibly be?* He has a familiar brown face. The dark hair, the nose. A face I know.

He looks away. Maybe not. *Maybe not.* The man beside him has his face turned away, a magazine in his hands. Yet also so familiar. The boy is so young, so fragile. Innocence in his face. Surely it could not be.

He looks up at me again. Right into my eyes. *It just can't be!* I know those very eyes. In Heaven's name! *It's me! It's really me! Thirteen years old and going to England for the first time!*

I try to say something but nothing comes out. I have to sit down, or I will surely faint. I find a seat three rows in front of the boy. Closing my eyes, afraid to open them, not believing what is happening. The plane, like a winged and fiery monster, roars into the night sky.

And I know it ... know it with a compounding certainty, that I will be there. Following him.

X

GRAVEDIGGER'S KISS

had not seen Lucas for a few days. It was his habit, /as mine, to stop at the Jolly Axeman religiously every evening for a pint. Even while nursing a bad cold, the old gravedigger would be at the corner by the window, his sandpapery voice quietly rasping in the pub's smoky haze. We did no more than exchange pleasantries on these occasions, for we gravitated towards different groups. Naturally, he mixed with fellow tradesmen while I huddled with shopkeepers and professionals.

Even so, it was obvious that Lucas was missing. His rasping voice, which I was told he acquired when a boot, studs and all, crunched into his neck during a rugby match, was gone. Word was that the man had locked himself up in his ramshackle cottage that ever threatens to collapse into the graveyard. Perhaps he wanted time alone.

I was surprised to stumble upon Lucas that Saturday. I had read the morning's papers with its usual depressing fill of car bombs, rioting youths, drugs and starvation in Africa. Even though a fog had fallen on the village, cloaking it in an eerie veil, I went out for a walk, my padded leather jacket keeping me warm. There is nothing like a park filled with luscious foliage to invigorate one's senses, to bring one's thoughts back to earth.

I beheld tall oaks shrouded in mist, their limbs stripped bare and shivering in the breeze. The lawns were covered in the browns and reds of autumn. But before I could go further, I found Lucas slouched upon a stone bench.

The old gravedigger had a stiff hat pulled tightly over his head. His dirty gray stubble threatened to swamp his haggard pinched face. His small shoulders were slumped within a tattered green coat covered in stains. It seemed too big for him. His boots were muddy, which was no surprise for a man of his profession.

"Hello there, Lucas," I said as jovially as I could.

His eyes darted in my direction while his body remained stooped in its sorry state as if he were frozen by the chill. He grunted and his eyes slid back to the cold hard ground. "I haven't seen you in a while. You been busy, Lucas?"

I stood in front of him, waiting for an answer. His ragged breath hung in the cold air. His eyes were glazed.

"What have you been doing with yourself?" I said. "You been ill?"

Lucas slowly took his gloved hands off his knees and clasped them tightly, his body shuddering forward as he did so. He coughed once. Twice. Still he said nothing. I was concerned by his behavior. This was very unlike the man.

I ran a small art supply shop in the village, selling mainly canvases, paints and brushes. I sometimes organize art courses, usually with a visiting artist from one of the other villages or a town nearby, the nearest being a good forty minutes away. Occasionally, we would set up our easels in the grounds of the church, for the old sandstone building on a sunny day was particularly striking.

Lucas would inevitably be there, raking up leaves, pruning roses, fixing the gate and all the other half-dozen things that needed his attention. He was both the gardener and the church handyman, but we all called him the gravedigger. That was the most important, though infrequent, part of his duties. Not being a particularly good artist myself, I would chat with Lucas on these occasions. Small talk of no consequence, really, although he did ask many questions about brush sizes and cartridge paper. He was an animated man with much to say.

"Lucas, aren't you going to answer me?" I asked.

The gravedigger cleared his throat and slowly looked up. How haggard he was! The man looked like he had not slept for days. His eyes were bloodshot and the creases on his face were more pronounced than ever. It seemed as though his face was cracking.

"I will answer you, Mr Wood," he said in a quiet voice, his rasp unmistakable. "But it's better you leave me alone."

"Why Lucas, what's wrong?"

"What's wrong?" he snorted. He pulled off his hat revealing a bald liver-spotted head surrounded by a messy tufts of gray hair. "You don't want to know. It'll only bring trouble, bad trouble."

"Oh, come off it, Lucas. Tell me what's this all about."

The gravedigger got up and pulled the hat back over his head. Mumbling, he brushed past me and hurried up the footpath, up the stone steps and into the gloomy street.

Perturbed by Lucas's strange behavior, I thought I should let him be. The man obviously had problems he didn't care to share. It was none of my business. So I ambled down the footpath into the park. The leaves rustled. I could smell the damp earth, the fallen leaves. In the distance I could see the lake and the forest beyond.

I stopped. I realized I had regressed into that big-city mentality. Anonymity. Non-involvement. Keep your distance. Those were its hallmarks. I moved here nine years ago to escape its rush, its numbing indifference, its unquestioning embrace of modern technology before all else. There drugs, crime and violence hid beneath advertising billboards and glittering shopping malls. And here I was harboring that same attitude as if I had never left that wretched place.

I leapt up the pathway, rushing up the short flight of steps to see Lucas's hunched figure a good fifty meters ahead, already veiled by fog. I darted past the old stone cottages, their small front gardens, the low wooden fences and mailboxes. Some had their lights on. I smelt chimney smoke and the stale dampness brought by the fog.

Lucas had slunk past the shops and taken a right turn at the post office. He was in a hurry, going at a quick pace for an old man. Some thought he was already into his seventies. He had been in the village for as long as anyone could remember.

I followed him. At the butcher's, I was surprised to see graffiti splattered on the wall. Big, bold and blue. The tag, its vicious curls and strokes were indecipherable.

That big city plague had arrived. Our village was changing. Children, the older ones, had taken to garbing in black, and swearing was the norm. There were rumors of drugs. This I found hard to believe.

At the post office I saw Lucas's hunched figure climbing the sloping lane, his long coat flapping in the wind. He had to be going home, back to his shack that bordered the graveyard. I decided to drop by later. I didn't want him to think I was following him.

It was almost 2 and, not having had lunch, I crossed over to Ma Deidre's tea rooms. I was welcomed by a warm fire, pretty curtains and cheerful paintings. Doris, the owner, had round glasses and gray hair. She was at the counter, in a white apron, chatting to Mabel. Mabel was a jolly woman in her forties, perhaps a couple of years younger than me, who always tied her hair in a bun. She ran the florist's next door.

"I really can't understand what they get up to," said Mabel, shaking her heads. "They hardly say a word during dinner. I don't know where they've been. Josie's become so rude. And the way she dresses ..."

"Maybe you should bring your girls back here," quipped Doris. "Get them to work for me again. My customers liked them."

"Until Belle spilled tea over poor Mr Bentley," said Mabel, eyebrows arching. "He was not amused."

The two women sniggered.

"And what can I get you today, Mr Wood?" asked Doris.

"How about some soup? It's freezing cold out there."

"Oh, we've got mushroom soup today," said Doris. "It's very creamy."

"How's everything going in your lovely shop?" I asked Mabel as Doris wandered into the kitchen.

"Oh, very well ..."

So it was after 3 when I left Ma Deidre's and started up the lane towards the church. As I passed the magnificent trees beside the road, their gnarled tree trunks, their bare limbs still shrouded in fog, I thought of my wife. I still lived in the flat above the shop with sticks of furniture she had left behind. I had bills to pay and business was slow.

I entered the church grounds and scurried past the squat building, its stonemasonry dark against the gray sky. I had painted it several times. How gloomy in was in this fog! The gravel path dragged me around the back to the cemetery, the gravestones in several shapes and sizes stood in rows, a few with dead flowers in vases.

This was not a place for the living. I suddenly knew I didn't belong here. But I couldn't let it bother me though. Lucas lived here and it didn't seem to worry him.

I followed the path and came to a grave, the tilted cross surrounded by dead weeds. It was the oldest one. I could hardly read the weathered inscriptions. *Mary Elizabeth Stephenson. Born 4th August 1821. Died 17th January 1839. Aged 18.* Beside it were newer resting places. The cemetery was filling up, the graves advancing full circle.

A little girl, Sara Batts, had been buried less than a week ago. The mist sat heavily upon her fresh mound of earth and the sad bouquets left behind. A wind swept up behind me and a chill slipped down my neck. I hurried away.

I was glad to reach Lucas's shack. Green paint peeled off its timber planks. Its roof was rusted. There was a crack in a window. A broken pot lay slumped against a wall. I knocked on the flimsy door.

The gravedigger was surprised to see me. He gruffly let me in. Despite the fire in the wood heater, it was cold in that small room. A wooden table and chair stood next to the tiny kitchen. His living area consisted of an armchair, a small coffee table with large stains on it and two stools. A door led to the bedroom. His home was damp and smelled of sour milk.

I sat on a stool which seemed solid enough, but Lucas remained standing, stooped in his tracksuit bottoms and thick sweater.

"I'm sorry for rushing off, Mr Wood," he muttered. "I just couldn't ... talk about it."

"About what?" I said. "What is it you can't talk about?"

"It's about—" he glanced out the window, "what I've seen in that graveyard. Ever since, ever since I buried that little girl."

"Sara Batts?" I asked. "The girl who drowned in the river?"

"Yes, her," he whispered. "I don't even dare say her name. She's ... she's ..."

He stared at me, despair in his eyes. His creased face looked terribly old.

"What about her?" I asked. "You buried her on Sunday, didn't you?"

"Yes," he groaned. "But I still see the girl out there!"

He pointed with one trembling finger at the window, at the pale headstones.

"Yes, I've seen her," he whispered, "stalking among those graves in the dark as if searching for something. No, don't look at me like that. Don't look at me as though I'm bloody mad. That I am not!"

"I don't think you're mad, Lucas. It's just ..."

"Oh, Mr Wood, I do think I've gone crazy half the time. Since I first saw her in that white dress. I can't think of nothing else. It's like she's locked herself right here in me brain and she won't leave!"

"How do you know it's her, the girl you buried?"

Lucas laughed in a croaking voice.

"Not difficult that one, Mr Wood. She hangs around that freshly turned grave over there beside that old grave with the leaning cross. Usually she comes just as it's getting dark."

"Every night?"

"For the past three nights," he whispered. "About the same time."

"Well, let's wait for her," I said. "It gets dark about 4. Only forty minutes or so to go."

"Are you sure you want to stay, Mr Wood? It's a terrible, accursed thing to see."

"Why don't you put on a pot of tea, Lucas. I've never seen a ghost. So it could be a first time for me."

"As you wish. And I thank you gladly, for being here, sir. Yes, I will put the water to boil. Yes, yes, tea. Of course."

He busied himself in his tiny kitchen, then placed two mugs on the stained coffee table.

I tried making conversation with Lucas, but the poor man grew more anxious as the minutes crept by, his eyes darting like those of an injured animal at the window, at the darkening vista of headstones.

Shadows filled the spaces, growing like an evil miasma over the graves, creeping through the undergrowth, grasping the dried-up bouquets left for the dead. Inside, darkness drifted over the moth-eaten carpet, claimed ownership of the kitchen, the dinner table, the lounge area, crawled upon Lucas's gaunt and agitated face.

"Shall we turn on a light?" I asked.

"Better not, Mr Wood. We can see better then. See ... outside."

"All right then, Lucas. Let's just wait."

Lucas really believed something would appear. I wouldn't say that I didn't believe in ghosts nor had I any evidence that spirits did exist. I would keep an open mind. I was afraid though that poor Lucas's own mind was coming unhinged. Spending his time alone in the graveyard, tending the garden, fixing fences, could not be healthy.

Just as I managed to get Lucas into some sort of conversation about his childhood in Eastern Europe, he abruptly stiffened. Even in the enshrouding gloom I knew his face had gone deadly pale.

His body trembled as it got off the armchair and he pointed.

"There," he whispered. "There you can see it."

I moved to the window and peered outside. At first I saw nothing in the foggy darkness.

Then, as I stared, a shadow emerged. It stood unmoving beside a headstone, as though watching me.

I swallowed. Unbelieving.

It was a small figure. Perhaps a child. Sara Batts.

She had ponytails, a flowing dress. Her arms drifted up, sweeping the darkness in front of her.

"Jesus," I whispered.

Lucas moaned.

The dark figure drifted past the headstones towards the shack, one hand touching the inscriptions as she came. Her dress caught by the breeze. A sleeve billowed.

And then, dear God, I heard a voice. It was hard to make out at first. Then I realized it was a sort of song.

Gravedigger's kiss
Gravedigger's kiss
Come hold me, come stroke me
The sound of thudding earth I miss

I turned to Lucas but he had retreated behind the armchair, seeking protection from the approaching horror. The voice grew louder. Closer she came.

Gravedigger's kiss
Gravedigger's kiss
Oh touch me, oh feel me
Open my coffin, enjoy our bliss

Then I leapt, bursting out the door. I ran towards the figure. She tried to escape but I caught hold off her arm.

"No!" she screamed.

"What the hell are you trying to do?" I shouted.

"Just a joke. Oh, it's just a joke!"

It was Belle, Mabel's daughter.

I was right. I knew that voice. She had served me so often at Ma Deidre's. They could have pulled it off if it wasn't for the singing.

"And you. Yes, I can see you. Come out from behind that gravestone."

A taller figure emerged. It was her older sister, Josie. Josie was about sixteen and Belle a couple of years younger. But from the way Belle dressed in her white-laced frock and hair in ponytails she looked much younger. From far away, especially in the dark, we easily mistook her for the dead eight-year-old.

Josie sauntered towards me, her long hair falling wildly to her shoulders.

"You should be ashamed of yourselves! Frightening poor Lucas. How heartless of you both!"

"We're sorry, Mr Wood," mumbled Belle. "It was a joke. Please don't tell mum."

"Hey, we were just mucking around," said Josie. "We're not harming anyone."

"You better come in and apologize," I said. I tried to keep the anger out of my voice. "That's the least you can do."

I led the two girls towards the shack. Lucas had turned the lights on. I could see his stooped figure pacing up and down, muttering to himself.

Belle hesitated at the front door. The light spilled on her face. I could see she was scared. Josie smelled of cheap perfume. Her hair was dyed black and she had thick kohl around her eyes. Her fingernails were long and dark. Her black dress which was pierced by at least a dozen safety pins, revealed her surprisingly ample cleavage. She sneered at me. She was obviously not in the least sorry for scaring the poor gravedigger.

"Please," said Belle. "It was just a joke."

"Oh shut up, Belle," snarled Josie. "You're such a bloody moaner."

"Go on in," I said.

Lucas sat in his armchair.

"What's all this?" he rasped. "What's going on?"

"A couple of ruffians," I said. "They've been pulling your leg. Real hard, I'd say. A very unkind thing to do."

I glared at the two girls.

"Sit down." I pointed to the two stools.

Belle sat down. Josie remained standing, pouting her lips.

"You better sit down, Josie. You're only making it worse for yourself."

"Screw you," she said.

This was unlike the Josie I knew. Maybe she was on drugs.

"You're caught trespassing," I said. "You better sit. I can call the police, you know?"

Josie tossed her hair to one side and made a big show of sitting down. She gave Lucas a suggestive grin and crossed her legs to reveal her smooth pale thighs.

"Well, what do you both have to say for yourselves?"

I was disgusted by their behavior. Scaring an old man so badly. I was sure Lucas was not far from a nervous breakdown. He sat quivering in his armchair, his trembling liver-spotted head was a testimony to his fright.

"We're sorry," moaned Belle.

"Bugger off!" said Josie, her arms tightly crossed. "We've got bloody nothing to say. He's just a shitty old man and you're a—"

"What?" I barked. "What am I?"

"A stupid lonely art peddler," Josie spat, "whose wife left you for someone else."

I stared at Josie, my anger rising. I clutched my hands behind my back and tried not to let any emotion show.

"Don't you want to touch me then, Mr Wood. Feel my body, my breasts, kiss my lips? You know you want me."

"No, I don't want to touch you," I said. "You're only a child. And my wife, she didn't like it here in the village. She went back to the big city. But that's got nothing to do with you."

"And us frightening this big loser here has nothing to do with you." Josie threw her hair back and stuck her tongue out at me. It was pierced by an awful-looking ring.

"Lucas happens to be a friend of mine. Are you going to apologize?"

"I'm sorry," sighed Belle, tears welling in her eyes. "It was Josie's idea. We just wanted to scare him. It was just for fun ..."

"He's a horrible old man." Josie stared at Lucas. The poor man still trembled in his armchair, lips moving but saying nothing. "We know what that gravedigger did."

She pointed a black fingernail at Lucas, her bright red lips sneering.

"What do you mean what he did? What are you talking about?" Again I thought that the older sister might have taken a drug of some kind. "Josie, tell me what this is about."

"We saw him by the river. That afternoon when the little girl drowned. We saw him in the woods."

"Oh, we just wanted to frighten him," moaned Belle. "We wanted him to leave the village."

"He's a murderer," said Josie, her eyes suddenly pleading. "He was there by the river when the little girl was drowned. We saw him there. We know he killed her."

"That's rubbish," I said. "Lucas has nothing to do with Sara Batts."

I was trying to remain level-headed in the midst of this stupidity. The girls were making it up, trying to worm their way out of their predicament.

"Lucas, please tell the girls you weren't in the forest that day."

Lucas was bent over, body quivering. All we could see was his liver-spotted head, the tufts of gray hair trembling. He clutched his knees tightly, fingers gnarled, shoulders swaying.

"Yes, yes, I was," he croaked. "I was there, Mr Wood."

"But you didn't kill her, did you? You didn't drown that little girl."

Making small trembling movements with his head, the gravedigger shook it from side to side. The man had been frightened so badly and now the sisters were making crazy accusations.

"See girls, he didn't kill her," I said. "He had nothing to do with her death. Did you, Lucas?"

Lucas got up. He grunted. He rolled one shoulder, stretching his long neck from one side to the other. He stared at the girls. I realized then, as my breath was caught in my throat, that his previous trembling, his swaying body had nothing to do with the man being afraid.

Fury hid in the shadows of his face. His eyes blazed like flames. Beneath the anger I saw an intelligence I had never perceived. He seemed to be tottering on the edge of some decision. He seemed taller. And stronger, too.

"Stop staring at me like that!" snarled Josie. "You drowned her, you ugly old man. I know you bloody well did it."

"I didn't drown her, you fool," he spat. "I spied the little girl playing so happily by the stream. She was singing to herself as she wandered along, getting her bare feet wet."

"See, he admits it!" said Josie. "He was following Sara."

Lucas ignored her. "She strolled by the water, throwing leaves into the ripples, dancing around rocks and fallen branches. How beautiful, so fair she was. So innocent in her white dress. Her blonde hair glowing bright in the shafts of sunlight. Oh, like an angel she was."

He shook his liver-spotted head. His eyes downcast as if the memory troubled him. Then he glanced at me, ever so slyly I thought, before staring again at the two girls. His tongue slid out and licked his tumescent lips.

"No, no, I didn't drown Sara Batts. Not that lovely thing. Any old fool could do that. What fool would want to fill her small lungs with water? No, her beauty, her radiance was something to be savored. Oh, I can still taste her in my mouth. No, the poor thing was already dead when she hit the water."

He glanced at me again. His eyes alive and bright.

"Oh, you don't understand .... Well, you see, my friends, I drank her."

Lucas grinned.

I couldn't believe his words. The girls said nothing but stared, eyes wide open.

For an instance, silence reigned and it seemed that its electrical charge would go on forever.

Until I cried, "You what? ... this ... this is crazy!"

And then, with great deliberation, like a coffin slowly opening, Lucas's mouth yawned before us.

The girls gasped.

"No," whispered Belle. "No, no ..."

"What are you?" moaned Josie. "Bloody fuck off!"

The gravedigger's fangs, long and gleaming white, glistened in the black cavern of his mouth.

"Girls, girls, you played a good trick," he rasped through the bowels of his throat.

"We have a legend. Every few hundred years a victim returns from the dead. Comes back to hunt, to feed upon the hunter. I am that hunter. And I thought my time was up!"

He roared with savage laughter. Its ghastly sound pierced horribly in my ears. Black spittle shot from his mouth. The two girls screamed.

Like a spider, Lucas leapt over the coffee table, his knees shooting up high, and he landed silently between the sisters. He spun, crouching as he did so, grabbed Belle by the waist and flung her over his shoulder. She crashed into the armchair.

Then, eyes blazing, he plunged his mouth into Josie's pale neck. Her wild screaming died instantly. He turned her body around in a slow circle as if they were waltzing. A romantic interlude to violins and champagne. Then he halted and his eyes were pressed up close against mine. I smelt his hunger and that metallic stench of blood.

The gravedigger's arm, gripped Josie's back to stop her from getting away. I could feel her silent horror, her helpless revulsion.

The gravedigger slurped greedily in a low gurgling noise. His mouth made small biting motions. All this while his eyes stared into mine as though conspiring, as though he were feeding for us both. I stared back transfixed by his eyeballs that seemed to grow bigger.

The years fell like rotten leaves from his face. The lines and crevices gave way to a stark smoothness. Dark hair sprouted long and abundantly from his skull.

Lucas, now a young man, was even handsome.

I stumbled back and struck the edge of the dining table, its corner struck my hip bone but I felt nothing.

Josie's arms, which until now had been feebly trying to push the vampire off, fell uselessly to her sides. Her body slumped forward and would have collapsed if it wasn't for Lucas's arm pinning her body to him.

When he had finished feasting, eyes still on me, he gently laid the girl on the floor. Blood, red and bright, trickled down his chin. A drop fell to her pale breast and stayed there unmolested like a single red rose. He wiped his mouth with a tissue from his pocket.

"That's better," he said in a clear, strong voice that bore no resemblance to the previous rasping. "Young blood, it's so sweet, Mr Wood. Almost tangy. Quite delicious. Unlike wine though, it doesn't improve with age."

He gave a small laugh.

"You, you're a ..."

"A vampire? Yes, isn't that obvious? I've been one for as long as I could remember. But I've only killed when it's been safe. How was I to know these two sisters were in the forest that day. Silly, silly girls they are."

"What ... what are you going to do with me?"

"I'm quite fond of you, my friend. We say hello in the pub, don't we? And I enjoyed our chats in the churchyard. It brought back to me memories of painting nudes in Verona. Such a long time ago now. What shall I do with you? I think I'll ..." he suddenly turned. "Ah, I see our young guest is waking up. Poor, poor beautiful thing."

Sure enough, Belle's arm pushed against the carpet. Her hand felt the armchair as if trying to work out her surrounds. She moaned. We watched her rise to her knees, one hand slowly rubbing her arm. Blood dripped from a wound on her forehead.

"Please ..." she whimpered. "Oh, please ..."

Her one eye stared through her fingers at the gravedigger. Wide and scared it was. She gnawed her pale lips. Her ponytails, like dead creatures, hung off her skull. Her frock was impossibly white.

Lucas turned to me and a grin flickered on his angular face. "We vampires have other needs too," he said.

He slid like a ravenous lizard over to the trembling girl. With one foot, he pushed Belle to the carpet. She made no sound in protest.

There followed an ugly ripping — clothes, then flesh. And throughout his intrusion, came screams that clawed my mind to madness. Blood, like graffiti, splattered the walls.

I stood, cold claws upon my heart. My eyes were snared by his brutality. How could any human being ... no! He was not human but a creature of evil.

And the foul smell of it!

I wanted to flee but my legs were frozen. Then, as if awakening from an imprisoning dream, I realized my head hurt terribly. I was still striking my head backward repeatedly against the shattered window pane. Warm liquid slid through my hair.

Something struck my cheek. I pulled it off and had to stop myself from vomiting. Wiping the gristle on my trousers, I stepped over Josie's dead body and grabbed the stool.

I raised it above my head. I could see the younger girl plainly now, her pale arm still shaking. Oh, the butchery! The blood, the open wound, the whites of bone, the slimy insides uncoiling upon the floor.

My knees buckled and I fell forward, the stool still over my head. My cheeks were wet.

"No ...," I whispered. "No, no, no ..."

The weapon slipped from my hands and crashed onto the coffee table.

"Ah, Mr Wood," purred the vampire, glancing back at me. He left the tortured body, the disfigured face and crawled to me on all fours, his body naked, smeared in blood.

He stroked me on the cheek.

"It is done. Finished now. No need to cry. It'll be fine. All so very fine."

Then, his cold, cold lips ...

Fell on mine.

MALAY MAGICK

London. A summer's afternoon. Crispin Birkenhead on his way to lunch, turns down an alley never noticed those six years of stamping books in the library. He brings ham sandwiches everyday but on Thursdays he hankers for a hot meal.

Following the cobblestones, his gray hair retreats like mist into smoke as his thin body is embraced by shadows cast by the two-storey terraces. The rumble of traffic is kept beyond these narrow confines and the shafts of sunlight retreat as though unwilling to fall beyond the steep rooftops. Most of these buildings had been used as offices at some time or another. All stand vacant now, their dust-covered windows, several with broken panes, like soft skin so promising and yet not without its inherent risks. His cardigan, a size too big for his thin body, twists and turns, as he glides dreamily on. The alley narrows, the shadows turn darker and colder until, eventually, the cobblestones meet a moss-covered wall.

He sighs and turns to go back the way he came, but not before his eyes catch upon a set of peeling yellow letters on an ebony board. **Malay Magick**. He approaches the window, this one oddly clean, and sees three knee-high puppets, their thick eye-browed faces staring at him, their headdresses standing aloft against their foreheads, long dangling arms attached to splints, their torsos turned like frightened birds within the clasps of their faded sarongs.

From the chipped paintwork, from the dull sheen upon their bodies, they are obviously antiques. Crispin is not interested in antiques. His salary, which does not leave much over to feed a cat, cannot permit such frivolities. He turns to go but his eyes do not leave the three wooden figures. Did they not move then?

He is unable to take another glance for a bell chimes and a door creaks. A face emerges from the darkness — hairless, large ears with thick earlobes, black bristle on his chin and oval, deep-set eyes. No Englishman obviously.

"Come in, sir," said the man in a deep, heavily-accented voice. 'My name is Samad."

"Oh ... eh, I was just looking." Crispin steals another glance at the puppets. They do not move but, instead, stare back expectantly.

"We have nice things here." Samad's eyes bulges out of its sockets. "Come in, sir. Please."

Samad's buffalo-like body follows his swiveling head into the alley, one pudgy hand holding the door open. Crispin mutters his thanks, looks back at the alley and enters the store. A musty smell engulfs him. He edges his way down the shadowy corridor, keen to get this over and done with. Behind him the door shuts, the bell jangling his nerves as Samad's heavy footsteps trail his. "Straight ahead, sir."

Crispin reaches the end of the corridor and is surprised by a huge cavernous room filled with objects, piled over one another, mostly covered by dust and time. A mountain of things. Leftovers from other people's lives.

Before Crispin can turn, Samad is already there breathing by his side. He smells of sweat. Buffalo sweat.

"My collection," Samad says with a grin, one fleshy hand sweeping out proudly at the forlorn mass.

"I see," says Crispin. "A lot of things you have indeed."

"Oh, yes ... collected over a long, long time. My mother started it and I took over. Please sir, have a look."

These things are of no interest to Crispin, but he wanders through the room anyway, making a pretense of examining some of the objects. A full-height mirror. A chest of drawers with missing handles. A valet of rosewood. Two porcelain figures of ladies with parasols sitting on a dresser. A crystal bowl. A doll's house with a broken window. A war medal. A hairbrush with strands of blonde hair still entwined. A silver locket staring from an open drawer.

"Beautiful, aren't they?" Samad's grin climbs like a lizard to his fleshy ears.

"Perhaps. But not really my cup of tea, I'm afraid."

"A pity, sir. They are beautiful, with wonderful memories attached to them."

"Well I must go. I'll see myself out ... thank you for asking me in."

Samad takes a step forward as if to block his path. "Wait."

One of Samad's eyes increases in size, a glutinous globe growing and pulsing. The grin is gone and in its place are white large teeth. "I want you to bring something for me, sir. Your most prized possession, please."

"There must be some misunderstanding, I'm afraid. I didn't realize you purchased collectibles. No, I have nothing to sell. You see, I'm really not in need of any money."

"Ah, then let me show you something!"

"Oh no, I don't think so. There's nothing here that can possibly interest me."

"Are you sure, sir?"

"Absolutely."

"Just a quick look, sir. Then you can go on your way."

"I really don't think so."

"Sir, I can guarantee that you will not regret it. Samad knows what his customers want."

Samad abruptly turns and without waiting for a response from his customer throws open what appears to be a wardrobe door, wedges his body through its aperture and is swallowed by darkness.

The brisk-rhythmic thumping of Samad's footsteps as he climbs the hidden flight of stairs compels the librarian to make a decision. His gut instincts tell him to flee into the alley, then down the street into the meager June sunshine, yet Samad's sudden indifference dissolves this sensibility. It is the allure of the mysterious object on the floor above which spurs him to pursue the buffalo-like man. A quick look, then he'll leave.

Crispin consoles himself with this notion as he slips into the wardrobe. Here the peeling walls brush their coldness against his clothes and as he climbs the creaky steps, dampness pours into his wretched bones. And wretched they are, for although Crispin is forty-five he suffers from osteoporosis—"an old woman's disease," he often chides himself—and he must take care or he will break his brittle bones again.

It is a suffocating climb in these dingy confines, which are only occasionally lit by narrow shafts of light from a lamp on the upper floor. As he winds his way up, Crispin is almost sure he is clutching part of a giant skeleton for the stair-rails feel unnaturally warm like bones recently hewn from living flesh. The steps narrow as they turn upon themselves and Crispin wonders how Samad is able to squeeze his buffalo-body through the coiling passageway. An image of a slithering python swallowing a struggling goat whole enters Crispin's head and he wonders if this could be the worse decision he has made in his uneventful life.

He reaches the upper level and is short of breath. Samad is stroking his chin and upon seeing his customer, the proprietor shuffles towards him, a grin alighting like a strangled bird on his face. They are in a long wood-paneled corridor where no paintings hang except for a yellowing map in a tarnished bronze frame. Crispin has only a brief moment to examine its tributaries, jungle-covered mountains and ports before Samad reaches him. It is time enough for him to realize that he does not recognize the country or region, yet its geographic scale demands that he should.

"Is this somewhere in Borneo?" Crispin asks uncertainly.

"No, sir," Samad whispers. "Somewhere else. No, not thousands of miles away but closer, so much closer than you think." He quickly turns, his chunky shoulder almost knocking the map off the wall. "Come, come follow me, sir," he says in a booming voice. "I have what you want. You won't regret it."

Samad thuds down the corridor and Crispin follows. He doesn't care for the proprietor's incomprehensible ramblings. The map has to be fictional. Why doesn't Samad admit it? Or is he just a Philistine selling whatever he can at as high a price as possible?

This corridor is better lit than the one downstairs. The red carpet is badly torn in several places and the tall windows are covered in thick layers of dust so that it emits no view but just a ghostly illumination.

He stops at an open doorway. A room piled with furniture covered in haunting white sheets. Propped on the floor is a portrait of a man in a black Victorian suit whose pockmarked face is all nose and chin. The troll-like man is sneering and Crispin is again sure that this must be a fictional character for no human could possibly look so repulsive. He promptly leaves to keep pace with Samad who is now moving quickly.

The passageway turns right, then a sudden left. The sweaty odor is still present yet less pervasive and Crispin's spirit lightens when they reach a well-lit hall where a broken chandelier hangs. He will write about this odd encounter in his journal and when he retires in Blackpool as he has always planned to do, he will read it beside his fireplace and, drunk with port, laugh at the memory.

Later he will take a long walk on a wintry beach, empty of soulless holidaymakers. Another ten years or so at the library. Not all that long to go.

"In here," whispers Samad, beckoning excitedly with one hand. He removes a large key and unlocks a heavy door. It creaks open to a dimly lit room.

"So what's in here?" says Crispin, now a little unsure of himself.

"Exactly what you need, sir. Believe me."

With that he gives Crispin a shove.

The librarian falls headlong into the room. He tumbles to the floor. His wrist breaks. His leg snaps in two places. Crispin hollers.

"Sorry about that, sir," continues Samad. "Now enjoy!"

Samad laughs and yanks the door close. The key turns. The lock clicks.

"Let me out!" Crispin yells. Hot pain-filled tears roll down his cheeks.

No answer. Only heavy footsteps moving away.

"Please, please, please let me out!"

Crispin knows he's a prisoner. But has to get out. Yet he can't even stand. His wrist, his leg is on fire ... his head spins ... a chasm opens to swallow him.

But he has to escape!

He looks around the room searching for another door. But heavy curtains, red and velvety, smother the windows, so all he sees are undulating shadows. He wipes the tears from his eyes and the shadows grow still.

Then he hears a rustling and realizes that someone else is in here with him.

From the shadows of a massive four-poster bed, draped with Indian cotton or perhaps Thai silk, a head lifts from the tumult of pillows to peer across the room. Sheets rustle like dead leaves as its occupant slithers across it and drops like an alligator to the floor.

Crouching, the figure flicks its head from side to side as though sniffing the air. When it scratches itself there is the grisly sound of sharp nails on leather. For a long moment, it just stares at the librarian, breathing heavily and occasionally snorting.

An animal, thinks Crispin, not daring to move. But before the thought even slinks out his head, he knows it can't be true, for he has never seen or heard of a form that moves in such a strangely fascinating manner or possesses a body as sleek as a dolphin's. Yet nor is the thing human, for no mortal can possibly smell so pungent or have such a protracted tongue that even in the half-light it can be seen quivering below its chin or flickering between its eyes.

It is the idea of a being, locked in here with him, that is neither human nor animal that causes the blood to drain from his face. Despite the shooting pain, he turns and, using his good arm, he tries to flee. He crawls towards the window trying not to breathe but ends up sucking great wafts of ammonia-like stink as a blinding terror takes over and his mouth begins an uncontrolled babbling. This thing that is neither human nor animal follows at a distance, creeping low on its haunches, stopping and then quickly shuffling forward, in bursts of what must be wanton curiosity.

As Crispin reaches the curtain, the thing steps into a crack of daylight and the librarian, glancing back to see if he will now be killed, sees the figure clearly for the first time.

There is not a hair on its skin. Instead scales, the shape and size of human ears — scales of iridescent and changing colors — cover its body. The inhuman is a shapely woman for it has two small cone-shaped breasts with black aureoles like midnight suns. But the creature is also a fully fledged man for between its sinewy legs, above the dangling scrotum, an erect and scale-wrapped penis gently sways.

Upon the oval head, eyes, composed of no more than slithers of gold, stare back intelligently. It lifts its snout-like nose and sniffs at him. Then, as if satisfied with its prey, the mouth, large and lipless, yet strangely cruel, curves into a delicate grin.

Then the inhuman hermaphrodite, for that is what it is and no idea or logic can banish it away, lifts itself into a sinewy crouch and leaps.

The librarian only begins to savor its caresses when the inhuman rapes him a second time. Thrills of quivering pleasure surge up his spine and he turns and pushes his tongue into the inhuman's lipless mouth. From then on it is a marathon of love-making in the soft comforts of the four-poster bed with the sheets billowing like sails around their hot bodies.

An hour or two later, the door creaks open.

"Your time is up, sir," says Samad, his bulky body filling the doorway. "If you stay any longer I'm afraid I'll have to charge you for another session with Warna."

"Warna?"

"Its name is Warna. It means color. I'm sure you'll agree, sir, that its name is rather apt."

Crispin turns to Warna but the hermaphrodite has withdrawn to a corner of the bed, eyes closed, scaly iridescent legs pulled up over its chest.

"Time to go, sir," says Samad.

Crispin gets off the bed and pulls his clothes back on. Some of the buttons on his shirt are missing and his trousers are ripped but no matter — stars are still exploding in his head.

"And how are your bones, sir?"

"What! Goodness ... they're perfect." Crispin examines his wrist and leg. "It feels like I never fell. What's going on here?"

"Warna can have that effect on clients. A form of sexual healing, I suppose, sir. But Warna's clients — both men and women — come here not for that but for the pleasure. And I'm sure you'll agree, sir, that Warna only delivers boundless joy. You'll still feel its heavenly caresses when you go back to stamping books in the library."

Crispin suddenly stiffens and he starts to shake. He's been asleep and is now awake, fully aware of his thoughts and actions. He had an exquisite dream. No, a terrible nightmare. But it wasn't real. He had fainted when he fell and dreamt it all. And if it did transpire, he was a mere observer for he surely wasn't the sick bastard putting his cock in the thing's mouth. It wasn't him straddling its firm buttocks while he caressed its breasts from behind. It wasn't him screaming as he ejaculated all over its leathery stomach.

Not believing that it happened, he peeks at the bed hoping, praying that Warna won't be there, just twisted sheets and pillows — that it was just some delusion, some insane hallucination induced by the proprietor.

But the hermaphrodite is of course there, squatting against a bed post, quite, quite real, eyes cast down and quietly sobbing. But ... but such a creature surely cannot exist. And surely, surely he did not have sex with that monstrosity!

That alien! That gargoyle! That freak!

Crispin screams and runs out of the room. He retches and, halfway down the corridor, tries to vomit but he expels nothing but air which whiffs of ammonia. He leaps down the flight of stairs, not caring whether he falls and breaks more bones. He gets to the bottom and flees the shop. He glances back and sees the sign **Malay Magick** and the puppets, he can't believe it, they are dancing. And there is a rhythm, a sweet sensual one, playing in his head.

He doesn't return to work. Anyway, the streetlights are on. Five hours have passed, not one or two.

He catches the tube to his one-bedroom flat, slips into bed and stares at the ceiling.

Daylight. Crispin rises. Has a shower. Gets changed. Scoffs down some cereal. Takes the tube to work.

The morning is a blur. His colleagues whisper. Beneath the steel-framed windows, Crispin can't stop staring at the dust motes that dance like fireflies in the morning sunlight. At 12:30 he flees down the library steps. He has forgotten to make his sandwiches. That doesn't matter. He is walking, almost trotting down the cobblestone alley.

He rings the doorbell. Are the puppets smiling ever so mischievously now?

Samad opens the door as if expecting him.

"Another session, sir?" asks the proprietor as he leads him down the corridor.

Crispin nods, sheepishly, foolishly. Samad, the buffalo man, has beaten him, humiliated him. Crispin wants to weep. Yet every object he has seen today is seen through new eyes. Every item burns with intensity. The streets hum like bees. The low gray clouds whisper. The artificial lights are knowing eyes that watch and wink. The people, the fleshy work-a-day mortals out there are weak, decrepit creatures.

Samad tells him the price while he opens the wardrobe-like doors. Crispin hardly hears it. Something about a portion of his income and that Samad knows his salary. "I know everything and more," says Samad with an ugly laugh.

Crispin will agree to any fee and so says: "No problem. I can easily afford that."

All he can think about is getting upstairs.

"Good," says Samad. "Follow me."

Crispin climbs the stairs, he glides by the strange map and the room with the portrait, except that the troll-like man is now bare-chested and grinning. Crispin shivers. He makes a right and a left; trying hard not to think, he enters the chandeliered hall. Samad unlocks the door and lets him in.

Warna stands by the velvet curtains, legs crossed, arms folded beneath its breasts, penis flaccid against one thigh. A yearning smile plays on its lipless mouth.

Crispin is already moaning before it begins undressing him, kissing his bare body as it does so. As usual Warna does not speak. Perhaps it is incapable or perhaps it has been silenced. But there on the bed Crispin is afloat on an enchanted lake that is warm and wet and deep, so very deep ...

All too soon, Crispin leaves two hours later. He floats down the alley, and up through the street. He feels like a balloon bobbing through perfume-filled air. It is only when he slips through the library doors does he realize how exorbitant the fee really is. But what choice does he have?

Crispin wanders past rows of books. Biology. Plants. Photography. Religion. Architecture. Computers. Biographies. Art. Sports. Film. Poetry. History. Fiction. In the reference section, he is rooted before the rows and rows of law reports where he caresses the thick old spines and gold lettering and imagines Warna stroking his member so delightfully while the creature penetrates him from behind. He pulls out a *King's Bench 1932* and, taking a seat, he leafs through pages which, although dry and crinkled, are pungently delectable. Warna has written the words. These pages are filled with adulations of love just for him. He can't take the books home so he copies the rivers of text onto paper. Their secret meanings will see him through the week until he is reunited with Warna. That is all he will now do. To hell with everything else.

Within two months of being fired by the Head Librarian, Crispin's account at Barclays is empty. He has been a loyal customer for over twenty years and they refused to give him a loan. No matter. He will take his possessions to Samad. His television, clock, dining table, chairs, sofa, vacuum cleaner, stereo, bed, posters, rugs, clothes, potted plants, kitchenware, family photos, stamp collection, fridge, watches, and CDs. Even his most precious items — a small collection of first editions — have found their way into Samad's cavernous room. When he is finally evicted, there is nothing in the flat but a cracked mug and a moth-eaten quilt.

Without a penny or a single material thing to his name, Samad forbids the former librarian from returning. Crispin tries to break in one night but he swears, as he lifts a hammer to smash the shop window, that he sees the three puppets pull knives from their sarongs. So, with his plans to rescue Warna thwarted, Crispin disappears into the maze of streets, weeping for Warna's wicked imprisonment and his unsatiated lust for it, all the while muttering blindly to himself and verbally threatening all those who stare at him.

Sometimes you can still see him in different garbage-strewn alleys and soiled pavements in London. Usually he is holding a bottle of vodka and swearing or shouting or pleading for a bit of change for a cup of tea. In his mud-splattered coat, he has grown a ragged beard and wears his dirty greasy hair to his shoulders. And he smells of maggot-filled meat. For many hours he rummages through rubbish bins beside the road, especially the ones outside McDonald's — they remind him of the ham sandwiches he used to make. He pushes a Safeway shopping cart along the streets piled high with cardboard boxes and assorted treasures, his spoils from digging through other people's junk.

Perhaps he still searches for that door to the other world where inhuman hermaphrodites and troll-like people live amongst the tributaries and jungle-covered mountains. But he is mostly found seated alone in municipal libraries across the city, hour upon hour, year after year, muttering while copying assiduously from the law reports in a scrawny jabbering hand. This month he has pulled out the *Weekly Law Reports 1974* and he is already four hundred pages through it. Many tramps will look like Crispin Birkenhead but if you gaze carefully into his bloodshot eyes you will see a curious yearning. A yearning for a bit of **Malay Magick**.

THE LAUGHING BUDDHA

Writing a good story, or any old story for that matter, is not a particularly easy task and mine had been missing from these pages for a dreadfully long time. My odd ones on the latest kidnapping on Weld Quay or old ladies getting cheated of their life savings deserved to be tossed into the bin, or perhaps used as toilet paper. That latter remark I overheard an insensitive young colleague remark but blissfully chose to ignore. It just wasn't worth the trouble any more.

I've been here ever since Mr Leong took over the company from his uncle. That was in my favor — you don't fire old loyal staff. Back then he wanted to turn this into the best newspaper in Penang. Honesty, integrity, independence — the lot. That was a long time ago, maybe twenty-five years now. He's given up that ambition for survival had become a challenge in itself. Circulation numbers were abysmal and advertising scarce.

As for me, I was a deadweight. A non-functioning cost center, to put it mildly. More so with my big black desk filled with books, papers and pencils dominating the office and the younger, ambitious journalists typing crazily around me, creating stories out of mere shadows, interviewing witnesses who don't exist. Hints had been dropped, heavy ones too — with Mr Leong pacing irritably up and down in white short sleeves and purple tie with laksa stains. It was time for me to find a story. And it had better be a good one too.

That was when Datuk Khoo came to mind. He would be the one to save me. It would be a scoop. Interviewing him would keep me employed for at least another few years, who knows, perhaps even until retirement. So I approached Mr Leong who approved the job grudgingly. He'd given up on me too soon, but I would show him — with the interview done and my article published he wouldn't dare fire me.

Little did I know that I was taking myself into the realms of utter despair. In ignorance I wrote to Datuk Khoo. He was well-known for being a private person and I prayed for a reply to my letter. Naively when he agreed to the interview, I jumped with joy, causing the furious typing to cease abruptly and bewildered young faces to stare at me as if two heads sprouted from my neck. I ignored them and laughed and re-read the letter. Looking back, I should have suspected something untoward when I found out that he wanted me to live with him throughout my stay in Kuala Lumpur.

As it was a Sunday, I telephoned Datuk Khoo's residence to be doubly sure. Datin Khoo picked up the phone.

"Oh yes, Mr Albert Chew, my husband would like you to stay with us. Just give me the dates you'll be in KL."

I told her that I would be there for three nights. Interviewing the Datuk would only take a day but I did not want to rush it. I wanted to travel at a leisurely pace, one of the few pleasures of being a journalist. And life at this age could not be rushed.

I arrived at the Moorish train station in Kuala Lumpur in the late morning and walked towards the entrance, admiring the splendid architecture. A taxi waited by the curb and I entered it with my suitcase trailing behind, relieved at having arrived at my destination. We drove out onto the quiet streets, overtaking a tired-looking rickshaw with an old bearded man wearing a torn hat at the pedals. His eyes spoke of a back-breaking tiredness and I slumped into the plastic seat, feeling an overwhelming weariness, my excitement at interviewing Datuk Khoo darkening into a feeling of dread.

Sparrows sat, incessantly chirping, unknowing on the electrified power lines overhead, large trees hung like silent stern guardians over the road. The sky was a mass of towering clouds which hid the blazing humid sun from my eyes. The Majestic Hotel was not more than five minutes away and was the best hotel in the city. Getting there seemed like forever.

The year was 1967 and Tunku Abdul Rahman was Prime Minister. The nation of Malaysia had only been formed four years earlier and then Singapore had decided to go its own way. These were exciting times, and my article on Datuk Khoo would brim with the energy of a young nation. Yet this feeling of dread crept all over me as I sat on that plastic seat in the taxi, wondering what this trip would bring.

Valerie Hallbrook sat at her mahogany writing desk trying to write to her mother, but not knowing what to say. All she'd written was, *Hope you are in the very best of health and As for me things are perfectly fine*. It was a complete lie, things were ... she could not even describe the awful feeling, that terrible knowing.

In frustration she crumpled the letter into a tiny ball and whimpered softly. After managing to hold back her tears, she looked up to meet the powerful gaze of the jungle, its entangling greenery, and she listened out for the strange noises she sometimes heard — monkeys, birds or bats. It was a beautiful country with friendly, accepting people and she considered it her own. Sure, the heat took a lot of getting used to, but it was better than the dreary cold of old England. In the reflection of the louvered glass she saw her short brown hair against her cheeks, her sad hazel eyes gazing out for help, from somewhere, anywhere.

She did not know what to do, and in desperation had replied to the man's letter. She should have crumpled it, just as she did the letter to her mother. And Valerie had spoken to him on the phone too, he would be well on his way. There would be trouble now, but so be it; what happened at the market the other day only confirmed her suspicion and she had to get help from anywhere, anyhow. There was a gnawing of fear deep in her stomach and the feeling of icy hands clambering for her throat. The thought of him made her tremble and the memory of his kiss on her cheek was like the rancid lick of the devil's tongue.

From downstairs came the muffled ring of the phone. Valerie leapt to her feet, hoping that freedom and safety would find her soon.

×

With relief, I entered the hotel and slammed the door behind me. Immediately, I felt the lightening of my spirit and the thought of meeting Datuk Khoo brought back that feeling of excitement. I reveled in the echoes of my footsteps on marble and the sparkling entrance pleased my eyes. Azmi was there lounging in the hotel lobby underneath a large, slow-rotating ceiling fan. He was my age but looked younger. I caught him in the middle of his yawn.

"Sorry I'm late," I apologized jovially, "but you know I'm always late."

"You've put on even more weight, Albert my friend," he remarked, staring at my paunch. I wouldn't say that I was fat, maybe a little chubby. I thought it suited my age — I was approaching fifty. "Don't you do any exercise in Penang?" Azmi said as he laughed, knowing that I didn't exercise at all. He had kept trim for his age and he loved to rub it in.

"Oh yes," I said proudly, "I exercise my mouth eating our delightful char kway teow. Hey, let's have lunch." The restaurant was inviting and the smell of roast lamb was irresistible. Any feeling of dread had long dissipated.

The rattan chair creaked uneasily as I sat down. The unsmiling Chinese captain with a crew cut in a smart white uniform took our orders. We talked about our old working days when Azmi was in Penang. Then I told him about my interview with Datuk Khoo.

"You're lucky to get an interview with him," Azmi said enviously. "He's a very private and wealthy man. Quite ruthless too."

"What do you mean?" This was interesting. I thought I knew all about the Datuk from my hastily compiled research.

"Well, he bought a small company last year."

"Yes, I read about it," I said through the spicy mouthfuls of my nasi lemak. "It was in the *Straits Times*. I have a clipping of it in my folder."

"Well, you know what that guy did? At their quarterly meeting last month, he fired everybody. All forty of them, including clerks and office boys. Just because the company didn't perform to his expectations. A very ruthless man. And everybody in KL knows how he deals in business. He's nasty."

I had heard about the Datuk's business methods. Azmi started telling me about some other tycoons when I noticed a pretty Mat Salleh woman wearing a yellow floral dress enter the hotel lobby.

She was in her thirties, not too tall. Her short brown hair was the delicate color of Anchor Beer. A white man in office attire was waiting for her. He kissed her lightly on her cheek, concern registered on his youthful face. I read his lips. "Are you all right?" They talked briefly and left the hotel in his car. I saw it all from my chair by the window.

"Albert, are you listening to me?" Azmi must have just realized I wasn't giving him my undivided attention.

"Sorry, old friend, I was just looking at some people outside. KL is such an interesting place." He laughed and told me I hadn't changed. We ordered dessert.

After lunch Azmi drove me to Kenny Hills. I had not been there before so it was a surprise when we turned the corner and was greeted by a jungle. Trees, dense and entangling, hung over on both sides and a monkey scampered playfully in some rich man's garden. Its round eyes stared mischievously back at me as Azmi's red Morris turned the corner. The road wound around a steep valley buried in a mass of green tree tops. Huge houses were scattered among the slopes above, their acres of gardens staking a claim on the pressing wilderness.

We reached the heavy black gates of 'Khoo Villa'. Azmi got out to press the doorbell. An Indian gardener in yellow shorts without a shirt peered out from behind a thick clump of plants. He spoke to someone we could not see, and then hurried over, the sun shone on the glistening sweat of his dark body. He unlocked the gate and pulled it open with a grating sound. As the red Morris entered the driveway, I saw the house loom up ahead behind the sprawling green carpet of grass.

The house looked recently renovated with modern glass louvered windows overlooking the garden. It was a large house with an extension at the back and a spacious verandah filled with plants at the side. The backs of two air conditioners protruded on the first floor. The garden was lovely with a large manicured lawn, orchids and tall majestic trees.

An elderly Chinese maid came out. She was lanky, and her face was covered in deep lines which looked like you could hang washing on. She looked as if she had never smiled in her life and her white hair and old gray clothes looked unwashed. She gruffly introduced herself as Ah Por and told me to come in. I thanked Azmi and waved goodbye, watching his Morris escape down the steep driveway. Ah Por escorted me into the house and immediately up a large wooden, almost unending, flight of stairs. She muttered something unintelligible. The stairs creaked beneath the red carpet. By the time we reached the top, my suitcase felt heavy despite containing only a few pieces of clothing, research and stationery.

"This is your room," she said roughly in Hokkien as she pushed opened the door to my room. It looked very comfortable with a view of the front garden and the vibrant mass of trees beyond. My eyes were led towards the jungle and gray clouds swirling on the horizon.

"Where is Datuk?" I politely asked, setting down my suitcase.

"Datuk has an appointment in Rawang and Datin is out. They will join you for dinner at 7:30. If there's anything you need I will be downstairs." She abruptly turned and left as if she couldn't bear to be with me another second, the heavy lines on her face disappearing with her down the great staircase.

I spent the afternoon quietly looking over my notes. Datuk Khoo was born in Ipoh. His family owned several mines there. He studied in Ipoh and later in Bristol.

He graduated from Cambridge with a first-class degree in Economics. Several years after he returned to Ipoh, his parents died in a car crash and being the only son he inherited the family fortune. He then moved the company to KL where he bought several large tracts of land. By the time he was thirty, he had sold most of them at handsome profits.

Datuk Khoo then moved into banking and housing development. His cunning and intelligence made almost all his ventures successful. He disappeared from the business scene at the age of fifty saying that he was retiring. It was more probable that no one would do business with him anymore. So it was a forced retirement. Or maybe he just got bored of making money. His tactics were not honorable but he retired a multimillionaire.

He married an English lady, Valerie Hallbrook, who was now Datin Khoo. They met at a business conference in London and married a year later. It was a small wedding for such a big business tycoon. Many thought it strange. Datuk Khoo refused to conform. His previous wife had been Chinese. She died two years before he met Miss Hallbrook. An interesting man and a good story for me, Mr Leong and the struggling paper.

When I finally put my journals away it was almost dark. The sound of insects began to fill that ephemeral purple darkness of dusk that now sat above the blackness of the jungle. I showered, put on a clean shirt and walked down the stairs. Ah Por, to my surprise, was waiting for me at the bottom. She showed me to the dining room which was dominated by an antique table that could have seated twelve to fourteen people. Silver cutlery had been set out amidst the crystal wine glasses. I sat down feeling lost and occupied my time admiring the grand crystal chandelier, enjoying the quietness of the location, listening to the vibrant calls of a million insects.

I heard the heavy footsteps first and then Datuk Khoo came into view. He was in his sixties but his gray beard seemed to belong to someone with one foot in the grave. He was an enigma, with eyes sharp like an eagle's circling a wounded animal. There was a wildness in that look, a secret animal instinct that permeated his very soul. He wore white cotton trousers and a casual shirt which looked crisp and new, but his shoes were slightly soiled. What was he doing in Rawang? Perhaps he was buying some land. I did not have time to speculate for what followed next was most unexpected.

"Mr Chew," he said in a soft voice, I almost didn't hear. "What are you doing here?" His unwelcoming words startled me.

"Sorry, but wasn't I suppose to arrive today?" I felt my cheeks flush. I was sure I got the dates right.

"Mr Chew," he whispered, "you weren't supposed to come at all." He folded his arms, an uncomfortable expression pressed upon his features.

"But I got your letter and I spoke to your wife," I answered defensively. I didn't understand what was happening. There must have been some mistake.

"My wife is crazy, Mr Chew ... she has started answering my letters." His voice continued in a low whisper, his eyes piercing me. "I don't know why she thought I wanted to be interviewed ... you'll go back tomorrow morning."

"What about the interview?" I asked, desperately trying to salvage my job. He sat down and stared at me in disbelief.

"There will be no interview. None at all." A noise at the door brought a strange and unexpected smile to his face. "And here comes my dear letter-writing wife Valerie."

I was startled by his wife — flashes of the day rushed through my mind — the train ride, the old rickshaw man, the hotel, Azmi. She was the lady in the hotel. Now I recognized her. She smiled awkwardly, almost apologetically.

"Hello, I'm Valerie," she said. "I'm so sorry about the misunderstanding. It's been a terrible mistake. But please be our guest for tonight."

Datuk Khoo kissed his wife on the cheek, then dragged out a chair for her. She thanked him politely and they both sat down. His smile made me feel even more uncomfortable.

"No, it's quite all right," I replied feeling both annoyed and bewildered. "I'll take a taxi into town."

"Oh, please do stay with us," said Valerie persuasively, "and you've already settled into your room here, haven't you?"

"Well, yes I have but I haven't unpacked yet. So it's no trouble."

Valerie gave me a disarming smile. "It's all my fault, please stay. It's the least we can do."

Against my better judgment I decided to stay. I was intruding yet I was annoyed at this so-called mistake. Everything had been arranged properly and carefully. I had spoken to Valerie and she confirmed the interview and the stay. Why this sudden change? I decided not to pursue the matter for now.

She was after all a nice lady and I didn't want to make a scene. Her short brown hair fell around her cheeks and her hazel eyes gave the impression of gaiety, yet I had been around long enough to see beneath the surface, long enough to see the sorrow hidden behind her pleasing looks. I wondered what she was doing in the hotel and who her companion was.

"Are you all right, Mr Chew?" she asked with concern. I looked down at the whiteness of my empty plate. I didn't realize I was staring.

"Oh ... yes ... I'm fine," I replied awkwardly. My annoyance turned to gloom.

Ah Por entered the dining room, the lines strong against her face, pushing a trolley with creaky wheels and three bowls of soup. I recognized the distinct aroma of Chinese clear broth.

Dinner was unpleasant. I felt upset over this whole episode. A waste of time, and I was now bound to lose my job. Even the good food could not lift my spirits. And Datuk Khoo remained silent through most of the meal, except for the odd questions he would politely throw my way. His demeanor was of one in deep thought; occasionally he would smile at me and his wife, that curling of his lips above the gray beard unnerving me. Valerie barely spoke to him. Perhaps the misunderstanding over my presence had something to do with it. The snippets of conversation never passed a sentence or two and after a while I gave up trying to talk to him.

I felt like an intruder. Fortunately, Valerie tried to make me feel welcome by chatting with me and asking me about my work and my family. I told her that my wife had died and that I had a son who was working in Singapore. I felt like I could tell her more about the problems at work and the difficulties ahead. Losing a job close to my fifties was not a good prospect. Nobody was going to employ an aging journalist who hadn't written a good article in years.

"Work is great," I lied competently, "I work with good young people and they treat me with respect and are always coming to me for advice."

"That's nice," Valerie said with a smile. But shadows swam in her hazel eyes.

After dinner the Datuk said he was retiring early as he was tired. Valerie suggested that we adjourn to the library for coffee. I didn't feel like it, but politely agreed.

I felt the leather sofa sink like my spirits as I sat down. There was a globe the size of a medicine ball, but it looked out of place. It mirrored my feelings and I wished I was back in Penang.

Valerie brought in two cups of coffee. She sat down with a pensive look and abruptly apologized for the misunderstanding. I saw no such misunderstanding.

"But you asked me to come to KL," I said. I wanted some answers and my voice did not hide it.

"Mr Chew, I must be honest with you. I did ask you to come. There was *no* misunderstanding." She lowered her voice and glanced behind her. Her voice was trembling. "I could not tell my husband. You see, I need your help. I have no one else to turn to." She put her cup down as her hands began to shake. "I have to tell you something. It is about my husband. You may not believe me but I think my husband is trying to kill me," she said in almost a whisper.

"What?" I couldn't believe what she had said. This was no joke. Her face was deadly serious.

"My husband wants to kill me," she said it this time in a stronger voice.

"How do you know?" I asked, bewildered.

"Because he thinks I'm seeing somebody else. He's always had someone follow me. I didn't find out until recently but it was too late. John is just a friend, someone I can talk to. I can't talk to my husband. He treats me like his private property."

"But how do you know he wants to kill you?" I asked. I hoped she was being irrational. I did not want to be involved.

"I knew it was him. Two Saturdays ago, I went to the market as usual. I brought Ah Por with me. We got out of the car at the market."

Valerie and Ah Por got out from the car. The smell of raw meat and fish greeted them. A Chinese man in a white singlet was weighing longans for an old lady. He yelled out "eighty sen" and stuck out his palm at her face. One crumpled ringgit exchanged hands. Valerie avoided the murky puddles and made her way into the noisy market.

The squawk of a chicken being slaughtered made her jump, followed by the loud thumps of its headless body against a rusted barrel. The chicken-vendor woman brought it out legs first. Blood dripped from its neck like a leaky tap. Valerie looked away. She hated the market. The noise and the haggling were so removed from the niceties of Kenny Hills.

They had stopped at a few stalls and Ah Por carried the shopping in pink plastic bags. She walked a few steps behind Valerie. The last stop was the vegetable man. Valerie liked him. He was polite and his vegetables were always fresh. "One ringgit twenty, please." He wrapped the vegetables in newspaper and put them into plastic bags which Ah Por duteously added onto her shopping weight.

As Valerie was putting away her purse, she saw a man wearing a rubber mask of the Laughing Buddha. The Laughing Buddha had a round large head, a huge mouth, large cheeks with blushes of pink and thin lips. The eyes were round and large with two holes for eyeballs from which the wearer could look out.

She thought it was a sales gimmick at first. Children were running around him yelling out joyfully. But he ignored them. The Laughing Buddha stared at her and Valerie saw into the darkness of the eyeballs and froze. She saw nothing but she could feel his hate emanating from within. He just stared and stared at her through the crowd of shoppers, ignoring the noisy children around him.

Her heart felt like it was being squeezed and before she knew what she was doing, she was heading briskly for the car. Velu had better not be late. She didn't like this Laughing Buddha one bit.

The Laughing Buddha was walking behind the stalls parallel to her. His rubber mask bobbed up and down as he walked. Valerie quickened her pace, brushing past shopping bags, baskets, shoulders and elbows. She heard Ah Por say something behind her but she didn't stop.

The Mercedes-Benz was waiting just beyond the longan seller. Just as she was about to rush up to it, she saw his insane smile. He was standing in front of the stall. She could see the eyes behind the mask.

It was mean. And utterly evil. "Hello bitch." His voice was deep and muffled. Valerie's eyes were locked into his. She saw the knife, long and rusty, come out from his crumpled trousers. He growled like an animal as he advanced on her.

Valerie stepped back, stumbled and fell hard into the puddle. Even as she faced her attacker she cursed the soaking mess. His fluorescent green slippers came forward and stared her in the face.

"Say goodbye to your lover," said the Laughing Buddha, raising his knife, its point aiming at her heart.

As it flashed down, she saw something pink shoot out. There was a thud and oranges and apples rolled over the murky water. One fell into the slimy drain.

It was Ah Por!

She stood in front of the Laughing Buddha, screaming at him in Hokkien. The knife lay on the ground. She had somehow swung her shopping at the knife and saved Valerie.

Velu ran towards them, shouting. The Laughing Buddha looked around in sudden panic. He adjusted his mask, picked up the knife and ran into the market.

Ah Por stared at Valerie, a look of triumph in her eyes.

X

"Of course I made a police report. But I didn't tell them I suspected my husband. He wanted me dead and got somebody to kill me. I know it! Nobody else knew I was seeing someone. Albert, you have to help me!"

"But why didn't you tell the police it was your husband's doing?" I asked, quite shocked and feeling completely helpless.

"I don't know. I was so scared. I wasn't so sure. I've had time to think about it now. And I know he hired that man to kill me. Please help me. John doesn't know what to do. He doesn't want to be involved. He's had threats over the phone and is afraid for his life. He flew to Singapore this evening." She looked desperate. I saw real fear permeate her face. "You see, I don't have any other friends. When I got your letter I thought that maybe you could help, you being a journalist and all. So I wrote to you. I didn't know what else to do. Albert, surely you can help me somehow."

I stared at her for a long time. I told her I had to think about all of this and would see if I could get some kind of help tomorrow. I hated this. I didn't want to be involved.

I slowly climbed the staircase, feeling dread sink deeper with every step. I did not disbelieve her story. If the Datuk wanted her dead, what could I do to save her? I really did not know what to do. I hoped that all this would go away in the morning.

Datuk Khoo was wide awake. He'd had an unusual day. He had not heard Valerie come up to her room yet. Instead he heard voices coming from the library below. He couldn't make out the words. And he didn't care what they were. The fat journalist was an inconvenience. But no matter.

It had been a short drive to Rawang. His car left the ugly construction sites behind. The road then wound through a Malay village and rubber estates took over. Rawang was a one-road town sitting in the humid sun. He hated the place.

He found the farm easily. The man he knew as So Kow dragged himself from the shed, his feet covered in mud. The smell of pigs and manure was everywhere. Datuk Khoo felt like vomiting.

"Oi, are you the one who telephoned!" So Kow called out as his finger pried into his left nostril.

"Yes, I am. Have you got what I wanted?" questioned Datuk Khoo as he strode pass the puddles of mud and feces. So Kow was a lowlife that could only live with pigs. He had better deliver as promised.

"Of course, I have it. Caught it yesterday. You have to be fast and clever you know. These things can be very dangerous. But I know how to do it. My father taught me." He brushed his slimy finger against his already soiled shirt and straightened up proudly. "My father was a real expert."

"So where is it?" Datuk Khoo questioned impatiently. "I need to go back to KL soon."

"In here, in here," So Kow replied as he pointed to the shed.

The shed was dark, dingy and smelled even worse than outside. Datuk Khoo kicked out at a chicken that wandered too close. It squawked loudly as it ran out into the blazing sun.

So Kow motioned to the basket with his muddy feet. "It is here as you wanted." He stuck out his grimy hand in expectation. Datuk Khoo paid So Kow twenty dollars and took the basket. Everything was going according to plan.

Datuk Khoo had always felt a deep power within him. It was so strong it could burst right out of his body. If he looked up at the sky, it would burst out of his eyes like fireworks. He fought with it every day. It would taunt him and in a rage he would scream obscenities at it.

It would disappear for awhile. Sometimes, he even forgot the power existed. Valerie had helped make it go away. But only for a short while.

He had married her two years ago. She was pretty and irresistible. Then something familiar started pulling at the back of his mind. *She is evil, she is unfaithful! She is a monster!*

He knew this thing and he would scream back at it. It would disappear but he could hear it laughing at him. Taunting him. He so very much wanted her to be faithful. It told him to watch her closely with other men.

It took awhile before he started seeing the little things. The neatly brushed hair. The new dress. The extra scent of perfume. The extra lift in her voice.

Did I not tell you so? Your wife is evil! Follow her and find out.

He had her followed and now he knew the truth. She was with that *gwei loh* engineer!

The power exploded out of him. His arms and legs were like pillars of fire bursting with light. He found a knife and went to the market. The power ordered him to wear a mask to hide the wonder of his being. He wore the Laughing Buddha because only it could contain his divine power.

The force of a million sinners is in you. Make her pay for her disloyalty. Cut her into a thousand pieces!

Yes, he would kill her. He had the awesome power. He remembered the first time he felt it so long ago.

He remembered the sounds of groaning. He had fallen asleep in the huge wardrobe. He was holding onto his mother's night dress which he found lying on the floor of the wardrobe. He was only four and liked to play hide-and-seek with himself. It was in the afternoon and his father had just left the house after lunch.

Father came home for lunch every afternoon and he would sit next to him, completely mesmerized by what father was saying to mother. He did not understand much but he loved the sound of his father's voice.

And his mother would open the car door for his father to get in. The driver would then take him away through the open gate and he remembered waving until the car had disappeared. It always seemed like many hours until his father's return.

Mother would usually take him for a drive or they would go for a walk. But these days she did not spend much time with him and he was always sent to the maid. He didn't like her much and played by himself instead.

Now he had woken up. And these sounds were terrifying. It echoed within the cathedral darkness of the wardrobe. He clutched his mother's crumpled night dress, his heartbeat racing. He silently peeped through the wooden louvers. He only saw shadows at first. Then he saw him.

The driver was on the bed, sweat dripping from his forehead. He heard a noise. It sounded strange but familiar. It was not from the driver. He squinted through the louvers but could not see who made it. He quietly crawled to the right and peered from a different angle. And then he saw her.

It was from his mother. Groaning. His own mother. Her face looked strange. Contorted and ugly. No, it was not his mother. It could not be his mother.

It was a monster. An evil monster. He stared at their writhing embrace. Fear turned to anger and anger turned to something strange.

He did not know what it was but it filled him with a burning sensation in his head. It was *power*. A deep dark power that grew. That told him things. Strange things and he felt comforted. When they left he sat in a daze until he heard the servants calling for him. He walked back to his toy-filled room and hid the nightdress. It had been bitten to shreds.

Monsters needed to be taught a lesson. He had poisoned his last wife. She liked artists. He hoped she liked the arsenic cakes. The power told him about that one. He laughed through his tears as he brought out the shredded nightdress. It felt so soft, so good. It made him excited and he eagerly responded until his power ebbed in its own stickiness. He was falling asleep when he heard the staircase creak. It was the bloody fat slob. A muffled sound came from his wardrobe. He remembered the basket and smiled.

Valerie felt the cold water enliven her body. It stroked every part of her. It was rejuvenating. She loved the crack of dawn. The soft sunlight played on her face. The cool breeze reminded her of home. The jungle beyond stirred as the leaves felt the dawn. Her lean body glided gracefully through the embracing water. She was on her twelfth lap. She would do twenty today. It was so quiet and peaceful. She almost felt safe.

Speaking to Albert had helped her to think. She was glad she spoke to him. He was a nice man but she got the impression that he didn't want to get involved. She had come to a decision on her own. She would leave her husband and fly to London. Then she would stay with her sister in Surrey. She needed time away from him, somewhere she could be safe. And then later on she would be able to think about her future and start living again. That would be the best thing. She should have done it a long time ago. She didn't know what her husband was going to do and she wasn't going to wait to find out.

Her hands gently moved the waters, pushing her body forward. Her face stayed above the wet surroundings, surveying everything calmly. The morning air tasted delicious and clean. She felt triumphant in making her decision. She swam faster and smiled. After eight more laps, she got out of the pool.

She dried herself, leaving the damp towel on the deck chair for Ah Por to clear. It was nice having maids pick up after you. She would have to get used to doing things for herself again. The newly washed bathrobe felt soft against her skin. She climbed the staircase to her room. She remembered when they had shared a room. That lasted only a short while. He said he wanted to be alone. There was no explanation, just a strange look in his eyes. The thought of him made her tremble.

Valerie tossed her robe onto her bed and entered the bathroom. She did not notice the open basket under the sink. She examined her face and smiled. No new wrinkles. Just as she was about to turn on the shower she noticed a movement from the corner of her eye. It was something black slithering next to the bidet. Her heart froze. She slowly turned around and saw the snake. It was long, its black and yellow body over three feet in length. It stared at her; its head hung in mid-air. Its eyes looked into her hypnotically. Venomously.

Perspiration formed on her forehead, she did not dare wipe it away. She felt her legs tremble as she carefully tried to edge to the door. The snake followed her every movement. Its tongue darted back and forth as it hissed out at her. She prayed it would leave her alone. She had edged past the basin, the brass doorknob was just within reach. She slowly reached out and turned it.

It did not budge.

She pulled at it again. It was locked! *Somebody had locked it!*

She then knew he had done it. He had done it all. He was the Laughing Buddha and was going to kill her this time. She pulled at the door as hard as she could, praying for it to open. The snake hissed again. She turned just it time to see its black shadow fly through the air.

A searing pain struck her left thigh.

She fell screaming as the stab from the bite seared through her body. The snake darted away. Within seconds she was in convulsions and foaming at the mouth. She tried to lift herself up but fell against the sink, her arms knocking over bottles of perfume which shattered onto the marbled tiles. Her lungs heaved for air and her vision swam into darkness.

I was just putting on my shirt when I heard her scream. I ran downstairs to see what was happening. Ah Por was yelling and pointing back upstairs. Fear was written on her face and I suddenly remembered Valerie's story. I heard the sound of glass breaking. I raced back up the endless flight of stairs, onto the landing and saw the door to Valerie's room wide open. I rushed into the bedroom. She wasn't there but the bathroom door was closed.

It was very silent. I approached it with fear, afraid of what lay beyond.

"Valerie, are you there?" I called out. No reply.

I knocked several times. "Valerie, are you there? Answer me!" Still no reply. I noticed the key in the lock and turned it. The door could not open fully. I pushed harder and to my horror saw Valerie's body slump forward. There was blood on her white swimsuit. Her eyes stared emptily at the ceiling.

The snake hissed in the corner. I froze. I recognized it as poisonous and dread drenched through my body. I knew Valerie was dead.

And the smell, an overwhelming concoction of expensive perfumes invaded my nostrils. Sweet and sickly. It gradually filled her bedroom and wafted its way down the stairs. It was like her goodbye, the last remnants of her life on earth.

Ah Por, in a rage and without any care for her own safety, killed the snake. She was still standing over it with the rake, trembling in fury, when the police came. The ambulance took Valerie's body away. It took the police at least half an hour to find Datuk Khoo.

The papers said that Datuk Khoo was so traumatized by his wife's accidental death that he went quite mad. They found him hiding in his wardrobe clinging to an old and badly torn nightgown. He wore a mask of the Laughing Buddha. Beneath the mask were the tears of a raving lunatic.

I knew he had killed her. But I kept this story to myself. It would have made little difference. Datuk Khoo spent the rest of his days in the asylum. There was no proof anyway. For myself, I had to live with her memory. I could have saved Valerie if I had done something that night she pleaded for my help.

When I got back to Penang I was fired. Not for losing the Datuk Khoo interview but for not writing the story of Valerie's death. It was inexcusable; I was there when it happened. But I could not write about her.

I later did more research on Datuk Khoo. A snake was also responsible for the death of Datuk Khoo's parents. It was hiding in the car, his father panicked and drove the car into a ravine. The car crashed and they died instantly.

I wondered who else this business tycoon had killed. All his money couldn't save him from his insanity.

Datuk Khoo sat Buddha-like in his cell. And when the monster-woman screamed from the bite, he felt the power explode in his head. His mind was one. He was very glad. And then he felt himself falling.

But now he had risen, stronger than before. He wanted to get married again but that stupid incompetent doctor said no. He had leaped at him, his fingers aiming to gouge out the eyes. They had pulled him away and kicked him until he vomited. They gave him drugs so that his mind went soft and thoughts fell through his brain like a sieve. Everything turned a dirty rotten black.

It did not matter. He was all right now. His power would not deny him anything. He yearned for his torn nightgown. It kept him safe from this wretched world, from all the monsters. His eyes darted back and forth looking for her.

He started to salivate as the power rose inside him. His body shook with hate. Monsters must be killed. They must be eaten alive. And there was one right here. He heard the pretty young nurse's soft footsteps and he laughed and laughed.

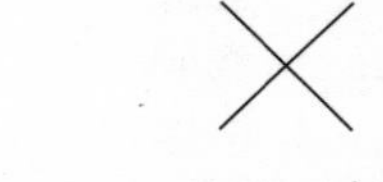

MR INSURANCE MAN

Putney Wong hated his name. He didn't really know where his father got 'Putney' from. He never asked and the information was never volunteered. He was tall and lanky and smoked too much for a man of thirty-five. He found his hairstyle in a magazine five years ago and had maintained it ever since. He always returned to the same hairdresser and paid thirty dollars each time. He bought his shoes at Scotts last month at the 'Price Countdown' sale. He grabbed the last pair of size seven. He smiled when he heard another customer curse at not getting his own seven.

Putney had reason to celebrate. He had sold two insurance policies today which was worth about a thousand five hundred each in commissions alone. His last prospect was in Science Park Drive. After taking her through the numbers, all the time emphasizing the large sums she would get, he used the 'minor-decision' closing technique. He didn't ask her whether she wanted the policy. That was for amateurs, too direct and often frightened them off. He just said in a smooth and sexy way, "Could I have your IC please?" When she timidly handed over her identity card he knew she was sold. He quickly filled out the details and got her to sign on the dotted line. He left with a grin carrying her cheque for three thousand two. He never once asked himself whether three thousand two a year was too much for a secretary to pay. That would be suicidal for Mr Insurance Man.

Leong, Andrew and Boon Siew asked him to join them for dinner in Johor Bahru. He declined, saying he hated the long queue at the causeway. He lied. The truth was that he hated them. They lived in HDB flats and ate at coffee shops with Pepsi-Cola neon signs. Putney was destined for better things. He had just bought a two-bedroom apartment on Bukit Timah Road with a view of the pool. On Sundays, he would sunbathe with his expatriate neighbors. The Coppertone 3 would glisten over his roasting body. With his Armani dark glasses and dangling gold chain, he would survey the bathing beauties while pretending to read W. Somerset Maugham.

Putney loudly ordered another beer. Party Jive was a small karaoke bar near Holland Village. It was a Saturday night and the place was packed. He knew that he would either bump into friends or he would make new ones. The crowd was singing and shouting to *Crocodile Rock* as they moved their bodies out of time and spilt beer everywhere. Tables were crowded and those not singing were yelling into ears trying to joke, impress or execute a new chat-up line. A table of white expats were celebrating a birthday and rapidly emptying jugs of Tiger. The one with the heavy mustache was clicking his heels and clapping his hands like a Spanish dancer on drugs. The fat woman with big earrings managed to grab the microphone and was singing in a croaky voice. It was horrendous. Putney put his fingers into his ears as the DJ tried to get the microphone back for re-distribution to more polished singers.

It was this drunken madness that Putney loved. Here he was the hunter. All kinds of prospects grazed at this watering-hole. He would look out for the well-dressed ones. And the greater the inebriation the friendlier they were, and ultimately the better the chance of a sale. Putney was always at work. And if the well-dressed drinkers wouldn't talk to him he would just move down a notch to the less well-dressed. Sometimes Putney ran into a terrible dilemma when he chatted up females. Should he try to sell her a policy or get her into bed? He had only managed to do both once. He now forced himself to decide what he wanted before making his approach. He usually found that the greater his bed counts, the less his month-end commissions were. Putney naturally preferred the commissions.

"Hello, my name's Putney," he yelled to the target wearing a smart jacket.

"I'm Andrew Loh," the target yelled back as he shook Putney's hand. Andrew was short, about five feet two, with round designer glasses and a chubby face. The striped jacket was expensive and the watch had diamonds. Andrew was drunk, which suited Putney fine.

They laughed and shouted at songs together. Andrew was spinning his overweight body to *La Bamba* and Putney danced Elvis style to *Hound Dog*. The two girls with Andrew started dancing on the stools until the waiter told them to step down.

Putney exaggerated his stagger as they tumbled out of Party Jive. They were almost the last to leave. Putney smiled to himself. This was a good prospect. In the two hours together, they had become 'friends.' He waved goodbye, and when he saw Andrew head for a Porsche, Putney's smile grew bigger. When he got home, he carefully inserted Andrew's business card into his card file labeled

SELL! SELL! SELL! Just before he fell asleep, he visualized Andrew handing him a big fat cheque. He had learnt that from the 'Master Your Mind and Increase Your Sales' seminar at Genting Highlands. It worked, sometimes.

The next day, he telephoned Andrew for lunch at the Hyatt coffeehouse. Through mouthfuls of his Chef Salad and sips of orange juice Andrew announced that he was in the textiles business exporting to Europe and the United States. Putney explained proudly that he was a successful financial advisor. That was always a good way to get the ball rolling.

"Don't you mean insurance agent?" asked Andrew with a grin.

"Yes, I'm an insurance agent, but I also advise on all aspects of finance," answered Putney readily.

"Really, like what?"

"Okay, take this example," Putney said, artfully gesturing with his hands, "say, if you accidentally died, what would happen to your business?"

"Well, I suppose we would have to fold up," Andrew said with a frown. "My sister doesn't know much about the business."

"Exactly! You see, big companies like yours always have business plans, annual budgets and visions for the future. Besides that, you also protect yourselves. For example, you protect your markets, your cash flow, your profits. But sometimes we look at all the details and forget the overall picture."

"What do you mean — the overall picture?" Andrew asked as he edged forward.

"You, Andrew, you are the overall picture. Without you, the business would die. We need to protect your company by having a policy on you. How much does your company make a year?"

"About five million," answered Andrew proudly.

"Well, that would mean that we would have to protect your company to the sum of at least ten million. That would become payable to the company should you, as the key man, die for any reason whatsoever." Putney studied Andrew, closely looking for a reaction; he had now reached a critical point. "Let me put a plan together for you based on ten million."

Andrew hesitated, then answered. "All right, let me see what's involved."

Got him! He was one step nearer the sale. "Look, Andrew, let's meet for dinner tomorrow. I'll have your plan ready then and we can discuss it." Putney scribbled down the necessary personal details.

"I'd like to bring my sister along tomorrow," said Andrew. "She's a major shareholder and I'd like her to be involved in big decisions."

"Sure," said Putney as he surveyed the menu for dessert. It had been a very productive lunch. He was going to sell the bastard! If he could cover Andrew for ten million he would be laughing all the way to The Million Dollar Round Table. That was the elite club for the top agents in the whole damn world.

X

Putney flicked the channels on his television, finally settling on tiny bodies chasing a football frantically. He sprawled on his black leather sofa, luxuriating in the coolness of his air-conditioned lounge. He wore his yellow boxers and could almost count the hairs on his smooth tanned legs. Yeah, those were good insurance legs. They would take him from the bigger sale to the biggest sales yet. Next year he would buy that thirty-thousand-dollar hi-fi. The shop assistant knew him well for he had gone over the amplifier, speakers and players, again and again.

Putney loved his work. He had been a trainee accountant for a year until he met Leong. Leong was very convincing until he started to pick his teeth, so Putney told him to buzz off. They ended up at a pub instead. They became friends and Leong introduced him to the world of insurance. Putney took the exams, passed and started to sell policies. The first policy he sold was to himself.

"It's important to have a policy on yourself," explained Leong in a Chinaman sort of way. "It's an important selling prop."

Leong was right. Putney was sitting anxiously at Mr Sivanathan's posh office. The coffee cups had long been emptied and the Standard Chartered Building across was red with the setting sun. Time was short. He had gone through the numbers carefully. Sivanathan was into finance. He now had Sivanathan agreeing on the numbers. Yes, it looked good. Yes, insurance is vital for protection. Yes, I must think of my family. Yes, I should be insured. But every time Putney tried to close the deal Sivanathan would come up with some excuse not to buy. If it wasn't the high premiums, it was the hassle of going for a medical, and if it wasn't the long-term commitment, it was whether it was the right type of plan. Finally, in the closing minutes, Putney decided to use the prop.

"Look, Mr Siva, if you died right this minute, your family would get nothing. But if I died," Putney now slapped his policy underneath Sivanathan's nose, "my family would get a quarter of a million." Putney hardly flinched as he lied about his family. He was unmarried and his parents were dead.

Sivanathan wrote out a cheque immediately to cover himself for half a million. *People were funny*, Putney mused, *they liked to follow the crowd*. They wanted safety in numbers. Sivanathan finally bought a policy because Putney himself had one. Naturally, he had to have more protection than a lowly insurance agent. Bloody fool! Sivanathan didn't know that Putney's policy was protected by only 'term insurance' which was much cheaper since it only bought protection without savings. Putney himself didn't sell term insurance since the commissions were lousy. No, he sold 'life insurance' where the commissions smelt of roses.

Putney had made it big in the insurance world. He now went for bigger catches and his prop had to be sizeable — it now stood at two million. He didn't care for the protection, only the size of the numbers. He just had to slap that on the table and any prospect would be impressed.

Leong was still struggling from shophouse to shophouse. He knew the sales techniques and could talk big but he wasn't the right class of person to sell to the bigwigs. Putney had learnt the ropes and was putting it to good use. He didn't think he'd need his prop with Andrew though. Andrew ate right out of his hand. Wow! Cover for ten million. That would be his biggest sale yet!

The next day, Putney dressed carefully for dinner. He wore his new Moschino tie and combed his hair again and again until it matched the photo in *GQ*. He put on a white jacket and grinned at his reflection. He even believed his teeth could sparkle. He was Mr Insurance Man, dashing and ready for the big sale.

June Loh was not beautiful, just simply pretty. She had short straight hair, was very fair and had large almond eyes. Her face was childlike and bright with innocence. If she wore pigtails and skipped down the block, you would have thought her no more than twelve. June therefore tried to look her age. She wore Estée Lauder cosmetics and attempted to dress in a sophisticated manner. And even though she wasn't short, she wore high heels as if it would increase her age. She looked much younger than twenty-five.

June's prettiness attracted a lot of attention. Last month, an old man, thinking that she was a Taiwanese actress, chased her down Orchard Road begging for an autograph. He refused to hear her words of denial, so in the end she just scrawled on the piece of paper he shoved at her. She was still trembling when she got home; holding the anger tightly inside instead of, as she had so needed to, unleashing punches into the old man's face.

June regretted taking the job at the dance studio. It was fun at first, teaching housewives aerobics and jazz dancing. Now she couldn't wait for the lessons to end and step under a nice hot shower. This evening had been tiresome. She had to repeat the steps over and over again. The beginners were the most difficult to teach. She felt more relaxed now. The soothing spray massaged her shoulders as it washed away the apple-scented shampoo. She dried herself and wondered what the insurance man was really like.

×

Putney did not believe in love. He believed in money. Love was just a sideshow. Love was what you saw in movies and read in books. It was not too difficult to understand why.

When his parents moved across the causeway to Singapore, they lived in an HDB flat. Both his parents went to work and came back bad-tempered and often shouted at each other. Sometimes they locked him in his tiny room with one window that opened up to a slimy algae-infested wall. One day, he felt like jumping out but vicariously threw his Ultraman down instead. When the door was unlocked many hours later, he ran down the fire escape and found the toy mangled and twisted in a drain minus an arm. His parents did not love him and he in turn hated them. He squatted on the concrete pavement and felt the acid tears of hate roll down his cheeks. He would love money. And he would love only himself.

X

June sipped her glass of Chablis while looking over the financial plan with her brother. Her eyes sparkled and Putney rejoiced, breathing in her perfume. She studied the plan the way she would have studied a *TV Guide*. He wondered how much she was worth. She taught aerobics to amuse herself while living off fat dividends and other perquisites. Some people had it lucky, silver spoon and all.

"Andrew, this looks interesting," June remarked politely.

"Well, I'd like to study it fully first at the office," said Andrew as he cut into his medium rare tenderloin. The meat was red like an open wound and the juice oozed like blood on Noritake white.

"That's no problem," answered Putney, "take as long as you like, there's no real hurry." Putney had within a long minute made a decision of major proportions. The mother of all decisions.

He deliberately kissed his Million Dollar Round Table goodbye. That had become secondary after all. Mr Insurance Man was Mr Marry-Money-Man. From the way she looked and spoke to him, he knew that June liked him and he stood a good chance. This was his opportunity to make it big. Putney was now selling himself. He was Mr MMM.

"June, will you have dinner with me tomorrow?" Putney smiled eagerly. June looked at him as if taken by surprise.

"Oh, I can't, I've got my dance class tomorrow," she answered shyly.

"How about lunch?" Putney asked fully concentrating on winning her. She was his prize money, there for the taking.

"Well, I usually have lunch at home."

"Have lunch with me. I know a nice Italian restaurant. Do you like Italian food?"

"Yes, I do," June answered with a smile and Putney knew he had a date with money.

Two months later, while waiting at the MRT station for a train to Raffles Place, Putney asked June to marry him. She shrieked with happiness, dropping her Ferragamo handbag on the clean square-tiled ground, and hugged him hard. Putney didn't care that everybody stared at them as if they were crazy. June had agreed to marry him and he was going to be rich!

She insisted they told Andrew straightaway and so they went up to the phone booths to make the call. June wanted a small wedding next month and chatted excitedly on the phone. Andrew was overjoyed and quickly planned a wedding venue for them. June started calling all their friends with the good news until she had exhausted all their telephone cards and coins. They celebrated at the Italian restaurant where they had their first date.

For their wedding, June bought him that thirty-thousand-dollar hi-fi. Putney was pleased. Soon, he would have much, much more. After their return, they would move into her million-dollar apartment. He had not seen it yet. She wanted it to be a surprise. Such a romantic. Such a child. A first-class fool. Putney was the hunter and she was the lamb for the taking. And he would take everything she had.

It was a beautiful wedding ceremony followed by a small dinner with close friends at a hotel. Leong, Andrew and Boon Siew were there and even Mr Sivanathan. Putney liked to keep in close contact with his big clients. They could still be useful later. Andrew, being the brother of the bride, was very proud. He told Putney to look after his sister. Putney smiled to himself. He would take care of her all right.

"And don't forget the insurance policy you're selling me," Andrew quipped.

"Oh, I almost forgot about that," said Putney. "I'll get round to that after the honeymoon, brother-in-law. As you can see, I've been keeping your sister busy. Hey, don't you think she looks pretty?"

June wore a white wedding dress and sat radiant as a bride should be. She was shy, and that made her even more beautiful. Putney had the grin of a hyena about to laugh. He had everything, a pretty wife and money, lots and lots of it.

The large ferry cruised down the Aegean Sea. Seagulls followed it, gliding in and out above the sun-drenched white deck. Their frequent calls broke the stillness above the sounds of the trudging engine. Looking back, the outlines of islands could be seen dotted against the background of darker clouds to the south. A young Greek boy not more than six ran across the deck with an ice cream cone, his corpulent mother chasing after him and his father, who must have been sixty at least, with a long gray beard, sat on a bench struggling to read a wind-blown newspaper. A few of the tourists, mostly white, some Japanese, were busy clicking their cameras while others just sat lazily soaking up the sun.

June leaned against the rail looking out towards the island ahead. Her pretty white dress fluttered in the wind. Putney was feeling satisfied. Two weeks cruising around the Greek islands was fun. They stayed at the nicest hotels, drank the finest wine and ate lobster, caviar and the most delicious and expensive foods. Yes, he could get used to such a life!

"Darling, we're almost there," June called out as she took off her sunglasses.

"It'll be awhile yet," answered Putney. "You'd better not get too excited." June sat down obediently and took out her Greece travel guide.

"You'll like Santorini, the hotel there is lovely and it's a lot nicer than some islands."

"June, it's been a wonderful trip," Putney said as he geared to change the subject, "but when we get back we'll have things to do. Like the apartment, I think it's best for me to handle that and all your other finances. I'll get the lawyer to arrange its transfer to my name. It'll be so much easier, you know."

"Anything, my darling, I normally let Andrew handle all those complicated things but now I've got you to do it for me. I'm so lucky. And you know what, I won't be going back to the boring aerobics class. I'll stay at home and make it beautiful for you." She snuggled up to him and kissed him on the cheek.

Easier than I thought, mused Putney, as he smiled and breathed in the delightful sea air. In three days, they would be back in Singapore. He thought about Party Jive. Now that he had money he did not have to sell anymore. He could focus on the girls and his bed counts would soar. He was so glad he kept his Bukit Timah apartment. June would never know, she was so naive. And even if she did, so what? He felt aroused at the thought of Singapore and grinned.

Putney climbed up the track wearing the walking shoes he bought in Athens. He regretted it. The pair would have a good label and be cheaper in Singapore. It didn't matter. Soon, he could have more shoes than Imelda Marcos. He almost laughed at the thought.

Putney could feel the light sweat on his back. June was right, the hotel was lovely. One of the best yet. She was not her normal self last night. She was unusually quiet, not her normal chatty self. Perhaps she was tired from the ferry ride. Or perhaps she was having second thoughts about putting the apartment in his name. She had better not. He would teach her to keep to her word.

June was climbing steadily behind him, with the aid of a walking stick, with a silver-colored metal duck's head as a handle, she had bought at one of the shops. He could see the ruins just up ahead. The two Doric columns framed the red evening sky and the sea beyond. This was a had-to-see attraction. One of the famous ruins on the island.

Putney got to the top of the hill and stretched out his arms triumphantly. The wind refreshed his face and messed up his hair. The sea crashed against the dark looming rocks below, its spray bursting towards the top of the cliff. It was a long drop down to that pebbled beach. Putney shuddered. Then he thought of June and smiled.

He turned round and saw June just reach the top. She took out her camera and started taking photos of the ruins. The temple from centuries past was scattered on the ground. Only a few foundation stones remained. The undergrowth was everywhere and ready to embrace the ruins.

"Darling, stand by the column, will you. I want to take your photo," she said as she approached. Putney moved towards the column which was set by the edge of the cliff.

"How's this?" Putney yelled, beaming in the glorious setting.

"It's lovely! I can get the sunset behind you." June came closer, bent down, focused and the camera clicked. "Another one," she said as she came forward. Putney put on his sunglasses and posed like a *GQ* model.

"Move back," said June, her voice seemed deeper. Putney took a couple of steps back and then realized that he was too close to the edge of the cliff. The blue waters crashed below him.

"Hey, I'm ..." Putney turned and saw June standing right next to him, her face contorted, her eyes narrowed, her lips pressed tight together. The walking-stick was raised with both hands, the duck's head reflecting the blood-like sunset was poised to strike. He almost expected it to go 'Quack.'

"What the hell are you doing, June?" yelled Putney.

"I'm going to kill you, Putney darling," she snarled. She suddenly seemed taller and stronger. The pretty girl was gone.

"What are you saying? You're mad."

"I'm going to kill you, stupid," she shouted loudly, "I'm going to push you down that cliff."

Putney trembled, suddenly realizing that his life was in danger. For the first time, he noticed how those aerobics classes had put muscles on her. June was ferocious. He realized that up until now she had been putting on a little girl act. That had evaporated and he now saw her true self. Why had he not seen it before? She raised the stick high above her head.

"Why, June? Why?" Putney's voice was shaking now.

"Your insurance, of course. Your two-million-dollar insurance. You're going to make us very rich."

"What do you mean?" He couldn't understand this. He was after her money, not the other way round! He couldn't believe that she was after his insurance money!

"We checked. You insured yourself for two million so it could help your sales. We've been watching you for a long time." June's voice was deep and mean. "You don't honestly think I fell in love with you, dummy. I fell in love with your big fat policy!"

"But you're already bloody rich," yelled Putney. He could not keep the fear out of his voice. He could not believe that this was happening. He was locked into this, the way he was locked in his room many years ago. He was a child again. He saw the algae-covered wall and the open window calling.

"Rich? You really believed I bought a million-dollar apartment?" June's high-pitched laughter echoed down the cliff. "The wedding, this honeymoon, it's all been an investment. We've had to rent everything, all our props! Your stupid hi-fi cost four thousand a month! It's time to reap the rewards!"

The metal handle of the walking-stick hit Putney hard on the head. He yelled in pain. Blood spurted out of his ear and stained the ground. Putney reeled as it hit him again and again. The pain exploded in his head. He heard the stick crack and felt a hard kick to his chest. He fell back and the ground disappeared. Putney grabbed at emptiness.

His body was dangling like a puppet in mid-air. One hand had grabbed desperately onto a rock, the other onto the undergrowth. The waters roared its warning below and the sharp boulders jutted out menacingly. His Armani sunglasses fell and disappeared into the void. Warm blood trickled down his cheek. The bitch was going to kill him!

June towered above him, a deadly smile on her lips. Her eyes blazed in triumph. The broken walking-stick was held in each hand like daggers.

"Oh, Putney dear, Andrew and I would like to thank you for the two million."

"No, June, no," yelled Putney as he tried to pull himself up.

June stamped hard on his left hand. He heard his bones crack and a sharp pain jabbed down his entire arm. Putney screamed in agony. His left arm fell and dangled uselessly by his side.

Even as he clung onto the creeper with one hand he knew he was going to die. He was indeed Mr Insurance Man. They were going to live on his death money. This greedy woman had outsmarted him. His perfect bloody wife.

"Damn you, June," he cursed.

"Goodbye, Putney," she said as she slammed her foot on his remaining hand, the shoe heel breaking his fingers. Putney screamed as he lost his grip and felt his body fall.

He plummeted head-first. The scream echoed all the way down. His body hit a jagged boulder with a thump, bounced off and landed on the pebbled shore. The waves rolled over him like a final ablution as its white froth washed over the bloodstained rocks. His body was mangled and twisted like a child's broken toy.

June Loh tossed the broken walking-stick down at the dead body. The crimson sunset was indeed beautiful. It was a wonderful day. She started to walk towards the village, where she would break down, and tell them of the terrible accident. She could just see the report in the *Straits Times*, **Honeymoon Couple Tragedy.** How sad. The insurance company would be very sympathetic to the new bride. Putney Wong was dead, poor foolish, greedy guy. She never really liked his name either.

STRANGLING THE SOUL

"Bloody hell," Jam cried.

He threw the pen on the table, and it rolled over his papers. He intended it to stop but it continued its roll, flipped off the desk and landed on the carpet with a muted thud.

He stormed out of his office, down the corridor and into the lift lobby, the security door closing with a bang. Whiffs of the stench had come his way the past hour, but since his colleagues left, it had turned stronger.

He opened the door to the Men's Room and flicked the switch. Two urinals confronted him, a puddle covered the tiles as if someone had stood between the urinals and pissed hard. A stream of toilet paper clung to the side of a sink, wet and crinkled. In the mirror, an image of a thin man with beard and round glasses stared back.

The perfume though had lost its potency. Jam turned and left the toilet.

Back in the lobby the odor turned on him. Gone were the subtle nuances. Gone was the seductive fragrance. It hit full steam. Like being in a department store with pretty girls in white spraying perfume in his face all at once.

Through watery eyes he saw lift doors and glass walls. A brass sign said **CORPORATE FINANCE** beside a framed photograph of the chairman smiling like a hairless Mona Lisa.

Where the hell's the smell coming from?

There was only one place left to check.

"The Ladies Toilet," he whispered.

No one could be in after midnight, the entire floor was deserted. He knocked anyway, just in case.

With a handkerchief over his nose, he called out, "Anyone there?"

No answer.

"Anyone in there?" He knocked again.

Still nothing.

He pushed the door, it creaked. A coffin opening.

Jam made the mistake of breathing in. Vomit swam up his throat. Rot clambered down his lungs and swirled around his mind like liquid shit.

Just get out of here! a part of him yelled. *It's not right, it's unnatural, it's ...*

He didn't dare think of what could be in the toilet. Of course, he knew the legends, the sweet perfume one shouldn't mention because to do so would only make the thing appear. And yes, he knew about ghosts and demons. His family was after all from a kampung in Kedah and as a boy he had heard many, many stories.

But this was KL. He was a merchant banker, this was a merchant bank. Those fables didn't exist in this world of put and call options, of SC directives, of bond yields and currency hedging. Those demons, those spirits couldn't exist in this modern world where the ATM machine was the altar, the KLSE index the spiritual pulse of the nation.

In his heart Jamal said a doa. He wasn't particularly religious and often skipped Friday prayers and he was proud if he did two out of the five daily prayers. But now he wished he had uttered every prayer, attended every religious class, memorized the contents of the Quran, then maybe he would be safe, then maybe he would find nothing in the darkness of the ladies' toilet.

Ya Allah, what will I find in there?

An image of an old lady stooped over a washbasin came to him, a clutch of gray hair scattered about her slippers, out of a wrinkled face beady eyes met his, while her bright red tongue licked swathes of blood from a sanitary napkin, flicking its pointed tip up at the ceiling as the organ finished each swipe. She dropped the pad back into the bin and smiled.

He shuddered. It was a story he had heard: the shopping-complex ghost who dug in sanitary bins all over the city. He had laughed when he first heard it, but now he wasn't so sure, he could believe in anything.

He pushed the door open a creak.

Please let there be no old lady here. No pontianak. No toyol. Just a dead rat.

He opened it wider and a watery blackness confronted him. One hand held the handkerchief over this nose, the other felt the tiled wall for the light switch.

He found it, flicked it. The toilet came awash in a bright yellow light.

He gasped.

A man straddled a woman's body, his weight pinning her down. Sweat dripped over his glasses, his face tightly bunched. Hands gripped her neck.

The woman opened her lipsticked mouth as if to scream but nothing came. Her eyes blinked rapidly, hands pulling at his shirt, fingernails painted red.

The man swayed, his hands squeezing her throat, her gold chain entangled in his fingers. It seemed as if it was the necklace that drew the man's digits together, as if it was the jewelry that was eager to kill its vain owner. Her head shook, hair mopping the floor, leaving curly black strands upon the tiles.

Jam stood by the door watching, finger stuck to the switch. He had to help this woman but in his paralysis of not more than four or five seconds, the woman succumbed to the strangulation, her arms falling to the floor.

The man untightened his hands, fell back on his knees and glared up at Jam.

Jam screamed.

He staggered back into the lobby. The door swung shut. He gasped for breath. His legs gave way and he fell to the floor.

He could not believe what he had seen. A man had killed a woman. But that was not all, that was not any man, that man was ...was ... *Ya Allah!*

Jam had seen his own face staring at him!

Jam scrambled away, pushing and sliding on the floor, half-crawling back towards the security door, gasping for each breath. He was only able to stand when he reached it, pulling himself up with the aluminum door latch.

He was about to open door and run back to his office when he realized a change had taken place. The smell ... it was gone!

Dinah sat up in bed and screamed. Her hands tore at the darkness, nails to bloody the face of her assailant.

She scratched the air, flailing her arms to keep him away. Whimpering. Then, when the expected assault didn't come, she fell, huddling upon her knees, breathing hard, tears streaming.

She turned on the bedside light. Her eyes darted to the corners of the bedroom. Bookshelf, writing desk, towel stand. Eleven dolls stared back.

No one's here.

She lay down on her pillow, her breathing more controlled. Perspiration ran down her neck, sliding down her gold chain. She wiped it with a tissue then, pulling an ashtray out of a drawer, lit a cigarette.

Just a dream. An awful, awful dream.

She held the smoke in her lungs for a moment, then blew it upwards to the rotating fan. From outside came the shrill sounds of insects.

She had never known such a nightmare in her twenty-five years of life. So real. She still saw the shadow of the man's face before her. Still felt his strong hands over her throat. Still tasted the sourness of his sweat.

Past midnight, said the bedside clock. She had gone to bed early, hoping for a good night's sleep so she'd be fresh for her new job tomorrow.

She liked new beginnings. It gave her a chance to start anew. After what happened in her last job.

Oh, I wish he's with me now. Just to have him to hold me.

It took little to recall his aquiline features, his intelligent eyes that devoured any books he could find. Her fingers remembered the thick curly hair entwined in them. It brought a thrill to her bones. A longing that stretched deep through the night, to the stars that peeked through her open window.

It had been six months, two weeks, three days since she spoke to him.

"I'm going to miss you," she had said, one finger running across his hairy chest, even as she felt the tightening in her belly. How could she have let it get so out of hand?

He had propped himself on one elbow, a hand over one cheek as if he wanted to strip his skin off like an orange peel.

"I can't believe this is happening. Don't you love me?"

"You know I do. But we can't. My parents ... it's just impossible."

"Dinah, I'm willing to do anything, anything for you."

"I know that," she said, avoiding his eyes. "But my parents ... you're not—"

"—Malay." Sivanathan fell on his pillow and stared at the ceiling. "I know I'm not. I'm a Malayali, a Hindu and proud of it."

"So you should be, Siva. But it means we can't be together. We have no future together."

"But we have the present, so why think of the future? I make you happy, don't I?"

"Yes, you do ... I want to spend all my time with you ... but I want more, I want to get married, I want a family. And that you can't give me."

"Yes I can. And I want to give it all to you. I'll convert. I won't eat pork. I'll get circumcised. I'll learn to pray."

"But my parents ... you're not ..."

"Malay." He sat up. His handsome features hung over the sheets, his jaw quivering as if his face was about to melt and fall away like boiling lava.

"No, Siva, you're not."

"Why can't they understand?"

"I'm their only daughter. These attitudes ... prejudices ... they'll disappear with time, but not in ours."

"Then I'm finished."

"We're finished."

But the relationship didn't die.

It just turned bad.

Seeing Siva every day at work skewered her heart. He worked in her department, several cubicles away.

The agony of seeing him, of not being able to hold him and kiss his ruby lips left Dinah lifeless, like a trodden doll.

The once-handsome Siva now turned up at work with hair uncombed, dark shadows beneath his eyes. She smelt beer whenever they silently passed in the corridors.

One sleepless night, she found herself wiping her dolls over and over until she thought she might be doing them damage. Enough was enough. Delicately, she rearranged them on the shelf. Some porcelain, some wooden, some plastic like Barbie dolls. All blonde.

All blue-eyed. All Diana. All showed beauty with sad, downcast eyes.

She adored them. Her mother said they were un-Islamic, but Dinah didn't care.

The next day she handed in a 24-hour notice and had not seen Siva since. She always wondered why she could defy her mother over the dolls but not for Siva. Not the one thing that really mattered.

It took her months to find a new job. Months in which she lived on her savings and her memories of Siva. Countless times she had been tempted to pick up the phone and call him. Finally, she did only to find out that he had left a month ago.

She only had one previous lover, a theology student in Ohio. She was in bed with him, when the news flash came on the country radio station, right after Dylan's *Love Minus Zero/No Limit*. Princess Di was dead.

She wept and so did he. He was an Anglo-Saxon American from Texas. He found her dark skin strangely compelling, her religion fascinating. She, in turn, loved his Southern drawl and the way he insisted on only playing his guitar arpeggio style. He said that was how his heartstrings sang. Then in the fall he left her for someone on the netball team. She cut the strings of his guitar and started collecting Princess Dis.

A new job tomorrow. A new beginning. She stared at the dolls. Death had come so suddenly in the midst of such happiness. Their babies would have been Muslim too. She turned off the bedside light and hoped the nightmare would not return.

The next morning Cynthia Lim, a clerk in accounts, came into Jam's office. As usual she was wearing those cheap green slippers. Jam felt his face flush. This was a merchant bank, not a bloody fish market. Dank puddles formed around those slippers, rickety stalls stood behind her, hawkers shouted their wares in Cantonese, chickens danced in rusty drums, thumping and banging as a haze of blood drifted upwards. Cynthia carried plastic bags, some brimming with vegetables, others laden with raw meat. She poked a handful of crumpled dollar notes at Jam's face.

"Encik Jamal, this is our new AFM," Cynthia said with a big grin. No plastic bags, no dollar notes, a thick file was held to her boyish chest.

Jam looked up to see a woman standing outside the door.

Cynthia motioned to her.

The woman came in wearing a baju kurung and tudung. A regal nose preceded a cloudless face of arched eyebrows and eyes so warm he found himself floating in them.

Jam blinked.

"I'm Dinah, pleased to meet you." The woman smiled and stuck out a hand.

Jam blinked again.

No. It can't be.

"I start today," Dinah said, hand dangling in the air.

"She's the new AFM," added Cynthia, one finger scratched an ear.

Jam stared.

Can't be.

Dinah's hand hung empty above his desk. Cynthia coughed and squeezed her nose.

Dinah's hand lowered like a feather falling. Cynthia clasped her file with both hands.

"AFM?" Jam jumped to his feet and, before Dinah could withdraw it, took her hand in a salam.

"Assistant Finance Manager," said Dinah, fingering her gold chain.

"I see." Jam wiped his forehead with a handkerchief. The gold glittered. Did it move then?

"Are you okay, Encik Jamal?"

"Er ... yes ... yes ... I'm fine, Cynthia. Just a little hot in here. Something wrong with the air conditioning?"

"It seems okay, but I'll check with maintenance."

Jam looked at Dinah again. "It's nice to meet you," he said and managed a smile. "Welcome to the bank."

"Thanks," she said. "Oh, your pen fell."

Before he could go around the desk, she had already handed it to him.

"Thanks, Cik Dinah."

"Welcome." She turned and left.

Jam fell into his chair. He wiped the sweat from his forehead.

She's the woman who got strangled last night. Ya Allah ... the one I strangled!

Last night when the smell disappeared, he had stood watching the door of the ladies' for what must have been an hour. Finally, he had summoned the courage to go back in. He found nothing. No one. It was empty. The toilet had no windows, so he would have seen anyone leaving or entering. Then he saw a bearded man with glasses staring back at him. He screamed, then realized it was only his reflection. He had cried, his tears captured by the porcelain sink, trickling into the plug hole.

For a long time Jam watched the screen of his computer, not reading the words of his report, just gazing into the space behind the glass where the cathode ray tube and the electronic devices lived, thinking about Dinah, her sparkling voice, her warm intelligent eyes, his hands around her neck ...

No!

It was crazy.

Why would he want to kill her? The vision. What did it mean? And the smell, what was that? How did it suddenly disappear? The questions leaped around his mind like monkeys, screaming and tearing his brain.

The rest of the day was a blur. The only thing constructive Jam did that day was to decide to keep away from Cik Dinah, no matter how alluring she was.

He succeeded until one day they bumped into each other at the pantry, his coffee falling to the carpet, her tea drenching his shirt.

"Sorry," he said.

"Oh shit!" she said, looking at the mess.

"I agree." The hot sticky shirt clung to his chest.

"But I think it's tea."

She laughed. "Sorry, my fault."

"No, no, Cik Dinah, it was mine."

"No, I'm guilty. You're all wet, do you have a spare shirt?"

"No, I don't normally expect to be drenched in tea. And you can call me Jam, everyone does."

"Jam, please borrow my T-shirt, it's one of those oversized ones I wear to the gym. I'm sure it'll fit you. I'm not going today so you can use it."

"Don't worry about it, I'm sure one of the other guys will have one I can borrow."

"Please take it, it was my fault after all. And you can call me Dinah."

Dinah's T-shirt was a perfect fit and pleasant too with her lingering perfume. Not like the sweet scent that night but a musky fragrance that reminded him of turmeric, fried onions and pounded chilies.

Despite his decision to stay away, on many occasions, Jam found himself standing by her desk talking to Dinah, taking pleasure from her voice. Later, he would find himself in the toilet beside a leaky tap asking his reflection if he knew what the hell he was doing.

Must keep away, he told himself. *The image must be a warning of some kind. I don't want to end up killing her.*

His eyes blazed back, filled with fear and longing. The door swung open, a colleague said hello, Jamal waved back and pretended to comb his hair. Then he relieved himself, but inside he felt his heart and guts being slowly torn apart.

Finally, as the weeks passed and the smell and image of him strangling Dinah faded and dismissed as nothing but his imagination, Jam asked her over for dinner.

The meal was at Jam's single-story terrace house where he lived alone. Jam knew he was paying his mamak landlord too much, which wouldn't have bothered him much except for the way that old toothless man, draped in white cloth, smiled so eagerly each month, time and again his long wrinkled hands like a snake stretching to pluck the cash from Jam's fingers.

Jam had invited another couple for dinner. The couple was now talking quietly between themselves, engrossed as those in love would be. Nothing remained of the daging rendang and kari ayam but bones scattered on the puddles of dark sauce. A fan spun above them, Céline Dion was singing about some old love.

"That was a wonderful meal, Jam," Dinah said. "You're a great cook."

"My mum taught me."

Dinah lit a cigarette with a yellow plastic lighter. "I can't cook," she said, blowing smoke over the table. "Never been interested in it."

"I didn't know you smoked."

"Picked up the habit in the States," she said.

"I stopped smoking two years ago," said Jam.

"Uh huh. So Jam, how long have you been with the bank?"

"Smoking's bad for you."

"So are a lot of other things."

Jam nodded and stared out into the night.

The neighbors were in. A light blazed. The TV flickered. A relative died there a month ago. It may have been the grandfather, or maybe the father, he didn't know for sure. They had set up a tent-like structure in front of the gate, there was a lot of banging and praying. An open-air truck, painted black, took the coffin away. The entire street smelled of incense.

Dinah was looking at him. He smiled happily. The image of him killing her faded to the dark confines of his memory.

X

They gathered in Dinah's garden in Gombak, beneath a canopy with fans blowing. They were at the VIP table with her parents, Jam's parents and a solemn-looking Datuk, high up in the UMNO division, accompanied by his jewel-fingered wife with a face flushed with rouge and mascara.

Was today the happiest day, her happiest hour? With her grandchildren all about her feet, would she look back through all the years at today ever so wistfully? Perhaps it would have been the same for Princess Di if she had married Dodi. If only. Tunnels, car chases, princesses. They didn't go together.

She loved Jam, she was sure of it. She loved stroking that beard of his, loved the way he wiped his glasses with his shirt. Loneliness slipped off her from the moment she spilt tea all over him. Another office romance, yes it was, but this relationship wasn't doomed from the start.

All that was missing was a spark, a quivering, an aching inside her — like just before jumping on a rollercoaster. Jam was a choo-choo train filled with babies and balloons — so very safe. This so-called spark would disappear with time anyway, so why insist on it as a criterion for marriage? Today was the happiest day, her happiest hour — she was sure of it.

Dinah glanced across the bunga telurs, the dishes laden with curries and, between the shoulders of her parents, saw a forlorn figure among the crowded tables.

She turned away. Part of her refusing to see, refusing to believe.

Today of all days!

"Please go ahead," her mother said, nodding at the guests at the table.

Her mother wore embroidered blue with a white scarf stretched from hair across breasts.

"But the wedding couple should be served first," said Jam's mother, smiling back.

"Of course."

Dinah thought it was perhaps memory causing his apparition to appear. But no, here he was coming towards them. She desperately needed a cigarette.

Dishes were held before them. Jam helped himself to some beef rendang. Dinah spilt some curry, a wing clung to the edge of her plate.

"Nervous on your wedding night?" asked her father, beaming from his songkok and mustache.

"Must be," said Jam's father with a twinkle in his eye. "My son's very demanding."

Everybody laughed.

Jam grinned shyly behind his beard. His head-dress pointed towards her house, where they would spend their wedding night. Between Jam's gold-threaded headdress and her mother's scarf, the figure came.

Quickly she retrieved the stranded wing. Said no to the vegetables and sipped rose syrup water. It felt very warm. Her glass sweated.

Siva's face had filled her mind so many times — hanging dreadfully over the bed sheets, as if his features were about to melt into boiling lava.

She looked up and there he was, standing over her mother and Jam.

"Dinah."

Siva wore a white shirt and looked thinner than she remembered. In his eyes she saw hurt, desolation.

"Hello," she replied, barely able to look at him.

"Congratulations," he said.

Was there an edge in his voice? A yearning, a craving, a boiling anger?

"Thank you," Jam said before Dinah could reply. Jam stuck out his hand and, slowly, Siva reached out and shook it.

He now offered her his hand. Hands she never wanted to let go of.

She took it as briefly as she could. Hands so warm, so strong ... By the time she had pulled hers back, Siva had disappeared.

"Who is he?" asked Jam.

"Old friend," said Dinah, fighting to keep the trembling from her voice. "From my old job."

Her mother had her nose stuck high in the air. Her father's mustache had lost its smile, his eyes met hers for a moment, then returned to his food.

Soon everyone was talking again.

"An angel has just passed," said Jam's mother jovially, referring to the old-wives' tale of sudden quietness.

To Dinah's relief, neither Jam nor his parents suspected that the love of her life had just come and gone.

The happiest day, her happiest hour? She didn't think so.

Her angel had disappeared forever.

Rosnah binti Jamaluddin sprang into the world with a sudden cry. Her birth, a joyous triumph for parents and grandparents, came shortly before midnight. Jam and Dinah left the hospital with glowing faces, cuddling their little treasure in a bundle.

Jam drove home, the car floating on air except when the baby cried, which made his insides squirm with worms of worry. For a while he forgot his wife was happily poisoning his baby throughout the pregnancy. Then one night he woke up with that memory ticking in his brain.

They had fought when Dinah was two months pregnant.

"I can't stop," she said. "I've tried but I can't."

"You must Dinah, it's bad for the baby. Anyone will tell you that."

"I know, but I just need my cigarettes. I'm only smoking seven or eight a day ... I'm sure it's not so bad. I've moved to low tar, anyway."

"It's bad, believe me. Don't you care for your own baby?"

"Of course, I do!"

"Then why the hell don't you do something about it!" He grabbed the cigarette from her mouth and stamped on it. It burnt his soles but he said nothing.

"You have no right to do that!"

"I have every right, it's my baby too!" He kicked the cancer stick, it flew under the dining table. "Don't let me catch you smoking again!"

"You go to hell!" She turned and rushed into the bedroom, spending the rest of the evening polishing her God-awful Princess Dis.

He now lay in bed watching the darkness, the memory turning clockwise in his skull. The air conditioner, a wedding present from his parents, hummed. The streetlight fell through the window, throwing claw-like shadows on the curtains. He closed his eyes, his head pounded, he wanted sleep but his bladder cried for relief.

He put on his glasses and got out of bed, making the well-trodden route to the bathroom.

A noise.

The baby crying?

He opened the bedroom door and stepped into the corridor. Then it struck.

No! Not the smell!

It tore at his face so he almost stumbled back into the bedroom. But he had heard a crying, didn't he?

Step by heavy step he willed himself to baby Rosnah's room, fighting his way through the thick sweet odor.

There it was again.

Louder this time. The baby crying out.

Where the hell's Dinah? Why doesn't she come out of bed? Doesn't she care?

A light slanted out the nursery. He grabbed the doorframe. The stench made his head spin. He pushed the door open. The crying was now a wailing. At first the light blazed upon his eyes so that he saw nothing. Then he saw the cot against one wall, a teddy bear covered in shadows sat expectantly in a chair.

Above the cot stood Dinah, a knife in one hand raised as high as the curtain rail. A shadow thrown on the wall. A hand. A baby's hand curling and uncurling as though pleading, as if baby Rosnah knew her time had come, that her brief time in this world was over.

Jam lunged forward just as the knife fell towards the baby. He grabbed Dinah's hand as the weight of his body slammed against her ...

... against nothing ...

... and he slammed against the wall, hitting his head. Jam would have fainted if it were not for the baby.

Got to save her!

He rose unsteadily, holding onto a shelf of baby lotion and nappies for support. The bright light had vanished.

"Where are you, Dinah?" he growled. His eyes searched the room for her, but he couldn't see her in the semi-darkness. How could she have disappeared?

Maybe she wasn't here at all?

He had grabbed her hand but felt nothing. His body had slammed against hers, but it was like doing a rugby tackle on empty air.

Slowly, he turned to the cot, expecting the worse, not wanting to see the blanket soaked a bright red, his baby tightly curled against a cot bumper, her little fingers still grasping a pink dummy. Her dead eyes wide open, begging her mother *Why?*

He didn't want to look. But he had to. At first he only saw her hand gripping the sheet, then he saw her face — *thank Allah!* — with a half-smile on her lips. She was wrapped in her blanket and he could hear her light breathing, a slow soft rhythm upon the night.

"Allah's mercy," he gasped.

The awful stench, there wasn't even a whiff of it.

Dinah was still in bed. Lightly breathing. He stood over her for a long time before lying beside her.

The next morning, Dinah wondered if Jam should call in sick.

"Didn't you sleep last night, darling?" she asked over breakfast. "Maybe you shouldn't go to work today." Baby Rosnah had just fallen asleep in her arms after breastfeeding. She was warm and soft and wonderful.

"I'm fine," Jam said, all ready for work in his office clothes. His bloodshot eyes were on the newspaper before him but Dinah could tell he wasn't reading it.

She didn't like his quietness, the ashen look in his face but mostly his eyes and how she caught them staring at her when she wasn't looking.

Everything was well in her life with Jam. She had made her decision and she stuck to it. She loved him, not like the way she loved Siva, but he was her husband and, in his own way, he made her happy.

They had never fought, except that one time when he tried to force her to stop smoking during her pregnancy. She tried to stop, she used the patches — but it didn't work. She was hooked like a whimpering fish to the lighted end of a cigarette.

In her guilt, she decided to breastfeed, better for the baby than the bottle, the books told her. She looked at Rosnah and wanted to weep with happiness. She would never do anything to harm her.

She turned back to her husband. "Are you sure you're feeling okay? I'll make an appointment at the clinic."

"I'm fine," Jam growled and left the table.

Maybe he's angry with me. But what did I do?

She followed Jam into the bedroom, placed the baby in the cot and got dressed.

Even though she spent most of her day at home, she liked to dress first thing in the morning as if she was going out; dressing up made her feel fresh. She penciled her eyebrows, lipsticked her lips, brushed her hair and sprayed perfume from a frosted glass bottle, a gift with the skin lotion she bought yesterday. A sweet, seductive scent.

She liked the way she looked. Liked her shoulder-length hair, even though it was always covered outside the house.

I must speak to Jam. Don't know what he's so angry about.

Jam was in the toilet, urinating with the door open.

I better talk to him now.

She followed him into the bathroom.

Jam felt his brain had been cut in two, not cleanly into right and left hemispheres, but sawed with a blunt razor into upper and lower clumps of meat.

Upper's words came in long trickling streams.

It's you not her. You're the one your mind tricking seeing things smelling things not there see a doctor a psychiatrist anybody just get out or you'll do her harm don't you see your mind playing tricks get help help help....

Lower was more to the point, simply repeating the same words over and over like a clock ticking the seconds over.

her kill her kill her kill her kill her kill her kill her kill her kill her kill her

The two had been upon him all night like worms devouring his brain. At breakfast, he was nothing but a zombie staring at the mess of words in the newspaper. He pleaded with them to stop but they went on and on, the Trickling Stream, the Ticking Clock.

Finally, as he combed his hair and trimmed his beard, they stopped. Just like that. And his thoughts were his own. A blank page. To think what he wanted. When he wanted.

Mostly, he needed to rest his mind.

Yes, that's it. Rest. Relax.

He zipped up his pants and flushed the toilet.

He turned.

Dinah. Standing there.

The smell.

Ya Allah, the smell!

He fell on the toilet seat. Images of her over the baby, a knife in her hand.

She made as if to help but he brushed her hands aside.

kill her

"I'll get you," he whispered as he stood up.

"Jam, what's wrong?"

kill her

The Clock ticking down.

"I know what you're going to do."

"What do you mean?"

"I know!"

"What are you talking about, Jam?"

kill her

He grabbed her by the throat and stuck her head against the wall.

Her eyes swam and her body crumpled to the floor like a ragged doll.

Jam bent over his wife and stared. Strands of hair like a net covered her face, her neck, so smooth and slender, the gold chain tight against her skin.

So pretty. So deadly.

The sweet stench made it hard to breathe. It was so thick he could almost see it swirling around him.

Jam straddled his wife and placed his hands upon her neck. It was warm to the touch.

He squeezed.

Dinah's eyes jumped to life and met his.

Confusion. Bewilderment. Fear.

Good. She knows what's happening. She knows she can never ever harm my baby.

Jam tightened his grip. His body rocking to and fro as his fingers crushed her neck.

Dinah tossed her head from side to side, strands of hair were left on the tiles. Her arms weakly hit his shoulders and chest.

Jam's tie flicked from side to side like a dancing serpent. He tightened his fingers as hard as could, tears falling. He didn't remember seeing himself crying, but here he was weeping away.

Dinah's hands flew at his face. One of her nails bit into his flesh beneath the eye. Blood poured down his cheek. Another scratched him deeply in the neck.

He punched her in the face. Her nose broke. Blood soaked his fist. Her eyes turned groggy again and her arms fell to the floor.

He continued strangling his wife. He didn't remember any of this. But the smell, it was everywhere, more sweet and more foul than ever.

Minutes passed.

More minutes.

Finally, Jam brought his breathing under control, took his hands off his dead wife's neck, wiped his tears with his sleeves and got up from her tangled body. He gave her bloody face one last look and left the toilet, kicking her arm out of the way as he shut the door.

The skin on his hands were burning. The joints felt like they were about to fall off.

Baby Rosnah was still asleep.

Sleep. Sleep. All is well. Ayah has taken care of everything.

He took the eleven Princess Di dolls off the shelf and placed them beside the baby in a circle.

"Mak's gone," he whispered. "What a bad woman she was. But these dolls are here to play with you. Ayah is going to have a rest now. So sleep, my baby. Sleep."

Jam lay in bed and closed his eyes. The Ticking Clock, it was quiet now.

And the smell was gone.

Then, like some sick joke, it returned.

Marching in like a conquering army.

Jam didn't know how long he slept. Perhaps ten minutes. Perhaps an hour.

Through his eyes, he squinted.

The smell was loathsome. It tightened around his neck like a noose. Swimming shit in his brain.

A noise.

A noise?

What can it be?

He peered between his feet and saw Rosnah's white cot at the foot of the bed.

He was sure it came from there.

A ruffling on the baby's blanket.

A shuffling. A scuffling.

A giggling?

What was it?

Not something. Many things. Small shadows moving.

Rats? Couldn't be.

What was it?

The cot rails rattled.

Upon it came a mass of orange blotches.

Hands! Many tiny hands clutching it.

Rising. Up and up like pink geckos on the trail of mosquitoes.

Climbing the cot. Through the rails, tiny blue eyes peered icily at him.

Ya Allah! The dolls!

Jam sprang up.

The dolls had reached the top rail. Some sat gazing at him, swinging their legs from side to side, smiling. Some stood balancing themselves like tight-rope walkers. Some wooden. Some porcelain. Some plastic. All blonde. All Diana.

All clutched glinting blades in tiny hands.

A chuckle.

Through the rails, Jam saw baby Rosnah lying there in her teddy bear blanket, her eyes staring right at him.

Anger. Hatred. Revenge.

All in one horrible look.

"No Rosnah," Jam cried. "It was ... was ... a mistake! An accident!"

The baby cried out a single command. More like a bark than a squeal.

The dolls leaped noiselessly onto the bed. Blonde hair, blue eyes closed in on him.

"Listen to me. It was an accident!"

Jam pushed himself away.

"Keep away from me," he yelled.

Still they came. Grinning. Hair streaming in the air-conditioned breeze.

He was trapped at the bedhead against the wall.

"No, no, NO!"

They fell on him.

He swiped at them, left and right, but they easily dodged his blows and kept coming.

He screamed. A sharp pain in his foot. Blood flowed onto the sheet. The doll that had stabbed him wore a triumphant smirk on its plastic face.

He kicked it and it fell to the floor with a high-pitched cry.

Then one stabbed him in his calf. Another in his thigh.

Jam yelled.

Tiny hands gripped his fingers, his hair, his nose, his ears.

And the knives.

Sharp. So sharp.

And plunging. Stabbing. Cutting.

He screamed and screamed.

His body, a hive of pain.

Still they crawled all over him.

Plunging. Stabbing. Cutting.

Blood, blood everywhere. Fountains and scarlet blooms all over the clean white sheets.

And the smell so, so awful.

Then darkness at last.

Sweet, sweet unconsciousness.

Another vision?

Of course, it is.

A warning?

Of course.

And Baby Rosnah?

He would get her.

Just you wait.

LADIAH

"Hey Eddie," I called out across the squash court.

Eddie turned, sweat on his face. He swung his racket over his shoulder, blinked, gave a boyish grin and said: "Ai ya, ai ya, it's you ..."

I figured it had been over thirty years since our schooldays and Eddie wouldn't remember. But he did. He called out my name as if it had always been there burning at the tip of his tongue. I shouldn't have been so surprised, after all, we were once best friends. Lost touch, of course, like so many school friends have done and will do, but it was great bumping into Eddie like that, not literally of course, for I'd be on the floor, my spectacles flying and breaking on the glass panes of the squash court.

Eddie, you see, is big — five foot eleven and strong — always had been, he was with the bodybuilding team. Some of it now turned to flab but he was still big. Me, I was puny with a dull accountant's face and only one child, not enough spermatozoa for another one, the doctor said. A few years later, he said I had something called erectile dysfunction. Why not just say I was impotent? I took every medicine known to man. Viagra did nothing for me and dried tiger's penis powder only gave me a bad cough.

Eddie and I headed to the terrace for a drink. To our surprise we found out we only lived one street away in OUG. I told him I had a small factory manufacturing electrical components.

"I own a restaurant," he said with a wide grin. "You know what, between you and me, business is so good I'm printing money there!"

"Oh ... that's great. So you're not a pharmacist?" I'd known since our schooldays that Eddie wanted to be a pharmacist like his father.

"No lah, I dropped out after a couple of years. Waste of time studying so hard, I was only doing it for the old man. No money there. Last year I bought a BMW, only one year old — 7 series. You know what BMW stands for?"

I shook my head.

"Big Money Win."

"I thought BMW means Best Man Win."

"Yeah, yeah, you're right. But the Best Man must first have the Big Money!" And he roared with laughter.

Eddie hadn't changed. So confident about everything.

"Hey, Eddie, why don't we go out for dinner next week."

"Ai ya, good idea ... come to my restaurant."

So my wife and daughter, his wife and three boys went for dinner. Four times at his restaurant famous for its abalone soup cooked with eggs, tofu and Chinese herbs.

Eddie was printing money here all right, the place was always packed and each time he insisted it was his treat. Magnanimous and generous, that's Eddie.

I invited them to our Chinese New Year open house. He said they would try to come. Try usually means no, but to my surprise he waltzed into my terrace house that afternoon and gave ten-dollar ang pows to all the kids.

He announced that his wife, Poh Ting, and the three boys were visiting relatives. Strange, I thought, putting our open house before his family.

Eddie stayed drinking Anchor beer, chewing nuts but took no cake or the spicy chicken wings my cousin brought. Guests and family came and went but Eddie, he stayed on and on. When everyone else had left and the children had retreated behind doors, I asked him why he wasn't visiting his family with Poh Ting and the boys.

"I don't like her brother's family," he said.

"Why's that?"

"Snobbish, you know. Think they're so grand with their Mercedes-Benzes."

"Ah ... don't worry, lots of Mercedes-Benzes in town these days—no big deal." My mud-streaked Proton in the porch caught my eye — it needed a wash but I couldn't do it on New Year's Day.

Eddie turned to me and whispered. "I took up your invite because I didn't want to stay alone at home with ..." he glanced around, "... the servant."

Then he grinned and for the first time I saw that strange look in his eyes. So unlike Eddie there was no confidence there, but rather a fearful yearning.

"Why's that, Eddie?"

Eddie took a long slurp at his Anchor, threw a handful of nuts into his mouth and chewed. Then he took another swig at his beer, looked at me, opened his mouth, and then I saw it, a tremor rose like a large caterpillar shunting its way up from his stomach to his face, the folds of his cheeks shook as though an earthquake was marching past.

"She's ... she's," he glanced around again, "... doing magic on me."

And there it was again, that strangeness in his eyes.

"I knew there was something not right with her when she first came to work with us."

Eddie told me, in between the slurping of beer and the chewing of nuts, of how Ladiah, from her first day had given him looks which made him sweat on his forehead and down the back of his T-shirt. And, if by chance, they were watching TV alone, Ladiah on the floor and Eddie on the sofa, she would stretch out her legs and allow her sarong to creep up one thigh, revealing smooth, smooth flesh.

Neither Penny nor I had ever seen Ladiah. But Eddie described her as no great beauty, dark face, squinty eyes, long crinkled hair, but at twenty-four she had a shape that Eddie had not had the pleasure of knowing for many years. Now his wife, Poh Ting, was a wonderful woman but she was overweight ... well, fat, to call a spade a spade ... and having Ladiah around proved a natural distraction. But Eddie was adamant, saying he would not have given Ladiah a second look if it was not for the way she looked at him and revealed her smooth leg all the way up those inviting thighs.

Two Sundays ago, while Ladiah was on leave, Eddie strayed into the utility room. Opposite the wall piled high with boxes which they had not opened in ten years, stood an ironing board, a set of drawers and her bed. He pulled off the thin blanket and upon the pale blue sheet, as if watching him like a vermilion eye, lay a menstrual stain. *Bad thing*, he thought, not knowing why. *Unholy woman's magic, woman's secret power.*

He felt idiotic to think such a thing, but this irrational idea stayed nailed in his head.

He turned to the drawer and pulled it open to reveal red panties and bras, all neatly folded. Before he could stop himself, he found himself fingering the soft material. Something caught his eye, a swath of yellow entangled in red underclothing. He pulled at it and let it hang in the air, not believing what he had found.

His yellow underwear.

What was it doing here?

He checked the label — sure enough it said Jockey. Poh Ting had bought it at a sale two years ago, came in a multicolored pack of six. They were big, XL, so how could Ladiah mistake them for her own panties? And she only wore red.

"So that's why I don't want to stay home alone with her," Eddie said, chewing the nuts a little too vigorously, bits of skin fell down his chin.

"What did you do with the underwear?"

"Ai ya, I didn't know what to do. I was standing in Ladiah's room with my yellow underwear dangling in my hands over a drawer full of knickers and bras, so I quickly left. Just as I shut the door, it hit me — she'd know. If I took the underwear she'd know I'd been in her room rummaging through her bras and panties. So I put it back."

"But why? She shouldn't have taken it in the first place."

"I know lah. I should have taken it back. I went to her room the next Sunday but it was gone. I thought she'd found out her mistake and put the underwear back in my cupboard, so I looked but it wasn't there."

"So what are you going to do about her?"

He looked into his glass of beer as if searching for answers within its dancing bubbles.

"I'm so ashamed," he said.

"Why?"

"I ... I can't take my eyes of her," he whispered. "She enters my dreams, dancing, naked, kissing me all over and I come, you know ... a wet dream."

His eyes met mine, searching for some understanding. I nodded sympathetically.

"I have to sneak out of bed and clean myself, so Poh Ting doesn't find out."

"But, Eddie, you didn't do anything wrong."

"I did. In my dreams."

"But only in your dreams."

"Don't you think your dreams reveal your real intentions, real desires?"

I thought about it. This thin puny body of mine held little physical desires. Impotent men knew not of such things.

"I'm not sure," I said. "Maybe it's just your mind in turmoil sending you all kinds of images, all kinds of feelings."

Eddie shook his head. "Ai ya, I don't know what to do ... she's driving me gila. I can't get her face out of my mind, I see her dark face, long hair, all day at the restaurant. I long to get home, not to see Poh Ting or the boys, but to see Ladiah. I spend hours in bed listening to Poh Ting snoring and I really want to, need to, go downstairs and join my servant in bed, in that dingy room. I'm so, so tired. And so scared."

For the first time I noticed the dark rings beneath his eyes and for the third time I saw that strange look shimmering there.

"Eddie," I whispered. "You have to get rid of her."

"Yes, I know ... but how?"

I'm the type who minds his own business. So I didn't speak to Eddie until a week later. I called him at work.

"Hold on," he said. "Let me get the other phone." I heard banging, loud yelling in Cantonese, a sizzling, more banging. "Okay, it's me," he said.

"Am I calling at the wrong time?"

"Ai ya, anytime is fine."

"So how are things going ... you know, Ladiah?"

"No problem now."

"She's gone?"

"No, no — we are together now."

"Together?"

"Ai ya, having sex lah. You see ..."

I said nothing while Eddie babbled excitedly. He had not been able to convince Poh Ting to get rid of Ladiah. Poh Ting got furious telling Eddie he had no idea how difficult it was to get good servants these days — some went on leave never to return, some brought men into the house, some were dirty, some lazy. Ladiah was perfect.

Eddie was not ready that day to tell her how strange Ladiah was and how he couldn't get her out of his mind. If he had only told her then, things would have turned out differently.

A few nights ago, Eddie couldn't sleep. Poh Ting was already snoring, she seemed to be sleeping so well these days. Eddie lay on the pillow thinking of Ladiah, lying in bed with her sarong tied above her breast. Once she had left her door open and he had seen her so attired for bed. Now, in his mind, he saw her with her legs splayed open — waiting for him. Her tongue rolled across her moist lips, her eyes dancing into his — it was that look in her eyes driving him wild. Her long lashes blinked, her hair flowed like a veil across her face and his stiffness pushed hard against the pajama bottoms.

He glanced at Poh Ting, still snoring, her fat bottom facing him, one fleshy arm strangling a pillow. He slipped out of bed, his erection pointing the way. He went past the boys' room and crept downstairs.

He crossed the half-dark living room, his bare feet not making a sound on the tiles. Around him were the bits of furniture they had acquired through the past fourteen years of marriage. On the wall was a photograph of the family — a devoted wife and the fruits of his loins: his three boys, all doing well at school, tuition four times a week was paying off. His family sat smiling within the silver frame, but their eyes were questioning. *Is this what you really want? Do you want to put all that you have at risk for your servant?*

But Eddie cared not. All the jewels nor all the love in the world could stop him. He pushed on. His penis still pointing the way.

To her door. The door to that cramped utility room. The door to boundless pleasure.

It stood a crack open.

He pushed it slowly, soundlessly and entered the dark. Ladiah's bed was pushed against one wall, half of the other wall was piled with boxes. The stuff people carry with them all their burdened lives.

On the bed lay the unmistakable shape of Ladiah. Young, slim body. Legs open. Head propped on a pillow. He approached now not knowing if she was awake or asleep. The outline of her face stood against the darkness, long hair falling around her bare shoulders.

She was breathing deeply. There was the smell of garlic, of a musty sweetness which reminded Eddie of the time when, as a twelve-year-old, he had smelt his sister's bra before it was sent for wash. It had given him a headache and an aching down below. That was the first time he had masturbated and that was the best sex he had ever had. But he was sure things were about to change.

Eddie reached to touch Ladiah's face but instead felt a hand meeting his. It softly caressed his palm, long slender fingers entwined within his. Slowly she guided his hand to an exposed breast.

Eddie gasped.

"Mari sini," she whispered.

She drew him to her several times that night, the bed creaking and creaking and creaking.

Close to dawn he returned upstairs to Poh Ting who still slept so blissfully. Eddie did not feel tired. He felt vibrant, so very alive.

"Poh Ting doesn't suspect a thing," he whispered over the phone. I thought I heard a giggle.

"But Eddie, you can't carry on like this."

"Oh yes, yes, I can. I go downstairs every night and join Ladiah. It's so wonderful."

"How much sleep have you been getting?"

"None!"

Again I thought I heard a giggle.

"But soon I will. When Ladiah and I are together for always."

"What do you mean? You're going to leave Poh Ting and the boys?"

"Maybe they're going to leave me."

And then he did giggle.

"Eddie, listen ... don't you think she might have put some kind of magic spell on you? You said so the other day."

"Ai ya, I was talking gila things then. I want Ladiah, she's all I want."

"What about Poh Ting and the boys?"

"What about them?"

I don't believe in magic. But I've heard stories about charms, potions, bomoh*s* and the more I thought about it, the more certain I was that Eddie was under Ladiah's love spell. She was Indonesian and Indonesians knew about these things, don't they?

I closed my factory early that day and sent my four workers home. I returned to OUG and watched TV for a while, helped my nine-year-old daughter with her homework, after which she gave me a kiss. I tucked her into bed, adjusting the fan so it didn't point straight on her face. She wanted to learn the piano, but I couldn't afford it, not until things picked up at the factory anyway.

Later that night I voiced out my fears to my wife.

"I think he's going to do something to them."

"Like what?" she said. Penny poured me a cup of ginseng tea. She first started giving it to me six years ago, perhaps hoping it would improve our non-existent sex life. It made me more alert, that I think it did but as for downstairs, it was still a dreadfully feeble affair.

"Kill them," I said and cradled the hot cup, wafts of steam spiraled upwards, my spectacles became misty. "He's going to kill his family."

Penny wiped her hands on her shorts. She had spilt tea on it. She placed her trembling cup on the table. "What makes you think so?"

"His voice. The tone of it I suppose. Just a feeling I have. A damn scary feeling."

"Why don't you call the police?"

"And tell them what? I've no evidence."

"But what if something should happen?" A fat frown sat on her emaciated face. Her hair was disheveled, and she didn't even bother using contact lenses anymore. No sex, I suppose, takes the woman out of you.

I shook my head and sipped ginseng tea. Most people would have left the matter alone — *none of my business*, they would say. I couldn't. It was none of my business, true, but I couldn't stand by and watch Eddie kill his wife and three boys.

But I did. That's exactly what I did.

Two nights later, Eddie came stumbling through our gate. He gripped onto the metal grille like an orang utan in a zoo and yelled for me.

I unlocked it and let him in.

He sat down on the sofa, bawling his eyes out.

"Eddie, what's wrong?"

He gulped breaths of air, shaking his head from side to side.

"Tell me what happened?"

"Ai ya ... ai ya ...ai ya." Tears meandered down the plains of his cheeks.

"What happened, Eddie?"

"How could it be?" He raised a large hand in the air, fingers gripping at an invisible thought. "How could it?"

"Where are Poh Ting and the boys?"

"Poisoned," he cried.

"How?"

"Poisoned at the restaurant. We ...we were having dinner there. I ... I was helping in the kitchen, then three or four tables started getting ill, stomach cramps and vomiting. I rushed Poh Ting and the boys to hospital but ... but they never made it ... dead, by the time I arrived."

His tears dripped on our floor.

"Dead?"

"Yes, they were all there in the emergency ward, dying all around me, on the beds, on the floor, in the corridors. Sixteen people ... sixteen people ... all dead ... all gone!" He wiped his tears with his palms and dried them on his shirt.

"My God, Eddie. My God." It had happened. I did nothing and now not only were his family dead but others had perished too.

Penny, face ashen and in a trembling voice, asked if he wanted something to drink. He shook his head and wiped his tears again.

"Eddie, can we help in some way, any way?"

"No." He shook his head. Then he looked up at me, that strangeness in his eyes. Then I recalled he had spent two years studying pharmacy.

"Eddie, how did the poison get in the food?"

His tears stopped — as though a blistering drought had come. "Don't know. Someone put poison in the abalone soup — it was simmering in the pot all afternoon ... anyone could have put it in."

Then I asked the question I dreaded to ask, but knew I had to ask it.

"And Ladiah?"

"She was helping in the kitchen all day. We were short-staffed."

"I see," I said. Was it Eddie or Ladiah, or both of them? I didn't know. Didn't want to know. But it was murder all the same.

And I did nothing.

Two months later Eddie was dead. I couldn't bring myself to attend the funeral of Poh Ting and the three boys, but I went to Eddie's.

A large crowd had gathered at the Catholic Church. Most people said Eddie died of a broken heart. From the death of his family and so many others. They were right. The coroner's report read *acute myocardial infarction*.

Heart attack.

Eddie didn't leave much behind. Some whispered that before he died he had been spending lavishly on clothes and jewelry. Those whispers said he had a mistress but no one knew who she was.

As for Ladiah, she had disappeared the week before, went back to Indonesia and never came back.

"Don't know why," said Eddie's elder sister, wiping a tear from beneath her dark glasses. "Poh Ting found her very good. Did you ever meet her?"

"No," I said, staring at the freshly turned soil. "But I heard she was good."

We stood in silence beneath a large tree, beneath a sky that said rain. I didn't tell Eddie's sister her unwashed bra had given her dead brother his first orgasm ever. It would not help her grief.

A few weeks later our servant went on Hari Raya leave and never came back. *So unreliable, servants nowadays*, Penny said after waiting two weeks for her to turn up. And so expensive too.

The agency quickly found us a new one after Penny demanded our deposit back. From the first day, our new servant stared strangely at me from her dark face, her squinty eyes and whenever, by chance, we watched TV alone, she would pull up her sarong and show plenty of her young smooth legs. I could do nothing but wipe the mist from my glasses and stare.

Now Penny is a wonderful wife, but I've been impotent for years and she is her disheveled self, doesn't even bother wearing her contact lenses ... but she's been sleeping so well recently.

At night I lie in bed and think of Liza. I see her dancing naked before me with that beckoning look in her eyes and I, I am so, so stiff below. For two nights now I had to creep out of bed to clean myself.

Yesterday, as expected, I found my underpants in Liza's drawer. I left it nestled amongst her red panties and bras whose soft silky material held such musky scents, such forbidden pleasures. My thoughts return relentlessly to Penny and electricity and accidents that happen at home.

But tonight, I will go down to the utility room. And I know Liza or Ladiah, or whatever her real name is, will be waiting for me.

THE WOMAN WHO GREW HORNS

One sultry evening at Coffee Bean in Jalan P. Ramlee, while I was complaining about the price of everything, especially the price of CDs and the iced coffee I was slurping all too quickly, Fong whispered that he had a secret. He leaned over and in a single hot breath, like steam from a wok stir-frying chilli and garlic, said that there was a monster where he lived.

I almost poked my straw up my nose as I craned my head towards Fong and said: "Hey, what are you talking about?"

"There's a monster living at my condo," he whispered again. This time he turned to stare at the other tables just to make sure no one was listening.

"A monster?" I said. "You really know how to talk rubbish, don't you?"

"I'm telling the truth," he said. "It lives in the block opposite. I can see it from my window."

"What do you mean 'a monster'? Get serious, okay?"

"Look, I'm really serious. It's a real monster, a woman monster. She's horrible-looking and thumps across her bedroom, you know. Swaying from side to side."

Fong tried to demonstrate but instead looked like a drugged-up elephant and almost tumbled from his chair. The three guys at a table beside us, who had been staring into their handphones as though the Nokias, Ericssons, Motorolas or whatever other bloody brand they ceaselessly caressed were their sexy plastic girlfriends, frowned desperately at him. They smelled of cigarettes and looked as though they'd just sauntered out of that meat-packed nightclub next door. Even though it was past midnight, there was a traffic jam outside and a crowd of locals and expats wandered the streets, sizing each other up.

"So Fong, you've been spying on your neighbor who just happens to look a bit weird, huh?"

Fong finished his coffee and wiped his mouth with a paper napkin. "Not just a bit weird. Very, very weird. She's a freak, I tell you. She should be locked up."

"So you think people who don't have your looks should be locked up?"

"Aiyah, you should see her. I'm not saying she's ugly. I'm saying she's a monster!"

"Come on. You're exaggerating!"

"Okay, why don't you visit me tomorrow night and see?"

I'd once been to Fong's place but after a cup of iced Milo he tried to take my clothes off, so I never went again. As if reading my mind, he said: "I'll be a good boy, okay? I just want you to see this horrible monster."

After some hesitation, I agreed. Tomorrow night at 9. Fong and his dumb stories.

I arrived at 9:20, parked beneath a sign that said **Visitor Car Park** and winced. The missing 'apostrophe s' never failed to irk me.

My mother's secondhand Kancil beeped twice as I locked it. At twenty-two, I spent my daylight hours in the telesales office of a credit card company where I got good commissions and praises from my bosses and in a couple of years, when I would surely be promoted to sales manager, I would get a car loan and buy a new Proton or a secondhand Honda and perhaps even move out into a condo of my own. I planned to work hard and smart, retire at forty, travel the world and write bestsellers like Amy Tan.

I went into a lift, pressed floor 13A and, seconds later, I found myself stabbing at Fong's door bell.

"Aiyah, you're late," said Fong. "Never mind, she's a bit late too."

Before I could say anything, Fong dragged me into the lounge dominated by a large television and a hi-fi system. "Now you sure you won't be shocked?"

"I'm not shockable," I said.

"Good."

"Where's Chong and David?" I glanced around for his flatmates.

"They've gone to the stalls for prawn mee. Hey, don't worry, it won't be like the last time. I said I'll be a good boy. Follow me."

I followed Fong into his bedroom which smelt of freshly sprayed deodorant. A glossy calendar of half-dressed models hung on a wall and on a side table, next to his recharging handphone, was a row of neatly arranged combs and a tub of hair cream. In one corner stood an ironing board where a crumpled office shirt hung. Like brushing his teeth or having a shower, Fong's morning ritual would include ironing one shirt for use that day.

Fong switched off the lights.

"Hey Fong, what are you doing? You said you weren't going to ..."

"Don't worry. I don't want the monster to see us."

Fong crept across to the window and drew open a gap in the curtains. Dim light slanted into the room. He pulled a stool for me while he leaned against a cupboard.

"Why do you keep calling your neighbor a monster? You know she isn't one."

"You decide, Nancy. You see that flat over there, the one with no lights on?"

"I see it."

"Okay, go three floors down. The lights are on. You can just about see the lounge with the rosewood furniture and the Chinese scrolls on the wall. Well, the window on the left is her bedroom. The curtains are normally closed but usually around this time she ... ah, there!"

The curtains suddenly opened and, because Fong's flat was a floor or two higher, we could see right into the brightly-lit bedroom which were filled with posters and books from floor to ceiling. A shadow turned from the window. Except for the fact that she was short and seemed to have a large head, I couldn't make out anything else.

"What's the big deal, Fong?"

"Here," he said and thrust an object into my hand.

It was a set of binoculars and, with it, I turned to the window. The tower leaped at me. The binoculars were powerful and, because of its magnification, at first I couldn't find the right apartment. Then I scanned down a couple of floors and posters of the latest popstars came into view. In one corner, was a desk piled with CDs and a computer with a screen-saver showing Popeye running across the screen. Beneath the shelves of books, the woman sat cross-legged on a bed, a couple of heart-shaped cushions beside her.

I saw her face.

"Shit," I whispered.

What threw me was not the matted flat top of her head, nor the eyes that bulged like a frog's, nor her pockmarked skin, nor the puffy lips that were covered in sores, nor the fact that her shoulders were hunched right up to her ears, but rather the thing that slithered out of the back of her shorts and which she now stroked so lovingly against her chest like a baby iguana.

I turned to Fong.

"Oh shit," I said. "She's got a tail."

"What?"

"A tail! Have a look!"

Fong grabbed the binoculars from me and turned to the window. For a long while, he was silent and all I could hear was his deep breathing.

"Take it," he finally whispered as he passed the binoculars back to me.

Adjusting the focus for a better image, I looked back into the woman's bedroom.

She turned to a small television, inserted a VCD into the player, then sat on the bed and watched. A minute later, she made a face, turned it off with the remote and fell on the bed. For a second I thought she was staring back at me but no, her eyes drew upward towards the night sky and her mouth began to open and close.

This poor woman, who must have been born an unfortunate freak, who must have drawn a mutated gene from that cesspool of human DNA, who must have surely cursed the heavens, opened her windows every night to converse with the stars. And if the sky was overcast, did she talk to the clouds? And if rain came down, did she address the individual droplets that turned to puddles that stalled the vehicles on the roads or the floods that drowned those that played by the river? And what did she say? Were they curses or piteous words uttered by probably the loneliest, saddest woman in the world?

Fong was but a twisted shadow in the doorway. His silence told me that he had been badly shaken. The fact that he was biting his nails confirmed it.

"Are you okay?" I said.

"No ... I've spied on her a few times but I've never ... never seen her tail. Shit ..."

He stumbled out of the room into the corridor. I followed him into the lounge.

He plonked himself into the sofa and ran his hands over his face. "Maybe that's why I've never seen her anywhere in the condo. Not at the pool. The cafeteria. The gym. The squash courts. I always wanted to get a good look at her monster face but I've never seen her."

"Her mother must lock her in the apartment," I said.

He stared at me and as our eyes met, we both knew that this was as true as the gray concrete that held up the apartment blocks.

"You can't hide a tail like that in your clothes, can you, Nancy?"

"No, you can't."

"That poor monster."

"Fong, why do you keep calling her a monster? Yeah, she's ugly like hell but that's no big deal. A bit of care and her face might be okay. Those hunched shoulders can be worked on. But that tail ..."

"They should cut it off."

"No ..."

Even if the old lady's daughter was a freak, I still felt it was wrong to keep her locked up, for surely she had a right to wander around the pool, stroll among the KLCC crowds, eat at the stalls, enjoy the cinema with its latest mindless blockbusters, drink exorbitantly priced coffee at Starbucks and watch the world go by, but mostly to play badminton over a gate on a street full of houses with new friends. And I was determined to be one. I would not let my prejudices, my irrational fears destroy my conscience, my humanity, no matter how I might inwardly be repelled by her hideous appearance and her rat-like tail.

And they were doing wonderful things these days in the medical world. If they could split Siamese twins, surely they could sever a mere tail? Thick and glistening though it was.

Fong begged me not to go. And I would rather not have gone except that I had little choice. How could I do nothing while that poor woman languished on the bed watching VCDs and conversing with the stars, never stepping a foot out of that prison of an apartment?

So the next evening, after work, I was back at the apartments. I asked Fong to come but he refused. He made a pretense of watching some local game show on TV while playing cards with his flatmates and barely glanced at me when I stormed out the door. I went down to Block B and took the lift up. The doors opened and I stepped onto the 12th floor. A part of me wanted to leave — admonishing myself that this was none of my business. Perhaps Fong was right. Maybe I should go back to the poker game, laugh at their stupid jokes and stare stupidly at the television. But how could I let another human being suffer before my own eyes?

I'd worked out which apartment to go to and so pressed the doorbell. It took a while before I heard footsteps. The door opened ajar and out peered a white-haired woman with a pair of steel-rimmed glasses attached to a cord around her neck. She frowned as she stared at me.

"Yes?" she said.

Then I realized I didn't even know what I was going to say.

"Can I help you?" she asked in a voice I thought sounded both educated and bitter.

"I ... I ..." Then, before I could catch myself, the torrent of words rushed out. "I came here to talk to you. It's ... it's about your daughter who you keep locked in the apartment. I ... I think it's wrong. I want to talk to you about it."

Now that I'd said it, I wanted to turn and flee, back to the poker game, back behind our grilled doors where everyone minded their own business, that secure place where we hoped someone else would right the wrongs of the world, that hideout where we kid ourselves into believing that as long as we're making money, or even as long as we're earning our keep, then everything else was fine.

Instead of screaming at me though, the old woman turned pale. She bit her lip and stared at the floor.

Finally, she whispered: "Come in."

The apartment was smaller than Fong's but ten times neater. The rosewood furniture gleamed beneath the fluorescent lights. Three large scrolls with Chinese characters covered one wall. I didn't know what they said. During my schooldays my parents always put off Chinese tuition as it was too expensive.

The old woman pointed to a black leather sofa and asked me to sit down. She took a seat beside me. "What's your name?" she said.

"Nancy."

"I'm Madam Liew."

Then she leaned close to me so I could smell her faint perfume and see the talcum powder on her cheeks and the flecks of skin on her skull. She whispered: "And how do you know about Mei?"

I assumed that Mei must have been Fong's monster.

"I saw her ... from my boyfriend's apartment, over there in Block C. We used binoculars."

"So you were spying on us?" Her voice toughened and her features hardened.

"No, my boyfriend, Fong, asked me to look. I ... I just wanted to see what he was talking about. I didn't mean to spy."

"But you still spied, didn't you?"

"Yes, I did."

"And you saw something you weren't supposed to. Something strange. Something that upset you?"

I nodded.

"I keep telling her to shut the curtains at night." Madam Liew sighed and she stared at her wrinkled fingers which knotted themselves into each other. "Mei was born eighteen years ago." She looked up at me and her eyes moistened. "I was pushing so hard on the delivery table. Then when her head popped out of me and all I could see was her face, you know, that was the most wonderful moment of my life. My baby was asleep and happy, eyes closed to the world. When the last contraction came and I pushed the rest of her body out, I screamed. Not because of the pain, which was very very bad, but because as my baby fell into Dr Lim's hands, I saw a tail slither out. It flicked blood up to the ceiling. The nurse fainted and Dr Lim staggered around before he found a chair to sit down. I think he cried."

"It must have been so terrible," I said, not knowing what else to say, but conscious that I needed to say something to console the old lady.

"I was glad my husband was playing golf that afternoon. If he had been there I know he would have run out of the maternity ward screaming, because a few days later he left us. I receive a cheque every month since then but, other than that, we've never heard from him."

Tears welled up in Madam Liew's eyes and I thought she was going to weep uncontrollably. But she just wiped them with a small white handkerchief with laced edges which she kept in the pocket of her cheongsam and tried to smile.

"I'm sorry," she said. "You know we're still married. I still wear his ring. I don't know where he is or what he does. I think he has another family now somewhere else."

"Madam Liew, I want to ask you a question."

"What is it?"

"Why do you keep Mei locked up in this apartment? Why don't you ever let her go down to the pool or take her out?"

The old lady drew back and her eyes hardened. "Why do you think? Because she'll be stared at. They'll whisper. They'll laugh at her. Do you think she can take it? Do you think my little Mei can go through life with all that abuse? She's all I have!"

"Can't the doctors operate on her and ..."

"Chop off her tail? Of course, if you want to paralyze her. After Mei was born, I took her to a few doctors. But her tail, you see, it's part of her spine, part of her central nervous system, they said. If they chop it off, she won't be able to walk ..."

At this point Madam Liew began to cry.

Then, after blowing her nose into a tissue, her eyes met mine and the flinching guilt I saw buried there sent a shiver down *my* spine. It had perhaps crossed the old lady's mind, more than once, that bringing up a paralyzed child was easier than raising one with a tail.

Before the feeling of suffocating despair could completely overwhelm me, I heard a door groan and from the corridor came a voice like an old man's.

"Mother? Is there someone with you? Can ... can I come out?"

Madam Liew quickly wiped away her tears. She stared at me before turning to the corridor.

"Yes, Mei," she said. "You can come out. We have a friend visiting."

Because the corridor lights were off, I first saw a stunted wide creature, emerging from the depths of a cave. A shadow that crept forward slowly, pressing tightly against the wall, occasionally craning its thick neck forward as it turned from side to side.

"Come on, Mei," said Madam Liew. "There's nothing to be scared of. This is a friend. Her name is Nancy."

The beast stopped beneath a hanging lamp with a scalloped lampshade of stained glass and, all at once, I could see her plainly and simply beneath its warm glow. I was shown a face from a book of children's stories — the wicked witch from *Snow White*, the ogre from

Jack and the Beanstalk — combined in a gruesome yet strangely human manner and, remarkably, it was this latter resemblance that I found the most horrible. Her bulging eyes, so much larger than what I'd seen through the binoculars, twisted towards the ceiling before falling on me and her sore-covered lips crept their way upwards into a semblance of a grin.

"Hi," she said in a low guttural voice. "I'm Mei. Is your name Nancy?"

"Yes," I said, and tried to smile.

Before I could back away from this unfortunate creature, she came up to me and shook my hand. I was surprised at the touch of her skin for I expected it to be tough like leather or coarse and furry; instead it was smooth and cool to the touch. Just like a real human's ... a girl's.

What else should it have been? And what should the label say? 'Girl hand' or 'Girl's hand'? Or 'Mutated monster girl's hand'? No matter what genetic mistake had spiked her DNA, the hand was still no doubt that of a girl's.

"I'm glad to meet you, Nancy. Thank you for coming to visit me. I know we'll have so much to ..."

There was a loud slapping sound.

The thing, which she must have tried to hide in her shorts, had flopped out on the floor behind her. The tail was thick and bore the paleness of a newborn baby.

Mei stared back, she made a yowling noise and burst out crying.

Madam Liew quickly got up and embraced her. She mumbled some words in Teochew which I didn't understand. They both whimpered and it was at this point that I felt ashamed of my revulsion for Mei. She was a human being that nature had cursed. She deserved my sympathy.

As tears rolled down Mei's cheeks, her eyes met mine.

"I'm so so sorry," she said. "My tail ... I was born with it. It's grown as I have grown. I didn't want you to see it because I want you for a friend. You see, no one's ever visited me before. Now you'll just laugh or stare or lower your eyes and pretend I'm not here. Just like the awful doctors and nurses at the clinics."

"That was a long time ago," Madam Liew said. "You were only six then. Nancy's not like them. She'll be a friend even if you have a tail. Isn't that right, Nancy?"

Madam Liew turned to me and her eyes begged: *Please say YES. Even if you leave tonight and never come back, just say YES! PLEASE!!!*

"I'll be your friend, Mei," I managed to say. "Even if you have a tail."

"Really?" she gasped, wiping her tears away with the sleeves of her T-shirt. "Do you mean it?"

"Yes, Mei. I mean it."

Although I really did try to be sincere with all my heart, I had no idea how I was going to be friends with a girl with a rat's tail. What was I getting myself into? Could I get over my revulsion or would I leave tonight and never return? To her I'd just then be some woman who came to visit one night. A memory quickly erased or perhaps, just perhaps, one that is cherished to her dying day.

Mei smiled and she slumped happily beside me, the last minute no more than an unfortunate blur that was easily forgotten. She was careful though to hide her tail from my eyes. I had another glimpse of it when she edged forward excitedly in her seat and saw that the thing was at least two inches thick and four feet long.

"The sores on her lips are from allergies," Madam Liew said. "But I don't know what she's allergic to."

"Maybe from being cooped up," I said, before I could stop myself.

"Maybe you're right," said Madam Liew, to my surprise.

I had expected her to tell me to mind my own business or launch into the terrors of a world full of prejudice.

Madam Liew put on her glasses, folded her arms and sighed. "Perhaps it really is time for my Mei to take the lift down. Maybe she should see the world again and maybe the world should see her. Nancy, you coming here must have its meaning. Will you come down with us tomorrow?"

"Yes," I said. "Tomorrow's Saturday. I'll come in the morning."

"Great!" said Mei. "I haven't been down for five years. The last time was when we moved to this apartment from our terrace house in Cheras."

Madam Liew nodded. Worry and sadness enveloped her face but what I saw most in her eyes was fear. Yet for a brief second, I saw more than fear. I saw terror as she stood trembling over Mei's cot with a cushion gripped tightly in both hands and a scream of hateful sorrow caught in her throat as she watched the tiny tail curled up against a soft rattle. It would only take a minute and the promised pain in the years ahead would just dissolve into nothingness, into everlasting emptiness. I shuddered and quickly looked to the floor.

"Is everything okay, Nancy?" Mei said in a guttural voice which I now recognized as filled with concern.

"I'm okay, just a headache," I said.

"How about something to drink," offered Madam Liew, who now seemed kindly and wise. How could I ever imagine her killing her own baby?

We spent the rest of the evening chatting over soft drinks and chocolate, which Mei was hopelessly addicted to. Mei had never gone to school, instead her mother had taught her since she was three. With no place to go and no friends to meet, Mei had spent all her time reading and studying. She ended up taking dozens of correspondence courses from various universities in Europe and America. She had several degrees and was working on a research doctorate at the University of Wisconsin. Through the Internet, she had made friends all over the world, friends which she would never be in danger of meeting.

"But now I have a pal I can see and touch," she said to me.

"Yes, Mei," I said. "A real friend." But I didn't want her to touch me again. A couple of times that evening, as she shifted happily on the sofa, her T-shirt had brushed mine, but all I could feel was her tail slithering against my skin. I tried not show it but I cringed.

It was almost 11 by the time I left Mei and Madam Liew. I promised to return in the morning. As I took the lift down, I wondered if it was a promise I could keep.

I left Madam Liew's with a dark confusion like bats swarming in my head. I didn't want to go home. Instead I just wanted to be held, consoled, comforted and loved. My parents wouldn't understand — how could I tell them that I desperately wanted to help Mei, yet I also wanted to flee in revulsion and fear? They would only tell me to not get involved, as they tidied up the bicycle shop for business tomorrow. There was only Fong and he was throwing down his Kings and Aces in the next block.

When he opened the door in his white singlet and shorts, the television was mercifully off and his flatmates had gone to bed.

"I want you to make love to me," I said.

Fong's mouth fell open. Silently, he shut the door and led me to his bedroom.

We made love. Our bodies soaring like kites across the beach, just above the waves that crashed the sand. We chased each other's lips, brushed each other's skin and let death take us by the hand and only came out the other side sweaty and sighing and startled to still be alive.

I fell asleep as dawn approached, listening to Fong's deep breathing and aware of a crack of pink breaking through the carved-up hills beyond.

I may have slept for two or three hours. I touched his naked body wet with sweat like dew on barren ground.

"Good morning," I said. "You're awake?"

"For a while. I was watching you."

"Why?"

"You're beautiful."

"Don't bullshit."

"You know I saw you last night. I used the binoculars."

"Spying?"

"Just looking ... you seemed very at home with the old lady and the monster."

"Don't say that. Her name is Mei and she's only a girl. She's eighteen. I know she looks sixty and hideous but ..."

"But what?"

"But I'm going to help her ... I think."

"What?"

"Fong, we're going to take the lift down this morning. Mei is going to show herself to the world."

"You can't. She's got a tail! Everyone's going to stare or laugh or who knows what. There'll be trouble."

Up to this point, I wasn't sure if I'd go. But Fong's objection, his arrogance in the belief that he was always right, made me want to go. I looked at my watch. It was almost 9.

I jumped from the bed. "Thanks for last night," I said.

"My pleasure. So are you staying tonight?"

"Maybe," I said, helping myself to his towel as I headed for the shower. "See you later."

When I got to the apartment, Madam Liew and Mei were already waiting for me. Madam Liew was in a light blue cheongsam and Mei wore a colorful top and baggy trousers, out of which her tail sprouted.

"I've tried tying it up and hiding it in her pants," Madam Liew said. "But it keeps flopping out. And if I coil the thing too tightly, it's too painful and Mei cries."

"Let's go down," Mei said. "I can't bear all this waiting. I'm excited and scared and who knows what else ... But if I don't go down, I'll never know."

"That's right," Madam Liew said. "You'll never know until you go down. I've kept you cooped up here for so long. It wasn't until Nancy came to visit last night that it truly hit me. Life is down there, it's not in the books or that computer of yours. It's time you really found out about it. Good or bad."

"Okay then," I said. "Let's go." I tried to contain the tightness in my stomach, like a hundred worms coiling in my guts, as I turned to the front door. I knew that if we didn't go now, I would flee and never return.

So we entered the lift and as it took us down I had the ugly feeling that my life was being torn away from me. Everything was going to change. And what would greet us out there in the big bad world? How would

Mei cope? How would I cope? Why, oh why, did I get involved? Before I could fortify myself, the lift, like a birdcage strung up in the trees, suddenly opened.

Madam Liew sighed, glanced back at me and then stepped out into the heat.

Mei followed and then myself. I tried not to look at the appendage that slid along the tiled floor but as it meandered like a sea serpent, my eyes became fixed upon its glistening skin.

The sun was beating down on the terrace and the water sparkled blue and, as it was a weekend, the pool was full of children laughing and splashing while servants and parents watched from the shade of the mildewed umbrellas.

Madam Liew followed a route, which I was sure she had meticulously planned, that took us as far as possible from the boisterous activity. We went past half-dead palm trees and low hedges, the cafeteria serving a nasi lemak breakfast, the towels and T-shirts hung on the plastic chairs, the slippers cluttered on the crisscross paving, and all the while my mouth became drier and drier and I felt a pressing need to urinate.

Just as we slid past the gloomy-looking gym, devoid of equipment, I noticed that a hefty silence had fallen over the pool. It felt like a hundred eyes were upon us. Or rather, on Mei and the flesh and bone trailing behind her.

"I want to see!" a little boy cried, his shrill voice echoing between the concrete towers.

I looked up and thought the sky was going to fall on us.

Like a giant octopus dragging itself to shore, there came the slapping sound of wet feet. Bodies, dripping with water, emerged, tentatively to begin with, but this was short-lived as they elbowed each other to scramble over to us first. Within seconds, we were surrounded by a crowd of wet bodies and gawking eyes with their parents and servants close behind.

A little girl squealed. "Why has she got a tail?" she asked as she clung to her mother who said nothing but stared open-mouthed. "I want a tail too! Mummy, I want a tail!"

"Ugly woman! Ugly woman!" a toddler cried.

The adults, who must have suddenly become overwhelmed by curiosity, pushed the children out of the way, leaving them screaming and crying to see more. This was better than a collection of blond-haired Barbie dolls, better than blowing up aliens on PlayStation 2, better than any profit-maximizing product the toy industry could ever dream up. A live freak show at the swimming pool.

A bald-headed man with glasses and a folded copy of the *Sin Chew Jit Poh* under one arm crouched down to examine the tail. An Indian man, holding a badminton racket, joined him and shook his head in awe. There was a flash of light and a Malay woman in a tudung with a camera in her hands grinned sheepishly.

Madam Liew attempted to block the crowd and Mei pulled her limb out of sight but the children and adults were already swarming all around her.

"Go away!" I yelled at the crowd. "Can't you people mind your bloody own business!"

But they edged closer with their disbelieving frowns, their pursed lips and greedy eyes, hands scratching their heads. They whispered and muttered and exclaimed.

"Owwww!" screamed Mei.

A boy of eight or nine, in swimming trunks and a Power Rangers T-shirt, grinned mischievously — his foot still on her tail.

I pushed him away and let loose a stream of Cantonese obscenities.

Mei knelt on the ground sobbing, clutching her appendage as Madam Liew held her, their bodies shivering.

"Don't touch my son!" a woman shouted at me, waving a video cassette as though it was a knife. "That freak doesn't belong here!"

"Yah lah!" a man yelled. "She's a bad omen. Bad luck for all of us!"

"She'll make us all sick, isn't it?" a young woman in a yellow blouse added, holding her plastic handbag to her chest. "A devil! She's a devil!"

"That's right! A devil!" another woman in sunglasses yelled, before bending over and spitting into Mei's face.

"A devil! A devil! A devil!" rang other voices.

A bald youth in a Tommy Hilfiger sweat-shirt shoved me backwards, his face a mixture of excitement and fear.

The crowd closed in.

They were now chanting. Eyes deliriously wide.

I grabbed Mei and Madam Liew. "We better go," I cried.

The route to the apartment was blocked by the crowd.

"This way," I yelled. I dragged Madam Liew and Mei through the lobby of the apartment complex, down the steps and through the car park, past the guardhouse and onto the main road with its whizzing cars, throwing hot dust around. All the while, the crowd followed, punching their fists in the air and chanting: "A devil! A devil! A devil!"

This was when Mei, sobbing and babbling, and not looking where she was going, tripped over her tail and fell into a monsoon drain.

There was a single, dreadful scream.

Sinseh Tai enjoyed humming along to the Chinese opera blaring from the speakers of his battered Toyota, and people stared when it rumbled by. Not only did he have a brown toy monkey clutching with its plastic suckers to a rear passenger window but his was also one of the few vehicles in the city without air con. This morning he was on his way to his herbal store in Jalan Petaling when, together with the stream of impatient cars behind him, he found his Toyota blocked by the crowd. To the sound of rampant honking, he jumped on the road and rushed to see what had happened.

As he was first on the scene, I pleaded for his help. Shaking his bald head and muttering something about getting his trousers dirty, he eased himself into the drain and, with me pulling from above and he pushing from below, we managed to drag a hysterical Mei out. The mob converged on her as she lay sobbing and bleeding on the grass. Then they started to hurl abuse at the four of us. Sinseh Tai's face went pale. One of them threw a slipper at Mei. It hit her head. She screamed and told them to go to hell.

Sinseh Tai pointed to his car and, in a stuttering voice, asked us to get in. We rushed to it and, when we had taken our seats on the hot plastic, he turned it around, honked at the crowd and sped us away. I looked back at the mob, which somehow seemed less human and more like a pack of frightened boars.

He took us to his narrow shop which not only sold herbs and dangling dried seahorses but also doubled as a foot reflexology clinic and the concoction of smells was evil and good and quite insane. He ushered us into a private room with a large poster of a human's organs, meridians and energy points and poured us Chinese tea from a teapot with a cracked blue lid.

Later, after he had placed antiseptic cream on the wound and wrapped a bandage around Mei's head, he stared at her tail as though it was just another medical problem. Up to this point, he had not mentioned the pale limb, yet alone looked at it.

"I can cure that," he uttered as he stared through the thick lenses of his aquarium-like glasses, before picking the tail up with one hand and sniffing at it as though it was an exotic dish he was about to eat. "If you let me, I can prepare a special ointment and bandage the thing up."

Madam Liew said yes straightaway. What was there to lose? She was willing to give it a go. After what happened this morning she was willing to try anything. She looked at me as if wanting my approval. I nodded over my cup of steaming tea. I was still shaken over the commotion but the hope of perhaps helping Mei lightened my spirit.

I helped Mei and Madam Liew move to a house in Bandar Utama. For the next two months, Madam Liew diligently attended to Mei as instructed by Sinseh Tai, with hours spent removing the bandage from the tail, rubbing the ointment up and down its smooth skin and rewrapping it with a fresh dressing. During this period, I would visit Mei at least twice a week. We would talk, watch television, discuss books, surf the web, even wrote a poem together and a snippet of a song. With the tail all wrapped up and hidden from view, I no longer had the same revulsion for her. It was like a plaster over a weeping sore, hiding the ugly wound and the fear of it.

It was towards the end of those two months that Mei was laid in bed with a fever. Her face had turned a bright red and her sheets were soaked in sweat. Madam Liew wanted to take her to the Policlinic around the corner but Sinseh Tai said no and instead gave her a cold herb drink and a foot massage. The fever was part of the cure and he was proved right. Three days later, while Mei huddled in the corner of her bedroom shivering so frightfully that I thought her body might explode and send blood and bone everywhere, the tail which was still wrapped in a bandage fell off and slithered like a dying lizard under the bed. None of us dared retrieve the thing because of its sporadic twitching as though it was trying to cling on to life. When the tail had finally stopped moving, Sinseh Tai buried it in the garden.

Now that the fever had broken, Mei looked up at me and said: "Never again will I have a tail. Never!"

This was the start of Mei's meteoric rise. With no such appendage to hold her back, Madam Liew took her to a plastic surgeon to improve her hideous appearance. Luck was with her, for the plastic surgeon said that Mei's facial bone structure was indeed promising and her features when worked on individually would combine perfectly and would create a creature that was so beautiful that people would cry on seeing her beauty. Those were his words and I thought he was exaggerating. Madam Liew too was most skeptical until a few days later when the bandages around her face came off to reveal a woman who took my very breath away. Madam Liew and I both wept as we knelt beside the hospital bed.

We found out that Mei was allergic to chocolate and with that banished from her diet, the sores around her lips disappeared and, to our surprise, her voice reverted not only to that of a normal girl's but one that was truly a pleasure to hear. "Like that of a canary released from a cage," were the words Sinseh Tai used. By sticking to a Fit for Life diet and jogging every morning with a stick she used to scare the dogs away, she began to lose weight. Her bad posture and hunched shoulders were worked on by a physiotherapist and within six months, and with a new hairstyle, she carried herself as confidently and elegantly like a model down the catwalk.

When I went with her to the shopping complexes to look for clothes, not only did all the men stare open-mouthed at her, but so did most women. She was simply stunning. And the green of envy was the color of the day.

Up until now, Fong wanted nothing to do with Mei. To him, she was once a freak and would always remain a freak. "I never want to meet her," he declared even after I told him about how she'd lost her tail and how she was now beautiful not only on the inside but outside too. But I persisted because Fong was my boyfriend who one day I would marry and Mei was my best friend and surely my two worlds should meet? So one day, after Chinese New Year we had lunch at KFC and I was delighted to see how Fong's mouth fell wide open when I introduced them. The Mei who was sitting in the booth waiting for us bore no resemblance to the monster he had seen through the binoculars. Fong was charmed and I was delighted that we could all be friends.

A few weeks after Hari Raya, Mei came to my house with a letter clutched in one quivering hand. She had been to an interview and was offered a marketing job with a European multinational. I was not surprised for Mei was not only a walking encyclopedia but also had an IQ of 180. I had to drum these facts into her head and after a few hours she left my house confident that she could easily do the work the company expected of her. I was glad. Now she could reap the rewards of all the studying she'd done in those years of solitude high up in that prison of an apartment.

Because of the long hours she worked, I began to see little of Mei. As Chinese New Year rolled around again, I telephoned her and she was thrilled to tell me she'd been promoted twice, was earning a good salary and was traveling around the region on business. Then, after some hesitation which I assumed was due to shyness, she said that she had found a boyfriend. I was thrilled. She agreed to bring him over to my house over the holiday period so that I could meet the lucky guy but, after watching two movies on HBO and trying numerous times to get her on her handphone, I decided that perhaps Mei had forgotten.

One day in a Guardian pharmacy, during my lunch break, I was flipping through the pages of the *Malaysia Tatler* when I saw her photo. I dropped the magazine and everyone stared at me. I quickly paid for the thing, sat in my car and screamed when I couldn't find the right page. Finally, I found it and wept. Mei was at a gala dinner for a charity for homeless children and standing next to her was Fong!

Fong who was supposed to be away in Myanmar for three months setting up an office for the finance company he worked for. I tried to telephone Mei but her secretary said she was in a meeting. I rushed over to Fong's condo but his flatmate, David, who was most apologetic, said that he had moved out a month earlier.

He knew Fong was seeing Mei behind my back and he had covered up for Fong many times. Then David said that he found me attractive and wanted to go out with me. He tried to hug me but I told him to go to hell and rushed out of the apartment.

I spent the next couple of months trying to telephone Mei and Fong but could never get hold of either of them. I didn't know any of Mei's new telephone numbers and Fong seemed to have just disappeared. I didn't know what I would say to them anyway. Perhaps I just wanted to know why. Perhaps I just wanted to understand. Perhaps I just wanted to scream and wail and ask Fong to come back to me. Didn't he say that Mei was once a freak and would always be a freak? No. To me she was once a monster and was still a monster. She had taken Fong away from me. My so-called friend had betrayed me.

The only place I saw her now was in the pages of the *Tatler* and Fong was always by her side, smiling and confident in his flashy clothes and a new greased-back hairstyle. As for Mei, the snob, the treacherous bitch, who must have been earning a packet, wore such finery and looked so happy that I wanted to scream until my lungs burst.

Mei and Fong were married six and a half months later. In spite of the rigors of her employment, in spite of the party circuit of fake smiles and tinkling cocktailed laughter, Mei managed to finish her doctorate and was, remarkably, commencing a new one at Oxford. Her three children were born in the UK where Fong had found a job with an insurance company with businesses in Asia. The last I heard was that she worked in a senior position in health management for the United Nations, where she was doing work in India.

Mei and Fong had by this time become staunch Christians and had started a retreat near Lumut, one of several throughout the world. I followed her success in *The Star*, the *NST* and on the Internet where her website had thousands of visitors a day. She had written three books — one on health management, one on leading a spiritual life and one enigmatically called *How to Make millions So You Can Give It All Away*. They were all bestsellers and translated into several languages.

During this time, I had send her cards, letters of congratulations and countless email messages. I never once mentioned Fong or called her a bloody whore. She replied once, in the form of a postcard, to say that she would call me the next time she was in KL so that we could meet up for lunch. Not surprisingly, she never did.

As for myself, I never made sales manager and was, in fact, fired when I screamed abuse at a prospective client. I had also fought with every one of my colleagues. I couldn't seem to let go of the anger. I drifted from job to job and ended up looking after my father's dingy bicycle shop.

So, as the years passed, I tried to forget about Mei and the man she stole from me and concentrated on spokes, chains, pedals, handlebars and reflectors, all the time wondering what had happened to the life I'd dreamt of. Then, around the time of my forty-second birthday, which would have made Mei about thirty-eight, I received a phone call.

"It's me," said a voice.

Even though we hadn't spoken for almost twenty years, I knew straightaway that it was Mei. I also knew, from the guttural sound of her voice, that something was wrong.

Mei was staying at a cheap hotel in Bukit Bintang. I took the lift up and found her room.

I tapped on the door and, after a few seconds, it opened a crack and I saw a shadow watching me from the cave-like darkness and I heard low muffled breathing like someone in pain or in labor. Then, after a moment, it opened fully.

For a second, I thought I was staring at Madam Liew, twenty years older and leaning sickly against the door frame, for the face that hung there was sagging and covered in clutches of straggling white hair and the body was hunched and bloated. But it wasn't Madam Liew. She had been coerced into a nursing home years ago where I once visited her among the puddles of urine, shit-smelling sheets and the wretched dog-like faces of its nurses. I told Madam Liew I would return but I promised myself never to go again.

As I stood by the door, I recognized the eyes that stared. They were Mei's. And the trembling sore-covered lips could not have belonged to anyone else.

She was a wretched creature now: a mummy with its bandages ripped open, a zombie stumbling through the swamp. It was as if some sadistic plastic surgeon had cut up Mei's beautiful face to make her as gruesome as possible.

Mei grabbed my hand.

With crusted sweaty fingers, she pulled me into a dark and drably furnished room with the curtains shut and a television blaring some product with free gifts of crockery. On the carpet was a box of half-eaten Nestlé chocolates. Two other empty chocolate boxes lay beside it.

The place was hot and Mei smelt of sweat and old urine.

"Look at me!" she said, tears welling around her bulging eyes. They spilt down her coarse cheeks. The Mei I met twenty years ago was hideous. This creature was even more repulsive.

"Mei, how did it go wrong? How have you ..."

"Lost everything? My looks, Fong, my children, my life? I'll show you."

She reached behind her and held up what looked like a dead iguana. She dropped the tail, fell on the bed, buried her face in a pillow and bawled.

At first the pale thing lay unmoving, then it throbbed and began to slither among the tattered white sheets sluggishly as if lazily looking for food.

What if the thing fell off, strangled me and swallowed me whole? But no, it would not because it had already feasted on Mei. Her spirit and faith had all been devoured.

I turned from the bed. I drew the curtains open, which revealed the mess: newspapers, magazines and empty packets of tidbits and sweets on the carpet, half-drunk glasses of soft drinks and wine on the table, one shoe and sock in a corner.

I eased into a creaky rattan chair and stared at my old friend.

"It just grew!" she cried as she thumped the pillow. "A month ago, I found a lump just above my backside. The doctors didn't know what it was but after a few days it was three inches long. A week later it was over a foot long. It just grew and grew!"

"But Mei ... why has it grown back?"

"I don't know, Nancy! I just don't know!"

"What about Sinseh Tai?"

"He's long dead. A lorry smashed into his Toyota on his way to Singapore."

I said nothing.

"What ... what do I do now?" she wailed. "I have no one! You have to help me ... you're the only one that wanted to help me. You're my one true friend. My dearest friend!"

I went to the bed and pushed my face an inch from her pockmarked nose. I could smell her fear and desperation.

"No," I whispered. "No ... no ... no ...."

I turned away, pushed open the sliding door and stepped out onto the balcony, glad to get away from the stink and heat.

Below me, cars and motorcycles, like miniature toys, plied the roads as they hummed and buzzed like angry bees. The apartment building beside us, dotted with air-con compressors and satellite dishes all blackening in the humid heat, stood empty. The skyline, filled with office towers, were a washed-out gray.

"What ... what do you mean, Nancy?" cried Mei from the bed. "What do you mean by 'no'?"

I said nothing but continued staring at the skyscrapers.

When I turned to face her, she was sitting up in bed, staring at the television where a Cantonese serial continued its ritual blaring about loss and abandonment.

"Come here," I finally said.

Mei got up and hobbled over to me, her tail slithering out of her shorts, leaving a wet trail on the carpet.

Mei stood barefooted on the balcony saying nothing, her eyes on the limestone hills in the distance. Part of me wanted to cry but I stood my ground up here on the fifteenth floor and cursed the very air I breathed.

I looked down at the road. It seemed so far away that perhaps it wasn't really there. It could have just been a photo or an image thrown up by a wide-screen television. Mei followed my eyes.

I turned to her and stroked her withering hair, the rough warmth of her cheek. Strands of hair came off in my hand.

"Jump," I whispered.

"What?"

"Jump!"

I grabbed her by the chin and stared into her crumbling face. "Mei, there's nothing left for you. You've enjoyed life and lapped it all up while I suffered all these years! Now you've got your tail back and there's nothing else for you!"

"Nancy ... but you're ... you're my friend! I'm sorry about Fong, I didn't mean ... it just, just happened ... I'm so sorry ..."

"Go to hell," I whispered. "Now jump."

"Nancy," she whispered.

I turned away and strode back into the hotel room. As I closed the door, I saw to my satisfaction that Mei was climbing the rails.

By the time the lift had taken me down fifteen floors to the narrow lobby, a gawking crowd had gathered on the street.

Days have passed and the dream keeps recurring. Mei's tail slipping downward, her body plummeting, arms flailing as though swimming through the air, the soft thud on the road below and the blood trickling from her broken skull. And I, running and screaming into the bathroom.

Above the free bottles of hotel shampoo, conditioner and body lotion, neatly lined up, I stare into the mirror and find two cartilaginous lumps have grown on my head, peeking from my tufts of hair, and, although fascinated at first, I whimper when they turn out to be horns like those of a wounded bull.

I've read somewhere — maybe *Times* or *Newsweek* — or heard somewhere — maybe CNN or ntv7 — that cancer is contagious, yet I need no scientific evidence, not from the Discovery Channel or any other broadcast — to know that betrayal is infectious.

Every morning, when I sweatily wake from this fetid dream, before brushing my teeth, before I even urinate the Tiger beers I gulped from the night before just to help me sleep, I run my fingers over my scalp to feel for the twin lumps. As I lay slumped on the desk at the shop, I can't see them nor touch the despicable mounds with the tips of my fingers but they are indeed there, sharpening and thickening as they grow in length, as real as Mei's slithering tail.

I look out for horns on the heads of people who bring their bicycles in for repair, on the shoppers who use the toilets where blank-faced headscarf-wearing women collect coins and issue tickets among the dark puddles of water. I search for the horn-headed humans in office buildings, their security cards dangling like leashes around their necks as they mingle by the lifts in herds. I wait for them among the plastic chairs of the cafeteria as they graze on their nasi lemak, fried noodles, nasi padang, teh tarik and discuss the latest sitcoms or the moving averages of the stock market. I seek them in their cars as they crawl the jammed-up highways and pot-holed neighborhood roads, using their Internet-enabled handphones to tell their loved ones they'll be late again, while above them the sky turns to dust.

These horns I bear are real if you look hard enough. We all have them jutting from our heads, for who has not betrayed? If not a friend then at least our own conscience, that irksome flame that flickers in that murky screwed-up depths of our hearts. So tell me, who has not betrayed? And betrayal, how it has ravaged us.

WATCHING THE DOLL

Supposing you were to know the horrible meaning behind that piece of wood, the long arms, lanky legs, oversized head, big eyes — that doll sitting in my living room shelf, peering from above, thin lips set in a grin. Recently sleep hasn't been coming my way, so I would leave my wife and two kids upstairs, creep down the stairs in my shorts and T-shirt and light a cigarette. I would sit by its amber glow watching the doll, watching me. Outside would be a dog howling or a noisy scooter, shooting past. Sometimes in the old musty armchair, when hours have crept past and I'm on the verge of sleep, I swear I see its fingers moving gracefully, delicately in the half-light.

The story. It was back in May 1997. The relentless heat poured itself like lava upon the rooftops of the terraced houses packed tightly together on a street with too much concrete, bitumen and Protons and just a few scraggly trees to count as landscaping.

There was Fakir, my oh-so-noble cousin. He was going to be a doctor, he was going to be the Mahatma Gandhi of KL, Mr Non-Violence, Brother Compassion. Twenty-one and already a pompous piece of shit.

One day, quite by accident, I stumbled across him at the mamak stall, stuffing his lean face with roti canai and dhal beneath a huge fluorescent blue umbrella. I caught him quite unawares for his attention was on his food and nothing was going to get in the way of the ghee-laced bread and his ever-welcoming stomach which never seemed to grow rounder. So I ambled up to the stall and plonked myself down in front of him.

"Oi, Fakir, you must be hungry," I said. "We only had fried eggs an hour ago, cooked by Mak." We all called my mother "Mak".

"Oh, it's you, the Struggling Auditor ... I'll be with you in a minute, let me finish this first." I didn't appreciate the reference to my mind-numbing vocation or the many long hours I put in, especially at the ridiculous hourly rate, if you worked it out. Fakir turned to the mamak and ordered a kopi-O. "Would you like something to drink?"

I shook my head. "Tell me where the money went."

"Why are you blaming me? You think I stole it? Why don't you look at yourself first before you go around casting aspersions."

"Hey, don't lie. I saw you in Yusof's room last night. You were rummaging around his desk."

"So what, Mr Trainee Auditor, that doesn't mean I took the forty ringgit. I was looking for a pen to write with."

I slammed my fist on the red plastic table. The mamak jumped back in fright, his white mustache bouncing lightly in the hot sunshine. "Don't you lie, Fakir. There are so many pens on the dining table. You didn't even own up to being in my brother's room, you just sat there on the chair looking dumb and stupid!"

Fakir jumped out of his chair and with a finger that trembled in front of my face, told me to go to hell.

He told me a lot of other things which I don't care to mention right now but all I can say is that the mamak had a most disgusted look on his face and I sat there certain Fakir had taken the money.

The next day, I was sitting in our terraced house with a cup of coffee watching the afternoon Malay serial (pretty girl meets handsome boy, parents don't approve, you know the type of show) when Fakir came in dressed in black shorts and a collared T-shirt. He seemed so thin, the wind could bowl him over.

"Is it true that Yusof only lost forty ringgit?"

"Well, isn't that enough?" I said. "Or do you regret not taking *all* the money?"

"Hey, look, it wasn't me, I keep telling you."

"Fakir, I can't prove it, okay? You and I know what's true. So we will leave it at that."

I had no intention of leaving it at that but there wasn't much I could do now. I would just have to keep my eyes closely on Fakir and hopefully catch him in the act one of these days. I hadn't told Mak. She wouldn't believe me for Fakir was her brother's son. His mother had passed away when he was very young and his father died in a car accident six years ago when Fakir was only fifteen. So Fakir came to stay with us and Mak treated him very well, even better than Yusof or myself, her real children. If only she knew what a damn thief Fakir was.

Beyond our metal front gate, a couple of cars passed, and a boy with a bright red baseball cap cycled idly by. Fakir lightly sat down next to me on the sofa much to my surprise. Before I could get up and leave in disgust, he turned to my direction.

"I know you hate me," he said.

"I don't," I said. "You're just such a ..." I didn't finish my sentence but looked up at the ever-revolving fan.

"I know who took it," he said.

"Don't joke with me, Fakir."

"I really do, listen to me."

"Okay, tell me then. Tell me who took it if it wasn't you."

"When I was at school this morning, I spoke to a couple of friends. I told them about the missing forty ringgit. They asked if all the money was missing and I said no, there was another forty which wasn't stolen. They were both quiet for a while, then one of them mentioned the word toyol."

"What do you mean toyol?"

"You know toyol. The doll bred by some Malays, the doll that comes alive at night and enters people's houses stealing money, but always leaving half behind."

"What a load of rubbish!" I said. "So if I had a fifty-ringgit note, it would leave twenty-five ringgit in change."

Fakir nodded. "Yes, it would. It would."

"You don't honestly believe this rubbish, do you? We're in the middle of the most rapidly developing city in the world and you're giving me this old wives' tale from the kampung."

"Look, it's true. I know." Fakir was looking at me so intensely that I believed Fakir had no doubts of the existence of the supernatural doll.

"How do you know?" I asked, taking the remote and switching off the television. The pretty girl and handsome boy were just about to discover they were brother and sister.

"That night when Yusof's money went missing, I was in bed when I heard the window being opened. I crept out of bed and opened the bedroom door. The corridor was dark except for a shaft of streetlight shining on the wall. Then I saw a dark shadow, jumping noiselessly from the window. It ran without a sound down the corridor. And I swear as it ran past the light shining from the street I saw the eyes. They were big and round, there was a button for a nose and crooked dark thread for the mouth. The hair was made of bits of string and there were no ears. This ... this *thing* was not more than two feet in height. Saw it all in a split second. Then Yusof's door opened and quickly closed. I was standing alone in the dark corridor wondering if I imagined the whole thing. Everything was quiet. The window I thought had been opened was firmly closed. I decided I'd been dreaming. In a daze I went back to bed. It was only when my friends mentioned toyol did the dream come back to me. I know now it was no dream."

I gazed at Fakir for a long time and finally decided that he *thought* he was telling the truth. He stared back miserably at me and suddenly he didn't seem like such a pompous piece of shit, maybe he didn't even take the money.

Then his eyes widened. I had no inkling of his thoughts until he said: "Let us catch this toyol!"

Fakir had told Yusof and Yusof, my foolish brother, instantly believed the story, that a supernatural doll had stolen his money. They excitedly told me their plans which they executed with great fervor, spending the day bragging, telling all the shopkeepers and everyone else that Fakir had been given three hundred ringgit cash by a grand uncle. These two clowns could hardly eat dinner that night. When Mak asked them what the matter was, they said they weren't hungry. Mak seemed a bit sulky afterward, perhaps thinking they didn't like her food. For me, I ate heartily, participating only to humor them. I didn't believe in such things, my cousin and younger brother were both twenty-one and I couldn't understand how two adults could believe in the supernatural; the toyol, along with the orang minyak and pontianak, were part of their everyday life.

Movies taught them a great deal. Excitedly, Yusof and Fakir placed what looked like a bundle of ten-ringgit notes on Fakir's desk. In fact, it was a stack of paper cut in the size of ten-ringgit notes with the real ringgit notes at the front and back. I taunted, saying the toyol probably watched the same movies they did.

At about 10 in the evening, Mak went to bed. Since about a year ago she had taken to sleeping downstairs — saying that she was too old to climb up and down the long flights of stairs. The three of us sat cross-legged on the floor of my room on the first floor. The air conditioner blew cool air over us, some of it was escaping into the corridor.

"Who do you think is keeping this toyol?" I asked in jest.

"Could be anyone," Fakir said, his thin face all serious. "Anyone who has the knowledge."

"People from the kampung know about these things," added Yusof. "They place the doll in miniature houses on the roofs of their kampung homes, this is how they keep them. They chant magic spells and give the dolls special food so that the doll will work for them."

"Like slaves," said Fakir.

"Yeah, just like slaves," agreed Yusof. "I'd hate to be a slave, toiling for your master with no pay or gratitude, doing everything that's asked without question."

"Sounds like any normal employee," I said with a grin. "Yes sir, no sir, three bags full sir. Ask me to jump and I'll say, *How high*?"

"The doll will do its master's bidding without question," Yusof said to Fakir, ignoring me. "It's completely obedient, it'll steal from whoever its master orders to steal from. I've heard there's this Datuk in our area who keeps a toyol, he lives in a huge house and drives a big Mercedes-Benz — that car costs more than two bungalows. He doesn't even work, he just sends out his doll to steal money."

"Like everyone else in KL," I quipped.

"Ha, ha," said Yusof sarcastically.

"Well, let's go find this Datuk then," said Fakir. "I'll tell him to give back your forty ringgit."

"You're nuts," said Yusof. "He's not going to give the money back. He won't admit to anything. Anyway, this city is full of Datuks who live in huge houses with Mercedes-Benzes costing more than two bungalows. We'll just have to catch the doll ourselves."

"So, how are we going to catch it?" I asked. The guys were going to be disappointed when nothing turned up but a rat and several curious cicak.

"We'll throw a blanket over it," said Fakir eagerly. "Bundle it up in a blanket and then tie it up."

"Yeah," agreed Yusof. "It won't come stealing again, from me or anyone else."

"It's time for bed, I think," I said with a yawn. "It's getting late." This toyol stuff was getting ludicrous.

Yusof opened my room door a crack to give us a view of the small window and the door to Fakir's room. Yusof took first watch, next Fakir, then myself. We agreed on an hourly watch.

At about 1 in the morning, Fakir woke me up. It was my turn to stand watch. I rubbed my eyes and yawned. I regretted agreeing to go along with the scheme. It was a lot of trouble to prove Fakir wrong. *It would be over in the morning*, I reassured myself. Fakir would have to admit that it was nothing more than a dream.

I sat beside the doorway leaning against the wall. Fakir and Yusof were lightly breathing, both of them asleep on mattresses. This really was a lot of bother. I was tempted to go back to bed and in the morning just laugh at both of them as I waved the fake wad of money in their faces.

I was turning this possibility in my mind when over the soft hum of the air conditioner, I heard a dog howling in the distance. It was a low moaning as if the animal was in anguish or pain. I listened closely but the sound did not repeat itself. Instead, the familiar and annoying sound of a revved-up scooter tore up the quiet night. Some guy heading home after a date perhaps. Wish he didn't have to wake up the whole neighborhood though.

I looked at my watch — 1:20, the digital read-out said, forty minutes to go and then I'd wake Yusof. Or should I even bother? I stifled a yawn and then heard it. Almost missed it.

A soft tapping. Like wooden wind chimes.

What was it? It couldn't be an animal, an animal would make a brushing, scampering sound, this was a tapping.

There, the sound again.

Louder this time. Irregular in its rhythm. Wood tapping on concrete. On *bricks*. Shit, something was coming up the wall outside!

Climbing.

I was sure of it.

"Something's coming," I whispered to Fakir and Yusof as I pushed and poked at them. Finally, they stirred, dragging themselves off the mattresses. "It's climbing up the wall outside the house."

I rushed to the door but saw nothing, just the corridor leading to the two other rooms, the streetlamp outside throwing a misshaped rectangular light on the wall.

Yusof and Fakir joined me, peering out the door.

"What did you hear?" Fakir asked.

"Shhhh ..." I said putting my finger to my lips. "Just listen."

There it was. The wood tapping, much louder this time as if it was in the next room.

"What is it?" whispered Yusof.

I shook my head.

"I'm sure it ..." Fakir didn't finish his sentence for there was another sound.

The deep groaning of a window being slowly and carefully opened.

And, this I swear, by the shafting light of the streetlamp, we saw a small, thin shadow coming through the window of the corridor. Its movements were awkward and it leaped noiselessly into the corridor. It was not more than two feet tall, creeping cautiously along the wall. The arms and legs seemed disproportionate and long compared to the body; the head was big, the size of a sepak takraw ball.

The creature, the monster, the doll, the whatever, stepped into the shaft of light. I held my breath. This was no dream. The toyol was as Fakir had described — big, round eyes, a button for a nose, crooked dark thread for the mouth, hair made from bits of string, no ears.

The door was shoved open and Fakir and Yusof were running into the corridor, shouting. The doll spun in their direction but before it could do anything, they flung the blanket over it. There was a mewing-like cry. It raised its arms as if to catch it but finally the doll just collapsed in a heap.

I joined them, flinging myself like a rugby player at the struggling thing caught within the blanket. There followed a muffled, cracking, splintering sound.

Yusof turned on the light. A rush of sanity came back to us. I was lying on the parquet floor. Fakir pulled the blanket away.

And there it was.

Sitting.

Damn it, sitting coquettishly, leaning against the wall. Its decapitated head on the floor, round eyes innocently looking up at us. One arm hung loosely by its side, broken in two places.

I'm not dead yet, it said in a high-pitched musical voice.

"Oh shit," Fakir said.

Yusof screamed and they both ran down the stairs.

And before I could move, the toyol stretched out its uninjured arm and grabbed its wooden head. I watched in horror and fascination as it screwed the head back on, the thing making three or four revolutions before grinning at me.

I hate working for him, the toyol said; the big round eyes were intense, full of quivering intelligence. *Hate stealing, stealing and stealing.*

The front door slammed, the gate creaked open and running footsteps echoed down the street. I knew Fakir was a piece of shit, taking Yusof and leaving me to die up here. The cowards. With my elbows and on my back I pushed myself trying to get away from the thing. I couldn't get far for my head met the corridor wall. I cried in both pain and fear.

Like banging your head on a brick wall, isn't it? it said.

"What do you mean?" My voice was hoarse, my throat like sandpaper. My heart a loud drum beating in my head.

Life. Full of bullshit. So damn hard to get by. Aren't I right?

"Eh ... if you say so."

I say so and I'm right. Why don't you take over?

"What do you mean?"

Be the Boss Man. Keep me for yourself. I'll steal for you.

"I don't want you to steal."

Why Boss Man? Stealing will make you rich — filthy, dirty rich!

"Stealing is wrong!"

Come on, don't be naive. Everyone steals, part of life. Corporate crooks, corrupt politicians. You name it, they're stealing.

"Not everyone steals. I don't want to own you, I don't want to be your Boss Man. I don't want to steal and I don't want you to steal. It's wrong!"

You really believe this? I didn't think anyone did. Then, my friend, you can set me free. I'll run into the jungle, you'll never see me again.

"And you'll never ever steal."

Never again. I'll live amongst the birds and trees — smell the blossoming flowers, dance with the butterflies. I will be totally free, to live my life for me and no one else!

"But ... but how do I set you free?"

Easy. Just repeat these words. I saw him write them in his book. I memorized them for a time like this. Hoping, always hoping I would be caught, and caught by someone righteous, someone who would not take advantage of me.

There was a look of great sorrow in its large, round eyes, the thread of a mouth curved downwards, the bits of string masquerading as hair fell just above the painted eyebrows. The wooden pieces it was made of were worn, old, with splinters here and there. The doll was neither a *he* nor *she*. *It* was the right word, but it wasn't a *thing*, it had a soul, it wanted to be free.

"I'll set you free," I said impulsively.

A bright light shone from its face. It was glowing with happiness.

Are you sure?

"Yes, I said I would — I'll set you free."

Thank you, thank you ... all you have to do is repeat these words after me.

I repeated the words, some familiar, others strange, neither Arabic nor Malay, they seemed ancient. When I was done, it seemed a cold wind swept down the corridor, and my hair flew in my face.

Thank you ... thank you, sir, it said, smiling and nodding.

There followed a sudden crack. The doll splintered, collapsing onto itself, falling in a ragged heap, legs and arms poking in impossible angles; the head slowly rolled down the body like a bowling ball coming to rest with a thud by my leg, eyes looking up at me, a serene smile on its face.

The toyol was dead. Did it know this was going to happen? Or did it expect to roam with the birds, trees, butterflies and flowers? It surely would not have killed itself ... surely not. But that smile said it knew.

The doll was created to steal. It lived to steal. Theft was in every grain of wood, every blink of its big round eyes. Once that deed could no longer be performed then it had no reason to live. But still in death, there should be a place for it to go to, some place where its soul could mingle with the birds, trees, butterflies and flowers. Some place for a toyol that didn't want to steal. I carefully gathered the pieces and put them in a box.

Years later, when I found the courage, I put the pieces back together and placed it in my living room. And if I'm ever asked about it, all I do is smile serenely. Yusof and Fakir asked what happened, I told them the truth. There is no point in lying for it's just like stealing. Stealing the truth.

So I sit beneath the fan on an old musty armchair watching the doll, listening for the cock's crow, but there is just the distant honking of Protons and revved-up scooters as they slip off to work just before dawn — to miss the inevitable traffic and the unquestioning rush of humanity.

That's where the story *should* end. But I might as well finish what I started. This is no easy thing for me. Three months ago, I was promoted to a senior position in the civil service, and a week later, a pockmarked contractor came to my house with a thick brown envelope. Before I could protest he thrust it in my hands and drove off. The next day, I went to the bank and deposited the ten thousand ringgit. Last month, another contractor came with twenty thousand. I asked him to stay for tea.

Then, like the inevitable haze over the city, came the giddy sleeplessness, the nights watching the dull wood in the half-light, the awkward arms folded on its lap, the legs hanging over the shelf, the big eyes looking intently, its brow creased into a frown.

What did it once say?

Like banging your head on a brick wall. That was it. *Life. Full of bullshit. So damn hard to get by.*

Yes, it was. Car loan, housing loan, school fees, credit card bills.

So I had taken. So I had stolen. Is it wrong? Is it so damn bloody wrong? Everyone's doing it, all of them, might as well be me ... might as well. Why let righteousness get in the way? The years of clean hands, of not taking despite the numerous hints and open offers, I took nothing. And where did it get me? Where the hell did it get me? Nowhere. I sat and watched my senior colleagues get fat climbing up faster and faster in their suits and cars and all those expensive functions and grand oh-so-bloody grand weddings. And where was I?

Nowhere.

And so I took.

Nothing wrong with it. Nothing wrong with it at all. Nothing wrong.

So I'll just sit here, watching it, watching me. On any night now it will leave those birds, trees, butterflies, flowers behind — fingers will move, legs will tremble, it will noiselessly jump to the parquet floor and with a scared and tired frown, say: *Hello Boss Man, from whom shall I steal today?*

I will stare blankly into its face and, without blinking, read from my list.

A SISTER'S TALE

1. WOMAN ON A TEA TOWEL

Dusk. A savage tear between light and dark, a transient strip in time of sodden gray creeping from the overhanging branches, from the crusted bitumen, from the deep murky drains running parallel to the wild grassy verge. Not a time to sleep for this is the time of spirits, roaming like hungry moths from their dwellings ... searching.

The Chinese woman with short black shining hair could not have been older than forty. Her clothing was that of a younger person — matching cotton pants and top in floral yellow with large green childlike buttons. Her fair complexion made her eyes seem dark and mysterious, like the shadows shifting uneasily around her. She sat on a tea towel laid on a raised section of concrete by the road, at the yawning entrance of a large house. On most evenings, at dusk, when the piercing heat had mostly dissipated, she would sit with a cup of steaming milky sweet tea in her small hands and watch the occasional passers-by heading home from work or sometimes wave to the old couple from No. 28 who usually took a leisurely stroll on the mostly empty road.

Her husband and two children were in the lounge watching a Cantonese drama serial, her two servants busied themselves in the kitchen noisily getting dinner ready. The woman was seemingly content with life, her children were healthy and did well at school, her husband provided generously, much better than she could have wished for when they'd wed seventeen years ago — a big house, two European cars, servants. What more could she ask for?

But she had asked. And it came in the form of a man ten years her junior, at a shopping center of all places. In the heady muskiness of the perfume counter, among the rows of shapely bright colored bottles, with a smile full of hidden caresses he asked her opinion on a particular fragrance new on the market; then asked her for a drink, and the rest followed.

She would wait for him every evening, just before darkness fell, sitting on her tea towel. On most occasions, he would walk past, with a note — sometimes a short poem, sometimes a love letter and always with details of when and where they could abandon themselves to each other again. Abandon themselves to the sweet and voracious passion. Weng Feh too was married and their affair required much forward planning and a whole heap of lying.

He had not come this evening. Perhaps his wife was in one of her moods and Weng Feh could not pretend to go out to the gym, could not drive the car with heart thumping wildly, could not park around the corner and walk dreamily down the road with a note in his hands, fervor in his eyes, gazing at the woman trembling on a tea towel.

"No show," she said to the shadows. "He's not going to come."

She had waited for more than twenty minutes. He was usually on time. The couple from No. 28 had decided to stay home too, the heavy threatening clouds hanging low in the sky were uninviting, now bearing the semblance of spilt ink for night had taken over — street lamps had come on, all except the one nearest to her. It pierced the air with defiance, with non-conformity.

Time to go back in, she thought. Back to that man she felt no love for, not the love of wild abandonment and honeyed kisses. Not the love she felt for Weng Feh. Maybe he was late. She decided to wait five more minutes. Oh, just to see his face, his smile, the longing in his eyes. She'd never felt like this before, she was like a teenager in the throes of love.

The woman shuddered, as if something cold and clammy had brushed her cheek. She turned and was startled by a tall figure. Though the figure was not more than twenty feet away, she couldn't see its face — it seemed to be cloaked in black shadows, as if every layer of darkness had been pulled in its direction. It? Why 'it'? This was a woman, that much was clear from the silhouette of loose clothes and the cascading hair falling below her bosom. The figure stopped and turned to face her from across the road.

"A nice evening," the figure said in a deep voice which seemed to come from further away, as if echoing up from the depths below the road. The voice was fluid — textured with a disturbing resonance, which made her shift uncomfortably on the tea towel.

"Getting late though," she replied politely. "Almost night."

"Waiting for someone?" That murky deep voice again. The figure took two deliberate steps forward, if steps they were, it seemed more like a slow gliding motion.

"No," said the woman on the tea towel, shaking her head. "Just spending some time out of the house ... Family's watching TV." She couldn't understand why she'd volunteered that last piece of information. She seemed to trust this woman whose face she still couldn't make out, but another part of her was saying she should hurriedly go back in — there was something untoward with the woman, an unnaturalness ...

"He must be late." The figure was standing directly in front of her, seeming to have grown taller.

The woman nodded. "I don't know why," she said.

"You really don't know?" the figure said. "That's a laugh."

The woman on the tea towel looked at her enquiringly.

"What do you mean?"

The figure leaned over and it was only then that the woman on the tea towel realized that what she'd taken for a shadow was no shadow at all. The woman's face was a putrid dark green, drenched in a thick slimy liquid.

The woman-thing opened its mouth to reveal a cavern of sharp teeth punctuated with two long ugly fangs.

"I know who you are," the woman on the tea towel gasped, the memories rushed at her just as the thing lunged forward.

2. ANNA'S DREAM OF PASSION

Seventeen years ago, Anna kicked off the blanket and turned in bed, the fan circling above her. Was it a vulture or helicopter? She wasn't sure. She could hear mother preparing breakfast, the frying pan clanging, heating on the stove. Jessica would already be there drinking coffee at the table, both mother and daughter chirping like senseless birds about the wedding. Jessica was twenty-one, only a year younger than Anna, but she was treated like a baby. Everything was given to Jessica and nothing to Anna.

And Jessica, of course, had all the men. She never stayed for more than a few months with any of them. She would start off with one, fall in love, meet another man, get embroiled in a passionate affair, then forsake old love for a new one.

Anna had no experience with men. But she had Kia Seng. He was her first love, her only true love. He was a smiling accountant who dressed well with a confident manner and a kind, generous nature. They had so many plans for life together.

That was until Jessica turned on her wily charms. And Kia Seng had succumbed.

Now Jessica and Kia Seng were to be married. Anna's world, her life, all hopelessly crushed. Did she scream out at her sister? Try to scratch out the bitch's eyes? No. Anna did none of those things. Instead she sat on the bed and wept her nights away. It would seem to anyone caring enough to look, that as the days and weeks passed, Anna would resign herself to this wicked fate and accept what had happened, that Jessica and Kia Seng were to be one and Anna would be left by the wayside and, if she was ever asked, pretend to be that happy bridesmaid walking down the aisle.

Until the dream. Anna had been dreaming of Kia Seng's naked and muscular body heaving on top of her, his mouth searching for her tongue, his large hands caressing her skin. She had never had such a dream. Of course, she and Kia Seng had made love several times, but that was exactly what it was, making love. A mere expression of emotion. This dream though, it was wild. It was animal. Passion aflame.

Anna was shaken into the realization that she could never give Kia Seng up. He was hers. Jessica had stolen her man but Anna would get him back. Those two were now together, to be married in a month, unless of course something went terribly wrong ...

Anna only thought out these things in bed as the sunlight came streaming in through the louvered window. Mere thoughts, doing nobody any harm. She saw them arm in arm, Kia Seng bringing Jessica home, Jessica with her ponytail, her dimples, lithe body and the colorful cotton dresses she wore. Jessica was always coming in from a beautiful summer's day, not that there were any summers in Malaysia — but there may as well have been. Jessica, always walking in an English garden with roses and trimmed hedges. And now she had stolen Kia Seng and was bringing him along with her; he would be dressed in a smart suit, a polka-dot bow tie and top hat, and they would be strolling on rolling lawns, holding hands, drinking champagne, giggling like children and eating ice cream.

And what about Anna? She would be squatting and weeping alone by a festering drain looking up at them, breathing exhaust fumes, tasting the phlegm of pedestrian spit, dirty flies swarming on her lips unhindered. This was her world.

But for the dream. For those hours when Kia Seng was upon her she had regained paradise. No, not English gardens, those were for Jessica, her pretty little world of niceties and politeness. No, Anna was on the windswept beach with Kia Seng, they were laughing in the water, splashing water on one another, falling on the sand with the tumultuous waves of passion pushing him into her. How she howled with delight, her quivering voice ascending over the trees and animals, drowning the sound of the insects. And Kia Seng ... oh, how he groaned. And they were together again. For always.

But it was merely a dream. Anna was thinking hard. And thoughts surely hurt no one. Anna would like to be waiting for them behind some hedge on some manicured English lawn, the sound of croquet in the background. Then as they turned the corner, hand in hand, she would swing an axe at Jessica's head and watch it cleave her skull and behold the bits of brain and blood slide down her face. Then she would turn to Kia Seng and she would tell him to remove his clothes at once. And Kia Seng would comply, just like in her dream.

Once Jessica was out of the way, all she had to do was reach out a hand and he would come back to her, and Kia Seng would not only find love but wild passion. She thought these things through in a slow and deliberate fashion, touching every thought with relish, enjoying the soft almost tangible feel of it. Ah, these delicious thoughts. And thoughts, of course, could hurt no one.

Until translated into action. And the thought of action made Anna's heart leap. Leap in hope. A leap for Kia Seng. Anna didn't even know how to swing an axe but she was a nurse in the General Hospital and she knew where poisons were kept. They weren't, of course, poisons by nature but a sufficient dose could easily kill. And a small bottle wouldn't be missed.

3. JESSICA'S ICE-CREAM SUNDAE

Jessica loved ice cream. She ate it all the time.

There was nothing like a chocolate Cornetto when she strolled down the shopping mall. She liked letting it drip down the cone so she could let her tongue roll up the wafer and catch the ice cream before it dripped off the bottom.

But at the table it was always a sundae, one with nuts, fruit and syrup. And three scoops with it too — chocolate, vanilla and strawberry. She would let it melt until it turned smooth and creamy. Only then would she bring the spoon up to her mouth, delicately sticking out her tongue and allowing the ice-cream to slide in.

And Anna knew this only too well. She waited for Jessica to come home from her job at the florist. Mother was at mahjong and wouldn't be home until after dinner. Anna sat at the kitchen table with two tall glasses, prepared just as Jessica liked. Tinned peaches, grapes and berries at the bottom, triple scoop ice cream on top, followed by a generous serving of chocolate sauce. As an extra treat, she had stuck a cinnamon wafer in each and sprinkled crushed macadamia nuts over them. Jessica loved surprises.

And what a surprise she'll have, Anna thought. *What an unpleasant surprise!*

"Hi Anna," Jessica called as she breezed in. Her intention was obviously to waltz down the corridor to her room and get changed. It was going to be a night out with Kia Seng, Anna could tell from that voice like a bird eagerly chirping.

"Jessica, look what I've made for tea."

"Sorry, I've got to ... oh ice-cream sundae ... looks delicious."

"Sit down. I only just made it."

Jessica came into the kitchen with that sweet smile. She placed her pink handbag on the counter and slid into the rattan chair facing Anna. She wore bright cherry-red lipstick, yellow earrings, a silver bangle, a yellow and red dress with lacy trimmings around her sleeves.

"How was your day?" Jessica asked, brushing her short hair behind her ears.

Anna smiled. *Not half as bad as yours is going to be, dear sister.*

"Well, how was it?"

"So, so," Anna chirped. Anna had taken the bottle from the restricted cabinet. She had whistled a pretty tune as she prepared the sundae, emptying the entire contents of the small blue bottle into Jessica's glass.

Anna slid the sundae across the kitchen table. "I've made it just the way you like it, and with macadamia nuts on top."

"Wow, you must be in a good mood. What's the occasion?"

"Oh nothing, just felt like it."

Jessica picked up the spoon.

Good, thought Anna. *Now eat away.*

Anna picked up hers and dug it into the chocolate and brought it to her mouth. "Nice and cold," she said licking her lips. "You'll like it."

Jessica scooped up some vanilla and placed the spoon on the edge of the bowl. "Looks just lovely."

Jessica and her silly ways.

Anna continued eating. She didn't much like ice cream. In fact she hated it. She found it too rich, too sweet. But she didn't want Jessica to get suspicious.

"We're going to the cinema tonight," said Jessica. "We're going to Rex, to watch *Kramer v Kramer*."

"It's *Kramer versus Kramer*."

"Yeah, it's so sad. About a little boy and their parents getting divorced."

Anna looked at Jessica's ice cream. Some of it had melted. "Why don't you eat your ice cream?"

"Oh yeah, it looks just delicious. Thank you Anna, you've never been so nice to me before." Jessica raised the spoon to her lips, pushed out her tongue and allowed the ice cream to slide down towards her cherry-pink lips. "Hmmm ... so nice."

Yes, it is. So nice poisoning you.

"Nice and cold, isn't it Jessica? Especially since it's so hot outside. You don't want to let it melt too much. It'll become watery."

"Kia Seng and I want to go to England for our honeymoon ..." Jessica continued eating the ice cream, placing spoon after spoon in her mouth, her tongue rising each time to meet it. "It'll be winter then, it'll be so nice and cold ... we want to go to Hampton Court ... cruise up the Thames ... oh it's going to be so lovely."

"Have you booked your flights?"

"Oh, not yet. We've been so busy getting ready for the wedding."

Anna had surprised herself. Despite hating ice cream she'd already eaten half a glass while waiting for Jessica to start eating hers. Perhaps it was nerves. Anna now took small mouthfuls of ice cream. Jessica helped herself to large doses.

Anna watched Jessica carefully, looking for a sign of the poison taking effect. But Jessica looked perfectly fine.

Bloody hell! What's wrong with the poison!

Anna sat back in her chair. She felt blood rush from her face, she clutched the sides of the chair.

"What's wrong, Anna?" Jessica said, frowning.

"Uh ... nothing. I just ..." The room was spinning. It felt like a sledgehammer was crashing into her skull. Anna could hear her heart pounding rapidly in her ears. "I think I ..."

No, it can't be ... It just can't be!

"... took the wrong one."

Anna fell off her chair, her arm hitting the glass, which flew and shattered on the tiled floor.

Stupid, stupid, stupid me!

Jessica rushed to her side and cradled Anna's head. "Took the wrong one? Anna, what do you mean?"

Anna opened her mouth, wheezing, taking in huge gulps of air. Her throat was on fire. "The wrong glass ..." she whispered. "... call an ambulance!"

"What?"

"Poisoned ... call an ambulance."

"How do you know, how do you ... my God ... you ... you were trying to *poison* me? You were trying to *kill* me?"

"Please Jessica ... call the ambulance now."

"Tell me ... were you trying to kill me? I want to know ... don't just lie there ... tell me now!"

Anna nodded. She closed her eyes, unable to look up at Jessica.

"You were planning to kill me ... poisoning the ice-cream sundae."

"Jessica ... the ambulance."

"Why? Anna. Why?"

Anna said nothing. Her heart was fluttering wildly. It felt as though acid had been poured down her throat.

She would die if help didn't come soon. "For Kia Seng ... please get an ambulance."

"You wanted Kia Seng to yourself?"

Anna nodded.

"I should have known!"

Jessica didn't reply, then Anna heard footsteps. She opened her eyes. Jessica was gone, she must have gone to the lounge to call 999.

Then the front door slammed.

No! Jessica what are you doing?

Jessica couldn't have called for an ambulance so quickly! She wasn't so foolish as to go out and *look* for an ambulance? Anna didn't think so ... unless ...

No, Jessica wouldn't do that!

Then to her relief, Anna heard a key in the front door.

Thank God! She's come back!

Footsteps. Jessica came back into the kitchen. She barely looked at Anna. She said nothing, instead she took her glass off the table and went to the sink. She ran the water, took a sponge and started to wash up the glass and spoon.

"What are you doing?" Anna whispered. Her voice hoarse.

Jessica said nothing. She rinsed the glass and dried it with a tea towel, crossed the kitchen and placed the glass back in the kitchen cupboard.

"You're ... not ..."

"No Anna, I'm not calling the ambulance."

"You're ..."

"I'm leaving you here ... it's that simple."

"You can't ..."

"You came home after work one day and killed yourself, put poison in your ice cream ... happens all the time. I'll write a little note. Remember how, as little girls, we used to copy each other's handwriting? Well, I can still copy yours."

"Please ..."

"I'll say you were heartbroken, after I took Kia Seng from you, that you couldn't live knowing he was getting married to me. It's the truth. Well, almost."

"Please ... Jessica."

"Goodbye, Anna."

"You don't ... even ... love him."

"I love him completely, with every part of my being. I'll love him forever."

"You'll only ... find ... someone else ... like you always do."

"Never. Those days are gone. It'll only be Kia Seng." Jessica laughed. "If I'm disloyal you can come back to haunt me!"

"No, Jessica. I'll come back to ... kill you ..."

Anna pointed a trembling finger up at her sister. Then she closed her eyes and the finger fell to the floor, curling into itself.

The smile dropped from Jessica's face. She shivered. Then hurried to Anna's room to write the note.

4. ANNA AGAIN

Jessica screamed and leapt off the tea towel.

"Get away from me!"

The thing lunged at her.

Shadows fluttered in the darkness.

Jessica raised her arms to protect her face, expecting the bite to rip out half her neck.

Death had come for her.

Seconds passed but nothing happened. No ripping of her neck, no excruciating pain.

She waited. Her legs trembling.

Still nothing.

She looked through the gap between her arms. Her knees buckling beneath her.

It was gone. The woman-thing. Nothing there but darkened street, rows of houses and streetlights.

Jessica got up from the road, wiping the dirt from her trousers. Her heart drumming in her ears, her breath short and quick. She suspiciously eyed every dark shadow about her.

For the moment, it seemed the thing had disappeared.

Did she imagine it? It seemed so real. Behind the putrid green face, she had recognized Anna.

Or had she really?

Hadn't she been thinking about Anna since Weng Feh came along? Since that first time in the five-star hotel room next to the department store.

Weng Feh had opened a celebratory beer. Jessica had laid there, her naked body beneath the sheets, staring at an oil painting of yellow roses. It reminded her of England, of lush green forests, of stone castles, mazes, statues and rolling lawns; they had seen it all when she and Kia Seng had gone there for their honeymoon. Her eyes were then drawn to a dewdrop hanging from a petal. In it was a shadow growing, forming a twisted face, she was sure of it. Then she heard what she thought was a breeze at first, shifting outside the window. But no, this was no sound of the wind, this was an acid whispering, coming from the rose ...

I'll come back to ... kill you ...

Jessica almost screamed. Then she turned to Weng Feh to see if he heard anything, but he just sat on a sofa, absorbed in a Chinese magazine. So it was her imagination. She stared angrily at the dewdrop, at the leering face reflected there. She wasn't going to let Anna's curse get to her. So she bought it from the hotel to show herself she wasn't afraid. Anna was dead and she would stay dead.

After all, wasn't Anna's curse seventeen years old? So much had happened since. She and Kia Seng had two kids and they went on with their busy lives.

He was contented. She wasn't.

Jessica's yearning for more had been bubbling in her veins for years. But she always remembered Anna's final words.

I'll come back to ... kill you ...

Stupid though it was, it kept her loyal. But how could she *really* be loyal? Her mind had strayed many a time. But physically, yes, physically she had been faithful. She had done nothing. Thoughts never became action. Sure, there was the odd remark, the odd look, the odd touch. Flirting was nothing.

Jessica, she had never done anything like this. This was the first time after seventeen years of marriage. Her sister's words had kept her faithful to Kia Seng, the sister that tried to kill her, the one that wanted Kia Seng to herself. What a joke!

But now it had happened and it was delicious, so delicious. She couldn't believe she had waited so long. This was Anna's revenge. Anna had turned Jessica into a nun ... except for Kia Seng ... and he could hardly perform these days. But Weng Feh ... what a stallion!

She must have imagined the woman-thing. Maybe it was her mind reacting to the disappointment of not seeing Weng Feh tonight.

Damn Weng Feh! Damn that wife of his!

Jessica picked up the tea towel and turned back to the house. She closed and locked the gate and walked towards the two European cars under the porch.

She took off her slippers, locked the metal grille and the door behind her. Kia Seng and the kids were still watching the movie. She thought she heard Jackie Chan's voice, followed by furniture being thrown and a lot of kicking, punching and screaming. And a car screeching.

No, that's not the TV. It's coming from outside the house!

She unlocked the door and grille, stepped into the porch and peered towards the front gate. A car sat at an angle by the entrance with lights blazing.

Who could it be? We're not expecting visitors.

She made her way towards the gate. A drop of rain fell on her face. Part of her wanted to go back and get Kia Seng. But there was something familiar about the shape of the car. She had been in it. It had met her at shopping complexes, at the Club, at every rendezvous point they could think of.

What's Weng Feh doing here?

She ran towards the car. He had to leave now or Kia Seng would find out. She took out the key to the padlock.

Something's wrong. Why's he still in the car? Why did it screech like that?

The key fell to the road. She bent down, picked it up and only on the third try managed to get the key into the padlock.

More drops of rain splashed on the road.

Why's he still in there?

She opened the padlock, pushed the gate open and rushed over to the driver's side.

The sky opened up and rain fell, drumming and bouncing off the roof of the car. Jessica's hair and clothes were completely soaked.

She could see Weng Feh sitting in the driver's seat. She knocked on the glass. No reaction.

He didn't even turn his head to look at her.

Could he be asleep?

"Weng Feh, open up. What are you doing here?"

No answer. Jessica's face was wet. Cold streams cascaded down her forehead, trickling off her nose.

"Open up, Weng Feh!"

Her heart thumped wildly in her head.

She pulled at the door handle. At first it wouldn't budge. Then she gave it a hard tug.

The door flew open. The interior light came on.

"No, Weng Feh ... no!"

Weng Feh sat in his office clothes, one hand gripping the steering wheel.

The yellowish light shone on his pale face. His eyes opened wide in terror. His lips twisted downward as if he'd just heard a tasteless joke.

Trickles of blood ran down his neck, soiling his Van Heusen shirt, the striped one she'd bought him from Metrojaya. Two dark gaping puncture marks sat on his neck.

Rain splashed into the car, splattering his trousers.

"What's happened to you ... my darling ..."

The night spun around her. Rain flew in all directions. Weng Feh's face danced before her eyes.

"My ... darling ... Weng Feh!"

Behind her she heard a high-pitched giggling.

She spun around. Nothing there but the dark wet street and a row of streetlights lighting up the falling rain.

She heard it again. This time the giggling was coming from inside the car.

She spun round, nothing there but Weng Feh gripping the steering wheel, blood still dripping down his neck.

Then she saw it. A movement in the back seat. She peered and saw a dark shape with flowing hair.

Jessica stepped back. "No, it's you. Get away from me!"

The woman-thing opened the door.

"I've come back to kill you, Jessica."

"No! No! No!"

"Yes, I have. I told you I would."

The thing glided out of the car.

Jessica raised her hands to her face. "No, Anna! No!"

Jessica spun and slipped on the wet road. Her body flew forward and she hit her head on the bitumen.

The world turned a hideous black.

5. DR PILLAY'S PROGNOSIS

Dr Pillay told Kia Seng his wife was in shock after coming across the dead man's body. Kia Seng nodded. He had read the police report. The man was on his way to the gym. He had a rare blood condition which caused a seizure and he died in his car. Jessica must have heard the car and ran out to see what was happening.

Dr Pillay said that Jessica's mind had reacted badly to it, withdrawing deep into herself to block out the horrid scene. Of course, the concussion was a contributing factor, but the physical injuries were superficial. She needed rest. Lots of it. Medication was necessary. Valzenol was a good non-addictive drug that would help bring her out of her catatonic state.

For many hours Kia Seng watched his wife lying on that hospital bed, her short hair disheveled, eyes wide open, spittle running down her chin. At first he couldn't bear seeing her with tubes sticking out her arms but he had gotten used to it. He could get used to anything as long as Jessica was getting better. But after three days in the hospital there was no sign of improvement.

"Why did you go out the gate alone?" Kia Seng quietly asked his wife. "Why didn't you call me? I would have gone out to see what was happening."

Jessica did not answer. She lay there silently looking at the ceiling, eyes occasionally blinking.

"My darling Jessica, get better. Please ..."

Kia Seng bent over and placed his head in his hands. He was exhausted, he hadn't slept for three nights.

"You must get better ..." he sobbed between his fingers. "Please get better, my darling."

She was admitted on Monday night. On Thursday, her condition remained unchanged. The doctor told him that his wife was of a fragile constitution and it may take awhile for her to get back to normal.

Exactly a week after she was admitted to hospital, Jessica started taking food from a spoon.

As soon as Kia Seng found out, he arranged for his driver to bring the servants to Gleneagles every mealtime with porridge and herbal soup for Jessica. Jessica ate and drank slowly and in small quantities to begin with. But with each day her appetite improved.

Dr Pillay strode down the corridor to Kia Seng, her hair tied in her bun, her glasses sliding to the edge of her nose. "I told you it's only a matter of time," she said. "This is indeed wonderful, she's making good progress."

"When do you think she'll start talking again, doctor?" asked Kia Seng as he stroked his wife's limp hand.

"It's difficult to say, it may take days, it may take weeks. We have to be patient, I'm afraid."

"I see."

"She has been in the hospital for over ten days now and I think there is not much the hospital can do in terms of medical treatment and, as you know, she no longer needs to be fed intravenously. I think we should consider taking your wife home to recuperate. It may be better for her to mentally recover in a familiar environment. You know this sort of healing does not happen quickly and of course staying here is no cheap affair."

"But what if something goes wrong, doctor?"

"I really doubt there will be any complications. You need not worry, we are on call twenty-four hours a day should you need our assistance."

So eleven days after being admitted to hospital, Jessica went home.

The servants had prepared the guestroom, making it as comfortable as possible. Kia Seng himself had put a nail in the wall and hung up her favorite painting, the one with the yellow rose that Jessica had one day brought home out of the blue. In the spare room she would have peace and quiet. It had a view of the palm tree and the lawn. Though Kia Seng knew this was no English garden, at least it was always kept neat and tidy and sometimes in the afternoon the breeze would stir the fronds.

Someone would be with her all the time, nothing was going to be left to chance. One of the servants would sleep on a mat at the foot of the bed. Jessica would be fed, changed and cleaned. The air conditioning would be on, she would be cool throughout the day even when the sun blazed its fury outside.

Kia Seng sat with her for many hours in that spare room brushing her hair and gently talking. He realized then, like many husbands did at such times, that he had never said so many words to his wife and it had been years and years since he last told her he loved her. Now his affectionate words were unending as if a valve of love had opened deep in his heart. Of course, he had always loved her, he just didn't know how deeply or how completely.

6. IN THE SPARE ROOM

The first change in Jessica's condition occurred about a month later. As was their routine now, Kia Seng and the two children, Andrew and Simon, would see her right after dinner, they would all sit and talk about their day, and, as recommended by Dr Pillay, they would joke and laugh as if nothing had happened, as if Jessica was perfectly fine. As always she would stare blankly at the ceiling, at the revolving fan, completely in her own world. After an hour the children would leave and Kia Seng would remain, sipping Chinese tea in the spare room with his wife.

That evening she was in her pink pajamas; the children had just left to do their homework. Somewhere from within the house, a gecko was calling. Suddenly, Jessica's head started to twitch in a spasm-like motion.

Kia Seng jumped out of the chair. "Jessica, are you there? Are you okay?"

Her head stopped twitching.

Then came the gecko's shrilling call.

Jessica's head twitched again.

"Jessica, can you hear me?"

The twitching stopped.

Her head twitched each time the gecko called out, as if it was the only thing in the world that could communicate with her.

Dr Pillay was there in less than an hour. She attempted reviving Jessica out of the catatonia by gently tapping different points of her body but couldn't obtain a reaction.

"Don't worry, it's a good sign," she said as she adjusted her spectacles. "She's starting to respond to the world around her."

"But why only to the call of the cicak?" Kia Seng asked as he paced up and down.

"Maybe it's the high pitch of it or maybe that particular sound, who knows for sure. But she's getting better, she's reacting to external stimuli. This is nothing, so don't worry about it, it's a good sign."

A week later, Kia Seng didn't think the sign was so good.

He was asleep when Elisa, the Filipino maid, came rushing into his room.

"Sir, sir, something is wrong with Ma'am!"

"What is it, Elisa?"

"Come, come, sir. See for yourself!"

Kia Seng jumped out of bed and in his pajamas ran down the corridor to the spare room.

Jessica was sitting up in bed. The outside lights threw a slanting ray of brightness into the room.

He rushed to his wife's side. "Jessica, can you hear me?"

Elisa followed him in. "Wait awhile, sir. Look what she is doing."

"What do you mean?"

"Please, wait and see, sir."

"Tell me, what does she do?"

"Mosquitoes, sir. It's the mosquitoes."

"Mosquitoes?"

"Look sir. Look!"

Kia Seng sat on the edge of the bed watching. Jessica's eyes were wide open looking blankly at the wall, but her right hand was trembling.

Then he heard it, the high-pitched whining of a mosquito. Suddenly Jessica's hand shot out and slapped her own cheek.

Kia Seng couldn't believe his eyes. "What the hell!" Slowly Jessica brought her hand down to the sheets where it sat nestled among the folds of her blanket.

"Elisa, turn on the light."

The light came on and Kia Seng gently took Jessica's hand. He opened her fingers and on her palm was a dead mosquito and a streak of bright red blood.

"I can't believe it," Kia Seng said shaking his head. "She just killed a mosquito but she's still in that state, still lost deep in herself. But how can she do that, how can she kill mosquitoes?"

Kia Seng called Dr Pillay. She arrived soon after.

"How is your wife?" she asked, looking weary, her spectacles seeming to be forever sliding down her nose.

"She's killing mosquitoes."

"What?"

"Killing mosquitoes. Come see."

Elisa brought chairs into the spare room and they both sat watching Jessica.

Dr Pillay turned to Kia Seng. "You mean she kills mosquitoes yet is still catatonic?"

"Yes, but how can this be, doctor?"

"It sounds incredible. I think that perhaps ..."

"Wait, doctor. Listen!"

It was the high-pitched whine of a mosquito.

Jessica's hand shot out and grabbed at the air in front of her face. Then, slowly, she pulled it back to her and wiped the pulped insect on her pajamas.

Dr Pillay jumped to her feet. "My Lord! I wouldn't have believed it if I didn't see it for myself."

"What does it mean, doctor?"

"It's hard to say. We could run tests but as you know this catatonia is caused by mental distress."

"But how can she catch mosquitoes like this? And why does she do it?"

Dr Pillay shook her head. "I don't know. We can only wait and see."

Kia Seng led Dr Pillay to the front door. It was already 3 in the morning when he went back to bed. He couldn't sleep so he went back to the spare room to sit beside Jessica. She had her eyes closed. She was fast asleep. This was the only time when she looked herself. He thought of many things as he sat, of their life together, of the memories they shared and then for one awful moment, he thought of Anna. He pushed it aside but before he could prevent the onslaught of guilt and ... something else ... was it ...

A sound.

He looked at Jessica. She was still asleep.

The sound again. Like someone weeping.

He turned to the window and thought he saw a shape moving, shifting darkly between the gap in the curtains. He rushed to the window and pushed aside the curtains. All he saw was the palm tree lit by the lamp outside, its leaves moving in a stroking motion. There was no wind tonight, an animal perhaps had brushed against it.

Kia Seng drew the curtains close and returned to his chair.

"Get better, Jessica," he quietly said. "Please get better."

7. BACK TO KIA SENG

For the next few days, Jessica's condition remained unchanged. She would sit up in bed hardly blinking, waiting for the high-pitched whining, then her hand would grab at the air and she would wipe the pulped mosquito and the blood of its victim on her pajamas. No blood-sucking insect could get near her, her hands tensed and twitched waiting for them day and night.

Kia Seng had been with her all evening. Dr Pillay had visited again but she was still confounded. She would consult with some of her colleagues before proceeding on any course of action.

Now, Kia Seng was alone with his wife. He turned to her. "Jessica, please tell me what is happening. Why are you killing mosquitoes? Please come back to us. The children need you. I need you."

Jessica remained silent, sitting up, looking right through her husband.

It was well past 11. Elisa was still tidying up in the kitchen, so Kia Seng put his arms around Jessica and gently slid her under the blanket. He adjusted the air conditioning with the remote, then tucked Jessica's blanket in.

"Sleep now, darling. You'll get better soon." As he turned from her he whispered to himself: "You just have to."

He switched off the light and was about to shut the door when he heard it.

At first he didn't know what it was or where it came from.

Then he realized the sound was coming from Jessica.

Jessica was whispering!

He rushed to his wife's side. Her eyes were wide open, staring blankly at the ceiling, lips twitching. What was she saying? He couldn't make out the words.

He placed his ear to her mouth. Then he heard it. She whispered the words over and over.

I've come back to kill you.

I've come back to kill you.

"Jessica, what's going on here?"

I've come back to kill you.

"You're talking! But why are you saying this!"

I'VE COME BACK TO KILL YOU.

Kia Seng rushed to the phone. As he was frantically dialing Dr Pillay's number he heard a scream.

He dropped the phone and ran down the corridor yelling: "I'm coming my darling! I'm coming!"

He rushed into the spare room. Behind him he could hear doors opening, Andrew and Simon coming out to see what was happening.

He flicked the light switch. The room was bathed in light.

Jessica was lying in bed. Her eyes wide open, but they weren't staring blankly at the ceiling, they stared right at him.

"Jessica, you're ... you're looking at me. I can't believe it! You're looking at me!"

But there was a strange expression in her eyes. Then she smiled and Kia Seng could have died from sheer happiness.

He knelt by his wife's side clutching her hands.

"What's happening, Daddy?"

Kia Seng turned to see Andrew and Simon and he didn't care they saw tears streaming down his face.

"Mother, she's awake! She's awake!"

The children rushed to their mother and hugged her. Kia Seng joined them and the four of them held each other. For Kia Seng it was a hug that ended all too soon, in that moment he experienced every wave of tumultuous emotion: happiness, sadness, triumph, relief, but mostly love.

"Let's get off her bed, let mother have some air."

"That's a great bed," Andrew said with a grin. "It could hold all of us!"

Jessica beamed.

Simon clutched his mother's hand, tears in his eyes.

Kia Seng laughed happily.

He hugged Jessica again. "Darling, I can't believe it, you're awake! Can you talk?"

Jessica slowly nodded, the smile never leaving her face. "Yes ... I can," she whispered.

"Mother, do you want something to drink?"

"Yes ... please."

"And something to eat?" asked Kia Seng, still holding his wife.

She nodded, looking awkwardly at the two boys.

Kia Seng stroked her hair, not able to contain his joy. "How about an ice-cream sundae with fruits at the bottom and nuts on top? Andrew can make if for you."

"Oh no, my darling. Anything, anything, but ice cream."

"But Jessica, ice-cream sundae, it's your favorite."

The woman in the spare room turned and stared at the darkness between the curtains. "No, Kia Seng, my love, not anymore."

Noel was Father Recycling. He'd go into a fit whenever someone threw stuff into the wrong bin. "Waste, waste, consumer haste," he'd mumble as he ripped open the plastic bag, pulling and sorting out the recyclables much to the dismay of the repentant unit-dweller. Yet when his passion wasn't being crossed, Noel was the most neighborly of neighbors.

The doors of the lifts would slide open and Noel would be standing there with three cartons. One laden with *Herald* newspapers, one piled with bills and junk mail, another full of bottles and jars. He'd prop the door open with one carton and slide the other two out. He did this in a little dance, stretching his eighty-one-year-old body in a blue track suit before spinning his way out, a box gripped in his liver-spotted hands.

"Top of the morning," he'd say to me, his eyes twinkling brightly behind his shriveled face.

"Hi, Noel," I'd say. "More boxes?"

"Yep, more happy boxes."

"You've got a lot of the stuff."

Noel laughed, his freckles jigging about his bald head. Yet the pallor of his skin was like a mist hiding the loss of his wife and child in a car accident forty years ago. Since then, life had lost its meaning, for Noel did nothing but stay in his unit all day with Matthew, his flat-mate, tending to rubbish and recyclables.

"Oh, they're not all mine," he said. "No, no, not at all. Some of these belong to Mrs Owen and Mrs Larousse."

Now, Noel is no close friend. But when you've known someone for fifteen years, whether bumping into him while waiting for the lift or chatting about the latest test results or what pot plants grow best on a southeast-facing balcony or complaining about those noisy construction trucks hurtling down the street, there is bound to be a closeness or perhaps, some sort of responsibility for the other bloke. You see that Noel, that Father Recycling, is truly gone.

And that's why tonight, on this New Year's Eve, when those of us on Eastern Standard Time count the seconds to 2000, I'll be here in my chair dreading the sound of a gunshot three floors below.

I only got to know Noel well a couple of years back. He invited me to that immaculately clean apartment of his to watch the New Year's fireworks with Matthew.

So armed with a bowl of potato salad and a bottle of Queen Adelaide, I arrived and joined a small congregation of acquaintances.

Noel told us that he was in the war in Malaya and how, because of an injured leg, he escaped on a ship a few weeks before Singapore fell. He even showed us his service revolver. Later, we all stood on the humid windless balcony, watching the showers of color burst over the harbor.

"Three hours to 1998," said Noel lifting up a glass of bubbly. "Another page in life's happy book."

"I suppose so," I said, wondering how joyous it could have really been. "Start of another chapter."

"Chapter 81 for me," smiled Noel behind those deep, trench-like wrinkles. I decided they could only have witnessed more tears than laughter.

"What do you reckon I'll be up for?" he added.

"Good things, I hope."

But it was not to be. I said the words flippantly, not knowing the next two years would see Noel's world crash about him again.

After the fireworks reached the climax, my image of Noel as the war veteran, the good bloke, Father Recycling, truly shattered.

Noel and Matthew stood by the sliding door, eyes skywards as if expecting more, fingers entwined in each other's.

"Beautiful, wasn't it?" he said.

I said nothing but stared.

"The fireworks," he said. "Beautiful, wasn't it?"

"Yes ... it was wonderful."

I left early that evening and saw 1998 in alone. I had nothing against gays. Noel was just a bloke you bumped into. In all my conversations with him there was nothing in his manner or anything he said that gave away his sexual preference. When did he turn? Was it after that car crash that wasted his life?

Over the next year or so, I continued my lift-lobby chats with Noel.

Then one day, after dragging his *Herald* carton out of the lift, Noel turned to me and said: "Matthew's left me."

"What?"

"He's left me. Matthew. Moved in with some bloody fairy in Paddington."

"Oh dear, Noel. I'm sorry to hear that."

"Had to happen sometime, I suppose."

Noel abruptly turned, dragging his cartons to the stand of plastic bins, but it was not before I saw tears welling in his eyes.

For me, the Spring of 1999 brought a month-long Western Australian tour with the Ballroom Dancing Section of the Leagues Club. When I got back, I carried on as normal, living the life of a new retiree — trying to make the hours pass constructively, to give meaning to the marching time. So it took me a few weeks to realize I hadn't seen Noel for awhile. I found out that he'd been holed up in his apartment.

And so the next day, I rang his bell and, after some delay, he door opened. Noel stood there in his pajamas. Patches of white hung from his chin, tufts of hair lay pasted to his scalp, dark lines were drawn beneath red eyes.

"Hello," he croaked. "Come in."

Clothes were strewn on the carpet, empty glasses and bottles dotted the coffee table. A mustiness clung to the air.

I sat down beside a pile of yellowing newspapers. "How are you, Noel?"

"Not so good. Haven't been able to do much ... excuse me." He rushed to the bathroom and vomited.

"You okay, Noel?"

Noel staggered back in. "For the moment. I've got Hepatitis."

"Ate a bad prawn, did you?"

"Wish I did, then it'd be Hep A. I'd be immune to it after the stuff I ate in Malaya. No, I'm not so lucky. It's Hep B."

"Hep B?"

"Spreads through blood. Matthew had it — he didn't tell me. Maybe he didn't even know."

"Isn't there something you can take for it?"

"Nope, the thing's damaged me enough. My liver's all shot to bits ... got liver cancer."

"Shit. That's not good."

"They give me three to six months."

"Oh God, I'm sorry."

He walked out to the balcony. "I've lived longer than some, I suppose. I just want to make it to next year — see 2000 roll in."

I didn't know what to say, so I just stood beside him, eyes meeting his on that bit of water beneath the hazy skyscrapers.

"Then I can go," he continued. "Don't wanna end up in some hospital bed pumped full of painkillers so I can't even think. I want to die right here in my unit looking at the view, seeing in the new Millennium. Happens once every thousand years. Some see it as a new beginning, for me it'll mark the end."

There is not much one can say when someone tells you he's going to die. Even less when he mentions taking his own life. My response was, therefore, nothing but trivial.

"What if they find a cure, Noel?"

"They won't, not for me anyway."

Noel then weakly shook my hand and showed me the way out.

After I left, I realized that New Year's Day was just a month away. I had no doubt that Noel was going to kill himself. Over the next few weeks, I stood outside his door trying to think of what to say to dissuade him, but nothing of any sense came to me.

I did not hear the gunshot. The fireworks at midnight drowned it out. I always wondered when he pulled the trigger. Was it at that climactic point when three enormous stars burst across the Harbor Bridge? That would have been the right time.

They found Noel's body slumped on a deckchair on the balcony, dressed in a moth-eaten suit, the service revolver gripped in one hand, dried blood pasted to his face, eyes closed as if in prayer.

On the coffee table they found photographs of his childhood days, Malaya, wife and child lost in a car crash and, of course, Matthew. Beneath these scraps of memories lay his journal, with an entry for January 1, 2000 — a scrawl in the center of a blank sheet.

IF YOU ENJOYED THIS BOOK,
DO CHECK OUT:

KL NOIR: RED

KL NOIR: WHITE

KL NOIR: BLUE

DARK HIGHWAYS

ALSO BY THE SAME AUTHOR: